"DANCING SOUNDS GOOD," SHE decided, needing the distraction.

His knowing gaze said he saw right through her, fully aware of his impact on her. "Allow me to lead, my lady." He held out his hand.

"Oh, is this the part where I call you *Your Highness*?" Stas recently learned about Issac's family ancestry. His father was a duke, making Issac the Duke of Wakefield after his father passed. Stas had yet to tease him about it, but now seemed as good a time as any.

"Technically, it's *Your Grace*, and no. You will not call me that."

"And if I do, Your Grace?" she asked, batting her eyelashes at him coquettishly.

He narrowed his gaze. "I'll be forced to punish you."

"This sounds enlightening. Please elaborate, Your Grace."

He looked her over, his stare assessing. "You want to play, darling?"

She smiled. "Always."

"Then we'll play." He held out his hand. "Call me whatever nickname you desire. I dare you."

Her skin heated as she accepted his palm, her stomach clenching for an entirely different reason than earlier. *Just the distraction I need.* "Introduce me to your history, Your Grace. Dance with me like you did centuries ago."

"We'll need to improvise with the modern music," he murmured, guiding her back toward the party. "But I accept the challenge."

Her heart fluttered in her chest. "Then take me dancing, Duke Wakefield."

"Happily, Lady Aya."

IMMORTAL CURSE SERIES

Angel Bonds

USA Today Bestselling Author

Lexi C. Foss

Angel Bonds

Editing by: Outthink Editing, LLC

Initial Content Review By: Allison Irwin

Proofreading By: Barb Jack, Joy Di Biase-Giachino, Katie Schmahl, & Laura Schoenfelder

Cover Design: Covers by Julie

Photography: Wander Aguiar Photography

Models: Thom Panto

Published by: Ninja Newt Publishing, LLC

Print Edition

ISBN: 978-1-950694-35-8

To Bethany, for tolerating the insanity in my head and all my mishaps with deadlines and for being the most thorough editor in existence. I love working with you! To many more books and punctual manuscripts… Cheers xx

Also, to Matt, for helping me stay alive during deadlines ;) I promise you still have a wife somewhere. When I find her, I'll let you know. And then we'll go on a very long holiday. <3

ANGEL BONDS

BOOK SIX

GLOSSARY

PRETERNATURAL BEINGS

Fledgling (noun): The child of a male Ichorian and a human female, who has not yet been reborn as a Hydraian; they do not typically possess supernatural or psychic gifts until their immortal rebirth.

Hydraian (noun): An immortal offspring of a male Ichorian and a human female, who possesses two supernatural or psychic gifts and does not require human blood to survive.

Ichorian (noun): An immortal being of unknown descent who possesses one supernatural or psychic gift and requires human blood to survive.

Immortal (noun): A general noun designating a being who does not age and is immune to natural human death.

Seraphim (noun): A being who belongs to the highest order of angelic hierarchy.

KEY TERMS

Arcadia: Notorious Ichorian club in New York City that also serves as the primary meeting location for the Ichorian government.

Blood Laws: A series of ordinances created by the Ichorian governing board in response to the Treaty of 1747.

Catastrophic Relief Foundation (CRF): A global humanitarian aid organization headquartered in New York City with a secret paramilitary unit designed to destroy rogue supernaturals.

Conclave: The Ichorian governing board.

Edict: A law or rule issued by the High Council of Seraph.

Elders: The original Hydraians who also serve as the Hydraian governing board.

Fated Line: Seraphim who can foresee the future.

High Council of Seraph: Seraphim governing board.

Nizari: Ancient Ichorian assassins who hunt and kill fledglings.

Nizari Poison: A green substance notorious for killing fledglings and preventing their rebirth.

Sentinel: A soldier in the CRF unit designed to slaughter rogue immortal beings.

Treaty of 1747: An armistice between Hydraians and Ichorians to cease fire and live in their designated areas. Those who opt to cross these boundaries do so at their own risk.

PART ONE
Holiday Bonds

"'Tis the season for chaos."

—Issac

CHAPTER ONE

Stas

"Well, that was certainly eventful."

Stas Davenport arched a brow at the handsome man beside her. The sarcasm in his tone wasn't lost on her. "Be nice."

"Is that a command, love?" He cocked his head to the side, an alluring smile playing over his lips. Stas loved this side of Issac Wakefield. The playful one that only came out when they were alone.

She slid into the passenger seat of their rental and buckled her seat belt while he watched. Those blue eyes seemed to trace every inch of her. "You realize I'm wearing four layers, right?"

He laid a forearm on the top of their SUV and leaned in

to press his lips to hers. "I'm looking forward to taking them off piece by piece later. Something I would have done already had you allowed us to travel my way."

"You're never going to let this go, are you?" Her adoptive parents had sent them plane tickets for the holidays, a gift Stas knew cost them a minor fortune. Hence the reason she'd begged him to just fly commercial. "We compromised by upgrading to first class."

"Business class," he corrected.

"And there's a difference?"

"Oh, Aya." He just shook his head and closed the door.

Spending the holidays with Issac in Montana would be interesting. Of course, he'd insisted on renting a house in Kalispell after her adoptive parents mentioned staying in a hotel. Fortunately, they'd been thrilled with the change in plans and were meeting them at Flathead Lake. Seeing as they lived in Havre, it was easier and cheaper for them to drive.

Issac buckled in beside her and started fumbling with the fancy controls. Stas had no idea how he managed to rent this brand of SUV in Montana, but it sat waiting for them as they exited the Glacier Park International Airport. At least it had seat warmers, an amenity they would need.

Issac muttered a curse just as the back doors popped open on either side. "Go home," he demanded as two familiar men made themselves comfortable on the plush leather seats.

"Yes, I believe we are headed to your new residence," Luc said by way of greeting, causing Stas to frown.

"New residence?" She flashed Issac a look. "I thought you were renting?"

"Peanut?" Luc held out a bag toward the front passenger seat.

Issac ignored the Hydraian King and smiled. "I said I acquired a residence for the holidays."

"You said you rented one."

"I definitely used the term *acquired*. You just inferred it to mean I rented it." His lips twitched. "It also happened to be a worthwhile investment opportunity given the rising costs."

"How did you even find one to buy?" Kalispell was one of those areas where the homes were traditionally handed down through generations or purchased by mega celebrities.

"Money speaks, darling," he replied.

Right. Billionaire boyfriend.

Sometimes she forgot that detail with everything else going on in their lives.

"I guess they don't want a peanut. B?" Luc held the bag out to his sidekick beside him, reminding her that they had unexpected company.

"What are you two even doing here?" Stas stared back and forth between the muscular blond and too-attractive brunet. If she brought them to meet her parents... *Oh God.* Her father would be going to the nearest gun store to pick up a new item for his extensive collection and offering to play target practice with their heads.

"Celebrating the holidays," Balthazar replied with a grin. "Amelia and Tom are already at the lake preparing the holiday home with the others, but Jacque dropped us off at the airport to ride with you."

Issac pulled out his phone to begin dialing while Stas gaped at the intruders.

"Define 'others.'"

"Germanic in origin, it refers to those remaining in a group or not already mentioned," Luc replied. "Or it can be used to refer to a person or thing that is different or distinct from another. Assuming you meant the pronoun, of course."

She blinked. "What?"

"This is unacceptable," Issac said to whomever he'd called. "Well, tell them all to leave." He pinched the bridge of his nose while Balthazar smirked from the backseat. "Amelia..." The female voice rose over the phone, suggesting Issac's sister didn't approve of his request, and the grins in the backseat grew.

"You're both trouble," Stas whispered.

Luc popped a peanut into his mouth and shrugged. "I've always been a fan of the pagans and their traditions."

"What does that even mean?"

"Christmas, sweetheart," Balthazar explained. "Sometimes we forget how human you are."

"Used to be," Luc added without apology.

Stas grimaced, not wanting to think about her current fate. This holiday was meant to be an escape. A way for her and Issac to truly determine their future together, but it seemed the immortals in the backseat had other ideas.

Most humans would envy her bloodline because it meant she would live forever. Unfortunately, it also meant she couldn't be with the Ichorian beside her. All because of some ancient laws and genetic bullshit that pitted the two supernatural beings against each other.

"It's a lot more than that," Balthazar murmured quietly.

Stas shot him a look. The mind reader heard everything. Always. He meant well, but sometimes she just wanted to keep her thoughts to herself.

"Yes, all right," Issac said softly. "Well, they believe he's dead, remember?" His head fell back on a sigh. "Yes, Amelia. I will."

A masculine voice came over the line.

"That should work. I'll talk to Aya. Put Amelia back on, Thomas." The last statement was said through gritted teeth, which unclenched when his sister started talking again. "Yes. Sounds lovely." He looked ready to punch something. "See you soon." He hung up the phone and glowered at the rearview mirror. "I will kill you both for this."

Luc finished off his peanuts. "A unique take on the whole ghosts-of-Christmas legend, Wakefield."

"Can we call him Scrooge?" Balthazar asked.

"Absolutely."

"Brilliant." Balthazar smiled. "Shall we go, then? I have a date in the snow with a to-be-determined guest of honor."

He waggled his eyebrows at Stas.

"No," she and Issac replied at the same time.

"You're turning down playtime in the snow?" He gave Luc an affronted look. "Who doesn't enjoy snowball fights?"

"Apparently these two Scrooges." He gestured to the pair of them in the front seat.

Issac blew out a breath and glanced sideways at Stas. "I suggest you call your mom and warn her that a bunch of adult toddlers are joining us."

If her parents weren't already on their way to Kalispell, Stas would have told them to stay home, and have Issac drive her to Havre instead. "How is this going to work? Where will everyone sleep?"

Balthazar's grin was absolutely wicked. "We'll just share your bed, Stas."

"The residence has enough room." He glared in the mirror again. "Lucian, the Christmas ghost you mentioned will become a reality if your second-in-command continues that train of visual thought."

The seductive Hydraian blew him a kiss while Luc produced another bag of airline peanuts from his pocket. Had Jacque snagged those for him midflight or something? "B, stop taunting Wakefield."

"Whatever you say, King Luc," Balthazar deadpanned.

Luc snorted and popped more of those damn peanuts into his mouth.

"Let's just go, Issac," Stas said, tired from traveling all day. A nap sounded great right about now. Or copious amounts of alcohol. "It's only thirty minutes."

"Right." Issac navigated away from the curb, giving up on the notion of expelling the two interlopers from the back. "You need to warn your parents and also inform them that Thomas is indeed alive since they believe him to be dead."

She gaped at him. "And explain that how?"

"By saying he was on a deep-cover assignment that

required the ultimate camouflage."

Her brows rose. "You expect them to believe that?"

"Thomas will help when he sees them. His gift for insinuating truth is begrudgingly useful."

"Right. Okay." She had no idea if her parents would buy it, but what choice did she have? "You two better be quiet back there." She needed as much focus as she could get.

Balthazar saluted her. "Yes, ma'am."

Luc just held up yet another bag of peanuts.

Well, at least it'll be a memorable holiday.

CHAPTER TWO

Stas

THIRTY MINUTES LATER and Stas still didn't know how to handle the problem in the backseat. She'd warned her mom that two of Issac's friends—a comment that had earned her a cocked eyebrow from the driver—were with them. But she hadn't exactly been able to add, *Oh, and by the way, they're abnormally handsome and are probably going to give Dad a heart attack.*

Having Issac home for the holidays had been challenge enough. Adding the entire gang? Yeah, well, hopefully everyone survived.

God, they didn't even know Stas lived in Hydria now. Or that she'd quit her job with the Catastrophic Relief Foundation (CRF). Or that Lizzie was pregnant and engaged.

Right, so her parents literally knew nothing and thought Stas still resided with Lizzie in New York City. Good thing they couldn't just drop by for a visit without a very long flight.

Issac reached over for her hand and gave it a squeeze as he turned off the road onto a long paved drive lined in snow-laden trees. When he mentioned *acquiring* a home on the lake, she expected a quaint cabin-like structure with enough room for them and her parents.

But no. That wasn't Issac Wakefield's style. Something she should have considered when he said there would be enough room to house the immortals as well.

Her jaw dropped as the lodge-style estate appeared, framed by Flathead Lake in the rear. Oversized windows, wraparound decks on the second and third levels, large double doors, wooden siding in between, and beautifully decorated with trees all around the property.

Issac backed into the garage off to the side, killing the engine. "As I said, it's a good investment." He smiled at her and lifted her chin. "Let's go explore, shall we?"

Balthazar and Luc were already out of the SUV, their chatter about snowballs, leaving Stas alone with her favorite demon.

She narrowed her gaze as he unbuckled her seat belt. "An investment," she repeated. "Are you planning to open a guest lodge?" Because the property was certainly big enough.

"The real estate agent suggested renting it out to celebrities or executive types." He shrugged. "I figured it would serve as a reasonable place to visit when you want to see the Davenports, while also making a profit on the side."

"A reasonable place," she parroted back at him. "My mother is going to lose her shit when she sees this."

"It's not as if my wealth is a secret, Aya." He kissed her on the cheek and opened the driver-side door. "Come on, I want to take a proper tour before Henry and Susan arrive."

She joined him outside, their luggage still in the trunk, and breathed in the cool, crisp air. Being in Hydria the last two months had not properly prepared her for the Montana winter, as was evidenced by the goose bumps trailing along her arm.

"Immortals still feel the cold," she said. "Good to know."

Issac chuckled, his fingers lacing with hers. "Oh, I believe immortals feel things more intensely." He tugged her to his side, his gaze suggestive. "Shall we start the tour with our bedroom?"

"I can't believe you bought a lodge."

"I imagine you'll want to visit Susan and Henry as much as possible over the next few years," he said quietly as they walked toward the gorgeous home. "Before they realize you've stopped aging."

Her heart stuttered with the words, her feet missing a step. She hadn't really thought that far ahead, despite it being the logical path.

"They can't know," Issac added softly.

"I know," she managed, her throat suddenly dry. "I just..."

"Hadn't considered it," he murmured. "I know. But I did, and I wanted you to have a place nearby that would be safe for them to visit."

Because the CRF was monitoring her home and her parents. "Has Mateo said anything?" she wondered, needing to change the subject to something safer. Such as her parents' pending arrival. Issac had tasked his technologically gifted progeny with the project of helping her parents leave without a tail.

"His last message said he managed to send the Sentinels watching your parents on a false mission north by altering the tracking device on Henry's car. And as far as surveillance goes, he hasn't seen anyone following them."

"Good." The last thing they needed was the CRF crashing the party. They had enough intruders already.

And two of those intruders were waiting for them in the doorway.

Tom at least wore an apologetic expression.

Jayson, however, did not.

The strong aroma of freshly baked cookies identified Lizzie's position in the kitchen. Even pregnant, the woman was still constantly cooking.

God, my parents are going to lose their ever-loving shit over all of this.

"Beer?" Tom offered, the question for Stas.

"Yes, please." She needed as much alcohol as possible, to… Her hand dropped halfway to the bottle. *Is that…?* "Oh, hell no. Issac, he can't meet my parents." She pointed at the smirking Ichorian lurking in the foyer.

"I believe I joined Issac's family long before you came along, little pet," Tristan replied, snagging the beer Tom had meant for her and taking a long swig. "Thanks, Thomas." He gave a salute and wandered off down the hall, leaving them all in the entryway.

"This can't—"

"I'll talk to him, Aya," Issac murmured. "It will all be fine. I promise."

She lifted her brows. "Fine?"

"He won't bite your parents," Issac promised. "Let's just go inside and take a look around, see how the living arrangements have been sorted, and go from there."

"Amelia made sure you have the master suite," Tom informed them. "Stas's parents will be in the basement bedroom suite, away from everyone else, with their own kitchen and exit onto the patio."

"Brilliant." Issac pushed Stas forward with a hand against her lower back. "We'll start downstairs so Aya can see that Susan and Henry will be safe and sound."

"In a house full of immortals, some of whom have a penchant for biting mortals," she added dryly. "Sure. Safe."

"They'll have a lock on their door," Issac said, guiding her into the main sitting area and toward a set of oversized stairs. Tristan was lounging on the couch, his sharp green eyes on the enormous Christmas tree by the windows and the Ichorian stringing lights around it. "Hello, Aidan."

"Issac," he greeted, a fond smile curling his lips as he glanced over his shoulder. "Lovely property investment, as always."

"I'm glad you approve." Issac eyed the male he considered his father with interest and arched a dark brow in silent question. He probably wanted to know why Aidan's hands were tangled up in cords. Stas wouldn't mind an answer as well. Given everything she knew about the ancient Ichorian, this seemed rather out of character for him.

And where is his harem? He rarely went anywhere without his beautiful trio, but perhaps he'd left them behind on Hydria, where they all were living now thanks to the fallout with Osiris—Stas's supposed grandfather.

"Amelia asked me to decorate the tree," Aidan explained. The words appeared to possess a hidden meaning, enough so that Issac paused at the top of the stairs.

"She did?" he asked, his sapphire eyes sparkling.

"Yes. She requested a festive atmosphere."

"And where is my sister?"

"Upstairs wrapping gifts," Tom replied. "She said anyone who disturbs her will be stabbed with her scissors."

Issac and Aidan both glanced at the blond male dressed in jeans and a sweater, nursing his beer. Too bad he hadn't procured another for Stas. She narrowed her gaze at the beer-stealing Ichorian on the couch who saluted her with the bottle.

Asshole.

Aidan held Issac's gaze, conveying some sort of unspoken message. "It almost reminds me of a former life, minus the life threat."

"Indeed," Issac murmured. "Can you have Jacque find me when you see him next?"

Aidan smiled, an understanding passing between them. "Of course."

"Cheers," he replied. "We'll just be downstairs a bit."

Stas waited until they were out of earshot before whispering, "What was all that about?"

"Amelia used to love the holidays," he replied just as softly. "Before, well, everything."

"Oh." Stas never met the old version of Amelia but had heard stories about her love for hosting parties and celebrating with family. Being held hostage in the CRF's basement for a few years had changed her irrevocably. "Aidan's surprised she's being festive."

"Yes," Issac confirmed, his hand finding Stas's again and giving her a gentle squeeze. "I am, too."

"It's why everyone's insisting on being here with us." Balthazar and Luc obviously enjoyed crashing their holiday plans, but their motives went so much deeper than a little fun and games. They wanted to give Amelia back a piece of her old self, to celebrate the way they used to.

To be a family for the holidays.

"All right," Stas murmured, turning to her demon and wrapping her arms around his neck. "My parents are going to be overwhelmed, but we'll figure it out. And"—she glanced around the spacious lower level—"I don't think they'll be able to complain about their accommodations."

His lips curled. "So you approve of my investment?"

She took in the windows overlooking the ground patio and lake, the giant fireplace between the empty bookshelves, the comfortable furniture, and the door she assumed led to the downstairs bedroom Tom had referenced. "I mean, it's all right. Could use some sprucing up."

He chuckled against her neck, his lips dangerously close to her pulse. "Are you offering to be my personal interior decorator?"

"Depends on how well it pays, job perks—you know, the important stuff."

"How about partial ownership?"

She froze. "What?"

He nibbled her earlobe gently, careful not to break the skin. They'd been growing more and more daring with each other over the last month, almost to the point of danger. One bite, one drop of her blood, and he would die.

But sometimes it seemed he didn't care.

"You can't be serious," she said, pulling back to study his expression.

Mirth danced in his gaze. "Any other woman would be over the moon, but of course, you balk at the idea of it."

"Tell me you're not serious," she demanded.

"I'm not serious," he replied. "Which I only said because you forced me to."

Damn it. Sometimes having the ability to compel someone backfired immensely. "Issac—"

He pressed his finger to her lips. "You can yell at me later. Lucian just showed me an image of Henry's car pulling into the drive. I suggest we greet them before the others do, yes?"

"This conversation isn't over."

"Definitely not," he agreed, his sapphire gaze glimmering. "You know how I adore our negotiations, Aya." He brushed his mouth over hers, silencing her retort. "Parents, love."

Right, time to celebrate the holidays.

With her human parents and her billionaire Ichorian boyfriend.

Oh, and a lodge full of a bunch of crazy, ancient immortals.

Yeah, what could possibly go wrong?

CHAPTER THREE

Issac

SUSAN DAVENPORT APPEARED ready to faint. Henry didn't look much better himself, his expression flickering between astonishment and concern.

Astasiya stood between them for the introductions, her green eyes meeting Issac's on several occasions, as if she craved his strength.

Balthazar laid on the charm.

Lucian remained cool and collected like his father, Aidan.

Amelia was warm, but not overly so.

Thomas and Elizabeth were already familiar with the Davenports, and Thomas worked his magic perfectly with his cover story.

Jayson gave Henry a strong handshake that seemed to intimidate the shorter, lankier human.

And Tristan merely smiled, his distaste for consorting so closely with mortals barely concealed.

Issac's phone buzzed, the incoming message from Mateo. *All clear.*

Brilliant, he typed back. Part of the reason he'd chosen Kalispell over visiting the Davenports' home was the CRF surveillance issue. As fun as it would be to kill a few Sentinels, Issac wanted Astasiya to enjoy the holiday. And she would be uneasy if blood were on their hands.

He made sure she saw him check the phone before giving a subtle nod, confirming they were safe. Her responding grin warmed his heart. She'd been concerned about seeing her family so close to home, but Issac knew how much it meant to her. While Susan and Henry weren't her real parents, they were the ones who raised her from seven years old onward, and she very much considered them her mother and father.

As such, he did, too.

Which meant he needed to turn Henry Davenport's opinion of him around because right now the male was thinking about clever ways to shoot Issac. Of course, he also imagined Balthazar's demise after he kissed Susan's hand— an image Issac quite enjoyed.

"This is a lovely rental, Issac," Susan murmured, admiring the living area of the main floor.

"Thank you." He didn't bother to correct her assumption regarding the so-called rental. Astasiya could correct her later once he informed her of the ownership agreement, a conversation that would likely infuriate his favorite blonde.

He couldn't wait to see her expression when he admitted that the home was in an alias he created for her, not one of his own. She needed to learn more about investments anyway. This would be her introduction to the game. What she did with the proceeds would be her choice; he would guide her only if she asked.

"We should probably get everyone settled," Elizabeth said, her brown eyes dancing nervously between the Davenports and everyone else. The blue dress she wore only barely covered her bump—an oddity considering she was only seven or eight weeks pregnant. Her Seraphim-altered genetics and Jayson's Hydraian genes made the outcome unpredictable, something Lucian and Balthazar were monitoring carefully.

But she seemed fine, if a little tired.

"Yes, Tristan, will you help me with the bags?" Issac gave him a pointed look, conveying that it was not a request but a demand.

His old friend sighed. "I'd be delighted," he deadpanned.

"Oh, that's not necessary." Susan looked at her husband, her eyes telling him to speak up.

"I insist," Issac replied before Henry could respond. "Astasiya can show you to your room." He'd gestured to the quarters earlier, before making their way back upstairs to meet her parents.

Tristan led the way, his shoulders stiff. Issac almost slapped him on the back just to loosen the bastard up but decided words would be better suited.

"Do I need to warn you away from the Davenports?" he asked seriously as they exited the home. "Or can I trust you to behave?"

His green eyes flashed. "So I'm a child now, am I?"

"You certainly treat Aya like a jealous sibling, yes."

He snorted. "That would imply we're equals, which we're not."

"No, you're not." Issac opened Henry's trunk and slammed a bag against Tristan's chest. "Astasiya could easily kick your ass if she wanted to, so you might want to show her some more respect."

He scoffed at that. "I'd enjoy watching her try."

"Oh, Tristan, so would I." Because Astasiya would flatten his arrogant ass in a second. Issac lifted another suitcase and set it on the ground before leveling his friend with a look. "Susan and Henry don't know anything about our lives, and we need to keep it that way. Surely you remember your final years with your family, because I do."

Issac had been patient while Tristan said his goodbyes, had consoled him when his parents died a decade later—alone, wondering where their prodigal son had gone.

"None of this is easy on her," he added. "She's trying very hard to pretend it doesn't bother her, that her world hasn't completely changed overnight—"

"Because of a decision she made," Tristan interjected with a growl that echoed inside of Issac.

As if he didn't know that.

As if he didn't think about it every goddamned day since Astasiya ran off to Bora Bora to save her best friend without thinking about her own future—*their* future.

"You have a right to be angry," Tristan continued, his shoulders tense, his gaze narrowed as he dropped the suitcase. "That woman puts your life in danger every day that you remain with her, and you just expect me to accept that. I won't, Issac. I refuse. And you can't ask me to."

He swallowed, his hands fisting at his sides.

"Hit me if you need to. I'll take it. But deep down, you know I'm right." Tristan punctuated his words with a sharp poke against his chest, his Irish lilt intensifying with each word. "You're giving up everything for her, maybe even your own life, and I cannot—will not—stand by and watch it happen."

"Then why are you here?" Issac asked through his teeth. "Why bother spending the holidays with us when you hate her so damn much?"

"Because you're my family and I worry every day that it might be my last with you. So yeah, I'm going to be here, and I'm going to watch you continue to sacrifice your own fucking happiness for a female who is nowhere near worthy of you. I'll do my best to steer clear of her, but do not ask me to be kind. Not when she's a living, breathing threat to the person I care about most in this world."

A sharp inhale had Issac cringing.

Astasiya stood just outside, her green eyes on a very unapologetic Tristan.

"Aya," Issac started, but she held out her hand.

"I just came to tell you my parents are downstairs for whenever you want to bring them their bags." She turned before he could reply, disappearing back into the house.

"You're an ass," Issac hissed.

"She knows the truth just as well as I do. The difference is, I'm not afraid to say it, because I actually care. She's just a selfish bitch who—"

Issac's fist connected with Tristan's jaw so hard it sent the man two paces back. "Never speak like that about her again." It was one thing to point out the concerns of their situation, but quite another to fling a derogatory label at Aya.

Someone started clapping, causing Issac to stiffen.

Everyone was in the house.

And the source of the sound was coming from the driveway.

Behind them.

He turned slowly to find Ezekiel leaning against the garage in his trademark leather jacket and jeans. "Nice form, Wakefield. Who knew you had it in you?" He applauded again, his legs casually crossed at the ankles. "Now, someone mentioned a holiday party, and I'm positively famished. Care to invite a lonely assassin in for dinner?"

Chapter Four

Issac

A BLADE WHIRLED THROUGH THE AIR, landing in Ezekiel's hand as he caught it by the sharp side. He eyed the metal, balanced it against his fingers, and smiled.

"Beautiful craftsmanship as always, Jedrick." He slid the knife into a pocket inside his jacket. "Perfect holiday gift. Unfortunately, I didn't get you anything."

"Oh, I have the perfect gift in mind," Jayson replied as he approached, Balthazar behind him. The mind reader must have heard Issac's mental curse at their unexpected guest's arrival.

"Do you?" The assassin looked positively delighted. "I'm all ears."

"Leave," Jayson growled.

"For a friendship as old as ours? That seems quite sad in terms of a gift." Ezekiel tapped his chin. "I know. How about you invite me in for dinner in exchange for some information you may find useful?"

"The last time you provided us with information didn't exactly work out in a positive manner," Balthazar replied dryly, no doubt thinking about how Osiris had forced Alik to use his torturing gifts against them all.

"Oh?" Ezekiel arched a brow. "See, now, as I remember it, Lizzie was returned safely and no one died. Oh, and Stas learned something very important about herself. A secret that's been kept hidden for nearly twenty-five years. Next week, actually." His dark eyes actually creased, his lips curling fondly. "That was a good month."

"Why are you here, Ezekiel?" Jayson demanded, taking the words right out of Issac's mouth.

"Why, to celebrate the holidays, of course. I mean, that's why you all crashed Issac and Stas's plans with the Davenports, right?"

A chill drafted down Issac's spine. "You've been watching Astasiya."

"For many years now," Ezekiel replied. "There's so much you don't know. I keep waiting for everything to unravel, but it's like watching a turtle cross the finish line." He gave a dramatic sigh and pushed off the garage. "So how about you let Uncle Ezekiel join the festivities? Maybe I can provide a few more hints to send you on your merry way, yeah? Besides, I've always enjoyed a good burning of the Yule log."

"No." The answer came from Jayson. "You are not getting anywhere near Red ever again."

Ezekiel snorted, those eerie gold-flecked irises finding Issac. "He's a protective one, isn't he?"

"You're not getting anywhere near Astasiya, either," he growled.

"Ah, now, how about we let her be the one to decide that?" His gaze traveled over them to the blonde in question, her ashen expression telling Issac exactly how she felt about it.

He moved to her side, his arm wrapping around her lower back on instinct. Tristan's words replayed in his mind, his accusations and frustrations.

If Aya was being selfish, then so was Issac.

He wanted this just as much as she did, if not more.

Being near her was akin to breathing. Without her, he would drown.

"Why is he here?" she demanded.

"He claims to have information and wants to join us for dinner."

"More like he wants to eat my parents for dinner," she snapped, some of her spirit leaking through her ghostly exterior. Ezekiel had killed her birth parents, or so she remembered. And the look in her eyes suggested she craved vengeance for them, for everything that had ever been done to her.

"They're not my type," Ezekiel murmured, his head tilting to the side. "Jedrick, can you ask your darling Red a question for me?"

"No," Jayson replied, not missing a beat.

Ezekiel ignored him. "Ask her about the man who helped her at Osiris's estate. Specifically, ask her for his name." His focus shifted to Issac. "Consider that your first clue. I'll return on Christmas Eve with a Yule log. That'll be my contribution to the festivities." He disappeared into a cloud of black smoke.

Astasiya melted into Issac's side, whatever harm Tristan may have caused disappearing beneath Ezekiel's unexpected visit. She pressed her forehead to his shoulder as he enveloped her in a hug.

Balthazar met his gaze, understanding bright in his features.

He picked up the Davenports' luggage without a word, handed one to Tristan, and guided the disgruntled Ichorian inside. But not before his oldest friend could pass him one final glower, the bruise on his jaw already fading.

Issac wouldn't apologize. Not after what Tristan called his Aya. The bastard deserved the hit and worse.

Jayson ran his fingers through his brown hair and expelled a long breath. "Right. I think it might be best to take Lizzie back to Hydria, where she'll be safe."

Ezekiel had tasted Elizabeth's blood, which explained how he found them all so easily in Montana. He could trace to anyone's essence he'd ever imbibed. But that didn't explain how he knew about Issac and Stas's original plans.

"I don't think he's here for Elizabeth at all." If that were Ezekiel's goal, he wouldn't have made his presence known until he struck. "This is about Astasiya."

"Maybe so, but I can't risk Lizzie being here." Jayson was already walking toward the house.

Issac couldn't blame the man for his concern. Osiris wanted their child and had already kidnapped Elizabeth once, but Ezekiel's side on this war remained ambiguous. While he resided with the evil mastermind and frequently ran his errands, the assassin offered intriguing insights that had proven useful over the last few months.

"Ask her the question," Issac said loudly, causing Jayson to pause at the door. "Ezekiel is clearly playing a game. I want the name so I know how to respond."

Jayson didn't move or reply right away, his emotions muddying his usual flair for strategy. Questioning Elizabeth was the correct path. However, her pregnancy overrode reason, especially in her fiancé's mind.

He eventually nodded before heading into the house, leaving Issac and Astasiya alone. She remained quiet, her body trembling against him as she no doubt lived through the horror of her memories. The fire that took her parents' lives haunted her nightmares, something very few knew. She confided in Issac about them, claiming they were growing worse, not better, with her immortality. Every time she woke up screaming, his heart broke a little more for her.

"Are you unhappy?" she asked softly, surprising him.

"What?" He pulled back to study her expression. "Why would you ask me that?"

She gave him a look. "You know why I'm asking, Issac." Pain flashed in her green depths, the edges of her lips curling downward. "He's right about me. I'm not—"

"If you tell me you're not worthy, I might break something." On that note, he strongly disagreed with Tristan.

She grimaced. "No, I was going to say I'm not good for you."

He groaned, releasing her and looking upward. "That's the same bloody statement, Astasiya."

"No, it's not. I could kill you, Issac."

"And I could kill you," he tossed back. "I could have killed you the day we first met. I could kill you now. The question is, do you expect me to?"

"Of course not."

"Likewise."

"That's not fair," she argued. "This is different."

"So I'm not entitled to trust you the way you trust me? Is that it?"

She growled, the sound normally one he enjoyed, but not at the moment. Right now, he felt like throttling her. "You're being purposely dense."

His eyebrows shot upward. "Excuse me?"

"First of all, you can't kill me. But I'd love to see you try. Second of all, my blood is toxic to you. One bite, Issac, and you die. Tristan's right. I'm a walking threat to you, one you dance with every day and sleep with every night. It's only a matter of time—"

"You think so little of my self-control?" he cut in, furious now. "After nearly two months of making this work, you're willing to throw everything away because of some foolish words spouted by Tristan?"

"No. No, that's not..." She deflated, her expression falling. "That's not what I meant. I just... He's right." Spoken so softly, her fire completely extinguished. "How could you possibly be happy with this?"

"No, Aya. That's not the right question." He moved into her space, leaving them a hairsbreadth apart. "The question you need to be asking is, how could I possibly be happy *without* this?"

She gazed up at him, her heart in her eyes. "I don't..." She swallowed roughly. "I *can't* lose you." She cupped his cheek. "You're my always."

He tried to smile, but his mouth refused him. "Then trust me to know my limits." He leaned into her touch, sighing. "Nothing worth having is ever easy, Aya."

They stared at each other for a long moment, so many unspoken words and emotions thriving between them.

Issac had never been one for commitment or relationships, finding them frivolous and not worth the effort. But Astasiya was different. From the moment they first met, she'd changed him irrevocably.

She'd been a pawn he meant to use in a revenge scheme but had blossomed into so much more. Fate dealt them a twisted hand, marking them as incompatible, but Issac never was one for following the rules.

He risked his life every time he kissed her, every time they touched, but he wouldn't be living if he let her go. That dependence terrified him. He'd never once relied on another being for anything. But Astasiya owned his heart. It would stop beating without her.

Their connection surpassed understanding.

It just was.

And he would do whatever he needed to hold on to it, to keep her by his side.

"I don't need or want anyone else," he whispered. "Only you, Aya. You are my happiness."

Her beautiful eyes glistened with tears. "Issac—"

The clearing of a throat from the doorway broke their trance, forcing Issac's gaze to the waiting male.

"We need to talk." Jayson's tone was underlined with resignation. "Stas is going to want to hear this, too."

Chapter Five

"Amelia is distracting Susan in the kitchen, and Henry is chatting with Tom," Lucian informed Stas before she could ask after her parents.

Everyone else was in the living area, including Jacque. He had a big pizza in his lap that Balthazar seemed to be sharing with him.

Aidan and Lucian remained standing, their identical green eyes brimming with knowledge and curiosity.

"What?" Stas asked. Everyone was focused on her. "What is it?"

"Tell Stas what you told me," Jayson murmured, his arms around Lizzie, who was seated in the oversized chair with him.

"I never thought it was important," she said, her cheeks flushing.

Jayson fondled a strand of her red hair that had fallen out of her makeshift bun. "It's okay, Red. You were focused on more important details." His palm fell to her belly, a smile lightening his eyes. "But tell them all now so we can discuss the matter."

She bit her lip and nodded. "Yeah, okay. Jayson said Kiel, sorry, Ezekiel, asked for the name of the guy from…" She trailed off and swallowed. "Osiris called him Sethios."

Stas's heart stopped beating.

"So rare, in fact, that they reveal your ancestry, daughter of Caro and Sethios." Osiris's lips had curled into an avid smile that chilled her to this day. *"Or would you prefer I call you 'granddaughter'?"*

"Ezekiel mentioned Sethios as well," Lizzie continued. "Said they grew up together, that Osiris was his father, but Jay said he meant *maker* or *Sire.*"

"What did Sethios look like?" Aidan asked, his words barely audible over the water rushing through Stas's ears. "Can you picture him?"

"Uh, yeah." Lizzie frowned, her attention shifting to Issac. He could see images, manipulate them, force people to dream… Was he seeing Sethios right now? "Brown hair, green eyes, tall, muscular in a thin way, likely because he couldn't eat with his mouth being wired shut."

Stas's focus snapped, the description bringing up memories.

Those features are common.
Don't get your hopes up.
He's dead.
You saw him burn.

Images assaulted her, plunging her into the past, the memory morphing into something harsh. Real. Overwhelming.

"You have to play today, little angel. For me and your mom. Just in case the bad men come, okay?"

Stas covered her ears, her knees giving out beneath her.

'It's the same as all the other times. Just hide and wait for us to find you. Then we'll get some ice cream."

"Now go, sweet angel. Hide."

Someone was screaming, so loud it hurt.

These memories.

She hated these memories.

The fire.

Ezekiel's face smiling in the flames.

The flare of red feathers beside her…

She shook her head, the nightmare morphing in her head, changing, never quite right. As if her mind had refused to comprehend that day. That night. The one that forever changed her life.

"Aya." Issac's voice was a breath against her ears.

But her father's screams were louder.

Writhing on the ground.

No flames.

This wasn't right. He burned… She'd watched her parents burn. But the fire didn't exist. Only *him.*

"Incendiary bullets," Ezekiel said. *"Jonathan's researchers developed them for the Sentinels at the CRF."*

What was this madness?

"Aya." Issac sounded insistent, his hands on her shoulders.

But she was running. Fast. Hard. Into the arms of an angel.

And nothing.

She gasped, her throat raw, her face damp with tears. Peppermint and sandalwood overwhelmed her, bringing her back, comforting her. "Issac," she breathed, her voice raspy as she buried her face in his sweater. His arms were around her, cocooning her from the nightmare brought to life by a description from her past.

Her mother had hurt so badly that day.

After her angel friend came to visit.

Stas fought for breath, her mind fracturing, unraveling, revealing an onslaught of memories that didn't exist—

shouldn't exist.

"What the fuck is happening to her?" Issac demanded, his voice a distant dream. She tried desperately to cling to him, but she hit a wall. It slammed down so hard it blinded her, throwing her away from the memory of her father, her mother, Ezekiel.

She clutched her chest, the pain of it searing a hole inside her spirit. Her world. Her life. Tears streamed down her face at the loss of what she didn't know, the reality slipping from her grasp, replaced by a blurry, false image.

Not right.

The fire isn't right.

A cloud enveloped her.

Warmth.

Issac.

She held on to him, surrounding herself in his familiar heat, the only truth in her existence. Her always.

"Distract them," he was saying. "I'll bring her out of it."

Someone replied. She didn't care who. All that mattered was Issac and that voice—a woman's voice.

Mom?

She followed the thread deep into the water, a familiar vision slamming into her heart. Trapped on the ocean's floor, a fragment of herself, lost to the depths of the sea.

Her body convulsed, begging for air, her lungs screaming in unending agony.

It burned.

It faded.

It flared again.

Over and over and over.

Issac's mouth covered her own, his oxygen becoming hers as she took what she needed, wrapping herself in him, his kiss grounding her in the land of the living. In his arms again.

His comfort.

His adoration.

His protection.

"Issac," she whimpered, burying her face in his neck, breathing him in, begging him to hold her in the present, to never let her go again. *What's happening to me?*

She trembled, horrified.

These terrors hit her at night, not during the day. Not like this. Not around a group of people.

The fear in Issac's eyes pierced her soul, locking her before him, under him, *with* him. He kissed her again, this time more forcefully, compelling her to relax, to feel, to lose herself in their embrace.

This was her world.

Her place.

Her Issac.

She returned his kiss with a fervor, forgetting the past, the present, and the future and focusing solely on him. The chaos slowly started to dissipate, replaced by a passion only her demon could excite. His tongue against hers, his hands roaming her body beneath the sweater, skin on skin. She arched into him, needing more. Needing him.

"Aya," he murmured, his mouth ripping from hers, his exhale heavy against her mouth.

Stas grabbed him, yanking him back, not ready to stop. She devoured him the way she craved, the way she used to, the way she adored. But he pushed her down, his hand on her chest, his breath hot against her neck. The tension in his touch told her something was wrong, his shoulders locked above her.

She tasted it then—the familiar iron fluid on the tip of her tongue.

Blood.

Her nails bit into his shoulders, her body frozen beneath him.

Oh God…

Don't let it be mine.

Please, fuck, don't—

"It's mine," he gritted out. "Just… I need a moment."

The air rushed from her lungs, tears filling her eyes. *So*

close. Too close. She shook, her soul ripping in half at the reality of what this could have meant.

I could lose him forever.

She knew that already, understood that, but the actuality of it shattered every truth she'd manufactured as to why this could work.

But they were just fooling themselves all along.

Issac held her close, his own shoulders shaking with hers. Because he knew it, too—how close they'd both just come to losing him forever. Stas could never live with herself if she killed him.

She buried her head against him, weeping beneath their crushing truth.

He can never really be mine.

Not again.

"I'm sorry," she cried. "I'm so sorry."

He just shook his head, his own tears falling soundlessly against her. Broken.

She'd destroyed Issac Wakefield with a kiss.

No, she destroyed him six weeks ago when she died before they'd had a chance to say goodbye. But would they have ever wanted to?

"Aya." He locked his arms around her, clinging to her as if she might disappear.

They were nearing the end.

And they both knew it.

She fell apart against him, unable to hide her agony. "I don't know how to do this."

"Neither do I," he admitted, his voice breaking.

Time escaped them.

Lost to their misery and pain.

Neither of them wanted to let go, to admit defeat.

"I can't lose you, Issac. I don't want to lose you."

She'd rather live a life without being able to touch him than to live a life without him at all.

"I love you," she whispered.

He nuzzled her neck, his face damp against her skin.

"I'm not ready to say goodbye, Aya."

"I know."

"Don't make me say goodbye yet." He sounded so fractured that it tore her apart. She could deny him nothing. Especially when she desired the same.

But one of these days, they'd have to be strong enough to walk away from each other. Because she refused to live in this world without Issac Wakefield.

Today doesn't have to be that day.

Another week.

Month.

"We have to be careful," she said, her fingers threading through his hair. "Far more careful than we've been."

He nodded. "Yes."

She nodded, too. "Not yet, then."

"Not yet," he repeated, his shoulders relaxing while his grip remained firm. "Not yet."

He said the words several more times, sounding less and less sure with every breath. But Stas refused to hear the doubt creeping in, refused to acknowledge the sense of foreboding settling over her, and instead chose to live in the moment. With her Issac.

Her love.

Her always.

Chapter Six

Stas

STAS BLINKED BLEARILY AT THE CLOCK, convinced it was lying to her.

Four? No, that couldn't be right. She squinted again at it. Still the same time. Had someone forgotten to set it when they arrived?

She shifted away from Issac's chest and glanced out the windows to see the moonlight dancing over the lake.

"Shit." Stas sat up and wiped her eyes, groggy with sleep. Her poor parents. What did they think? Were they worried? Oh, fuck, were they safe?

She started to climb out of bed, only to be yanked backward into Issac's hard body.

"Everyone is asleep," he murmured against her ear.

"Including Susan and Henry."

"Crap," she grumbled, her palm slapping her forehead. "What a great hostess I've been."

"Amelia told Susan you weren't feeling well and I was tending to you. She's fine, as is everyone else." He rolled her to her back to hover over her, his palm against her cheek. "But how are you?"

She swallowed, her throat dry. "Honestly, I don't know." The emotional upheaval had left her unsettled and hollow. "I hate this, Issac."

"Me, too, love." He brushed his lips against hers, far too soft for her liking. But they'd agreed to be safer. She couldn't risk him. Not now. Not ever. "Can we talk about what Elizabeth said? About her time with Osiris?"

Stas frowned, trying to recall the conversation. Yesterday had melted together in her mind, from getting on the plane to ending up in bed with Issac. It felt like sorting through years of memories, not a day's worth of conversations.

"Aya?" Issac prompted, the moon shining brightly enough outside to highlight the concern in his blue eyes.

"Yesterday feels like a dream," she whispered. "A bad one."

He drew his thumb along her lower lip, his gaze tracking the movement. "You fell into a trance and woke as if from a nightmare. I didn't know what to do, so I handled it the only way I could to ground you in the moment."

It was all so hazy. Something about her parents and the fire. "There weren't any flames." Her brow furrowed as she tried to remember, but the memory eluded her, slipping into the recesses of her mind behind a wall she couldn't penetrate. "It's strange, like my past has been altered somehow." She poked at the barrier. "I sound crazy."

"No," he murmured, his blue eyes lifting to hers. His palm slid over her sweater to her hip, pulling her onto her side so he could slip beneath the fabric along her lower back. "This rune proves someone altered key parts of you as a child, perhaps your memories as well." His touch tingled against the base of her spine.

"Can immortals do that?"

"I know an Ichorian who can tamper with perceptions of the past, and there's a Hydraian with a similar ability. But we're not talking about average immortals, Aya. A Seraphim placed this rune on you—a powerful one. Maybe he or she altered your mind, too."

Stas considered the possibility, a flurry of red feathers painting her vision for the barest of seconds. "Why would I be remembering these things now?" All her life, she'd been certain of the past. But these last few months had transformed her on a base level, leaving her more unsure of herself by the minute.

"If I were to guess? Your rebirth." He continued to trace the pattern along her skin, his touch hypnotic and soothing. "Or maybe newer developments have triggered your true memories to rise to the surface. Meeting Osiris and Ezekiel, for example. Hearing the names of your parents—Sethios and Caro." He studied her intently, as if waiting for a reaction.

It took her a moment to follow, yesterday proving too overwhelming to recall every detail. But one stuck out in the sea of confusion, prompted by Issac's silence. "Lizzie said the man who helped her was Sethios."

"She did, and the one she envisioned is the same Sethios that Aidan and the Elders have known for over two thousand years. He was considered Osiris's favorite protégé but disappeared about twenty-five years ago. Everyone assumed he'd gone into hiding, like Ezekiel, but recent events suggest that might not be the case."

"You think he's my father."

"I do." He flattened his palm against her skin, branding her to her very soul. "Sethios could persuade others through hypnosis, which is quite similar to compulsion."

"Is it possible that, with Osiris being his Sire, creating me mingled the abilities somehow?" she wondered.

"Allowing me to be more persuasive than hypnotic?" Because her power was definitely underlined in command, not trickery.

"Yes, but I find Osiris's terminology to be rather intriguing. He called you his granddaughter, as if by blood."

"But he's an Ichorian." And they couldn't procreate.

"Yes, but what if he created Sethios prior to being turned into an immortal?"

Stas considered that. "You're saying Sethios might be his biological son."

Issac nodded. "We don't know how old either of them truly is, and it would suit the story Ezekiel told Elizabeth. He said Sethios was Osiris's son, and Osiris was known to refer to him in that manner as well."

"So you think Osiris became an Ichorian after his son was born and then later turned that son—Sethios—into an Ichorian," Stas deduced.

"It seems quite plausible, yes. And would explain how you inherited gifts from Osiris."

She agreed, but what a convoluted parental history. "If that's all true, then Lizzie..." She couldn't finish the thought, the words sticking in her throat.

"Saw your birth father less than two months ago," Issac murmured. "Yes."

"And you're certain it's the same Sethios?"

"The one she imagined matches the man I've seen, just with a few odd details."

"Details?" she repeated.

"Yes, it would appear he's being punished for something."

The way he said it sent a chill down her spine. "Because of me?" she guessed, her voice barely a whisper.

Issac shook his head. "No. Osiris didn't realize who you were until you used your gift against him. His shock was clear. Unfortunately, that does leave us without an answer as to why he sewed Sethios's lips shut."

Stas shivered, the image leaving a gruesome stamp on

her imagination. "If he's really alive, and my father—"

"I see where you're going with this, but trust me, Aya, Sethios can take care of himself. If he wants to escape Osiris, he will."

"How do you know that?"

"Oh, Aya, his reputation is… intense."

Intense? "How so?"

"Let's just say he's his father's son."

"Are you telling me that my father is evil?" she demanded, feeling innately defensive. The father of her memories, as muddled as they might be, did not remind her of Osiris in the slightest. Her dad was honorable and affectionate, always calling her his little angel…

"No, I'm saying Sethios has a formidable reputation, just like his father. If anyone could stand up to Osiris, it's Sethios."

"Except his lips are sealed," she reiterated. "Why would anyone agree to live like that?"

Issac studied her for a long moment, his sapphire irises swirling with experience and an intelligence she envied. Luc and Aidan were known for their strategic gifts, but her demon always considered every angle, his steps always measured, his decisions never emotionally driven. Practical, passionate, and perfect.

"It pains me to say this, but I believe we need to take Ezekiel up on his Christmas Eve offer. He clearly has information, and while I have no doubt his motives are purely self-fulfilling, we may be able to glean some pertinent details from him. If we play the game right."

"Between you, Luc, and Aidan, I think we have the strategy realm covered."

He didn't look nearly as certain as she felt. "Ezekiel isn't one for predictability."

"No, but neither are you," she pointed out, brushing her lips over his. "My rule-breaking demon."

He chuckled. "Are you flirting with me, Aya?"

"I'm just identifying one of your finer attributes." Her

hand slid to his ass, squeezing it through the boxer briefs.

He pushed her onto her back again, his gaze glittering. "Now you're definitely flirting."

"No, just acknowledging yet another very fine attribute," she teased.

"I was trying to have a serious conversation."

"And you did a fine job of it. The conclusion is to have Ezekiel over for Christmas Eve." Something that would require a large group discussion, including parameters to be taken to safeguard her adoptive parents. However, as it was not even five o'clock in the morning yet, they had time to prepare for that conversation. "I'm ready for a diversion now."

Amusement shone in his features. "A diversion, hmm? To keep your mind off Sethios, you mean?"

Some of her playful energy left. His ability to see through her was uncanny. "I can't afford to hope, Issac."

He palmed her cheek. "I understand, love. It's a lot to consider, but if it's true, it would confirm your childhood memories were altered."

"I know."

"And it will necessitate looking into your past even more. Because, Aya, Seraphim do not interfere in immortal or mortal lives without cause."

Seraphim were near myths to Ichorians and Hydraians, their presence thought to be extinct eons ago. But her rune suggested otherwise. As did, perhaps, the meddling of her mind.

"Why me?" she whispered, gazing up at him, wishing he had all the answers.

"I wish I knew, Aya." He brushed his lips over hers. "But I can't deny that there is something breathtakingly unique about you."

She started to question that until she caught the smile playing over his lips. "Now you're flirting with me."

"Some would call it 'courting,'" he murmured.

She snorted. "Only old men from a very different time

period."

"How about 'seducing,' then?" he suggested, his lips a hairsbreadth from hers.

"That depends on your goals, Mister Wakefield."

"Well, for one, I'd like to divest you of these clothes, Miss Davenport."

Warmth spread through her veins, her lips curling on instinct. "I think I would like that."

"I think you would, too."

"Then stop talking about it and get to work." Persuasion trickled into her words, forcing his hands to start moving. *Undress me,* she whispered to his mind, his darkening gaze confirming he sensed it and approved.

"Mmm, a command," he murmured against her mouth. "My favorite."

Chapter Seven

Astasiya's blonde hair glowed in the sunlight, reminding him of the way she'd looked in his bed earlier this morning. Except she'd been naked then. Now she was dressed in a sweater and jeans again—a new pair thanks to Balthazar leaving their luggage outside their door.

Issac sipped his coffee while admiring her smile. She appeared so carefree and relieved beside Susan, discussing holidays of Christmases past. Something about sledding in Havre before visiting the tree downtown. He'd have to take her there next year, just to see if the images matched the ones blossoming in Susan's mind.

Assuming he and Astasiya were still together.

His chest ached at the thought of her being with anyone

else, the wrongness of it twisting his gut. But that kiss last night had been eye-opening. She'd barely nicked him in her eagerness. Had it been the other way around, he wouldn't be breathing right now.

How could something that felt so right be unsuitable?

There had to be a way for this to work. A way around fate.

His heart yearned for her and her alone.

It had taken him three hundred years to find her, to feel like this about another, to *love*. He couldn't give her up because of some ridiculous blood right.

That was what no one understood—their connection went deeper than any other, as if their souls were joined.

Her green eyes rose to his, the secrets in them making him smile. Because he knew how her mind worked, what her mother's comments about the seriousness of their relationship implied.

Susan wanted to know about marriage.

Astasiya had no desire to marry—ever. It wasn't her style. Nor was it his.

"Mom," she groaned. "Stop."

"What?" She glanced at Issac. "He rented a house for us to spend the holidays in. He clearly sees this being a long-term thing."

Astasiya's head fell to the table as Elizabeth entered. "We're not getting married, Mother."

"I didn't say that, did I? I just wanted to know what your next steps are. That's all." She gave Elizabeth a beseeching look. "You understand, right, Lizzie?"

Astasiya groaned louder while her best friend giggled, clearly enjoying her torment. Issac couldn't help but chuckle as well, earning him a glower from his favorite blonde.

"Stas isn't the marrying type, Mrs. Davenport," Elizabeth said. "But I think what she has with Issac is very special."

Yes, she'd made it quite clear that she was cheering for them even while everyone else expected this to blow up badly. Elizabeth Watkins was a true romantic, her own happily-ever-after only days away.

Jayson joined them, unable to stay too far away from his bride-to-be and the mother of his unborn child.

Issac had spoken to him briefly this morning about Ezekiel, telling him their plan for tomorrow night. He'd agreed on the play and also said they were staying, something Issac guessed Elizabeth had demanded. She wouldn't want to leave her best friend after learning her biological father might still be alive.

Of course, that meant the grounds were now flooded with Guardians—all here with the purpose of protecting their Hydraian Elders, and Elizabeth.

Not a horrible reaction so long as the Davenports didn't notice.

"So where is it going?" Susan pressed, looking between them impatiently.

"Where is what going?" Henry asked as he entered with his arms full of groceries. Thomas sauntered in after him, his load noticeably heavier. Henry had wanted to go on a beer run, which turned into a long shopping list from his wife, and Thomas had offered to accompany him—for protection.

"This relationship between our daughter and Issac."

He set down the bags and met Issac's gaze. "They're clearly getting married. Right, son?"

Astasiya bolted upright. "Dad!"

"What? You're practically living with the boy, and if he's the gentleman you claim him to be, then he'll make an honest woman out of you."

"What century are we in, again?" she demanded.

"One where 'courting' is considered outdated," Issac reminded her helpfully.

She glowered at him. "Do you want to get married?"

"Do you?" he countered, smirking.

"No!" She looked imploringly at Elizabeth. "Please help me. Please."

"By doing what?" she asked, her brown eyes glowing with mirth. "I already said you're not the marrying type."

"Of course she is," Henry put in. "All women want to be married."

"Not Stas," Thomas and Elizabeth said at once.

Astasiya waved her hands at them as if to imply that was proof enough of her argument.

"Then what are your intentions?" Henry asked, his eyes on Issac and not Astasiya.

So it was going to be that kind of day, then. Her adoptive father had made no secret of his distaste for Issac from the moment they first met after her graduation. Of course, he wasn't actually dating the man's daughter then. He'd merely been planning to use her for a revenge scheme. Not the best introduction, to be sure.

"Dad." Astasiya's green eyes were narrowed, the fun of the moment gone, seriousness taking over.

"It's all right, love," Issac murmured. "He has a right to ask, and a gentleman would answer."

Henry arched a brow. "I agree."

He stood to be on the same eye level, not liking the dominating angle her father had taken over him.

"While I have no qualms with the sanctity of marriage, it has never been a desire for your daughter. Nor has it ever been one of mine."

"Exactly," Astasiya muttered, her relief palpable.

"What I do desire," he continued, "is a long, prosperous life with the woman I adore at my side, and I will do whatever I need to ensure that happens. We don't require a ceremony to prove ourselves to one another or anyone else. What matters is Astasiya trusts me and I trust her, and we will remain together until she says otherwise."

He held Henry's gaze, allowing the man to see and feel the sincerity behind his words, as well as the resolve underlying his tone. Issac would be respectful to a point, but he would not be intimidated. Not even by the male who adopted Astasiya.

"So you're agreeing to take care of her." Not a question, but a statement.

"Oh God." Astasiya turned to her father. "I can take care of myself, thank you."

"As far as she'll allow me to, yes," he replied, not breaking eye contact with Henry even when Aya turned to glare at him. "But if you think Astasiya needs me to take care of her, then you don't know your daughter that well." The challenge sizzled in the air, Thomas and Jayson both taking a step backward while Susan's lips parted.

Astasiya, however, appeared quite pleased.

And Elizabeth was grinning from ear to ear.

Issac raised a brow, waiting for Henry's next test.

He would pass.

There was no other outcome in regard to his Astasiya. *Mine.*

"I've read about you."

"I'm sure you have, Henry. Astasiya did, too, when we first met." He purposely smiled at her, recalling a conversation they once had about how he never grinned in photographs.

Her lips curled as she shook her head. "He's not the man portrayed in those tabloids, Dad."

"I'm starting to see that." He looked Issac up and down. "I'd like to continue seeing that."

"I'll answer anything you want," he replied. "Consider me an open book." Within reason, of course. He couldn't exactly come clean about his Ichorian roots.

Henry nodded, seemingly satisfied for the moment. "Help me unload the rest of the groceries."

"Uh, there are none," Thomas interjected, gesturing to the bags littering the counters.

"You carried them all?" Henry's eyes were wide.

Thomas merely shrugged. "I'm young. Strong. Long arms."

Susan admired said arms, causing Astasiya to push away from the table. "Yeah, so, Issac, weren't you going to show me the grounds?"

"I was." A lie, as they had no such plans, but playing along came naturally to him. "Are you ready now?"

"Yes, please." She held out her hand and he gladly accepted, pulling her to his side to kiss her cheek. So warm and soft. Perfect. His Aya. "We'll be back in a bit."

She started walking, her boot-clad feet moving quickly over the marble tile of the extravagant kitchen. The table they'd been sitting at was really more of an island made of granite, but it was large enough to seat ten. A fascinatingly modern style that Issac enjoyed. He might have to remodel his own kitchen to match, then use the dining space for something else. An extended entertaining area, perhaps?

"You have a weird look in your eye," Aya murmured as they exited onto the main-floor balcony. It was cleared of snow and ice, a task that was completed before their arrival, and thankfully the weather had remained otherwise dry. And cold.

"Just thinking about my other properties. I like the layout of the kitchen."

She raised her brows as they descended the stairs. "Really?"

"You don't approve?"

"No, I mean, I'm surprised you're thinking about home remodeling now, of all times."

"What else would I consider?"

"Oh, I don't know, the fact that my father just tried to demand we marry each other?"

He chuckled. "Henry doesn't frighten me, darling." Now Sethios, if he proved to be her birth parent, might. Maybe. He frowned. What would Sethios think of Issac dating his daughter?

"Okay, now you look worried," Aya said, reaching the bottom deck.

"Just considering how I would handle Sethios if he tried to play the protective-parent card."

She stopped walking, her skin paling. "Do you think…?"

She swallowed. "Do you think he would?"

"I don't know," he admitted. "It would be interesting."

"Interesting bad? Or interesting good?"

Bad. Definitely bad. "We'll cross that bridge when we reach it." He pulled her into a kiss, brushing his lips against her temple. "If we concern ourselves with all the what-ifs in this life, we'll never be able to enjoy the moment. I say we push it all away and just be."

Her green eyes held his for a long moment, her lips curling. "I think I like that."

"Yeah?"

"Yeah." A full smile blossomed on her face, a devious twinkle tinting her irises. That was an expression he liked on her. Very much. "Live in the moment, right?"

"What did you have in mind?"

She pushed him away and darted off into the snowy grass, her blonde hair trailing behind her as he watched.

"Where are you going?"

"To live in the moment!" she called back to him, disappearing into the trees.

He started after her, bewildered by her antics. "Aya, I—" A ball slammed into his face, cutting off his words. It was cold and fluffy. "Did you just throw a snowball at me?"

Her responding laugh touched his heart.

Thud.

This attack came from the left and was a significantly harder throw.

Balthazar.

Fucking prat, Issac thought at him as he flicked the ice off his shoulder.

"Hey!" Astasiya returned fire at the smirking jackass. "That was a cheap shot, B."

Balthazar dodged her snowball with a chuckle. "You nailed him in the face while he was midsentence."

"Yeah, but I'm allowed to do that." She was already making another one.

Jacque appeared behind her with a bucket and dumped

it over her head. Fluffy white flakes stuck to her hair and blue sweater, giving her a winter appeal Issac found far too sexy.

But he had to punish the teleporter for the cruel move.

He engaged Jacque's vision, sending him backward into the snow with a mental shove that had the Hydraian yelping.

And he sent one to Balthazar for good measure as well.

"Now who's the prat?" the mind reader grumbled.

"You use your gifts. I'll use mine," he replied as he moved to Aya's side to help brush the snow from her shivering shoulders. "Are you all right?"

"No, but I will be once we take them all down," she murmured.

"Are you suggesting we join forces, love?"

"I am." No hesitation, just pure confidence.

"And who are we taking down?"

"All of them."

He smiled, sensing several more players in the field, their sights on them. "Can you feel them all?"

She nodded.

"You and me against the world?"

"Always."

"Always," he agreed, feeling her power radiate around them. "Try not to show off too much, love. You know how much I adore your commands."

She smiled. "That sounds like a challenge I have to accept."

"I hope you do." He tripped Balthazar with his mind, causing the snowball the mind reader intended to throw to go wide to the left. Issac turned to catch Lucian's attack with his right hand. The powder exploded on impact, the snow here not meant for packing. But it would make for an entertaining game.

Time to live in the moment.

Because who knew what tomorrow would bring.

Chapter Eight

Gabriel

"WHAT ARE YOU DOING, EZEKIEL?"

The dark-haired assassin didn't flinch or outwardly react to Gabriel's abrupt appearance; he merely squinted at the horde of immortals throwing snow at one another. "I'm watching Stas annihilate the competition. I daresay your sister is quite gifted in strategy, Stark."

Gabriel followed his gaze to the blonde in question, her face lit up in a way he hadn't seen in quite some time. She turned just as Jacque teleported behind her. He dumped a bucket of snow all over himself while she laughed.

"She's certainly learning how to control her power," he noted, somewhat impressed. "One of them, anyway." Stas didn't have a clue as to what she was capable of doing yet, her gifts only just now rising to the surface.

"So it would seem." Ezekiel smirked as Stas sent Lucian into a nearby snowbank with a mental command, her eyes glowing with power even from this distance. "She's nowhere near ready for Osiris, though."

Gabriel nearly snorted. "Obviously." She was a baby Seraphim, not even sprouting wings yet. But soon. "Why did you approach them yesterday?"

"I knew you were spying on me." Ezekiel tsked, his long hair waving as he shook his head. "If you missed me so much, you could just drop in to say hello."

"Hello," Gabriel deadpanned. "Now answer the fucking question."

Ezekiel grinned, his eyes alight with amusement. "Humanity looks good on you, Stark."

Gabriel didn't bite. Didn't even comment, merely stared at him emotionlessly, knowing it was the best way to counter the assassin's games.

"Boring," Ezekiel scoffed, returning his focus to the show down below.

No one suspected them on the nearby roof, the Hydraians roaming the perimeter too untrained to catch a Seraphim and an ancient Ichorian. Not that the Guardians were completely useless. Most of them contained unspeakable power that could protect Stas in a heartbeat. Just not against her own flesh and blood.

"If you must know, I decided to speed some insights along. They should have put Sethios's presence at Osiris's estate together by now, but of course, they hadn't."

Gabriel agreed with him there. "How did they miss that element?"

"Lizzie never mentioned it, her mind too preoccupied with the pregnancy. And they've not spoken much of Osiris's statements regarding Stas's birthright."

Gabriel had noticed that. "Any idea why they've avoided the topic?"

"Because they believe Sethios is an Ichorian and Caro a

mortal. They've completely missed the obvious truth before them."

"That my mother is a Seraphim."

"And that Osiris is one, too, making Sethios part Seraphim." Ezekiel shook his head. "I'm not quite sure how to make this any more obvious for them."

"They'll realize soon enough." When his sister sprouted wings, likely.

"You know, you could just tell her," Ezekiel suggested for the thousandth time.

"She's not ready yet."

The assassin faced him again. "She turns twenty-five next week."

"I'm aware."

"Perhaps you could be a good big brother and tell her how that's going to go in advance?"

"Why?"

Ezekiel snorted. "Right. Of course. I'm dealing with an emotionally stunted Seraphim." He crouched, his elbows resting on his knees. "She's your sister. Some might say you owe her an explanation."

"I intend to give her one when she's ready."

"So, I ask again—when will that be? Because I'm awfully tired of watching my best friend's continuous torture."

"As I am tired of hearing my mother's screams in my head, but we all do what is destined." Gabriel's feathers ruffled at his back, the cold air irritating his senses. Why anyone would choose to play in this weather, let alone live in it, was beyond him. He much preferred his quarters in the South Pacific. "What will you tell them tomorrow?"

Ezekiel shrugged. "Whatever comes to mind. I'm sure they'll ask me about Sethios."

"Will you give them the truth?"

"To the extent that I'm allowed." He glanced over his shoulder. "But don't worry. The Seraphim facts I'll save for you." True annoyance underlined his tone, the gold flecks in his dark eyes burning in the sunlight.

"You're displeased with me."

"So you can discern emotion," he murmured. "Fascinating."

"And now you're being sarcastic."

"Bloody brilliant, you are." Ezekiel smiled but it lacked warmth. "Do you have any idea what Osiris is doing to Sethios right now?"

It couldn't be worse than drowning over and over again beneath the water. "No."

"He's attempting to force him to procreate again."

Gabriel's brows furrowed. Sethios and Caro were forever bound. His body would never respond adequately to another. Not to mention, creating a Seraphim was a rare occurrence. "That's an impractical task."

"No shit," Ezekiel replied.

"Then why bother?"

Ezekiel gave him a hard look. "It's a mindfuck, Stark. Osiris is compelling his son to fornicate—or try, anyway— which hurts enough with unwilling subjects. Couple that with Sethios's inability to act on the persuasion, and it's excruciating. And just when he's about to break from the confusion and pain, Osiris allows him to remember Caro, which sends Sethios over the edge into insanity. His agony and screams are why I volunteered to watch Stas this week. I needed a break."

A foreign pang settled inside Gabriel's chest, his heart reacting to an emotion tied to his family bond.

Caro.

He ran his fingers through his hair, his gaze falling to the woman he vowed to protect for a lifetime. "Stas is still not ready." Not until her wings set. "But soon." *I hope.*

A small worry, one that had haunted him for years, itched to take root inside him, but he swallowed it.

She will fly.

She had to.

"I'm sorry about Sethios," Gabriel admitted. He was sorry about a lot of things.

Ezekiel said nothing, his arms straining around his shins.

"How is your Skye?" he wondered softly.

"Do you really care?" Ezekiel returned. "We're all in hell, and you're the only one who holds the cards."

"She's not ready," Gabriel growled, irritated by the accusation that he was the reason the plan could not move forward. "She has to evolve."

"She looks pretty fucking evolved to me," Ezekiel said, pointing to Stas as she glowed in the sunlight.

Angelic.

Ethereal.

Corporeal.

So close, but not quite.

"I'll return for an update later this week," Gabriel said.

"And do what in the interim?"

"Watch Jonathan." The CRF CEO was up to something but was not being all that forthcoming with information. After the fallout with Osiris over Elizabeth, he'd been quite determined to prove himself. "He's planning something."

Ezekiel snorted. "That idiot should be put out of his misery."

"Yet, Osiris left him alive."

"Of course he did. He wants another Seraphim." The assassin shook his head, standing again. "I need to find a proper Yule log."

"A what?"

Ezekiel smiled. "Sometimes I forget how young you are, Stark. How about you walk with me while I explain the old Nordic custom and regale you with stories of a lifelong past, yeah?"

"Why on earth would I want to do that?"

"Because I asked you to. Because you owe me. And frankly, because I could use the distraction." He stared at him. "It's the least you could do after everything we've been through."

That last part rankled.

Stark's time around humans had changed him

irrevocably. He felt things so differently now than thirty years ago. A part of him… *cared.*

"You act as though you're the only one who has made a sacrifice," Gabriel replied softly, his gaze flicking to Stas again. "That you're the only one hurting. I, too, feel pain, Ezekiel. More than you'll ever realize." He lived with it every day, the agony of his mother drowning over and over again, her soul deteriorating in his mind. "I left my home, everything I knew, and vowed to protect a woman who despises me."

He saw the hatred in Stas's eyes every time she looked at him. She thought him a monster. And maybe she was right. He'd done horrible things under Jonathan's rule, hurt countless people to escalate in the ranks, just so he could position himself in the right place to properly guard her.

"We've all given up key pieces of ourselves for her," he added softly. And even if he could, he wouldn't take anything back or do it any other way. Just as he knew Sethios and Caro would feel the same. "Astasiya is the future."

Ezekiel followed his gaze, his lips curling slightly, the heaviness of their conversation giving way to a somber resolution. "I just wish that future could arrive faster."

"It'll be here before you know it," Gabriel replied, his blood humming with the coming of her age. "She's nearly there."

As if sensing his presence, she whirled to face them, her eyes finding his. He went ethereal on instinct, his red feathers flaring in the daylight.

She didn't look away.

Her eyes holding.

And then she fainted.

"Yes," he whispered to Ezekiel on the wind. "Soon."

Because she'd seen him in his Seraphim state, just for a moment, the power of it rendering her unconscious.

That was why she wasn't ready yet—her mind was unable to process the truth. But every day they grew closer to the inevitable.

Her wings would be here before she knew it.
See you soon, little sister.

Chapter Nine

ISSAC RAN HIS FINGERS THROUGH HIS HAIR and expelled a long breath as he sat beside the man he considered his father.

Astasiya was in the main room with Susan and Henry, reminiscing over the fire. He'd left her to it, knowing she needed as much time with them as possible. The years would pass so much differently for her now, something she would begin to understand in a decade or so.

Aidan poured a fresh glass of brandy and handed it to Issac. "How's she feeling?"

He took a long swallow, his throat craving the burn. "That's an excellent question, one she seems to be avoiding."

She'd lost consciousness while playing in the snow and came to with no recollection of what had caused it. Of course, she'd brushed it off, saying she was fine, but Issac knew better.

"Aya's been seeing things, possibly visions of her past she didn't know existed." Issac paused to evaluate how he wanted to word this. He didn't want to break Astasiya's confidence, but he also needed to give Aidan all the facts to surmise potential causes. If anyone would know, or have an inkling of what might be happening to her, it would be his maker.

"I think she saw something outside—another vision—which knocked her out. She doesn't remember the details this time, but she believes someone may have altered her childhood memories."

He continued by recounting their conversation from earlier this morning, including all the pertinent details and their speculations. As well as his own personal theories.

"Osiris being Sethios's birth father." Aidan scratched his blond stubble. "That's an intriguing notion. I don't recall him mentioning a biological son in our younger years, although I didn't spend much time around him then. I ventured north while he stayed in the south. It would explain Stas's gift for persuasion."

"Yes, and also explains why he referred to her as his granddaughter."

"True." He observed Issac for a long moment. "What has you concerned, son? Aside from her night terrors, I mean."

Concerned wasn't the right word. More a predicament that Issac first thought to be a coincidence or a side effect of some kind. Now that it'd festered, he knew it had to be related in some manner. "There is something else," he admitted softly. "Something I've not told anyone yet."

Aidan stretched his arm out along the back of the sofa, hooking one ankle over his opposite knee. "You can tell me anything, Issac. Always."

He knew that. He trusted Aidan implicitly, which was why he sought him out. Not just for his knowledge and experience, but for his infallible loyalty. Issac lost his birth father at a young age and grew up with Aidan as his paternal guardian. Their bond was finalized when Aidan turned Issac into an Ichorian, and they'd been connected ever since.

If anyone could help him discern his unique situation, it was the male beside him.

"The last time I imbibed blood was from Aya, before the incident." Issac waited for the shock to settle between them, but Aidan's expression remained unchanged, his green eyes flickering with knowledge. "You already knew." Of course he did. The man knew everything.

"I suspected it, yes." He drummed his fingers over the back of the couch, curiosity highlighting his features. "Why haven't you told Stas?"

"I don't want to worry her."

He raised an expectant brow. "And?"

Issac blew out a breath, his head falling back, his gaze on the ceiling. She was sitting right above him, beside her family, pretending to be fine while the world broke around her. "She'll force me to feed, but I don't require it."

"Tell her that."

"I did." *During Elizabeth and Jayson's engagement party.* "She insisted I feed anyway."

"But you didn't."

"No, I told her I was handling it." He glanced sideways at his maker. "Not technically a lie since I don't appear to require blood at the moment."

His lips quirked at the sides. "Son, if there's one lesson I've learned through the ages, it's to never lie to your woman, even technically. You need to tell her."

"I know, and I will, but I wondered if this has ever happened to you. Is it a result of aging, or could it be related to, well, her?"

Aidan considered, his irises swirling with ancient history as he peered inward, sifting through thousands of years of experience. He remembered everything, just like Lucian, which was why everyone considered them to be omniscient. They lived through so much, cataloged every detail, and could process all that information in a flash. The avalanche of thoughts would crush most minds, but they withstood it with ease.

"The longest I've ever gone without blood is three weeks," Aidan murmured, the memory written into his visage. "But I've known Osiris to administer punishments with longer sentences. Most weaken after two or three weeks, the side effects increasing afterward by the day until they're rendered almost mindless with need."

"What's the longest sentence he's given?"

"A decade, but he gave the Ichorian blood every month to bring him back from insanity, just to drive him over the edge again." He cut him a look. "Osiris favors mental games, as you know."

"Yes." And that he administered it monthly said that was the standard tipping point. "I've not imbibed in nearly six weeks, almost seven, and I feel stronger than ever before."

"Do you crave it at all?"

Issac shook his head. "No. The only one I want to bite is Aya, and it's not for feeding purposes." A blunt statement, one he knew Aidan would understand.

"And she's the only one you've fed from in the last several months?"

"There's not been another since the moment I first tasted her in June, no. She's all I want."

Aidan smiled. "You wear monogamy well, just as your mother once did." He disappeared into his mind again, his eyes grinning through the memories. "She would be proud of you, the man you've become. She would approve of Stas as well."

"My mother wanted me to marry a female of title," Issac reminded him, grinning as images of his mother's lectures rolled through his mind. "She was obsessed with that Earl of Dangerfield's daughter—Lilliana, if memory serves."

Aidan chuckled. "I do remember that. She fancied you for monogamy at such a young age."

"Eighteen." He shook his head. "I protested quite a bit."

"You did. A product of your mother's stubborn nature, I believe." He sighed, his heart heavy in his eyes. "Still, title or not, she would approve of your Stas. If anything, because of the way she makes you smile. All your mother ever wanted was your happiness, son. Amelia's, too. And mine." Sadness colored that final word, his emotions high whenever they spoke of Issac's mother.

"You still miss her," he murmured, recalling their fondness for one another. Aidan had tried to convince her to accept immortality, but she steadfastly refused despite both her children joining the immortal ranks.

"Every day," Aidan replied softly. "And she would tell you to talk to Stas."

Issac chuckled. "Yes, she would." And he intended to, but he wanted more information first. Worrying her when she already had so many other concerns in her life seemed cruel. This was a burden he could bear for her, especially as it pertained to himself. "Do you have any idea what has caused this?"

"I have several theories, all of which will require blood samples to test." He glanced at the windows, noting the bonfire outside where the Hydraians were gathered. Tristan, too. "I'll need to discuss it with Lucian."

"Of course." He already assumed the Hydraian King would need to be involved. "I would like you both to be discreet."

Aidan nodded. "Agreed. But Astasiya will need to be included as well."

"I know." He finished his drink. "I'll talk to her." Just after the holidays were finished. She needed to focus on her family right now. Not to mention Ezekiel's impending visit. "But you think it's related?"

"To her night terrors and the possibility that someone altered her memories? Absolutely. Nothing about her has ever been normal—not her ability to compel prior to resurrection or her protective rune. That her blood also appears to have sustained you long-term, or at least for now, has to be connected. It's the only possible conclusion."

"What are some of your theories as to the cause?"

"That her birthright isn't a standard one," he replied without hesitation. "The Seraphim are thought to be extinct, but that rune on her back proves otherwise. And I suspect we'll be seeing them again very soon with Elizabeth's altered genetics and Stas's abnormal abilities."

Issac frowned. "You think Astasiya might be related to a Seraphim?"

"Yes." His fathomless green eyes fell back to Issac. "Yes, I do."

"What would that mean?"

"That, my son, is what I would love to understand myself." He took on that faraway gleam, his mind working through the puzzle pieces before Issac's eyes.

"You've suspected this for a while," he realized. "And never thought to mention it?"

"My suspicions are young and undeveloped." Aidan refocused, blinked. "You know I prefer concrete facts to speculation. But yes, I have considered this avenue several times since you showed me the rune on her back. She's clearly marked for protection, and from my experience, Seraphim never do anything without purpose."

Issac set his empty glass on the table, his thoughts spiraling, hope lingering in his chest.

If Astasiya was part Seraphim, what did that mean for their future? Could he be with her completely and not worry about biting her?

"What all do you know about Seraphim?" he asked, his heart desperate for details.

"Not very much," Aidan admitted. "I've only met a few in my lifetime, and they weren't the chatty sort. Very stoic beings who only operate with a purpose. And they tend to disappear before you can ask them anything."

Issac pondered deeper, another thought occurring to him—one he'd considered after Astasiya mentioned some of her mother's attributes. "Could Aya's birth mother be a Seraphim?"

Aidan chuckled. "I suppose if anyone could seduce one, it'd be Sethios, but I highly doubt the relation is that close. It's more like that whatever technology Osiris and Jonathan used to create Elizabeth was also applied to Stas in some form."

"Then why bother with a rune? Why protect her?"

"To hide her from Osiris," Aidan replied. "Sethios and Osiris have a notoriously unpredictable relationship. Some believe they're battling each other for power, while others consider them strong allies. My theory is Sethios created Stas without Osiris's knowledge and hypnotized a Seraphim into marking her with the protective rune."

A plausible hypothesis, but… "Where the hell would he find one to hypnotize?"

"Likely from the same source they're pulling genetics from for the CRF's testing."

Issac considered that, his mind blown by the possibility. "So you think Astasiya might be a lab experiment of some kind."

He nodded. "One Sethios created himself, yes."

That didn't add up in Issac's head, not with everything he knew. "Aya speaks of her birth parents with such love."

"Which may also be the case, but as you already pointed out, her memories have been altered. What's truth from fiction?"

Issac sighed, his palm sliding over his face. "What a bloody fucking puzzle."

"Indeed." Aidan grabbed his shoulder, giving it a reassuring squeeze. "But we'll solve it together."

He nodded slowly, trusting his mentor implicitly. "I hope so."

"We will," Aidan promised. "And in the meantime, talk to her."

Issac chuckled at the not-so-subtle order. "I always do." More than any other female in his existence. "Thank you."

"Anytime." He released Issac's shoulder. "Now, shall we join them upstairs? Help you continue winning over that father of hers?"

"You heard about earlier?"

His eyes beamed. "I did, and from what I hear, you handled him well."

He shrugged. "Just gave him the truth."

"No, you showed how much you love his daughter, and she displayed her affection for you in return." He stood, his expression softening. "All a father ever really wants for his children is to see them happy. It's the greatest gift in the world." He gestured to the stairs. "Show them how much you adore her, Issac, and they will be forever grateful. Trust me."

Chapter Ten

Stas

SUSAN DAVENPORT HAD FALLEN HEAD OVER heels for Issac Wakefield, much to Henry Davenport's chagrin.

Stas watched the three of them interact, a warmth entering her chest that trickled into her veins. She'd worried a little about what her parents would think of him, but he'd won them both over in the last twenty-four hours.

They were all seated around the fire, enjoying a variety of drinks, appetizers, and discussion. The perfect Christmas Eve, aside from the guest they were all waiting for to arrive.

Jayson had Lizzie at his side in the oversized chair. She'd insisted on staying, saying if Ezekiel wanted to harm her, he wouldn't have scheduled an appointment to do it. A fair statement that no one could argue, but the assassin was known for his games.

And he'd killed Stas's parents.

Maybe.

Her mind kept showing her images that suggested her memories weren't fully accurate. But he was there that day. She knew that in her gut.

Issac glanced over his shoulder, his blue eyes glittering in the firelight. She left the wall to join him on the couch and rested her head against his shoulder.

"Are you all right?" he whispered.

She nodded. "Just waiting." *For Ezekiel.* They'd told her parents that Jayson was expecting an old friend to stop by, something that had more than surprised her mother. Kalispell wasn't necessarily a common place for passing visitors. Tom had intervened then, lacing his words in truth, convincing her parents that it was entirely normal and expected. He stood against the wall Stas had just left, his arms folded, expression alert.

Amelia was with Lucian and Balthazar in the kitchen, something about helping with a gift. And Tristan sat beside Aidan.

She met the former's forest-green gaze. He'd avoided her the last two days since the words he exchanged with Issac outside. They didn't seem to be speaking to each other, either. While she wasn't particularly fond of Tristan, she didn't want to be the source of contention between them.

They were best friends. Why, she had no idea, but she respected Issac's choice.

Tristan arched a brow, his face handsomely arrogant. She could see why women found him attractive. Too bad he frequently ruined the appeal by opening his mouth.

And here she always thought an Irish accent was sexy.

Not on him.

His gaze narrowed as if sensing the direction of her thoughts, probably because she'd displayed them through her eyes. Issac brushed his lips against her temple. "He's behaving, Aya," he said softly for her ears alone. Tristan would still hear them, his gift being the ability to manipulate sound. The knowing glint in his green depths confirmed it.

"I know," she murmured. "And I appreciate it."

The Ichorian scowled. "It's not for you."

"What isn't?" Aidan asked, feigning interest for the benefit of her parents, who overheard the comment.

"Nothing," Tristan replied, pushing away from the couch and leaving the room.

Stas sighed. She hadn't meant to upset him.

"If you'll excuse me for just a moment," Issac murmured, following his friend.

Her mother watched him go, admiration shining in her eyes. "That man really loves you," she said wistfully. "Do you remember loving me like that, Henry?"

He gave her a playful look. "Once upon a time, before my wife asked me silly questions, yes. Yes, I did."

Aidan chuckled. "Love never fades; it merely evolves and strengthens. That's what makes the bond so special. No two loves are alike."

Her mother gazed affectionately at Aidan. "That's very wise."

"Just speaking from years of observation," he replied.

Henry gave him a doubtful look. "You're not even forty yet, right?"

Tom covered a laugh with a cough, causing Stas to grin.

"Looks can be deceiving" was all Aidan said, his focus shifting to the foyer. "I believe your friend is here, Jayson."

Stas's spine stiffened, the energy shifting in the room as Issac and Tristan returned with Ezekiel between them carrying what appeared to be a recently stripped tree that was a foot taller than the rest of the males in the room.

"A proper Yule log," Aidan said, his lips quirked upward. "Perhaps you should take that out onto the deck, Ezekiel? The boys can help you cut it."

"I miss proper fireplaces," the assassin grumbled, causing Aidan to chuckle.

"Some would argue the upgrades are more efficient."

"Not me."

"No, likely not," Aidan agreed.

Stas's parents observed the exchange with confusion, unable to see the dark-haired Ichorian behind the oversized log he was holding.

"This way," Issac said, leading Ezekiel to the glass balcony doors with Tristan at his side. That must have been why Tristan left abruptly moments ago—he'd either heard or sensed Ezekiel and told Issac with a vision. Even angry, he still protected his Sire, proving loyalty outweighed all emotions between them.

"Did I hear Ezekiel?" Balthazar asked, joining them in the main room and catching the tail end of the log going through the door. "Oh, that looks fun." He took off after them, his excitement palpable.

"Perhaps I should join them as well," Jayson murmured, standing. "He is my friend, after all." The latter was said through his teeth as he forced his mouth to smile.

Stas knew what they were doing. A four-on-one discussion meant to ensure Ezekiel was unarmed and aware of the mortals in attendance.

Tom watched them through the glass, his dark eyes harboring the soul of a true soldier. His job was to protect the living area. Stas and Aidan would help him.

But all Ezekiel did was laugh outside and help the men chop up the tree into smaller pieces for the fireplace. His presence didn't chill her like it once did, her mind no longer convinced of his guilt.

He caught her gaze through the glass and held it, those eerie black eyes flecked with gold filled with knowledge and secrets.

So old.

Just like Aidan, but more lived somehow.

And sad.

Such intrinsic pain swam in those cruel depths, hidden behind a mask of nonchalance. Just for a moment he allowed her a glimpse, the truth awakening between them and snapped away with a blink.

Her heart hurt from that brief look into his tortured soul.

The assassin she'd met was so carefree in an almost terrifying way. But the male who stared back at her just then possessed a history of agony, underlined in apology.

She'd seen that expression once before.

On him.

Years and years ago.

The memory teased the edges of her mind, refusing to elaborate. But she *knew* that face. Those eyes. Haunting pain swirling in gold and black.

How do I—

"Stas?" Her mother's voice drew her back. "Are you all right?"

"Hmm?" She blinked a few times, focusing on her mother's concerned features. "Uh, yeah. Sorry, I was lost in thought."

"Issac does that to her often," Tom remarked, helping her cover. "Constantly daydreaming."

Lizzie scoffed at him, catching on and lightening the mood. "You're one to talk, lover boy. This one practically follows Amelia all over the island." Her gaze widened at the slip. "Uh, that'd be Manhattan, I mean, to nonlocals."

A nice cover, one that had Tom's lips twitching. "Have you seen Amelia's ass?" he asked. "Can't blame me for following it."

"I heard that," she called from the kitchen.

"Good," he returned, genuine amusement radiating from him until he remembered Aidan was in the room. "Uh, that is, I mean…"

"As I said a bit ago, love evolves in all different forms," Aidan said slowly, his green eyes narrowed slightly.

Tom cleared his throat. "Right. Yeah. I very much love your, uh, *Amelia*." He couldn't exactly say "daughter" with Stas's parents in the room. Poor guy.

"I know you do," Aidan replied dryly. "Or you wouldn't

be here."

"I thought Amelia was Issac's sister?" Stas's mom asked.

Ezekiel and the others returned before anyone could answer, each of them carrying a few pieces of wood.

"That was fast," Stas's dad said, his eyes wide.

"There were a few of us helping out" was Balthazar's easy reply, his lips curled in one of his famous smiles. "Amazing what we can accomplish when working as a team. Right, Wakefield?"

"Depends on your definition," Issac replied, his blue eyes swirling with energy as he manipulated whatever image Balthazar had sent with his words.

The mind reader flinched. "Scrooge."

Issac ignored him and returned to Stas's side on the sofa. "Susan, Henry, this is Jayson's friend Ezekiel."

"They work together," Lizzie added, her brown eyes narrowed at the assassin.

"Indeed we do. How lovely of you to remember, Red," Ezekiel replied with a cheeky grin. "I'm actually more of an associate in a similar profession." He held out his hand for her parents to shake. "Nice to meet you both."

"What is it you and Jayson do?" her father asked in lieu of a formal reply.

Stas bit her tongue as Ezekiel sat beside her, his leg brushing hers. "We're both contractors in the defense industry." Such a smooth phrase that technically wasn't a lie. "It's quite boring, really. Long hours, a lot of travel, negotiations, and some unfortunate dealings. Right, Jayson?"

At least he managed to get the name right. Ezekiel usually referred to Jayson as Jedrick—his original name.

"Right," Jayson agreed as he joined Lizzie in her chair.

Balthazar tossed a log onto the fire, causing Ezekiel to flinch. "That's all wrong, mate. You're supposed to decorate it first, smother it in alcohol and dust it in flour, *then* burn it."

Stas's parents both raised their brows, while Aidan

chuckled. "I do miss that tradition. Far more fun."

"Exactly." Ezekiel gestured with his hand, amusement giving him a young appearance. "Twelve days of fire and smolder. A proper Yule log."

"I've never heard of that tradition," Stas's mom said, frowning. "Where is it from?"

"Babylon," Lizzie muttered.

Ezekiel smiled broadly. "Actually, it's an old European tradition. More pagan, really. But a hell of a lot of fun."

Stas's parents shared a look.

Issac cleared his throat. "Aidan, didn't you say something about there being a football match on the tele?"

"American football," Aidan corrected. "Yes."

Stas's father perked up, some team name falling from his mouth.

"That would be the one, yes," Aidan confirmed. "I believe the game starts in about fifteen minutes. I was going to watch it downstairs if anyone is interested in joining me."

"I'm in," Tom replied.

"Of course you are," Amelia replied. "Better than that dreadful sport with the bat. Has anyone else tried to watch a baseball game? It goes on and on and on for hours."

"The Yankees is a religion, sweetheart. It's meant to be worshipped and adored."

She snorted. "It's the most boring service I've ever attended."

He clutched his heart as if she'd struck him. "You're insulting my first love."

"You'll live." She kissed him on the cheek and danced out of his reach before he could grab her. "I'm going to help Balthazar and Luc make dinner instead."

"Oh, me, too," Lizzie said, hopping off Jayson's lap.

"That sounds more fun than a football game," Stas's mom said, standing to go with Lizzie and Amelia. "You have fun with whatever team it is you just said, dear."

She patted her husband's knee and joined Balthazar behind the couch. He offered his arm, which she happily accepted, and escorted her through the open dining area to the kitchen while Stas's father watched through narrowed eyes.

"What was that bit you said about love, again, Aidan?" he asked dryly.

He laughed in reply. "Come, we'll discuss it over the game. I believe the fridge downstairs is already stocked with beer as well."

"It is," Issac confirmed. "You all go on ahead. I want to catch up with Jayson and Ezekiel."

Which, of course, was all part of the plan—distract Stas's parents while the assassin explained his purpose here. And the glimmer in his gaze said he knew that was exactly what they were doing, too.

Tristan remained with them, taking over Aidan's seat, leaving just the five of them in the room together.

Jayson broke the silence, his patience the lowest in the room. "All right, Ezekiel. What the fuck do you want?"

Chapter Eleven

Stas

Ezekiel's chuckle chilled the room. "You all truly think the worst of me, which is fascinating considering how much I've actually helped you over the years."

"Helped?" Jayson repeated. "Need I remind you what happened the last time we saw each other? After your owner—Osiris—took me and my brothers hostage?"

"I recall giving you Elizabeth's location for a rescue and then leaving a bit of evidence behind for your people to track you afterward." He cocked his head to the side. "If that's not helping, what would you call it?"

"A game," Jayson growled. "One I don't understand."

Ezekiel's lips curled. "Because you're not really playing

yet, old friend. You all still have so much to learn, to discover. Especially you, darling." His eerie eyes pinned Stas in her seat. "But I have a choice for you all to make before I divulge anything else."

"A choice," Stas repeated, her throat dry from the intensity of staring directly into his eyes. So much pain and anger lurked in his irises. And lethality. He was the deadliest one in the room and did nothing to hide it.

He sighed. "Yes, it's a term that means—"

"I know what it means," she said, not liking his chastising tone. "What's the choice?"

"Direct." His gaze roamed over her with interest. "You truly have turned into an amazing young woman, Astasiya. Your father will be quite pleased."

Issac pulled her back, his growl not at all friendly. "Get to the point, Ezekiel."

"Relax, Wakefield. As beautiful as she is, she reminds me too much of her mother to be interested."

Stas's lips parted. "You knew my mother?"

"You already know the answer to that," he replied, a knowing glint in his gaze. "Now, since none of you seem interested in spending the holidays with me—which is quite rude, really, considering our backgrounds, but alas, here we are—your choice is simple. Would you like me to give you details that will assist with Elizabeth's pregnancy or more information on Astasiya's parents?"

Stas's lips parted as Jayson growled.

Ezekiel relaxed beside her, lifting his ankle to rest on his opposite knee. "A good teacher encourages his students to learn for themselves. A *helpful* one at least provides a few clues. I consider myself the latter."

"You should consider yourself a dead man if you don't start talking. Now." Jayson twirled a blade between his fingers for emphasis, his brown eyes darkening with rage.

"On which topic?" Ezekiel asked casually.

Stas's heart skipped a beat. *Lizzie or my parents?* There wasn't a choice. Not really. Not when her best friend had a baby growing inside her that no one knew anything about.

But my parents… Stas had wanted to know more about them for nearly two decades, and Ezekiel clearly had some answers.

Your father will be quite pleased. An indication that he did know her father *and* he was still alive.

She reminds me too much of her mother. Meaning he knew her mother as well.

But he also might be able to help with Lizzie's pregnancy. *Assist* was the word he'd used.

Stas frowned. "How do we know we can trust your advice regarding Lizzie?"

"Because I'm familiar with Seraphim births." He held her gaze. "Intimately familiar."

"You know a Seraphim."

He grinned. "Several, sweetheart." He leaned closer, his voice dropping. "As do you."

"Who?" she demanded.

"Is that your choice?" he countered, not at all impacted by her persuasive skills.

She nearly growled at him. "You're infuriating."

"It's so nice to see you unafraid of me," he replied, smiling. "Although, this hatred isn't all that much better, if I'm honest."

"Get used to it." Because this conversation wasn't endearing him to her any more.

He sighed. "I expected that might be the case. All right, darling Stas, choose. What would you like to know?" Jayson started to speak, but Ezekiel held up his hand. "I'm sorry, Jedrick, but this is Stas's decision. Woman's choice and all that."

She glanced at the brown-haired male, knowing exactly what he wanted her to do. Issac's grip loosened, his thumb drawing a soothing circle against her side, while Tristan observed them all with a bored expression. He would be absolutely no help to the conversation because he couldn't care less about Stas or Lizzie.

And Issac would be inherently biased on her behalf. Same with Jayson, but on Lizzie's behalf.

"You can really help her?" she asked softly.

"I wouldn't offer if I couldn't," he replied.

"Yes, you would." There was an edge to Issac's tone. "You love mind games almost as much as your maker does."

Ezekiel snorted. "Not nearly as much, actually." That speck of anguish lurked in his eyes again, despite the smile quirking his lips.

Did he mean to let her see it? Was it a trick? A way to lull her into a false sense of comfort?

No. No way could that kind of suffering be faked.

She didn't know much about his past other than he used to hunt and kill fledglings before they could be reborn into Hydraians. He'd disappeared for a while, according to Jayson, many thinking the assassin just retired due to having no one else left to kill. But he was clearly very much alive.

And so very sad.

"Tell me about Lizzie," she said before her heart could convince her otherwise. Lizzie's pregnancy was the more imminent issue, while the mystery of Stas's parents could wait. Her best friend's health was more important.

"Selfless, loyal, and direct," he murmured. "Yes, Sethios will be impressed indeed. Once he remembers, of course. But that's a conversation for another day." He took a deep breath, as if readying himself for a lecture. "How far along is your Red, Jedrick? Nearly two months now, right?"

"Lara said Lizzie seems to be around four months pregnant already, which is impossible considering our timeline." He'd calmed down marginally, his gaze still simmering with unveiled fury, but his tone lacked the growl from earlier.

"Your Lara is treating Elizabeth as a mortal patient, of which she is not." He shifted his legs, lifting his other ankle up to his knee, his gaze going to Jayson. "Your Red is part Seraphim, which means her pregnancy will be significantly escalated because a Seraphim's gestation period is roughly eight weeks. Given she's only four months now, according to human technology, I'd say she has another two months before she gives birth."

"That can't be healthy," Stas said, shocked by the escalated timeline.

"She's not human," he reminded. "Her body is equipped to handle it. But might I suggest you marry sooner rather than later? I hear women dislike showing in their bridal gowns. Virginity standards, thanks to the puritans."

Jayson just stared at him. "Any other words of wisdom before you leave?"

Ezekiel sighed. "I've not even finished burning my first log yet. You remember this tradition is a twelve-day one, yes?"

"We're two thousand years in the future, Ezekiel," Jayson replied. "Try joining us."

The assassin snorted. "I'd really rather not. Do you know they have gas fireplaces now with fake logs? It used to be considered bad luck to buy your wood. Can you imagine what it means to burn fake wood?" He shook his head. "A sad society, if you ask me."

"I didn't." Jayson folded his arms. "Do you have anything else useful to say?"

"You think I'm here to cause pain when I'm merely seeking a break from it." He was quiet for a long moment, his gaze finally lifting to Stas. "Your father is my best friend. I look forward to the day when you see him again because only then can we truly begin."

He stood, leaving Stas gaping up at him. "Then why did you kill him?"

"We both know you don't believe that. Not really. Not anymore." He fixed his leather jacket. "The truth is coming, Astasiya. Soon. And trust me when I say I can't wait for it all to unravel."

She shifted to her feet, blocking his exit. "If you know so much, why not just tell me? Why draw this out?"

"Because it's not my place to tell you," he said softly, sincerity mingling with his lethal energy. "And you know in your heart you just need to embrace it."

He tried to move around her, but she stepped with him.

"You came all the way here to spend Christmas Eve with us, just to give us some menial information about Lizzie and leave?" She wasn't accepting that. "No, you want something else. What is it?"

He moved into her personal space, causing Issac to stand at her back. "You're not ready to fight me yet, little darling. Or Osiris. Or anyone, really. Don't make the mistake of thinking that your new power is enough, because it's not. You're only just beginning to grow into your potential. Don't spoil it by listening to your emotions."

His belittling speech lit her blood on fire. "You underestimate me."

"Oh, no, sweetheart, I truly don't. I know exactly what you'll be capable of, just as I know you're nowhere near that point yet."

Her fists curled, irritated by his proclamation of knowing these things about her. Frustrated that he could be right. Angry that he wouldn't tell her more. She tried to compel him with her mind, force him to give her details, but all that did was earn her a glower and a tsk.

"Don't disappoint your parents by getting yourself killed too early, little angel. They sacrificed everything for you, as have several others. We're relying on you in ways you'll soon understand." He cupped her cheek, his touch cool and unexpected. As were his words.

"Ezekiel," Issac warned.

The assassin ignored him, his dark eyes glimmering with emotion. "Happy early birthday, little angel." His lips brushed her forehead just as he started to disappear. "Look for the red feathers. He'll have all the answers you seek."

Her heart stopped beating.

Red feathers.

That was what she saw on the roof yesterday.

"Well, he didn't stay long," Luc said as he joined them in the living area.

"He wasn't very useful, either," Tristan remarked. "I'm going to watch the game now."

Stas blinked, ignoring them all, her focus on Ezekiel's words.

Little angel.

Her father used to call her that as a child. Did Ezekiel purposely use it to drive home his point? To prove that he *knew* her? He claimed her father to be his best friend. Claimed to know her true potential. Claimed that she still had a lot more growing to do.

And she felt it in every fiber of her being that he was right.

That persuasion was just the beginning.

She could feel something awakening deep inside of her. The truth. Strength. A new power.

Issac wrapped his arms around her from behind, his face in her hair. "Aya," he breathed, calling her to the surface. Back to reality. Away from her inner musings.

Everyone had left them.

His warmth a comforting presence at her back.

"I... I believe him, Issac," she admitted in a soft whisper. "What he said about my father, my powers." She turned in his arms, his sapphire gaze burning into hers. "I saw red feathers yesterday on the roof before I passed out."

"Why didn't you say anything?"

"Because I thought my mind was playing tricks on me again, but something is happening to me." She clutched his shoulders. "Maybe it's related to my secondary power?" They had yet to discover what it was, but all Hydraians possessed two.

"Or something else entirely," he murmured, his palm circling her neck. "When we return to Hydria, we'll run some tests and talk about this more. All right?"

She swallowed, nodding. "Yes." She went onto her toes to kiss him softly, craving his familiarity. This week was supposed to be about forgetting their problems and enjoying each other. Instead it had derailed into immortal madness with her seeing strange visions that shouldn't exist. "I just want to forget for a little while." Was that so much to ask?

He smiled against her mouth. "I can help with that, Miss Davenport."

That was the answer she desired. "Promise?"

He nodded, lifting her into his arms. "Always."

"Always," she repeated. "Take me to bed." She purposely wove persuasion through the words, knowing he would approve.

"Keep commanding me, love. See what happens."

She lightly nibbled his lower lip. "A dare I accept."

His midnight gaze gleamed with wicked intent. "Please do."

Chapter Twelve

Issac

ASTASIYA APPEARED ANGELIC in the rising sun, her blonde hair splayed around her, the sheets revealing glimpses of her bare skin. It almost hurt to leave her naked and alone, but he wouldn't be far.

He closed the door softly and crept downstairs to find Jacque waiting for him in a pair of pajama bottoms, his dark hair wild with sleep.

"The only reason I'm not going to punch you right now is because I already opened my gift and I liked it."

Issac grinned. "I thought you might approve of that." He'd bought him a pair of high-tech headphones for his music obsession.

"Yep." He gestured to the pile of wrapped gifts beside

him. "I grabbed all the items you requested."

"Brilliant. Cheers." Issac had purchased several items for his family before leaving on holiday with Astasiya but hadn't brought any of the items with them, as he hadn't expected the Montana ambush.

He sorted through all the items on the floor, finding the most important ones and setting them aside. Then he carefully arranged everything beneath the tree. His gifts for Aya were upstairs as they all required private explanations.

Jacque had fallen asleep on the couch, one arm hanging off the end, his leg kicked out at a weird angle.

Issac chuckled at the sight, not used to seeing the hyper teleporter rest. But he clearly crashed hard. He draped a blanket over the lanky male and wandered into the kitchen to play with the coffee maker. Aya liked hers black with a few teaspoons of brown sugar, while he preferred his with no additives.

He fixed their cups, snagged a large muffin, and carefully carried all the items upstairs.

Astasiya was sitting up in the bed, waiting for him, the sheets around her waist. Her eyes lit up at the items in his hands. "I knew I loved you."

He chuckled and handed her a mug. "Merry Christmas, love."

Her responding smile warmed his heart. "Merry Christmas," she murmured before blowing across the steaming liquid.

Issac set the muffin on the nightstand and joined her on the bed with his own coffee.

They drank in companionable silence, something he adored about their relationship. Astasiya didn't require constant conversation or attention, she just enjoyed being in the moment. Like now with the way she admired the snow falling outside the windows, her lips curling into a secret grin. What he wouldn't give to be able to see inside her mind, just for a moment, to know what caused that look. A memory? A dream? Him?

He pictured her from the other day, the way she'd played with him and the others while throwing snowballs. Such a carefree passing of time, one he never would have indulged in without her.

She'd reawakened his youth, his will to live again.

Issac's world had grown mundane over the last century. Then revenge had consumed him these last few years, fueling his purpose.

Until her.

Astasiya changed everything.

Changed him.

He tucked a stray blonde strand of her hair behind her ear, his gaze tracing the movement. "Can we exchange our gifts here instead of downstairs?" he wondered, craving this moment between them and longing to extend it. Soon the house would be overwhelmed with noise and excitement, and he wanted to stay here just a little longer. With her. With his Aya.

She smiled over the rim of her mug with her eyes. "I like that idea." She took another fortifying sip before setting the coffee aside and climbing out of the bed. "You can open your presents first."

Issac admired her athletic form as she wandered through the room to the walk-in closet and disappeared. He finished his drink and placed it beside the untouched muffin as she returned with a gift in each hand. Neither of them compared to the confidence she exuded while walking around in the nude, or the beauty of her long, shapely legs, or the subtle curve of her waist.

Fuck exchanging gifts.

He wanted to nibble every inch of her.

Memorize the taste of her skin.

Kiss her until she couldn't remember her own name.

And fuck her so hard she thought of him all day, every time she moved.

Astasiya set the presents on the foot of the bed before crawling up to join him, her breasts swaying with the movement. He wrapped his palm around the back of her neck and pulled her up against him.

"Gifts," she reminded against his mouth as he rolled her to her back beneath him.

"I'm unwrapping the one I want first," he replied, his palm sliding down her side to the top of her bare thigh.

"I'm already naked," she pointed out.

"Trust me, I'm aware." He settled his hips between hers, eliciting a low moan in her throat. "Very, very aware."

She arched against him, her hands on his shoulders, tugging at his shirt. "I think it's you who needs unwrapping."

He smiled against her neck and lifted as she pulled the fabric over his head. "Does that make me your present, then?"

She pushed him to his back, her heated gaze admiring his bare chest and abdomen. "Yes. Yes, it does. Which means I can do whatever I want."

Issac arched a brow. "Is that how this works?"

She nodded, her lips curling.

"I thought I was opening my gifts first?"

"You are." Her eyes glimmered deviously as she pressed an open-mouthed kiss to his sternum, her hands pulling his pants down over his thighs. "Consider it opened and soon to be delivered." Her tongue traced a wet path down his abdomen, leaving no question as to what she had in mind.

"Aya." He threaded his fingers through her hair, his head falling back onto the pillows. Her mouth was his addiction. Every lick and nip against his skin a reminder of how well she'd come to know him, his tells, his preferences.

Nothing between them was ever gentle, even when they tried.

And Astasiya made no exception now.

She finished removing his pants, her lips right where he desired her most, hovering but not touching. Her smile said it was intentional.

"Do you want your present, Issac?" Her voice vibrated

against his shaft, causing him to groan low in his throat.

Aya loved to tease him, to try to take control, to bring him to his knees. And while he adored her mouth and skill, he didn't have a submissive bone in his body. Not even desire could crumble his strength of will, and he reminded her of that by tightening his hold in her hair and yanking her back to meet his gaze.

"All I've ever wanted is you," he said softly. "You know that."

"Seducing me with words?"

He smiled. Yes, that was most definitely his goal. "Suck my cock, darling."

Temptation darkened her eyes to a sultry green. "Such sweet things you say to me," she murmured, her lips brushing his sensitive skin.

"Now, Aya." He applied pressure to the back of her head, which only deepened the sensuality in her gaze.

She licked the arousal seeping from his tip and hummed in approval. "Merry Christmas, Issac." Sin underlined her tone, lighting his blood on fire.

Jesus, he adored this woman.

He tightened his hold as she took him deep, her name falling from his lips with a curse. Issac never wanted a woman more than once, always bored after the first time. But Aya gifted him with new perspective. Every time with her felt new yet experienced, and yielded the most intense pleasure of his life.

"More," he growled, needing everything she could give him. Sensation, emotion, passion. All of it.

His fist guided her movements while her tongue and mouth mapped every inch of his shaft. He thrust upward, his hips driving him to the back of her throat.

Yes…

She took him, her nails drawing down his thighs, her eyes locking with his. He nearly came from the image she represented alone, those lust-dilated pupils driving him to the edge of insanity.

"Fuck, Aya," he whispered, his muscles tensing as flames destroyed his being.

He swore she was smiling up at him, knowing what that look did to him.

And that only made him harder.

Only had him clutching her hair like a lifeline as he escalated her pace, forcing her to take more of him, needing her to swallow him down to her very core. To be inside her. To be with her. To own her the way she did him. To mark her as his in the darkest of ways. To keep her with him always. To forever remain with her.

His head fell back on a growl, his stomach clenching, his balls tightening. And fuck, she knew, her mouth already hollowing, her tongue stroking him exactly where he desired.

"Aya," he breathed, his jaw clenching. It almost hurt, that moment right before… and then she carried him over with another trick of her mouth, a hum in the back of her throat that encouraged him to explode.

He held on to her, forcing her to swallow, as he shook with his release. So much more powerful, more intense, than the night before, and yet he had no idea why or how that was even possible. Every experience deepened their connection, destroying any semblance of his ability to let her go. He'd forever be bonded to her. There would be no other. Not even if she commanded it.

Adoration mingled with relief and firm desire to return the favor. Just as soon as he could breathe again.

Astasiya climbed over him, her lips swollen from the way he'd fucked her mouth. She straddled his hips, her damp core against his erection. He wasn't ready yet, but knowing the way she excited him, he would be again soon.

"You have two more gifts to open," she said, her voice a low, husky sound that went straight to his groin.

How did she do this to him?

Sometimes he thought her second power might be related to sex because everything she did consumed him.

From her smile to the subtle way she clenched her thighs around him, all the way to the innocent excitement highlighting her gaze as she held out the gifts she'd retrieved from the bottom of the bed.

He could deny her nothing.

Ever.

Issac forced himself to sit up, feeling as if he'd just run a marathon despite it being her mouth that had done most of the work. He took the gifts and set them on the bed beside his hips and circled the back of her neck with his palm. "Thank you, Aya."

She smiled. "You're welcome."

He kissed her softly, loving the way her recently fucked lips felt against his. *Mine*, he thought possessively, tracing her mouth with his tongue.

She grabbed his biceps. "Gifts."

"Yes, it was quite a gift," he agreed.

She opened her mouth to say more, and he took advantage, dipping inside to properly taste her. Her responding groan reverberated against every inch of his body. She'd thought to give him an orgasm without reciprocation. Mmm, not on his watch. He might not be able to properly take her, but he could certainly return the favor in other ways.

He pulled her beneath him, away from the gifts, and slid his still-hard cock between her slick folds, massaging the sensitive spot that made her ache and scream. She quivered, her body already so close to the edge from her oral ministrations.

"I love having you like this," he whispered against her mouth. "Quivering with need. It's sexy as hell, Aya."

Her nails bit into his lower back, then his ass, as she encouraged him to give her more. His name left her lips on a moan, the sound being one of his favorites in existence.

He rocked into her harder, forcing his head to hit her clit on each thrust. She cradled him with her thighs, her chest arching into his as he dropped his mouth to her neck. He longed to bite her, to use his teeth to send her over the edge.

If she's a Seraphim, I might be able to.

A dangerous thought, one that lingered in his mind while he took Astasiya over the edge with a final shift of his hips against hers. She shattered on a spasm he felt down to his very soul, the call to claim her loud in his heart.

One bite.

God, he wanted to.

Needed to.

His resolve shook around him, his incisors aching with the need to mark her. It was not about her blood but about *her*. As if he would lose her forever if he didn't lay claim to her now.

Issac's hands fisted as common sense warred with his innate need for possession.

She's mine.

Not entirely.

Finish it.

"Issac," she whispered, her fingers combing through his hair, the other trailing down his taut back. "Are you all right?"

No.

They'd been together several times since her turning, and never once had he felt the need to bite her.

Until right now.

And it consumed him.

Overrode logic.

Tore right through his walls of control, penetrating him deep.

"You're starting to scare me." Aya's touch had stilled. "Issac?"

"I…" He had to clear his throat, his mouth watering with the desire to taste her again. To imbibe her blood the way he used to.

Why now? Why after two months of controlling it am I failing now?

He shook above her, his self-discipline shredding inside

of him.

He felt compelled to bite her.

Possessed by some unknown entity that presided over them, dictating his actions.

What is happening to me?

Just one bite.

No, he couldn't. Wouldn't. Not with his life in the balance.

And what about her life?

The pull tugged him forward, her pulse singing beneath his mouth. Just—

"Remove your mouth from my neck," Aya demanded hoarsely, her words laced with power.

Issac lifted, unable to resist the call of her persuasion.

Her eyes filled with tears, her lips trembling from what it took to force him away from her in that manner.

"Fuck," he breathed, the spell broken as he rolled away from her.

He'd nearly bitten her.

Had scraped his teeth over her skin, ready to take her.

"*Fuck*," he repeated, his palms digging into his eyes.

This is never going to work.

Chapter Thirteen

ASTASIYA REMAINED UTTERLY still beside him, her hitch in breath breaking his heart. She was crying because of him. Because of *this*—their relationship. The fact that he'd nearly risked his own life to taste her.

And the guilt she would bear if her blood killed him would destroy her. He knew that. Yet, he'd nearly bitten her anyway.

"I don't know what happened," he admitted. "It's never been like that before."

She said nothing for so long he worried she might be unable to speak.

"Aya," he whispered.

"I think... I think I was compelling you." So soft, he

barely heard her. "I d-didn't mean to. I just… I was thinking about it, how it used to be, and…" She broke off on a choked sound that broke his heart.

"Oh, Aya." He pulled her into him, her head going to his chest as he circled his arms around her. A part of him acknowledged the danger of that move, especially after what just happened, but his soul begged him to console his other half. Her pain was his pain. That was how this worked.

"I'm sorry, Issac." She buried her face against his skin, her body trembling against his. "It just happened. I thought about the last time you bit me, and the urge to finalize something, us, our blood, just slammed into me. It doesn't even make sense. I don't even know what we would be finishing."

He combed his fingers through her hair, considering her words. They matched his experience, but he hadn't *sensed* her compulsion. Not in the way he usually did when she persuaded him to do something, even mentally.

No, this had felt different.

Not compulsion, but something much more instinctual. As if his very soul had begged him to mark her.

He kissed the top of Astasiya's head. "It's not your fault, love. I think we both were caught up in the moment."

"What are we going to do?" she whispered. "If I have to choose between keeping you alive and our relationship, I'll always pick your life. Always, Issac."

"I know, Aya," he murmured, hugging her harder. "I know."

They clung to each other as if it might be the last time. Their hearts beating as one. Minutes passed, turning into an hour. No words were needed, just the comfort of their silence.

His family began to wake.

Images of conversation in the kitchen.

Breakfast.

Mingling by the tree in the living area.

So many smiles, not a single person aware of the pain

upstairs. Except for Balthazar, who thankfully kept his mouth shut.

"Christmas has officially begun downstairs," he advised softly.

Aya nodded. "I still want to open our presents up here."

"Me, too."

She tilted her head, her green eyes a softer shade, almost jade in color. "Do you want to open your gifts first?"

"I can," he murmured, stroking his hand down her arm. The artfully wrapped packages were still on the bed, sitting in the same spot Astasiya placed them before he requested a present of a different nature.

She slid away from him to sit up, and he followed suit, his thigh brushing hers. "Here." She snagged the two items and handed them to him, her cheeks reddening. "I've, um, never bought for a boyfriend before."

He chuckled at the frivolous term. "Boyfriend."

She gave him a look. "You know what I mean."

"I do." He grinned at her. "But I prefer *demon* as a pet name."

"How about *jackass* as a nickname?" she asked cheekily. "Since you're being one right now and all."

He laughed outright, his heavy heart lighter with her humor. "I'll answer to whatever you want to call me, love." He kissed her crimson cheek and started on the first box.

She bit her lip, her gaze uneasy as he lifted the lid to reveal a pair of black swim jammers, the brand a popular swimming company in the States. Beside it were a pair of goggles and a new cap, all seated atop a plush towel.

"I noticed you hadn't been swimming as much in Hydria and thought you might need some supplies." She sounded so nervous he couldn't help but give her a side hug.

"I love it, Aya." Even the size was right. She'd clearly done some research.

Her eyes lit up with pride. "Jacque helped me figure out what brand you preferred. I had no idea there were so many styles of swimming trunks on the market."

"You selected correctly." He kissed her cheek. "Thank you, love."

He tucked the items back into the box and started unwrapping the second present while she observed nervously. The woman faced Osiris without batting an eye, but watching Issac open gifts escalated her heartbeat. Fascinating.

That pull to bite her still lingered, but far more tame. Which confirmed his suspicion that it wasn't Aya at all that tempted him. Another topic to discuss with Aidan because Issac rarely felt this way around Hydraians. His logic always overrode his drive in the past. Why should this be any different?

Because I haven't fed in nearly two months.

He ignored the thought and finished revealing the picture frame. Aya stood smiling in a sapphire silk gown, her cheeks flushed alluringly. He grinned beside her, his arm around her lower back.

"This is from The Pierre." He recognized the stairs behind them, as well as her dress. "From the CRF gala."

"Technically, our first date," she said, her cheeks pink. "Right after you delivered that cheesy line."

His eyes narrowed. "I believe I proved quite thoroughly that I don't require such frivolities."

Her lips curled. "You did, and then they took that photo of you actually smiling. I thought it should be framed in memory as the one time that billionaire playboy Issac Wakefield actually smiled in a photograph."

Yes, she'd mentioned his lack of amusement in tabloid photos, as well as his playboy-handbook biography. That conversation still made him laugh. Astasiya was refreshingly honest.

"How did you acquire this?" he wondered, noting the high quality of the photograph.

"Uh…" She pinched her lips to the side. "Yeah, I may have agreed to an interview in exchange for the printing rights to that photo."

His eyebrows shot up. "An interview? With a tabloid?"

Her nose scrunched up adorably. "Just a few questions."

Oh, now he needed all the details. "Where can I read this brilliant literature?"

She huffed out a breath and grabbed her phone from the nightstand. It was one Jayson had given her that couldn't be tracked. A few clicks later and an article titled "Wakefield's Latest Conquest Speaks Out" appeared on the screen.

He snorted. "This should be an enlightening read." He skimmed the words, his lips twitching at Astasiya's clear sarcasm. "A demon in the bedroom, hmm?"

"Try denying it," she deadpanned.

"Absolutely not." He was quite satisfied with that description and the mention of his pet name. There were several questions about his dating preferences where Astasiya noted his penchant for control, specifically in terms of wardrobe for events. "You're the only woman in my existence who criticizes my extravagant gifts."

"Thousand-dollar dresses that I'll never wear again is wasteful."

He flashed her a devious glance. "Those gowns were worth more than a few thousand dollars, darling."

Her eyes narrowed. "I should have told her you enjoy throwing money away for no reason."

"I consider dressing you an investment."

She scoffed. "In what?"

"My personal pleasure," he replied, his lips quirking. "A very worthwhile investment, if you ask me."

She rolled her eyes. "You're incorrigible."

"When it comes to you, yes." He kissed her temple and handed back the phone. "I can't believe you subjected yourself to that filth."

"It was the only way she'd let me have the photo." She gave him an apologetic look. "I tried not to divulge anything of actual interest. You're not mad, right?"

He laughed. "I think you were punished enough by having to answer all those ridiculous questions." The interviewer had even asked Astasiya for tips on how to land a billionaire. *Demand a date*, had been her cheeky response.

He kissed her softly on the lips, entertained immensely by both the photo and what she went through to obtain it.

"Thank you for the gift. I'm putting this in our bedroom." And he'd be framing quotes from the article to go with it. "Now time for your gifts."

"A dress?" she joked.

He nipped her earlobe in reprimand and slid out of the bed to find her gifts. They were hidden in the closet as well.

She eyed the items with interest when he returned.

A small box.

A flat one.

And a carefully wrapped rectangle that he handed her first.

She eyed it curiously. "This is heavy."

"Yes. And fragile, too."

Her lips curled down, her fingers carefully moving over the paper to expose the contents within. "*Vita mutatur, non tollitur*," she read, tracing the inscription on the cover.

"Life is changed, not taken away," he translated. "I kept a journal for many years after Aidan turned me, and I thought you might want to have a piece of my past as you live through your present."

Her green eyes lifted, wonder turning her irises a luscious green. "You documented your first years as an immortal?"

"My first decades, yes." Men were often required to conceal strong emotions. He hid his in the form of a journal. "No one knows this exists except me, and now you."

He drew his finger along the old binding, the item one he hadn't touched in nearly two centuries until he wrapped it for her last week.

"There will be passages you may dislike," he warned. "But I never want to hide from you, Aya. And I want you to know that you can come to me with anything. No matter what happens, I'm here for you."

Tears gathered in her eyes as she held the notebook to

her chest. "This is a beautiful gift, Issac."

He smiled. "Just do me a favor and try to remember I wrote those words many years before you existed."

"The scandalous adventures of Issac Wakefield." Amusement shone through the dampness in her gaze. "I can't wait to start reading."

"Open the others," he encouraged, wanting to see her reaction. It would change drastically, and he couldn't wait to begin the debates. His Aya despised extravagance, but he'd gifted these items with a practical twist he hoped she would appreciate.

She carefully set the journal aside before picking up the smallest box.

"This better not be a ring," she muttered as she revealed the familiar jewelry encasing beneath the paper.

He laughed. "Wouldn't that be a thrill for your mum?"

"Not after I killed you," she replied sweetly, her nimble fingers carefully lifting the lid to reveal the necklace inside. The heart-shaped blue diamond glittered in the light, the white gold chain offsetting the color beautifully.

"It's gorgeous, and way too much, Issac. I bought you a swimsuit and you bought me a, a"—she waved her hand—"whatever that gem is. Aquamarine?"

He chuckled, loving that she knew nothing about jewelry. "The stone doesn't matter. It's the secret hidden inside that does. Here, let me show you. See this?" He pointed to the metal rung at the base of the heart. "It moves, but only with your thumbprint. Try it."

She frowned at him. "What does it do when it moves?"

"Trust me and try it." He retrieved his mobile while she tinkered with the necklace. It buzzed the second she figured out the switch.

"Okay," she said, staring doubtfully at the slightly crooked diamond. "Is that supposed to be exciting?"

Issac showed her the display on his screen.

Her eyebrows flew upward. "It's a tracking device? Are you fucking kidding me?"

He laughed outright, adoring her reaction.

"It's not funny. This is like stalker technology."

That only made him laugh harder. He wrapped his arm around her when she made to move, and held her to him. "It's a tracker that's only activated by you when you want to be found, Aya. Current technology can't sense the device because it's idle until your thumbprint activates it. And if you ever do, I will receive an alert, as will Mateo."

"So it's a fancy stalker device," she deadpanned.

"That might one day save your life." He tucked a blonde strand behind her ear. "You don't have to wear it if you don't want to, love. It's your choice. I just wanted you to have something to rely on if you're ever in a situation where you need help. It's something that could have saved Elizabeth sooner when Osiris took her."

Issac added that last bit to drive home the reminder that the infamous Ichorian had set his sights on a new target— Astasiya. And his current whereabouts were unknown since the manor was destroyed during Elizabeth's rescue.

"It's exactly the kind of gift a man in my position is supposed to give his lover," he continued, his voice softening. "No one would ever suspect the alternative use."

Aya eyed the necklace, then him, and then the necklace again. "A practical gift disguised as extravagance."

"Exactly."

"That cost a small fortune."

He shrugged. "If I gave you anything cheaper, it would be obvious." Not exactly true. He could have given her a sapphire, but that felt beneath her. "You're my heart, Aya. Now you can wear it for all to see."

"I thought you were better than cheesy lines," she replied, her eyes twinkling again. Which had been his goal with the word choice.

"Just giving you the backstory for when anyone asks. May I?" he asked, gesturing to the necklace.

"Only if you show me how to turn off the tracker first."

"By straightening the stone," he murmured. "Which is

brilliant because it means you can activate it to send a distress signal, then deactivate it before anyone can scan you again."

Mateo's technological abilities continued to floor Issac at every turn. This product was no different and one of the best items to date.

Aya righted the heart and looked at his screen for verification that it fixed the signal. "And only I can activate it?"

"Yes. Mateo wanted to put in a backdoor protocol, but I refused the enhancement." Issac knew she'd refuse to wear it if anyone else could switch on the tracking technology. "That's not to say Mateo couldn't finagle something in an emergent situation, but nothing exists today. It's a normal necklace until you make it otherwise."

She considered and slowly handed him the box. "All right, but only because it's practical." She pulled her hair away from her neck, her invitation clear.

Issac removed the chain from the box and secured it around her neck before drawing a finger down her exposed spine. She turned to face him, the heart nestled above her breasts. Right where it belonged. "Mmm, I sincerely approve of you wearing only my gift, darling. Perhaps you can model it again for me later."

Aya's gaze heated with promise. "I'll consider it."

"Do." He nudged the final gift to her. "But open this first."

"Should I be scared?" she asked as she unwrapped the final package.

"Just keep an open mind."

"Famous last words," she grumbled. "I gave you a photo and swim gear."

"Two gifts I adore." He kissed her shoulder. "It's the thought that counts."

"That's about the same as the 'size doesn't really matter' myth."

He chuckled. "Stop stalling and open the envelope." It'd

been idle in her hands for a long moment, her mouth trying to distract them both from the task.

She upended the contents onto the bed, making him glad he'd used paper clips to keep things separated.

The passport caught her eye first. "Aya Davenfield," she read, her lips twitching. "Clever."

"Every immortal needs a new identity," he explained. "Mateo helped me build yours."

She picked up the driver's license next, and then the assortment of bank cards. "Did you reroute my old accounts?"

"Not exactly," he murmured.

The statements were next, followed by an array of legal documents that had her eyes widening by the second. "You didn't… Oh, you didn't." She kept scanning and repeating those words, her head swaying back and forth. "Issac, this is—"

"Necessary," he completed for her. "You're going to live forever, Aya. That means investing now in preparation for the future. And as you have no assets, I'm lending you some of mine to begin the process."

"Lending," she repeated. "That's a lot, to, uh, *lend* to someone."

Amusement touched his chest. She truly had no idea how much he'd acquired through the centuries. This was just a small piece of his investments. "It's enough to start you down the right path and teach you the financial market."

"And the deed to this house?" she asked, raising a brow.

"I needed a name to put it in, and yours seemed appropriate." He maintained several aliases, and Aya Davenfield would be the newest player in the game. He may eventually create an Issac Davenfield as well.

Investments were one of Issac's favorite pastimes, as was company acquisition. Wakefield Pharmaceuticals was only one entity of several that he owned.

"Aidan taught me quite a bit about how the markets

work, how to spot trends, and where to invest. If you're willing, I would like to teach you as well. And we can use the alias I've created—Aya Davenfield—as the principal account."

She stared at him. "You want to make me a billionaire."

"No, I want to show you how to survive for eternity," he corrected. "Money isn't everything, Aya. You'll eventually crave a hobby or a career, and I want to show you how to accomplish that as an immortal."

"I… I don't know what to say." She took in all the documents again—the passport, the deed to the house, and the bank statements showing the amounts waiting for her chosen investments. "This is overwhelming."

"Yes," he agreed. "I felt the same when I took over my father's estate, and again when Aidan began training me. But it is worthwhile, love. Trust me."

"I do," she whispered. "Very much. I just don't know how to accept… *this*." She gestured at the papers.

"They're just numbers, darling. And as I said, it's a loan. You can pay me back when you're ready." Not that he necessarily wanted her to. It was Aya's independent instincts that required it, and he respected that. "The real gift here is that I'm offering to show you how it's done so you can do it yourself." Something he knew she would respect and desire.

And the look she granted him after hearing his words confirmed it. "I would like to learn."

"I thought you might." He cupped her cheek. "We can begin when you're ready, but everything is in place. And this home is yours to be used however you desire, whether it be to host an annual Christmas, or to rent, or even to sell."

"My parents will lose their ever-loving shit if I tell them you bought me this house."

Humor caressed his heart. "Yes, I imagine they would. We don't have to tell them."

"Good."

"You can claim I rented the same property for next year

if you want a repeat performance. They don't need to know."

"Okay," she agreed softly, her arms winding around his neck. "I'm not ready to join the others yet."

"We will have to soon," he murmured against her hair.

"I know. Just a few more minutes alone?"

"All right." He pulled her onto his lap, his arms circling her as she laid her head against his chest. "Merry Christmas, Aya."

"Merry Christmas, Issac."

Chapter Fourteen

Stas

THE JOYOUS ATMOSPHERE in the main area was almost too much to bear. It physically hurt to smile, but Stas managed it for her parents. For the Hydraians. For her friends. For Issac.

He knew, though. She could see the same pain lurking in his blue eyes. This trip had proven their relationship to be an impossibility. They would try because they had to, because there was no other choice for them, but this would eventually have to end.

Just not yet.

Tristan was right—she was a selfish bitch. She couldn't push Issac away even though she should. He'd come too close to biting her earlier, all because she craved it.

The way they used to be. The heat, the intensity, the passion.

It felt as if only a quarter of their previous chemistry existed now because of all the safety wheels they'd applied to their relationship. Issac couldn't even go down on her.

She didn't necessarily require the physical connection; it just wasn't the same. They were essentially walking around with this wall between them, too afraid to cross it. And whenever they came close, something reminded them of why they couldn't.

Issac squeezed her hand, his sapphire irises capturing hers for a long moment. He knew. "Not yet," he whispered.

She nodded, agreeing. "Not yet."

"You bought me my own Smith & Wesson?" Amelia squealed with delight, throwing her arms around Tom's neck, causing Issac to tense beside Stas.

"Yeah, and a holster so you can stop hiding mine in your pants." The taunt in Tom's voice earned him a slap against the arm.

"Arse," Amelia accused.

"Asset," he returned, his dark eyes grinning while everyone gaped at them.

"You bought my sister a gun for Christmas?" Issac sounded appalled, his tone matching Luc's expression. Aidan merely appeared amused.

"It's what she wanted." Tom winked at her. "Right, sweetheart?"

She beamed. "I did. I keep stealing his to practice, but now I have my own." She practically melted against him, her excitement palpable.

Issac shook his head, while Stas's father nodded in approval. "That's a good series." He started discussing one he owned in the same brand while Jayson handed Lizzie a ribbon-adorned bag beside them.

"Merry Christmas, Red," he murmured, a devious twinkle in his gaze.

She narrowed her eyes. "Is this family-appropriate?"

He smirked. "Yes, sweetheart. Now open the bag."

She gave him a doubtful look and peeked under the paper, her lips pulling into a frown. It took her a moment to undo all the ribbons, Jayson grinning the whole time, and she pulled out a binder. January first with the coming year's date was inscribed on the cover.

Lizzie turned the page and her lips parted. A ring glinted in the light with a ribbon strung through it, securing the item to the page. "Jayson," she breathed.

"Don't stop now," he murmured. "Flip the page."

She did—to a wedding invitation with next week's date on it.

Tears welled in Stas's eyes at what this signified.

The following page was a ceremony itinerary. The subsequent pages contained a seating map, a food menu, floral arrangements, the beverage chart, and a list of wedding-appropriate songs.

"You planned everything," she whispered, her nails trailing over the page.

"All except the dress," he replied. "But there's a team meeting us in Hydria this weekend for you to pick a gown. They're bringing bridesmaid dresses, too, assuming you want Stas in the wedding." His eyes lifted to Stas, happiness radiating from his features as Lizzie burst into tears on his lap. He smiled and shook his head. "These hormones are killing me, Red."

"Me, too," she said on a sob. She turned to bury her face in his neck, attracting everyone's attention to the happy couple beside Stas.

Issac squeezed her hand, his lips curling with amusement.

"What did I miss?" Amelia asked, the firearm safely tucked back into a box.

"Jayson just surprised Lizzie with their wedding arrangements," Balthazar said, his brown eyes gleaming proudly. "That's why he asked me to cancel the New Year's Eve bachelor party."

Luc nodded. "I see. I accept that reason."

"I do, too," Balthazar replied.

"Lizzie and Jayson are getting married?" Stas's mom asked, her eyes wide with surprise. "I didn't even know they were engaged."

"It's a recent development," Issac replied, his thumb drawing circles against Stas's wrist.

"Oh, you have to open your gift!" Lizzie tried to grab it, but Balthazar was already there, handing it to her. He winked at whatever she told him via her mind.

Jayson toyed with the bow, making a show of being slow until Lizzie cleared her throat. He chuckled and finished ripping the box open to reveal a dozen chocolate chip cookies. "Ah, cookies, Red? It's like you know me."

"Eat one," she encouraged, causing him to raise a brow. "Go on, try it."

"All right." He selected one from the middle and started to put the whole thing in his mouth, but Lizzie grabbed his wrist.

"Just a bite."

His brow furrowed. "I thought you wanted me to eat the cookie."

"I do, but just try it first."

He appeared doubtful but did as she asked, and stared at the item in his hand. "It's pink."

She smiled. "I know."

Stas's lips curled down, not understanding why... *Oh.* Her eyes widened. *Oh!*

"But why would....?" His lips parted. "It's... it's..." His gaze misted with tears, his heart in his eyes. "Oh, it's a girl?"

She nodded. "Yes."

Balthazar was grinning so widely. Amelia, too.

"That's what you were busy baking yesterday," Issac said just as Stas thought it.

Both of them nodded, their focus on the embracing couple.

"She's pregnant, too?" Stas's mom loudly whispered to

Tom.

He just nodded, his own emotions keeping him from speaking. It looked like he'd just opened a gift from Amelia before Lizzie and Jayson exchanged their presents. Stas saw a copy of a recently released movie, a Yankees cap, a New York–style pizza key chain, a toy motorcycle, and a few other random items that must have held some secret meaning between Amelia and Tom.

"So what do you say, Red. Will you marry me next week?" Jayson asked, the ring now in his hand.

Lizzie nodded, her smile bigger than Stas had ever seen it. "Yes. A thousand times yes."

He slid the ring over her finger and kissed her soundly, clearly not caring at all who was watching.

Issac brushed his lips over Stas's temple. "Be right back."

He crept over to the tree to retrieve a bag with Amelia's name on it, as well as a gift for Aidan and one for Tristan. He handed them out, then gave a fourth to Lucian and a final one to her parents before joining her again.

They all opened their presents at the same time.

A bottle of brandy for Aidan.

Red wine for Tristan that Stas guessed was laced with blood because he opened it and poured himself a glass.

"Canada's finest. Excellent," Luc said, eyeing the large glass container of maple syrup he'd just unwrapped.

Plane tickets and a hotel reservation for Stas's parents— in Greece. Which earned Issac a side-glance from her. He merely smiled. "We'll meet them in Athens for a week in the spring."

They were in the middle of gushing over the items when Amelia began to cry in earnest. Issac turned to her with a sad smile. "We always exchanged ornaments every year, even as children," he explained softly. "I never stopped collecting them."

"Issac." Her voice broke as she stood. He was there before she could take a step, his arms around her, his lips at her ear. Whatever he whispered only made her cry harder.

Stas's parents glanced around them, their confusion almost ruining the moment, but not quite.

Everyone around her was so happy, even through the tears.

Stas wanted to smile.

She tried.

But inside all she felt was hollow.

Because while everyone else could have their happily-ever-after, she would never have hers, and seeing all these exchanges just drove that point home so much harder.

Jayson and Lizzie were completely in their own little world, joyous in the occasion, so madly in love and about to have a baby girl.

Issac had his sister back after seven years of agony. Aidan had his daughter.

Tom was alive, the love of his life standing before him and thriving.

While Stas's stood at arm's length, unable to truly embrace her because of life's cruelty.

She tried to ignore the pain burning along her skin, centering in her heart, but it overwhelmed her mind.

Tristan met her gaze, his eyebrow cocked. *I told you so,* seemed to settle between them.

And she hated him for that. Hated that he couldn't see how much this hurt them both, how much she wanted this to work, how much she loved his best friend.

But all he did was smirk and look away.

Because he knew the guilt had finally won, and when Issac glanced back at her, he saw it, too. His expression fell as he gave a slight shake of his. *Not yet.*

But when? she wanted to ask, her soul splitting in two.

How can something so right be so wrong? How many times had she thought that over the last two months?

It wasn't fair.

Life wasn't fair.

He knelt before her, his gaze strong. "No, Aya."

"When, Issac?" she whispered, unable to bear this much longer, her forehead falling to his.

God, this wasn't the day to realize their fate. She knew that. The holidays were meant to be filled with love and joy and happiness, not this heart-wrenching pain destroying her inside.

"There's another gift under the tree," Balthazar was saying, his voice barely piercing the beating drum in her ears.

Issac's palms were on her cheeks. "Not yet, love."

"But when?" she repeated, her voice cracking.

"It's for Stas," Balthazar said.

What? She'd already opened all her gifts. Her parents had bought her socks and clothes, as they always did. Aidan had given her a pretty scarf. Amelia had given her Argentinian chocolates, claiming they were the best in the world. Lizzie and Stas had agreed not to exchange gifts.

So who was left?

The red package dropped into her lap, Issac still kneeling before her with his heart in his eyes. "This isn't from you, right?" she asked.

He shook his head. "No, not from me."

The package just said *Stas* in a masculine scrawl.

She fingered the edges, uncertain.

Who is it from, B? she asked, her gaze flicking to him.

He shook his head, saying he didn't know, either.

From no one here? she thought, frowning.

She stroked the finely wrapped item, the pattern oddly familiar. A memory flashed to her childhood, someone handing her a gift. *Red feathers.*

Gone in a blink.

Odd.

She tore through the paper to reveal a frame, one she recognized from her dreams.

A photo of her with her birth parents.

Her mother staring adoringly at her father with Stas nestled between them holding an angel doll with white, fluffy wings.

This was taken shortly before their deaths. Maybe a month before.

Her lips parted, shock overwhelming her. Everything had been destroyed in the house fire. Including this.

But it wasn't burnt at all, the frame still a beautiful bronze, etched with feathers.

"Aya?" Issac moved to her side, his hand curling around her wrist as he studied the photo with her.

"It's my parents," she breathed, her voice barely registering to her own ears.

"Sethios," he murmured, tracing the dark-haired male she only saw in her dreams. "I don't recognize the woman."

"My mom," she whispered. "Caroline." Or Caro, as Osiris had called her.

The room had gone still around them.

"What is it, Stas?" her adoptive mother asked.

"A photo of us," Issac replied for her. "May I?" He gestured to her gift, his intention clear.

Stas nodded mutely, unable to speak, her heart in her throat.

Her demon lifted the item, his gift causing the rune on her back to flare to life. He was manipulating the visual for the others, or perhaps just her parents.

A card caught her eye, taped to the back of the picture frame.

Beside it was a red feather shifting in and out of focus, reminding her of a hologram.

"Issac," she whispered. "Do you see that?"

"The card?"

She swallowed, shaking her head. "No, the feather."

He frowned. "No, darling. Only a card."

She blinked but it was still there.

Issac slowly lifted the paper beside it to reveal a note that stopped her heart.

Soon, Stas. I promise.
Love always,
Gabriel

106

PART TWO

Alis Volat Propriis

She flies with her own wings…

Chapter Fifteen

"The sun is glorious in the afterlife, painting the sky in shades I never noticed during mortality. Waking to this sight is a gift of life, a miracle, not a burden."

—*Issac Wakefield*
Vita mutatur, non tollitur

JAYSON really outdid himself. Tropical flowers decorated the path to the beach, where several rows of chairs sat vacant in the black sand. More floral arrangements adorned the backs, with dark pink ribbons, some splashes of white, and seashell embellishments.

And the altar framed by the sea behind it… It took Stas's

breath away.

She stood taking it all in, her heart in her throat.

It's perfect.

Tranquil, secluded, and bathed in the sounds of rolling waves. Stas never wanted a wedding, but this almost made her yearn for one. Almost.

A hot palm slid around her waist to rest on her abdomen as a sturdy chest pressed into her back. She melted against the familiar warmth, craving his heat. January in Hydria might be more temperate than New York City, but the beach held a slight chill that scattered goose bumps down her exposed arms and legs.

"Lizzie is going to cry," she whispered.

"I know." The two words were against her ear. "Thomas has several handkerchiefs for the occasion."

Stas smiled. As Lizzie had no family to speak of, Tom had offered to walk her down the aisle. It seemed appropriate for his big-brother role in her life.

"This dress is gorgeous, Aya." Issac kissed her neck, igniting butterflies in her stomach. They'd kept their physical distance after the near-biting incident last week. It only left her craving him more, and if the reaction she felt against her backside was any indication, he felt the same way.

"It's pink," Stas said, concentrating on a safe topic—her dress. "But I like the material."

"Hmm, and I like the length." The hand not on her stomach met her exposed thigh, sliding up beneath the fabric. "It displays your legs beautifully."

"You would be focused on that." She turned in his arms, which was a mistake.

Issac in a suit almost left her speechless.

Issac in a full tuxedo? Well, that just left her unable to think at all.

He even had on a bow tie.

I wonder if he'll let me remove that with my teeth later.

"You're staring," he murmured, his lips curling at the

edges.

No point in replying to that because obviously she couldn't take her eyes off him. She traced the handwoven silk of his jacket, indulging in the rich texture, down to his waist and the belt around his hips.

I'd rather remove that…

"Shall we skip the ceremony?" he asked innocently, his hand catching her wrist as her fingers slid across his lower abdomen. "Head back up to Balthazar's house instead?"

That was where they were staying while all the living arrangements were sorted on the island. While Balthazar and Issac may bicker like brothers, there was definitely a bond between them—something that came to fruition when Balthazar offered them the guest suite in his home. Aidan and his harem were staying with Lucian.

"Lizzie would kill me," she finally replied after thinking about his offer. It would be so tempting to lose herself for a few hours in his touch.

But that was exactly what couldn't happen.

Not after last week.

And they both knew it.

She met his sapphire gaze on a sigh. "I miss you, Issac."

"I'm right here, love."

"You know what I mean."

His smile was sad as he cupped her cheek, his forehead resting against hers. No words, just gentle understanding and a myriad of unspoken words and emotions flowing between them.

Not yet.

When?

Just not yet.

I can't live without you.

I love you.

We have all the time in the world to figure this out.

I know.

What if we don't?

That's not an option.

Maybe the conversation was all in her head, but she swore his voice infiltrated her thoughts on a few of those replies.

Or maybe she was losing her mind.

After that gift from the mysterious Gabriel, she'd been a mess. No one could see the red feather. Yet it sat on the dresser in her shared quarters with Issac, no longer flickering. The silky texture reminded her of dreams long forgotten, one where her father had described her mother's wings.

Except that dream was starting to feel like a memory, one that had been repressed for nearly twenty years.

And with that realization came more, rendering her confused and alone. She told Issac everything, speculating long into the twilight hours every night and coming up with no answers.

The Elders recognized Gabriel as the shell corporation that funded Owen's bar, suggesting a link between the two. But who—or what—was Gabriel?

And why am I the only one who can see the feather?

"Eliza is looking for you," Issac whispered. "It seems she and Amelia have finished with Elizabeth's makeup and hair, and they want to do photos with the maid of honor."

"This is all so surreal," Stas marveled. "My best friend is getting married today to an immortal of three-thousand-plus years."

"She's also pregnant with what might be a variation of a Seraphim," he added helpfully.

"Minor detail." Stas laughed and shook her head. "A year ago, I knew nothing about this world, and now…" *It's everything. My life. My purpose. My world.*

"I know." He brushed his lips over hers softly, tenderly. "I'll see you during the ceremony." Another kiss, this one lingering. "Save me a dance afterward." Not a question, but a command, one that caused her lips to twitch at the sides.

"You're supposed to ask, not demand."

"Amelia would be so disappointed," he teased. "Promise

me anyway."

Her heart soared with the playful nature of his tone, the way he taunted her in private when no one else was near. "You can have all my dances, always."

Happiness radiated from his features, his fingers curling around the back of her neck. "Mmm, I may just hold you to that, Aya."

"I hope you do."

His mouth captured hers, sealing off her need for air and filling her with his energy and life. Her soul wept for him, longed for more, urged her to finish something she couldn't quite define.

And then he released her.

"I really do love that dress." The devious twinkle in his gaze had her glancing downward at her skewed neckline. It revealed far too much of her breasts from this angle.

She fixed the halter top while he watched, and gave him a reproachful stare. "Behave."

"Never." That devilish smile of his had her thighs clenching. "Run along, Aya, before I decide to make use of that short dress."

She swallowed. Issac never bluffed and he certainly wasn't now. He cocked a brow as if daring her to stay. She took a step backward instead. "See you after the ceremony."

"Oh, you'll see me during." His heated gaze ran over her. "I'll be the one fantasizing about your legs and how they feel when wrapped around my waist. Or maybe I'll think about your mouth..."

Stas flushed hot, his words making the ache inside her worse. If she didn't leave now, they'd end up naked on this beach. Certainly not the ceremony everyone wanted to witness today.

"Leaving," she managed through her tightening throat.

"Watching," he called after her as she darted up the path, his hot gaze singeing a hole through her dress.

She'd chosen the short length because of the sand. Rustling skirts over the beach hadn't appealed to her. It now

served the dual purpose of taunting her favorite demon.
Maybe I'll play with that during the ceremony…

* * *

"You look beautiful, Liz," Stas said, catching her friend's gaze in the mirror above the dresser. Alik had offered his home to the wedding party since he lived closest to the beach, and the girls were in his guest suite, while the men took over his master bedroom.

"I just feel so… exposed," her best friend mumbled, lowering her hand from the bump beneath her Grecian-style gown. She was convinced that everyone would see right through the off-white fabric to the growing child beneath, and not see anything beyond it. But the flowing style hid everything, giving her the appearance of a Greek goddess.

Amelia had styled Lizzie's hair in long, red ringlets, clasping them loosely with pins in a variety of places. And Eliza had left Lizzie with a natural glow, the makeup subdued and allowing the bride's innate beauty to come through.

"Jay's jaw will be on the floor when he sees you," Stas added. "Trust me."

Eliza smiled wickedly. "And then again when you reveal what's beneath the dress."

The French designer who helped fit Lizzie with the dress had also gifted her with matching lingerie. All the girls had approved, especially the bride.

Lizzie blushed. "Well, at least Amelia and Eliza worked some magic on my hair and face."

The fledgling turned makeup artist snorted. "Pretty sure genetics gave you all that, Lizzie. We just perfected the masterpiece."

A knock sounded before Stas's best friend could refute the claim, which she'd clearly been about to do.

Luc popped his head in with an adorable grin. "Can I interrupt for a moment?"

"Did the Hydraian King just ask permission to do something?" Eliza asked, her gorgeous features twisting into a scowl. "Because I thought he thrived on dishing out commands without regard to anyone else's feelings."

His lips flattened. "Eliza. I didn't realize you were in here."

"I bet not." She faced him with a flip of her long, dark hair over a slender shoulder. "You do have a tendency to interrupt without thinking, after all."

His square jaw tightened. "I came to deliver a gift."

"Oh, is it another edict?" She fluttered her thick lashes at him. "How fucking thoughtful of you, *Your Majesty.*"

"From the groom," he added, his broad shoulders appearing wider, harsher, as he approached Eliza. "Keep pushing me, princess. See what it gets you."

She didn't appear at all fazed by the close proximity of his muscular form to her much smaller frame. "A spanking?"

His resulting smile was reminiscent of a panther sizing up its prey. "You'd like that far too much."

She snorted. "Not from you."

He took another step, crowding her up against the makeshift makeup counter in Alik's spare bedroom, his hands clasping the table beside her hips and caging her between his powerful arms.

Lizzie raised her auburn eyebrows, her expression rivaling Stas's feelings.

Luc *always* exuded a calm presence, yet there was nothing relaxed about his position now. Intimidation and fury rolled off him in waves, not that it seemed to bother Eliza. She held his gaze with a steely one of her own and arched one perfectly sculpted brow, awaiting his retort.

"No, it seems you'd rather have one from a boy at a club." His gaze raked over her in clear disapproval. "Pity when there's so much potential." He pushed away from her and left without a backward glance.

Stas frowned. *What just happened?*

Eliza huffed, her tan skin darkening. "That man is *impossible*." Her fingers clenched into fists at her sides. "What did he expect me to do last night? Just wait around on the island for everyone to come back after going into Athens to celebrate the New Year? No. I went out, too, because I'm an adult capable of making her own fucking decisions. And that asshole"—she pointed to the door—"has the audacity to chastise me for it? At a nightclub?" She scowled. "Fuck him."

"You all went out last night?" Lizzie asked, her forehead crumpling. "After the party on the beach?" There'd been a big bonfire with music and dancing in Hydria to ring in the New Year. Nothing extravagant, just a relaxing evening of champagne and conversation. Stas hadn't felt much like celebrating, her mind still wrapped up in the holidays from last week.

Gabriel.

Who are you?

"Yeah, Jacque took a group out," Eliza muttered. "I went with them, only to be tracked down thirty minutes later by..." She trailed off, shaking her head. "Never mind. This is your day. I won't let talk of the *King* ruin it."

Balthazar's chuckle preceded him as he entered the room. In a tux.

All three of them openly gaped at the too-handsome man. He resembled a god in whatever he wore, but that suit was sin personified. It should have been illegal.

He and Issac beside each other would be—

"Utter perfection," he finished for her with a wicked grin. "Now imagine what we'd look like with each other."

"I really hate when you do that," Stas growled, referring to the mind reading, not the very sexual image he'd just provoked in her head.

"You were the one thinking my name, sweetheart." He unbuttoned his black jacket to pull a package from the inner pocket. "Luc meant to give you this, Lizzie. Before he became otherwise distracted by the beauty in the room, I mean." His dimples appeared, earning him an appreciative sigh from Eliza. "Now that I've seen you all for myself, I can understand why." He pressed a kiss to the bride-to-be's temple as he handed her the gift. "You look stunning, Lizzie."

"Thank you," she replied, flushing. "What's this for?"

"Open it and find out," he encouraged, his chocolate eyes glittering.

She drew a manicured finger over the long package, her lower lip catching between her teeth. "Okay." Lizzie always loved presents, and it showed in her smile now as she lifted the lid. A necklace lay inside with a heart-shaped ruby pendant encrusted in diamonds.

Her gasp had Balthazar's lips twitching. "I'll give him an eight point seven. Points deducted for not delivering it himself."

"What?" she asked, her eyes fluttering upward with tears glistening in their depths. "Why did he do this?"

"Because you're his heart," Balthazar replied softly, cupping her cheek. "Welcome to the family, Lizzie."

She sniffled and threw her arms around his neck, her words unintelligible against his chest.

"Really glad I chose waterproof mascara," Eliza said, causing Balthazar's lips to curl into one of his devastating grins.

"Emotions are more than acceptable today." He kissed Lizzie on the head and released her. "I'll tell him you like the necklace."

She nodded. "Tell him I love it. I love everything."

"Which means I have to upgrade the score to a solid nine. I'll let him know, but I expect a ten from him tonight." He winked and ducked out of the room.

Lizzie stared after him. "He didn't just imply… I mean, he's not really going to, like, grade our…?"

"Jay is the only one you need to be thinking about," Eliza replied. "He won't let anyone, or anything, make you uncomfortable."

The bride-to-be's cheeks reddened again, her attention falling to the box in her hand. "You're right. He's made everything so perfect." Her brown irises locked on Stas. "I didn't plan anything."

"I know."

"Like, not even the food or the wine or the flowers."

"I know," Stas repeated.

"How is this my life?" She touched her belly, the open sleeves of her gown flowing around her like angel wings. "How did this all happen?" Her lower lip wobbled. "Oh God, I'm going to cry. *Again.*"

"Uh, then I'll just come back," Tom said from the doorway, Amelia beside him.

She caught him by the arm as he tried to escape, and pulled him over the threshold with her. "Nice try, arse."

"What? I was just giving her privacy."

"You were running." Amelia arched a brow, daring him to argue. When he didn't, she nodded. "That's what I thought."

Lizzie grinned at him through her watery gaze. "I'm so glad you're here."

"I wouldn't miss it for the world," he replied softly. "You look stunning, Lizzie."

She glanced down at her bump. "You can't tell?"

"Even if I could, it would only make you even more beautiful." He held out his arms for her. "Come here. I promise not to mess with your hair." A habit formed between them from years and years of brotherly affection.

"He knows better," Amelia added.

Lizzie giggled and accepted Tom's embrace. "Thank you," she whispered.

"For what?"

"Walking me down the aisle."

"Ah, Liz, I should be thanking you for the honor." He held her tighter, kissing the top of her head very carefully. "I'm so happy for you, sweetheart. So, so happy."

Stas teared up at the display, the reality of today settling over her. It hadn't been the decorations or even the dress, but Tom's embrace with Lizzie conveying the love of a man finally letting her go. Their relationship had always been platonic, even when Lizzie pined after him, but this felt like a final moment. A private one filled with joy and acceptance, and underlined in adoration.

"Love you," he murmured, his eyes falling closed.

"Love you, too," Lizzie replied just as softly.

A comforting silence fell over the room, Tom's eyes stilled closed as he lent Lizzie his strength one last time. This wasn't a goodbye between them, but a rebirth into a new life, one where he trusted another to protect her and cherish her the way she deserved.

He met Amelia's gaze over Lizzie's shoulder, and she gave him a nod. Some secret message Stas couldn't decipher. But it was clear that Amelia approved.

"It's time," Tom said quietly, slowly releasing Lizzie. "You ready?"

She nodded, no hesitation in her features. "Yes."

Chapter Sixteen

Stas

"Amelia is quite besotted with the Elder, Eli. She's mentioned the exchanging of vows on several occasions, desiring the promise of eternal love. This is not something I've ever desired for myself, but if it is my sister's wish, I shall endeavor to accept it."

—Issac Wakefield
Vita mutatur, non tollitur

"Do you, Elizabeth, take Jayson to be yours forever, to love and to hold dear, from this day forward, for the rest of eternity and beyond?" Luc's voice carried across the beach, his position at the altar fitting.

"I do," Lizzie replied, her hands clasped in Jayson's

palms, his smiling eyes holding hers. He hadn't stopped grinning since she appeared at the end of the aisle, had even shed a few tears at the sight of her walking toward him.

"And do you, Jayson, take Elizabeth to be yours forever, to love and to hold dear, from this day forward, for the rest of eternity and beyond?"

Adoration graced Jayson's features as he said, "Absolutely, I do."

Stas met Issac's burning gaze. He sat in the second row of the groom's section with Aidan beside him. She stood behind Lizzie, holding two bouquets of flowers.

Are you all right? he seemed to ask with his eyes. Or maybe that was her imagination. She seemed to have something caught in her throat, some sort of emotion she couldn't name. Because everywhere she looked, she saw a future that would never be hers.

Yet, elation also filled her chest at the love radiating between her best friend and Jayson.

So why do I feel like I'm about to cry?

Maybe it was the emotions of the day, the embrace she witnessed between Tom and Lizzie, the undeniable devotion thickening the air before her.

And the realization that Stas would never experience a moment like this for herself. Not the marriage, but the vows—that sense of having someone for eternity without any strings or concerns.

I'll never have that. Her heart ached with the thought.

Issac must have seen it in her expression, even though she tried her hardest to hide it, because his lips curled down at the corners. She swallowed and refocused on the ceremony, needing not to consider such things. Not right now. Not on Lizzie's day.

Because she truly was happy for her best friend. Lizzie deserved this moment more than anyone Stas knew, and she was so thankful to be a part of it.

"Jayson?" Luc prompted.

The groom's eyes glistened with warmth as he lifted

Lizzie's hand to his mouth to kiss her wrist. "From the moment we first met, you captivated me in a way no one else in my very long life has ever accomplished. I had to know you, Red. Every detail, key words that make you smile, why you care so much for others, what makes you so uniquely *you*, and how to be the best man possible in your life. And I've only begun achieving those goals, and with each one, I have a thousand more I want to experience and understand."

He cupped her cheek, his thumb brushing away the tear beneath her eye.

"I want to spend the rest of our very long lives creating a new history together, Red," he continued softly. "Loving each other, raising our beautiful daughter together, and spending every waking moment treasuring this unique and special bond between us. I won't let anyone or anything harm you, your heart, or your soul. I will never forsake you. I will always be faithful to you, to our family, to the bond between our souls. And I will forever love and adore you, as you are my heart, my love, and my life."

Balthazar—the best man—handed him a box, inside it a ring that Jayson slid over Lizzie's finger.

"*Vena amoris*," he murmured. "A tradition younger than me, one that states the vein of your left finger is tied to your heart. That's the purpose—to secure the other's heart. But, Lizzie, *you* are my heart. Therefore, this is merely a symbol of my devotion to you, and with this ring, I vow to spend eternity with you and you alone. Always. Forever. For all the centuries and millennia to come. You are my Elizabeth, my Red, my wife." He kissed her wrist again, adding a nibble to her pulse that left her smiling through the tears.

"You said we weren't doing vows," she whispered.

"I never said I wasn't," he clarified, the words only audible for those standing near the altar.

Clever man, Stas thought, smiling as Balthazar winked at her from over Luc's shoulder. *I hope you have more handkerchiefs*, she thought at him.

His responding grin held a note of confidence and a knowing gleam, as if to say, *Of course.*

"God, Jayson," Lizzie said, fanning her face with one hand. "I can't follow that."

The groom chuckled and kissed her hand again before releasing it. "I don't expect you to."

"But you just said all those things, and all I had planned was a standard vow that is so boring in comparison, and, oh…" She touched the back of her hand to her cheek, which was flushed a traditional Lizzie red. "I love you so much. You're going to be the most amazing father and husband, and I'll make you as many cookies as you could ever dream, and, and, I'm totally fucking this up right now." She pressed her palm to her mouth. "Oh God, I said *fuck* in my vow…"

Several chuckles came from the audience while Stas tried to hide her own amusement behind the bouquets of flowers in her hands.

Balthazar cleared his throat and handed Lizzie a box that matched the one he'd given Jay. "It's not official until you're holding the ring," he murmured, his voice warm and encouraging. "Just speak from your heart, sweetheart."

She nodded, taking the box and stealing a deep breath while everyone around them quieted themselves.

Stas risked another glance at Issac, and he tilted his head to the side, a deep curiosity in his gaze. *What would you say?* he seemed to be asking. Or maybe he just wanted to know her thoughts, or why her own eyes were tearing up yet again at the proceedings before them.

Because I'll never have a chance to say these things to him. They couldn't have eternity.

"Jayson," Lizzie started, pausing to swallow and straighten her shoulders. "I've spent my life not belonging, an outsider playing the part I was groomed for from a young age without ever understanding why. I thought I understood a lot of things, like love, but I didn't. Not until I met you."

He squeezed her hand when she paused again, the smile

in his dark eyes genuine and encouraging. She responded in kind, her expression glowing with warmth and conviction.

"You taught me how to feel, Jayson. To *really* feel. And you taught me how to live, as if I'd never been living at all. I can't wait to explore the future with you, with our new family, our daughter, to watch you become a dad, to live with you every day for the rest of our lives. God, there's going to be so much pizza and cookies, and I'm going to get fat, but I know you won't care because you're my Jay and I'm your Red, and together, we are one giant heart. Because you own my heart, too, Jayson. You always will, for richer, for poorer, for eternity. I will always be yours." She slid the ring over his finger with her words, handing the box back to a waiting Balthazar. "I love you."

"I love you, too." The tears were back in Jayson's eyes and his voice, but so was his smile. So much worship and devotion that no one would ever be able to question how he felt. Because it was written in the way he looked at Lizzie, just as it was obvious in the way she gazed up at him.

He didn't wait for Luc to make it official, his mouth claiming Lizzie's in a heated moment that left the audience *aww*ing at the sight.

"Well, I suppose that's it, then," Luc said, his dimples flashing. "As you've already kissed your bride, I now pronounce you Jayson and Elizabeth, husband and wife."

They didn't stop kissing or acknowledge the round of applause surrounding them, too lost in each other, their love, their future. One they would cherish forever. Nothing standing in their way. An everlasting partnership.

Stas smiled through her own emotions, happy to her very soul for her best friend while feeling utterly broken inside. Because she wanted this with Issac. Everything had always been so limited between them, an expiration date looming over their heads. And while they'd fought it for months, it would inevitably end.

"Walk with me." Balthazar's voice came from beside her as he held out his elbow to escort her back up the aisle behind a retreating Lizzie and Jayson. The bride hadn't even thought to grab her bouquet, too lost in her elation to realize Stas still held it.

"Love makes us blind," Balthazar said, responding to her thoughts.

Stas threaded her arm through his without a word. He knew everything. Her broken heart. Her frustrations. Her fury at fate. Her concern over what the future held.

What would happen when Issac found someone else?

Would he have a wedding such as this?

Don't be ridiculous, she chastised herself. Issac wasn't the marrying type. And more than that, what they had between them ran far too deep, to the depths of their beings. Stas knew with every breath she'd never find another like Issac. He was her only, her everything.

If I ever lost him... She bit her lip, focusing on her steps as Balthazar guided her blindly up the aisle.

"I cherished someone once, many, many years ago," her escort said, quiet, for her ears alone. "Some might even say I loved her. I was young, not even a hundred years old, but she reached a part of me few others have ever touched. And she was perfect in every way. Gorgeous, salacious, adventurous. I've not thought about her in some time, but I've found myself reliving our final moments a lot lately. Mainly because I fear you'll end up in a similar situation and I wouldn't wish that feeling on anyone in the world."

They reached the end, but he kept walking, his arm holding hers with ease as they wove a path away from the party along the shoreline. "What was her name?" Stas wondered, her gaze on the setting sun over the horizon and the beautiful colors painting the evening sky.

"Nythos," he murmured. "I've not said that name out loud in centuries, maybe even a thousand years." Reminiscence filled his tone, giving him a somber glow that Balthazar rarely exuded.

"This isn't a happy story, is it?"

He shook his head sadly. "No, it's not. It's a tragedy."

They continued walking in silence, Balthazar's gaze taking on a faraway gleam that touched Stas's heart. The flirtatious male with suggestive comments had disappeared behind a mask of sorrow and pain, his emotions palpable even unspoken.

"You don't need to talk about it," she told him. Especially not tonight, not while everyone should be celebrating. He was the best man, she the maid of honor. Surely there was a better time than now.

"On the contrary, it's the perfect moment," he replied, clearly listening to her thoughts. "My best friend of several millennia has just decided to spend an eternity in monogamy. Part of me envies him, while the other part is wary. I've seen so much, experienced true loss, and I don't want to see that for him or anyone else I care about. And, Stas, that includes you and Issac, too." He finally stopped walking, turning to face her. "You're not going to like what I have to say."

She could see in his eyes that he meant it. "I know."

"Nythos was killed in retaliation to something I did, but not after indulging in a little blood play with Aidan. She became the first made Ichorian, teaching us quite a bit about immortal rebirth. We thought she might be a Hydraian at first; of course, we didn't have that term yet. But she was an Ichorian of Aidan's line. And none of us knew the impact of Hydraian blood at the time."

Oh no… She could see why he'd chosen this story before he even finished.

"She bit me, Stas," he finished, confirming what she already suspected. "She died in my arms."

Stas's heart stopped, the pain in his expression halting her breath. And the reality of what he was telling her carving a hole in her very soul.

"I know you love him," he continued. "We all do, but you most of all. I would never want you to experience what I went through that day. To be honest, I'm not sure you'd survive it."

She swallowed, her stomach twisting in knots. "I don't know how to do this. I don't know how to say goodbye to him."

"I know, sweetheart. I know." He pulled her into his arms, his chin resting atop her head. "I'm not saying you have to, but you need to be careful. I can hear the urges between you. The fight is palpable, and it scares me. For you both."

"He almost bit me last week."

"I'm aware."

"But we've not…" *We've been celibate ever since.*

"Yes." He ran his hand over her back, lending her the comfort she so badly craved.

"I hate this, B. I hate it so much."

"I know, sweetheart, and I wish I could do something for you. I really do."

Of course he did. He heard her every thought, which was why he walked her away from the party, to give her a moment to collect her thoughts. And also to let her know he understood, in his own way.

She let the tears fall, her fists in his jacket. The need to strike something overwhelmed her, to scream, to curse, to let out the furious energy building inside her. It wasn't fair. None of this. And she despised it, loathed every fucking second.

They stood like that for several minutes, his arms around her, the waves rolling over the sand, the air cooling from the disappearing sun. Soon the glow of candles from the reception would be their only source of light besides the moon. A romantic evening to celebrate the union of two worthy souls, one of whom was her best friend.

Stas needed to be strong, supportive, give Lizzie the night she deserved.

"Let Jayson manage that," Balthazar whispered. "Take the evening, enjoy it with Issac. There's always tomorrow, Stas." He pulled back to cup her cheek. "You have an eternity. All I'm saying is, don't rush it and be careful. And if you need someone to talk to, I'm here. All right?"

She nodded, releasing him and stepping back to drag her thumbs beneath her damp eyes. "I'm a mess."

"You're gorgeous," he replied smoothly, his gaze twinkling. "You always are, and I believe there's someone here who would agree with me on that front."

"Indeed." Issac's voice came from several feet away where he stood with his hands tucked into his pockets, his burning gaze filled with questions.

Balthazar smirked. "If that were my goal, Wakefield, she'd already be naked." He winced at whatever reply Issac leveled at him, or perhaps it was an image of some sort. "Yes, I should be returning to the party now. Otherwise, Jacque will put on gothic metal, and I doubt Lizzie will approve."

Stas chuckled. "No, she definitely won't."

He winked at her and chucked her beneath the chin. "You know where to find me."

"Thank you."

"Anytime." He saluted Issac as he strolled past. "All yours."

Issac said nothing, his gaze on Stas, hands still tucked into his pants.

She blew out a breath. "The ceremony left me feeling emotional. He was just giving me a moment to collect myself."

"You don't need to explain, Aya. I trust you."

"Do you?" Because she really wouldn't blame him if he didn't. Especially around a male like Balthazar, one renowned for seduction and bedding every person in his path.

"Yes." He moved into her space, close enough to touch, but not quite. "When I didn't see you afterward, I wondered if you were all right. Balthazar showed me where he'd taken you."

"He did?"

Issac nodded. "Are you all right, love?"

She started to bob her head, then stopped, shaking it slowly from side to side. "No. I'm not. Not even a little bit."

His arms opened just in time to catch her as she stepped into him, her head going to his chest. Balthazar had offered her a semblance of comfort, but Issac... Issac felt like home. *Her* home. Her safe place. Her haven.

He said nothing as he held her, already aware of her troublesome thoughts. It felt as if they were on repeat, constantly, killing her with every moment. And she knew he had to be experiencing the same.

This agony.

Insecurity.

Heartache.

His lips were in her hair, kissing her softly, grounding her to him, reminding her why she'd chosen to fight. But her future refused to agree. How could she battle fate?

"Do you want to retire early?" he asked softly.

"I don't think that'll help."

"Then how about an evening of wine and dancing?" he offered. "On the beach, beneath the stars, without a thought of tomorrow. It seems the right way to celebrate your birthday, yes?"

She started, lifting her head. "My birthday?"

"You thought I forgot?"

"With all the festivities... I barely even considered it. Does it even count anymore?" She was immortal, forever twenty-four. Why bother?

He shrugged. "Doesn't mean we can't indulge a little bit, yes?"

She withdrew from him just enough to meet his gaze. "You didn't get me a gift, did you?"

"Of course I did. But it's back in the room."

She groaned. "Issac, you've already given me too much."

"I'd argue I've hardly given you anything at all."

Stas's lips flattened. "I'm not a materialistic person."

"Who said it's a materialistic present?" he countered.

She twisted her mouth to the side, considering. All right.

Now that intrigued her. "Now I want to retire early."

He tsked. "That's too bad, as you've already agreed to dancing on the beach, and if I recall, you promised me all your dances as well."

She narrowed her gaze. "Why do I feel like I was tricked into this agreement?"

"Perhaps because I'm a master of words and compromises."

"Or just a devious enigma capable of always obtaining what he wants, no matter the situation."

His adorable dimples appeared, devastating her female senses. He really should not be allowed to smile. Ever. It was dangerous to women—and men—everywhere. "A clever description. I approve."

She stole a deep breath, suppressing the need burning inside her. One look and he had her ready to lie out naked on the beach, consequences be damned. And he wasn't even trying. "Dancing sounds good," she decided, needing the distraction.

His knowing gaze said he saw right through her, fully aware of his impact on her. "Allow me to lead, my lady." He held out his hand.

"Oh, is this the part where I call you *Your Highness*?" Stas recently learned about Issac's family ancestry. His father was a duke, making Issac the Duke of Wakefield after his father passed. Stas had yet to tease him about it, but now seemed as good a time as any.

"Technically, it's *Your Grace*, and no. You will not call me that."

"And if I do, Your Grace?" she asked, batting her eyelashes at him coquettishly.

He narrowed his gaze. "I'll be forced to punish you."

"This sounds enlightening. Please elaborate, Your Grace."

He looked her over, his stare assessing. "You want to play, darling?"

She smiled. "Always."

"Then we'll play." He held out his hand. "Call me whatever nickname you desire. I dare you."

Her skin heated as she accepted his palm, her stomach clenching for an entirely different reason than earlier. *Just the distraction I need.* "Introduce me to your history, Your Grace. Dance with me like you did centuries ago."

"We'll need to improvise with the modern music," he murmured, guiding her back toward the party. "But I accept the challenge."

Her heart fluttered in her chest. "Then take me dancing, Duke Wakefield."

"Happily, Lady Aya."

Chapter Seventeen

Stas

"Okay, okay, I give," Stas said as Issac whirled her back into his arms for the thousandth time. "My feet need a break."

"Ah, but in my time, we would dance for hours on end, nonstop, as it provided the only semblance of foreplay." He pulled her flush against him, his thigh between hers. "I thought you wanted a proper old-fashioned seduction?"

"And I do, but I need a break."

His sapphire gaze twinkled in the moonlight. "Astasiya Davenport, are you attempting to woo me away from the party to entice me in private?" He sounded so aghast that she couldn't help but laugh.

"God, you really were a duke."

"Indeed." He nuzzled her cheek. "Technically, I still am since I never died."

"Did no one ever question your dukedom?"

"Ah, the benefits of living during a time with no electronic records. It was far easier to manipulate the financial system and pass on family estates. Most of my investments were funded through land sales, but I do still own quite a bit of property in Southern England, through various corporations and such."

"More than Wakefield Pharmaceuticals?"

"That's just my current cover, love." He spun her again, bringing her back hard against him, his lips at her ear. "One day, I'll show you everything. If you're interested."

She was. Very. Not because she wanted his money, but his manipulation of the system fascinated her. "I—"

"Stop," a deep voice to their left snapped.

Luc had Eliza by the shoulders, her glower and flushed cheeks indicating some sort of heated debate.

Several others noticed the altercation near the side of the dance floor, but many just continued enjoying their evening, swaying along to the beats Jacque wove through the air. Jayson and Lizzie were in the center, Balthazar beside them with several others. Alik was nowhere to be seen, his disinterest in social gatherings clear.

Amelia lounged with Tom, Aidan, Anya, and Clara at a nearby table, all chatting over their glasses of wine. Stas smiled at them, feeling slightly envious as her feet screamed at her for still standing. But this had been her idea, after all. Or was it Issac's? She could hardly remember.

"I really need to sit down," she told him. At least she'd

ditched her heels before treading barefoot into the sand.

"All right, Lady Davenport. If you—"

A pop to the left startled them apart.

What the fuck was that?

A bad speaker? No, the music still played, drowning out the sound for many on the floor. But Issac heard it, too, his focus on their surroundings.

The hairs along her arms danced. *Someone's coming.* She tried to lock on the source but couldn't find them, the energy around them too chaotic.

Another shot cracked through the air, eliciting a shout from Luc as Eliza crumpled in his arms.

Everyone started moving, the Guardians forming protective rings around their respective Elders as mayhem erupted on the beach.

Issac yanked Stas into a crouch beside him, his gaze searching as Hydraians ran toward the waterline.

Rapid-fire shots sliced through the night and the first line of defense, embers floating in their wake, igniting the night in flames. Stas's nightmares threatened to rise, her memories sparking to the surface.

A bullet taking Daddy to his knees. Mommy screaming in agony, writhing on the ground. Stas wanted to help but didn't know how.

Then red feathers appeared at her side, taking—

Not now! She stole a deep breath through her nose, focusing on the present, scanning her current surroundings.

Fatigues.

An army.

Sentinels.

Dotting the beach, running toward the party, firing their pistols without care for whom they hit.

"They're blocking us somehow!" Balthazar shouted.

"I know!" Issac returned from beside her.

A block?

Like a rune?

She frowned. Had Doctor Fitzgerald perfected the Sentinel technology enough to withstand Hydraian and

Ichorian gifts?

"Heads up," Jacque announced, dropping weapons before them and disappearing in a flash.

Luc was already there, picking up a gun and taking aim, Balthazar by his side, their Guardians around them.

Lizzie...

Stas swung around to see her cowering behind an enraged Jayson, another row of protective Hydraians in front of them. Jayson seemed focused, his gaze ignited with power.

He's trying to manipulate the metal.

Is it working?

Stas followed the line of his sight, to the twisting gun in a Sentinel's hand. It fell to the sand, his hand already holding another that fired with ease.

An indication that it worked or not? She couldn't tell, could hardly see in the dark.

What about mine? she wondered, digging deep, calling her power to life as she aimed her gun at an approaching Sentinel. A clean shot to the head sent him to the ground.

Focus. Try. See what happens.

Stas called on her ability to compel, laced it through her aura and outward, searching...

There.

A hint of malice not belonging to one of her own.

Drop your weapon, she urged, her gaze seeking the source. *Now,* she demanded.

The gun fell to his feet just in time for one of the Hydraians to ignite him in flames.

Had he dropped the gun in error, or—

A familiar shriek pierced Stas's ears. She turned just in time to see Aidan take Lizzie to the ground, his body covering hers as he took a series of bullets from behind.

"Lizzie!" Stas screamed, already on her feet and running, the gun still in her hand as she aimed it at the Sentinel who had somehow appeared behind the group. Anya fought another, her hands bare.

No gun.

She didn't typically need it, her touch being able to kill a person on contact, but the Sentinel was completely clothed.

Stas took aim just as Tom appeared, pistol in hand, sending a bullet through the soldier's skull.

But not before he pulled the trigger.

Anya fell to her knees, her palm at her chest, her expression horrified.

Clara collapsed beside her, hands on the other woman's face, tears tracking down her own.

Incendiary bullet.

Oh, shit. Aidan!

Stas didn't think.

She just reacted—running to Lizzie and Aidan, falling to the ground next to them. Amelia appeared beside her, helping to roll the ancient Ichorian to his back.

His glassy eyes stared up at them lifelessly.

"Dad..." Amelia choked on a sob.

Lizzie cried, her white dress covered in sand and black soot.

Aidan's blood... burned...

He's dead.

"I d-don't... I d-don't... How?" Her best friend wept, her attention shifting between Aidan and Amelia. "Oh God..."

Stas bit back a cry, her gaze searching for Issac, who fought on the other side of the beach, his jacket gone. He aimed his weapon, firing it with ease, holding his own.

Completely unaware that his Sire, the man he called Father, was gone.

Oh, Issac... Stas's heart broke for him. *And Luc...*

"Amelia," Tom breathed, immediately taking her into his arms despite the warfare erupting around them. "I've got you. I'm here."

"He's... he's..." Amelia shook violently, her shock melting into hysteria.

"Jacque!" Jayson called. "Take them!"

The teleporter appeared, grabbing Lizzie and disappearing in a flash. Tom and Amelia were gone a second later, then Aidan—Jacque moving too quickly for Stas to comment, to even think.

She stared at the empty space, her heart in her throat. *Is Lizzie even okay?* There hadn't been a chance to ask.

More screams bellowed across the beach, cascading goose bumps down Stas's spine. *People are dying.* The Hydraians weren't prepared for this, didn't have enough weapons, and with their psychic gifts not working, their primary line of defense was worthless.

Jonathan knew… He'd planned this perfectly, choosing a moment when everyone would be preoccupied and celebrating. *Evil son of a bitch.*

Stas stood, her ire rising by the second. These Sentinels had come here to destroy. She'd trained with some of them, knew they didn't care that the Hydraians were decent beings. They just liked to kill.

Jonathan had recruited them for a reason.

But he didn't count on *her*.

Stas's instincts fired to life, her persuasive skills streaming energy through her veins to her very soul. She felt alive, a beacon of power channeling some ancient beast inside her that yearned to be set free.

Now, her gift whispered cruelly, reaching around her, searching for all the malevolent minds she could find. Not the Hydraians. No. The Sentinels.

Those here with a single purpose—to kill.

There.

She latched onto them, driving herself into their thoughts, weaving persuasive bindings into their very beings. So easy. Too easy. And far too powerful.

Stop! she shouted through her psychic links, sweat dripping from her brow.

Several did, freezing in action, their connections snapping as their lives ended. She didn't know how she managed to push through the runes, why her psychic talent worked while the other immortals' powers didn't.

Doesn't matter.

Just compel.

More…

She found additional minds, securing them, readying her compulsion to—

A flash of purple gave her pause.

Wings.

She gaped as a Seraphim appeared beside Balthazar, her lips curled into a snarl. Murderous rage was etched into her features, but he didn't see her.

No! Stas started toward them, needing to warn him. To stop whatever the angel intended.

The female swirled in a cloud of purple mist, her feathers flaring outward and absorbing a bullet from a Sentinel who'd made it through the line of Guardian defense. Another hit the woman's side, a bullet that would have pierced Balthazar's chest had she not appeared. Her face contorted in agony, her fingertips brushing Balthazar's jaw as she fluttered backward, a third shot going into her back instead of him.

Stas froze.

Balthazar hadn't seen a thing, completely unaware of the glowing shield before him, his focus on the Sentinel charging toward him.

The angel fell to her knees, her pain palpable in the night, the glow of her wings dulling even as she flared them upward to save him from another bullet.

Stas focused on the Sentinel charging toward them, latching onto his being and commanding him to cease moving. His feet rooted to the sand, his arm locked just long enough for Balthazar to throw a knife into the man's chest.

Then another Hydraian was on the Sentinel, destroying him.

Stas heaved a breath, the mental exertion leaving her light-headed and weak.

The angel…

She looked for the purple, finding nothing but sand.

Where did she go?

Stas spun around, searching, needing to understand. Murder painted the beach all around her, no signs of ethereal energy, just violence and pain and blood.

What—

"Aya!" Issac yelled, causing her to twist toward him, her steps clumsy and disorientated.

Something sharp pierced her chest, causing her to gasp and stumble back. Another harsh jolt penetrated her stomach.

Bullets.

She fell to her knees, the impact shocking her into stillness.

So much heat.

Like her body was being eaten alive from the inside.

Hot.

She pressed her fingers to the wound, her blood an odd shade of charred black that she didn't understand.

Like the soot on Lizzie's dress.

How… fascinating… and so, so hot!

Issac appeared in front of her, his hands on her chest, her sides, her face. He blurred before her. She couldn't focus.

He said something, but the rushing in her ears drowned him out.

Focus, she told herself.

His sapphire gaze blinked in and out, disappearing behind a fog of smoke.

Issac?

He shouted her name, the strength of it reminding her of gunshots.

Fire.

Death.

I can't… Not yet.

A foreign part of her, anchored in her heart, flickered and burned, calling out to the minds she'd touched only briefly before. It stole her breath, halted her every thought, consumed her entire being. But it felt *right*. This was who she'd been meant to become, if only...

No time.

She called all the remains of her energy, her power, her life force, and channeled it into one final persuasive wave, needing her enemy to fall, needing to save those who were left, including her Issac.

Drop your weapons, she demanded, blasting the compulsion into those sent to destroy. The Sentinels. Jonathan's pet army.

They. Would. Not. Win.

Don't move, she added when she felt their combative response ignite to life. *You will die. All of you.*

And she didn't feel a single ounce of remorse.

Not a tear.

Only intense satisfaction.

Because somehow she knew it had worked. She *felt* their acquiescence, followed swiftly by their loss as their lives ended around her.

Or maybe it was all a dream.

She didn't know. Couldn't truly tell beyond the fire licking through her system, destroying her body. The essence slithered upward, threatening her mind, the pain suffocating.

No.

Not like this.

Please, not like this.

The voice reminded her of Issac, his presence beside her there... yet not. She tried to see him, to touch him, but blackness met her senses, wrenching her into an abyss.

I'm dying, she realized. *Really, truly dying.*

She'd been so caught up in revenge, the need to take everyone out, that she'd ignored the obvious.

And she'd missed her chance to say goodbye.

Issac!

A moment of panic hit her chest, the burning of air

infiltrating her lungs. Not of her own doing, but of someone else's…

He's trying to save me.

Oh God, Issac. Issac!

All that energy wasted on her own selfish need to take out the Sentinels, and not spent with him.

No!

Her chest cracked beneath the pressure, her soul slipping… disappearing…

She fought the darkening spell of sleep, refused to let death take her.

Balthazar! Oh, she hoped he could hear her. *Tell Issac…* She paused, her thoughts vanishing.

What had she wanted? What's happening?

Her soul wept, broken, losing touch… *Issac!*

Tell him I love him, B. Tell him… Help him… Fuck, the loss he'd experienced today… Aidan… *Help him heal,* she begged. *God, B, please be there for him, and tell him… tell him goodbye for me.*

Her world shattered.

Shadows lurking alongside her, guiding her, forcing her toward the glowing light. A gorgeous shade of blue. *Feathers.* A halo of gold. *Mom?*

An angelic face turned toward her, eyes a familiar shade of blue, holding tears of agony. "Oh, Astasiya… I'm so sorry," she whispered. "I'm so sorry we failed you."

Chapter Eighteen

Issac

"Mother's preference for mortality has impacted me of late. It's the stark realization that her years are numbered and time pauses for no one. Aidan calls this the consequence of our chosen fates—to live forever with memories frozen inside our hearts."

—*Issac Wakefield*
Vita mutatur, non tollitur

No.

Astasiya needed to breathe.

She needed to move.

She needed to live!

Issac refused to accept this, increasing his compressions

and ignoring the black substance oozing from her wounds.

No!

Fuck!

He gave her another breath, continuing the motions.

But nothing.

She just lay there, eyes closed as if asleep.

She'll wake up… She has to wake up…

He wiped the mist from his eyes, rejecting this fate. They weren't done yet. She was too young. This… this wasn't the right way.

They never said goodbye.

His chest ached, his stomach heaving as he collapsed on top of her. "Aya," he whispered. Her name a prayer, a benediction, his last wind of hope. "Don't do this to me. I can't…" His voice broke, his fingers digging into her hair to hold her to him. "Aya!" he screamed, his body wrecked from the pain, his lungs ceasing to work. He couldn't move, couldn't think, couldn't function.

Not without her.

Not without Aya.

Not without…

His soul splintered, his other half *gone.*

He shook his head, his heart in tatters, his world blackening.

This wasn't the way.

This shouldn't be…

No.

"Aya…" God, she needed to breathe. Why wasn't her heart beating? He started the compressions again, needing to do something, *anything.* She couldn't be… No. He rejected it. This wasn't, *couldn't,* be. He just needed—

A hand on his shoulder jolted him. He stood and swung backward without thought, only to be caught in Balthazar's arms, unable to move, unable to fight, his chest heaving with the exertion.

"She's gone, Issac."

"Fuck you," he growled, fighting him, needing to go

back to her, to save her, to—

"There's nothing you can do. She's gone."

Issac rejected the words, his fists swinging, Balthazar taking the hits and continuing to hold him.

"I'm sorry," he whispered. "I'm so sorry, Issac." Balthazar kept repeating the words, but Issac refused to hear them.

It felt *wrong*. Too soon.

"She can't be dead," he cried, collapsing to his knees again. "Balthazar, tell me she's not dead."

"I can't do that," Balthazar whispered, having followed Issac to the ground. "I wish I could, but I can't. She's gone."

Issac's head swayed back and forth, his face against the other man's shoulder. "I can't…"

"I know."

"This… it wasn't…"

"I know." His arms tightened. "I know."

Issac's heart ached inside him, a key piece of his existence missing from his soul. "We didn't…" God, he couldn't say it. He couldn't fucking say it.

"She loved you." The words were soft. "She begged me to say goodbye for her, Issac. Her last thoughts were of you."

Issac broke, his limbs losing feeling, every part of him destroyed. *Her last thoughts were of you.* Oh God, his thoughts for eternity would be of *her*. Of the time that was robbed from them, the end that should never have happened.

His teeth chattered, the drumming in his ears washing out everything and everyone around him. He didn't want to feel. Didn't want to experience another second of this agony. The pain of having his other half ripped away from him.

Aya…

How could you leave me like this?

But he knew it wasn't her fault. Someone else had taken her from him. *The Sentinels.*

"They're all dead," Balthazar said.

That wasn't good enough. Issac shook his head. *Not fucking good enough!* "We'll burn them all." Still not enough. "Jonathan…"

"Will burn, too," Balthazar agreed. "But we have to think—"

"What the fuck is there to think about?" Issac demanded, pulling away from the man, only to see the torture etched into his expression.

There's more.

Oh, fuck, Aya wasn't the only one…

"Who else?" he asked, needing to know. "Who else did that bastard take?" *If he took Amelia…*

"She's fine," he promised, his tone and words doing little to cease the storm brewing inside of Issac.

"Then who else?" he demanded, knowing from his expression that Astasiya… He couldn't finish the words, his heart unable to take another second. *Jonathan will pay for this.* In blood. And Issac wouldn't just shoot him. No. That'd be too easy. He'd mutilate the bastard first, feed him his own blood, and then, when he begged for death, he'd finish the task.

Issac allowed the grotesque picture to paint his vision, needing something—someone—to focus on, to push away…

Think of Jonathan.

His assassination.

Retribution.

Astasiya…

No. Mourn her after the task. Mourn her when this is done.

"That's not how this works," Balthazar replied softly. "And it's not what she would want."

God, he was right. Astasiya wouldn't want him consumed with revenge. But she wouldn't want him sad, either.

"She'd want you to be smart," Balthazar finished for him. "She begged me to guide you, Issac. Those were her final wishes—to say goodbye, to tell you she loved you, and to help you."

A sob ripped from Issac's throat, his anger giving way to despair. How was he supposed to do this? To live with this pain? To live with the agony of her loss?

Not even Amelia had crippled him like this.

And he loved his sister more than life itself.

But Aya… She'd been a part of him, his heart, his soul, his reason.

And she's gone.

The words reverberated in his mind, Balthazar's arms coming around him once more, holding him while he wept, no judgment between them. And Issac didn't care who saw him, didn't care who felt his torment, because he couldn't bear it alone.

His Aya… *My Aya…*

"We'll seek vengeance together," Balthazar vowed. "Jonathan has hell to pay, and I will not rest until we deliver it. Together."

Issac heard him, understood the words, but his mouth refused to work. His mind consumed. His being… broken.

Help me, he begged. *Help me.*

"I can't," Balthazar whispered. "I can't take this pain away from you, even though I want to…"

But you can. He could control emotion. *Why won't you help me?*

"Because it would be taking away your love."

Issac fractured, the devastation taking him under a wave of darkness. He didn't want to love anymore, didn't want to feel, didn't want to experience another second.

And yet, he wouldn't trade it for anything in the world.

Astasiya had been a gift, one he'd never expected to enter his life. To numb that, to numb her, would be a disservice to her memory. It would be selfish. It would be wrong. It would only hurt him more.

She would want him to be strong. To push through the pain, to carry her in his heart, to avenge her the right way.

But what if I can't?

You can, he heard her say, that voice forever in his mind, never to be heard again.

"I don't know how to do this," Issac admitted, feeling vulnerable and weak.

"I'll help you." Balthazar tightened his hug. "I'm here and I'll help you."

Issac shuddered, his body completely useless to him. His mind unfocused. His heart demolished.

They stayed like that for what could have been minutes or hours, Balthazar's presence the only thing keeping Issac from falling apart completely. His strength all that kept him breathing.

"Who else?" Issac asked after a long, long while, knowing the answer would hurt. Otherwise, Balthazar would have already told him. He'd been protecting his fragile state, and for that, Issac was grateful. But he needed to know. "Tell me who else he took from us."

"Eliza, but the incendiary bullet went through her and didn't ignite her blood. So Luc thinks she'll still wake Hydraian." Balthazar paused, swallowing. "Anya is dead. Jeremy, Grace, Sebastian, and Flora, as well."

All Guardians. They'd served their purpose, but their deaths would surely be felt.

"And," Balthazar continued, his voice lowering. "And Aidan."

Issac's breath caught. "Aidan?"

"He saved Lizzie's life."

He didn't…

Aidan?

He blinked, his heart in his throat.

My Sire, my father… Aidan?!

Fire poured through Issac's soul, the initial shock morphing into unadulterated fury. *Jonathan took Aidan from me, too?*

"Tristan? Mateo? Where the hell were they?" Issac demanded.

"They went into Athens with Alik and Nadia for a bite."

To feed.

His progeny had abandoned everyone *to feed*.

"Issac, they had no way of knowing. You can't—"

"I can," he seethed. "They should have been here."

"Alik couldn't stand the merriment, Tristan and Mateo offered to take him into town, and Nadia went, too, for security purposes. You can't hold that against them."

Logically, Issac knew he was right. Emotionally…

"Aidan died because—"

"Of Jonathan," Balthazar finished. "Because he sent an army to take us out while we were weak and distracted. Don't you dare blame anyone else. This is Jonathan's fault, no one else's."

Issac closed his eyes, pain mingling with a deep-seated need to kill, to blame, to maim.

Aidan.

His maker.

His father.

Dead.

One of the oldest Ichorians in existence, slaughtered.

Why doesn't this hurt more?

"Because you're already in agony," Balthazar whispered, his arms still loosely around Issac.

How long had they been sitting like this? Embracing?

Does it matter? No.

Issac thought of the man he considered his father, contemplating a memory from long ago, from the night they buried Issac's mother.

"She could have chosen life," Issac had said. "Why didn't she join us?"

"Because immortality isn't for everyone, son. She didn't desire the pain of loss—what you're experiencing now. Giving her the choice was the best gift of her existence, and she lived a full, loving, amazing life. And one day, I'll join her in the afterlife."

"You believe in that?"

"I do. Our souls were always meant to find one another. I'll never love another like I loved her, and when the time is right, I'll find her

again."

Aidan had been right. He never loved anyone more than he loved Issac's mother. Anya, Nadia, and Clara were all just diversions he enjoyed while biding his time.

All that ancient knowledge and wisdom shared with Lucian, everything Aidan had taught Issac, and the love he bestowed upon Amelia were all ways Aidan had secured his memory in each of them.

Just as he promised he would.

Issac finally took in the destruction around them, the bodies littering the beach, the pale moon shining morbidly down upon them. Ghostly. Deathly. Eerie. No signs of life other than Balthazar and Issac.

Astasiya remained unmoving beside him, her eyes closed, her body unhealed.

She's not coming back.

Was Aidan with her in the afterlife?

Did it truly exist?

Issac wanted to believe, to picture her in a happier place, surrounded by light and love. Would he ever find her again?

A buzzing in his pocket distracted his dazed thoughts, the vibrations unpleasant. "Do Tristan and Mateo know?" he asked as he took out the phone to glance at the unknown number.

"They're with Amelia."

Issac nodded. That was exactly where they should be.

He glanced at the local time, translating it to the current time in New York. Not a typical business hour for work to be calling. Especially, on a holiday. He was also on a three-month sabbatical from his position as CEO of Wakefield Pharmaceuticals, meaning they shouldn't be bothering him at all.

The phone stopped and immediately restarted.

His heart skipped a beat, understanding dawning.

This could only be one person.

He stood and brushed the sand from his trousers when the vibrating ceased again. The bastard would call again. He wouldn't be able to help himself.

Balthazar joined him, standing, arms folded across his chest, one eyebrow arched. He also clearly knew who was trying to reach Issac.

Only Jonathan would be this brave and stupid.

The device buzzed.

"Jonathan." The name burned Issac's tongue, sending white-hot rage to every nerve.

"Good evening, Issac," the bastard replied, sounding as formal as ever. "Or perhaps *early morning* is better for your time zone? It's well after midnight there, yes?"

So flippant.

So carefree.

As if Issac's world hadn't just crumpled down around him. As if Astasiya wasn't lying dead at his feet.

And the insolent ass decided to call him, to open the line with some idle chitchat.

"I hope you're hiding, Jonathan. Because you just incited a war that your little army cannot protect you from."

Jonathan chuckled, the sound grating on every nerve. "I take it my wedding gift arrived, then?"

Issac's blood ran hot and cold. The asshole thought this was all a game, considered it to be one big fucking joke. "Aidan is dead," he growled. *At your hand. Because you sent Sentinels here to destroy. And I will make you pay if it's the last thing I ever do.*

"That's a shame," Jonathan replied, sounding not at all disappointed. "He lived such a long time, too."

"No regard for how he saved your sorry excuse of an existence?" Issac asked, disgusted. "You would have died without him."

Jonathan snorted. "I'm a survivor, Issac. I always have been, always will be. That's the difference between us—you rely on others; I rely on myself."

"That's not the only difference." Issac had family, he cherished others, and he *lived.* Jonathan just wanted power, something Issac never required because he already possessed it in spades.

And Jonathan had harmed that which he held dear—his love.

Astasiya.

Aidan.

"Gloat while you can," Issac told him softly. "Because it'll be short-lived." Killing Aya was the worst move Jonathan could have made. Now there were no distractions, no wondering about the future, allowing Issac to focus on the single task of demolishing Jonathan. "You chose the wrong enemy, *old friend.*"

His nemesis laughed. "Hardly. I'm looking forward to our game of chess, Issac. It'll be entertaining having a worthy opponent on the board."

"You know what will be entertaining? Me finding you, Jonathan. Because your death will be slow, thorough, and so excruciating that you will beg me to stop, but I won't. You will feel pain unlike anything you've ever experienced, and I will enjoy every fucking minute. So I advise you to hide, Jonathan. Hide well."

"Hmm, so much emotion," he replied. "That'll be your downfall."

Wrong. "It's my strength and it will be what destroys you."

"We'll see about that, then, shall we?" he mused. "Oh, before I go, could you do me a favor and pass my regards on to my son? I hear he's quite well and enjoying life, with your sister, if I'm not mistaken. Clever ruse, that. Inform him I'm proud that he finally managed to pull one over on me, if you please."

Issac met Balthazar's gaze.

Osiris knew Tom was alive, yet he knew nothing about Amelia. Meaning he could have given Jonathan some of the pertinent details, but not all of them. Such as the wedding date and Amelia being alive.

We have a traitor in our midst, Issac thought.

The mind reader responded with a curt nod, his

expression darkening.

"I'll be sure to let Thomas know," Issac replied to Jonathan, referring to his request.

"Excellent. Well, I believe that's my cue to drop. Do enjoy your evening, Issac. I see a bonfire in your future."

The line went dead, sending a tremor down Issac's arm. He threw the phone into the crashing waves in a fit of rage, his growl vibrating his insides. "He will pay for this."

"He will," Balthazar agreed. "But first, we need to honor the dead."

Issac's heart fell, his gaze finding Astasiya a few feet away. Gorgeous, even in death. "Yes," he whispered, his soul fracturing all over again. He couldn't face Jonathan like this, his mind unable to properly form a plan beyond the grief.

And Aidan.

Jonathan had taken so much. So very, very much. He didn't even know about Astasiya, didn't know just how horribly wrong his plan had gone. Because now Issac had nothing and no one to hold him back. Amelia would understand. Balthazar and Lucian, too.

There was nothing stopping Issac from ripping Jonathan apart. Burning him from the inside out. Destroying everything he'd ever built and forcing the bastard to watch it all crumble to the ground.

Vengeance was a powerful tool, and Issac's was fueled by love.

Jonathan didn't stand a chance.

He would die.

And soon.

Chapter Nineteen

"The Earl of Sanford passed today. He will be the first of many, and while I mourned his loss, it will be nothing compared to those closer to me. Aidan says there is no preparation, that we live to endure. Such morbidity in the immortal life. It sometimes makes me wonder if I made the right choice."

—Issac Wakefield
Vita mutatur, non tollitur

Wakefield Estate.

Still vast, secluded, and gorgeous as ever.

North West England would always be home, these grounds Amelia's ideal safe haven. There were many memories here. Balls, societal events, stolen kisses with Eli. She smiled at the familiar gardens, all dusted in a light January snow, the fountain flowing because of the heated water beneath.

I've missed all this, she thought, squeezing Tom's hand as he strolled along beside her with that permanent air of vigilance about him.

"This is where you grew up?" he asked. It was more of a rhetorical statement than a question, as he already knew the answer, but she confirmed with a nod anyway.

"I've not been back for quite some time. Issac mostly maintains the estate, even had it all renovated again about a decade ago. It requires constant upkeep considering the age."

"Why don't you visit more often? Aside from your recent stay with the CRF, I mean."

She snorted. *Stay* was such a humane term. Jonathan had kept her prisoner, let his lead researcher torture her for years on end. *Imprisonment* was a much better word for it. Not that she bothered to correct him. Tom didn't want to upset her, and she adored him for it.

"Eli preferred Hydria," she murmured, replying to his inquiry.

Tom pulled her closer, wrapping his arm around her waist as they ventured toward the four-story manor before them. Wakefield Hall, a gorgeous home boasting a massive ballroom, three kitchens, several lounging areas, and more bedrooms than she or Issac could ever fill. But the estate had belonged to their family since the fifteenth century, and it meant too much to them to sell.

"And what about you? What do you prefer?"

"I miss it here," she admitted, gazing at the surrounding trees and vast landscapes. "I wouldn't mind visiting more. Especially now..." Her lips twisted, her heart aching at the reminder of why they were all here.

To bury my father.

She tripped over her feet, landing against Tom's solid

chest as he immediately wrapped her in his arms.

When would it stop?

When would the pain end?

All she'd done for the better part of three days was cry.

And Tom, as strong as ever, lent her his comfort and love, holding her as her shoulders trembled, her heart shattering all over again.

She'd just been reunited with her father after what felt like a century apart. In reality, it wasn't even a decade. Torture could make even the shortest of seconds resemble hours or days.

"Talking helps," her father had murmured only weeks ago. "And I've always been a good listener."

"Yes." She'd smiled sadly. "But discussing what happened—what he did—makes me feel weak as well."

"Because of the emotions the memories evoke."

She nodded, biting her lip.

"Well, in my experience, emotions are what strengthen us as well. They might hurt at first, but you can use the knowledge and experience tied to those sensations. Harness them, sharpen the tools, and create stronger building blocks to stand on. You're one of the strongest women I know, Amelia. And while I wouldn't wish your circumstances on anyone, I also recognize that they've crafted the brilliant woman before me. We are not what others make us, but what we make ourselves."

Amelia blinked back tears, his voice so strong and alive in her head. He never pressed her for details on what happened at the CRF, never tried to psychoanalyze her, either. He was just her dad. Her mentor. Her forever instructor.

Except it wasn't forever anymore.

"That's not true, love. Your mum will always be with you. She's here, right now, in your thoughts, your heart, even in your actions. Our loved ones never really leave. They are part of us forever, just as I will one day be part of you and your memories, when my time comes."

Amelia had frowned. "Your time? You're immortal."

"Yes, but that only means I've enjoyed an extended life. Even immortals can die, darling."

His words the day of her mother's funeral whispered through her mind, foreshadowing today and his own burial.

"He always wanted to be buried beside Mum," she whispered, something Tom already knew, something she'd said probably ten times now.

"And he will be," he replied, his palm rubbing her back.

She nodded. They were preparing the service now. It would be small. Personal. Heartbreaking.

Stas would be buried today as well, in the same private cemetery as the rest of Amelia's family. Issac hadn't asked for permission, not that he'd needed to. She would have agreed anyway. Stas was family. Plain and simple. Amelia just wished Issac would pause for a moment to grieve rather than throw himself into the funeral arrangements. It was as if he wanted them done so he could move on to something, and Amelia suspected that something to be revenge.

She understood that plight.

Jonathan will die.

Her fists clenched at the thought of *him*, her need to kill the bastard suffocating her sadness, drowning her in a murderous rage.

First, he took Eli from her. Then he stole years of her life that she would never get back, torturing her for *research* and personal enjoyment. And now Aidan. Stas. Her fellow Hydraians. Anya.

He had more than earned his punishment.

And she wanted to deliver it. Amelia wanted to gouge his eyes out, take samples of his ribs, carve her bloody name into his chest. And stare at him without remorse while he writhed in pain. Maybe even laugh the way he did all those times in her cell.

I'd put him in a cement cage.

Douse him in bleach.

Leave him in a filthy shirt.

Shoot him full of various drugs just to watch his heart react on a monitor.

Cut off his hand to see how long it took to regenerate.

Beat the living hell out of him due to boredom.
Turnabout is fair play, after all.

"John?" Tom asked, leaning back to cock a brow at her. He no longer referred to the Ichorian as his father, always John.

"Yes," she said, her voice low, growly. "It's like I can't breathe when I think of him. All I want, no, what I *need* is for him to die. Horribly. Slowly. I *need* to make him suffer. To find a way to take out his heart and burn it without killing him, because it'd be too easy. Pain, Tom. I want to give him *pain.*" So much pain. So much horror. So much *blood.* She thirsted for it, her heart racing with the thought of Jonathan spread out in agony.

"I'll help you," Tom murmured. "I'll help you find him and kill him."

She studied his sharp features, the chiseled shape of his jaw, his striking brown eyes, and long blond lashes. "Will that be hard for you? To hurt your own father?"

A sadness filled his expression, one he couldn't hide from her, not that he tried. Honesty was their foundation, a deep-seated vow between them that neither would ever break. "I don't know. He's done such horrible things, but he also created me."

And for that, Amelia was grateful. A part of her would always love Eli, her first partner in life, but her heart and soul belonged to Tom. He completed her in a way no one else ever would, understood her on a level very few had ever reached, and strengthened her beyond comprehension.

"He deserves to die," Tom added. "I want him to die."

"But torturing him?" she prompted.

"Might be outside my realm of abilities," he admitted softly. "However, I understand why you want him to suffer, and I'll help you seek retribution." He brushed his lips over hers, sealing the promise.

She returned the kiss, her arms twining around his neck. "Thank you."

He responded by deepening their embrace, his tongue

sliding into her mouth in a distracting manner that took her breath away. It left her light-headed and dizzy, causing her to sway into him. He chuckled, the sound delightfully knowing and underlined in arrogance. Tom knew his effect on her.

Hmm, two could play this game. And she could use the diversion to keep her mind off the afternoon's events. Plus, it would benefit her later.

"There's a field beyond those trees," she said, nodding to her right. "I don't suppose you're up for a little sparring in the snow?"

"An invitation to roll around on the ground and soak that pretty white sweater you're wearing?" He pretended to consider. "It's almost as if you're trying to flirt with me."

"Flirting?" She scoffed at that. "A lady never flirts. She seduces."

His lips quirked up at the edges. "In that case, consider me aroused, Miss Wakefield."

"There's just one thing," she said, stepping away from him and testing the paved walkway beneath her flat shoes.

He arched a brow. "A challenge, asset?"

She smiled. "You'll have to catch me first, arse." She took off toward the tree line, channeling all her hurt and rage into her pounding heels, determined. Just as her father had taught her—to use her emotions as strengths.

I'm proud of you, she imagined him saying. *I'll always be with you, love.*

I know, she whispered back at him. *Forever in my heart.*

* * *

The bonfire blazed in the cool air, sending dancing embers into the midnight sky around them. Each spark resembled a memory on the breeze, all centered around one man— Aidan. He affected the hearts of so many, his words and wisdom living on in everyone he touched.

Amelia added another paper to the fire, smiling through

her tears as it sizzled.

This had been Luc's idea—to write down all their fondest recollections of Aidan and celebrate his life in a positive manner. The funeral and burial this afternoon fulfilled the Wakefield legacy, something Aidan would have wanted because of his ties to Amelia's mother. Tonight was for everyone else, to grieve with one another and remember a man who impacted so many.

"What memory did you share?" Tom asked softly, his arms coming around her waist as he rested his chin on her shoulder.

"One of Aidan dancing with my mother," she whispered. "They caused quite a stir with the tango during the Summerlins' Ball when I was twelve. Society frowned upon my mother for remaining a widow and taking a clear consort."

"They never married?"

She shook her head. "It wasn't Aidan's style, nor did my mother wish to remarry. I think they rather enjoyed the forbidden, too." Her lips quirked. "They truly loved one another. I hope..." She swallowed, her gaze going to the stars. "I do hope they found each other again."

Tom brushed his lips against her jaw, hugging her close. "I would never stop searching for you," he whispered. "You know that, right?"

Amelia relaxed against him on a sigh. "I do."

The somber atmosphere surrounding them was a stark contrast to her memories of this estate. But the last few days had been spent grieving the lives lost. The Elders held a memorial in Hydria yesterday for the deceased, while Issac took care of the arrangements for Astasiya and Aidan here.

Anya's memory was celebrated with the Hydraians who lost their lives to Jonathan's Sentinels. While she served as a consort to Aidan for several decades, his feelings for her never reached the deepest levels of his heart. That love remained for Amelia's mother. And Luc had confirmed Aidan's dying wish would have been to be buried on the

Wakefield Estate.

Such a complex history.

One that raised so many morbid thoughts.

Would Amelia choose to be buried here with Eli and her family, or elsewhere with Tom? What about Luc? Balthazar? Alik? Issac and his progeny? She shivered, the notions leaving her cold inside.

A war was coming and not everyone would survive.

I've already lost so much, and we've only just begun.

"Write another memory," Tom encouraged, his lips at her ear. "I want to hear more."

"Do you fancy anything in particular?" she wondered, turning in his arms, thankful for the distraction.

His hands settled on her hips. "One of your favorite moments."

"Him meeting you," she said immediately, her lips quirking. "You were terrified."

He looked positively affronted. "I was not terrified."

She arched a brow. "You called him 'sir.'"

"To be polite."

"And you bowed."

"Because he's old and I assumed that was his preference."

She shook her head with a snort. "You were practically shaking."

"And this is a fond memory?" he countered, humor in his voice. "I'm second-guessing our relationship, asset."

She narrowed her eyes. "You love me, you arse."

"Only when you're nice to me."

Another snort. "You mean only when I straddle you."

"That, too." He pressed his mouth to her ear. "Especially when naked."

She giggled, a sound only Tom seemed to inspire.

He kissed her neck before pulling back with a smile, his nose nuzzling hers. "Better, sweetheart?"

Amelia nodded, tears welling in her eyes again, this time happy ones. "You always know how to pull me back from the darkness." Soft words, spoken only for him.

He cupped her cheek, bending to press his lips to hers. "I love you, Amelia."

"I love you, too," she whispered, returning his embrace.

The clearing of a throat had her glancing left to find Tristan standing awkwardly beside the fire, his expression sheltered. "Sorry to interrupt, but I was wondering if you've seen Issac?"

Tom's arm slid around Amelia's waist as she moved to his side. "I've not seen my brother since the burial," she admitted. "I think he wanted to be alone."

Tristan nodded, palming the back of his neck. "I'll see what I can do." He left without another word, his shoulders hunched in a way that hurt her heart.

"I hate this," she whispered, her focus shifting to Luc as Tristan passed him. The stoic expression on her older brother's face pained her even more. He was doing everything he could to hold it together, at the expense of his own sorrow. His father, a man he'd spent over three thousand years with, and he couldn't even grieve him. Because Luc was the one everyone relied on, the King they revered and looked up to for guidance.

Balthazar stood at his side, nursing a glass of Aidan's favorite scotch. His eyes lifted to hers, understanding flickering in his dark depths. Amelia could only imagine the thoughts he overheard from his best friend, not to mention the pain he had to be harboring deep inside.

Luc nodded at whatever Balthazar said, his hands tucked into his trouser pockets. Both men had lost their ties but remained in button-downs with jackets. A show of respect. Or perhaps they hadn't desired to change.

"He hates me," a soft voice said to Amelia's left. Eliza stood just off to the side, dressed in a black dress, her long hair pulled back into a ponytail. Her ebony gaze locked on Luc, her lower lip trembling. "I-I didn't mean for this to happen. I d-didn't meant to distract him."

"Oh, darling, no." Amelia pulled the woman into a hug.

"This isn't your fault. He knows that."

Eliza shook her head, her voice dropping to a whisper. "He won't even look at me. He hates me."

"No, it's not you." She glanced at Balthazar, but his focus was on Luc, who appeared to be saying something important. "There's a lot going on right now. He's just trying to keep everyone organized."

Another shake of her head as she pulled back, her attention shifting to the ground. "You didn't see the way he looked at me after… after I woke up." She meant as an immortal, causing Amelia to frown.

Luc had been lost in funeral arrangements for the last three days, yet he made time to visit Eliza? That alone said everything.

"He doesn't blame you," Amelia promised. "He just has a lot going on right now."

Eliza didn't seem to hear her, the words spilling from her mouth on a wave of shame. "Aidan would be alive if I hadn't been fighting with Luc. I wouldn't have gotten shot. I wouldn't have died. He would have been there for his father. He—"

"Would have died regardless of your interference," Luc finished for her, having approached while Eliza wasn't paying attention. "Not everything in this world revolves around you, Eliza. Aidan died protecting Lizzie and her unborn child. He would not appreciate you blaming yourself for his chosen actions."

The admonishment in his voice made Amelia cringe and Eliza freeze.

"Luc," Balthazar started, but a glance from her brother silenced whatever he'd been about to say.

"I'm sorry for your loss," Eliza whispered, then turned and fled for the house.

Amelia sighed and gave her brother a stern look. "That wasn't very nice."

He cocked a brow. "She's a selfish brat who only thinks about herself, Amelia. It is neither my job nor my responsibility to cater to her needs. She needs to grow the fuck up. I have too many other tasks to handle to be concerned about her feelings right now."

The harsh summarization shocked her. This was not her brother but a man relying on cold practicality to survive. He'd turned off his emotions to function. "Avoiding your pain isn't the solution," she advised softly. "Perhaps you should heed your own advice and realize Aidan wouldn't appreciate *that*, either."

A stoic expression met her words. Followed by an emotionless blink that broke her heart. "What our people need is a strategic leader who can focus and sharpen the pain into a plan for vengeance, not an emotional son who just lost his father. There will be time for mourning. That time is not now." He left her gaping after him, her hands fisted at her sides.

"I'll talk to him," Balthazar murmured.

"It shouldn't be on you to—"

"Amelia," he cut in gently, cupping her cheek. "We all have our purpose. You, more than anyone, understand mine. And what your brother needs right now is a friend. He'll be all right. I promise."

She stared at him for a long moment, reading between the lines. If anyone could provide Luc solace, it was Balthazar. Not because of his gifts, but because of his way with words. His heart. His presence.

"Take care of him," she said softly, allowing him to see the worry in her gaze. "He can't bottle this up forever." Or his treatment of Eliza would just be the beginning.

Balthazar's smile was sad. "Honestly, love, I'm more worried about your other brother."

Issac.

Her heart panged heavily in her chest. His face during the funeral… She swallowed. God, he looked a right mess. "I don't know how to help him," she admitted.

"I don't think any of us can," he replied. "But I'll never stop trying." With that, he wandered off after Luc, who had disappeared beyond the trees.

Tom folded Amelia into his arms, his cheek against her hair. "One day at a time, sweetheart," he whispered. "We'll take this one day at a time."

She hugged him back, thankful for his strength. Thankful for his life. Thankful for his love.

Somewhere, Aidan smiled. She felt it in her very soul, his approval radiating over her. Or maybe it was all in her head. But she swore she heard him murmuring positive words, praising her choice.

"He liked you, you know," she murmured.

"Who? Balthazar?"

She chuckled, shaking her head. "No. Well, him, too. But I meant my father. He liked you."

Tom stared down at her, his eyes holding a touch of disbelief. "Are you sure about that?"

She nodded. "He told me during our holiday in Montana. Nothing profound, just a statement, that he liked you." She smiled, tears gathering in her eyes. "I think I should write that down. To add to the fire." Because it was a memory she would cherish always.

Just three words.

I like him.

Her gaze lifted to the starry night again. *You're forever in my heart, Papa. And Tom will always guard it.*

Another wave of acceptance settled over her, warming her heart. Her father was definitely there, watching over her, hugging her with his soul.

I like him, she wrote on the paper Tom had handed to her. With a watery smile, she wrote beneath it, *Yeah, I like him, too.*

~*~

TOM watched Amelia add her memory to the fire, his chest aching for her. For everyone. For the losses created by his father. It took everything within Tom not to outwardly react, to show his anger, his fury over everything Jonathan Fitzgerald had done.

To Amelia.

To Stas.

To Lizzie.

To Aidan.

To the Hydraians.

I have to kill him. A verdict underlined in blood. *There's no other alternative.*

Jonathan Fitzgerald had created Tom to be the perfect soldier, a master on the chessboard. Those traits were about to bite the old man in the ass because Tom would be using them to the fullest extent to seek justice.

His father had to pay for what he'd done.

And Tom would be the one to deliver the punishment. It was his duty as the man's son.

He plucked a paper from the pile to jot down his own memory, but it wasn't of Aidan. No, he wrote about his own father. About the man who crafted the weapon Tom had become.

Five words, spoken to him several times over his lifetime. Always a taunt punctuated by a threat.

Where would you go, son?

Tom finally had an answer.

To hell.

And he would take his father with him. Bloody, screaming, and begging for mercy.

Folding the paper carefully, he dropped it into the fire and watched it burn, picturing Jonathan Fitzgerald's agonized face dancing in the flames.

Soon.

"What memory did you choose?" Amelia asked, her arm coming around his waist.

"I created a new one," he murmured. "With a very satisfying ending."

Chapter Twenty

"There are certain aspects of my former life that I miss. One such item is the ability to lose myself to oblivion. Immortality heals the body too quickly to experience inebriation, and after the day I've endured, I could use the old-fashioned remedy."

—*Issac Wakefield*
Vita mutatur, non tollitur

"You would have liked it here, Aya," Issac murmured, his gaze on the stars above her grave. "It's been a while since I visited—perhaps a decade ago? We try to keep our presence here quiet, to not draw attention to ourselves for obvious reasons. Amazing what an annual contribution to charities will do to keep the public satisfied."

He took another fortifying sip of his—he eyed the label—whiskey. Ugh, he'd clearly hit rock bottom if this was all he had left of his stash. But he couldn't seem to drink the liquor fast enough.

"I want to feel numb, you see." He took another sip. "But this shite isn't doing it, darling. It's just burning my throat and insides at this point." He couldn't remember the last time he imbibed such copious amounts of alcohol. Perhaps after he turned Tristan? The two had gone on a drinking binge for entertainment purposes. It ended in a tangle of blondes.

Issac snorted. "That's not happening again. Ever." Another drink, followed by a sigh. The ground was cold beneath his jacket. Dead. Because it contained all his loved ones—Aidan, Mum, Aya.

"Fuck, I miss you," he whispered, his chest aching. "I miss all of you." At least with his mum, he expected her passing. It didn't make it easier, but it was far more bearable than Aya's and Aidan's.

"I'm going to kill him," Issac told them. "Jonathan, I mean." His lips curled down. "I should be out there searching for him right now." But Lucian demanded a wake in Aidan's honor, stating it was what his father would have wanted. Tradition. Fucking tradition.

Issac finished his bottle and added it to the rest. "I've run out of liquor, Aya." Four bottles. He'd collect more, but he preferred the solitude of the cemetery around him. Aidan would have preferred a wake, just as Lucian said. However, Issac didn't know what Astasiya would have wanted. They never discussed death. "You weren't supposed to die."

His lips curled down, his gaze shifting to the headstone he'd had engraved for her just yesterday.

Aya Davenfield.

"I couldn't put your real name," he whispered. "I should. Fuck. How am I going to tell your parents?" Elizabeth had volunteered, but Issac knew it had to be him. "I want to tell them the truth, Aya. Should I? Or will they be unable to handle it?" He sighed, long and sorrowful. "It's the kind of inquiry I would ask of Aidan, but…" He swallowed, his focus returning to the stars overhead.

Issac didn't believe in the afterlife, aside from the resurrection aspects of immortality. As for religions and gods, he knew too much about the history of the world. So many of those theories stemmed from the act of a Hydraian or an Ichorian.

"But I want to hope," he admitted quietly. "I… I understand why people believe, Aya. It helps them hold on to the past, to know the soul is still thriving." He placed his palm over his chest. "I feel you here." He knew it sounded crazy, but he couldn't deny the very real sensation of her being a part of him. "You can't be *gone*." His voice cracked on the final word, his heart shattering for the thousandth time.

I don't accept this, he thought. *I don't accept that you're gone.*

His vision blurred, the moon smearing across the sky.

"Fuck." He dug his palms into his eyes. "I feel…" *Lost.* As if a part of him had fractured, never to be recovered.

A familiar approach had Issac stiffening, his instincts flaring.

"Don't," Tristan said gruffly. "I just brought you some proper whiskey, not that shite you found earlier."

Issac lowered his hands to see the bottle above his head. The label wasn't one he kept on the property, which meant Tristan had ventured over to Ireland—likely with Jacque—to pick up the decent brand.

"Thanks," Issac managed to say around the knot forming in this throat. He accepted the gift and downed several gulps as Tristan took a seat beside him.

"There's more in the house, if you need it."

Issac nodded, the liquid a welcome burn. He closed his eyes again, imagining a life where he could actually become drunk off a few shots and longing for the ability to lose feelings. "I fucking hate immortality."

Tristan grunted. "You'll enjoy it when you find Jonathan and force him to suffer."

"Cheers to that," Issac agreed, saluting his progeny.

They sat in silence, beneath the stars, ignoring the icy winter air.

Are you up there, Aya? Issac wondered, not for the first time. *Is that why I still feel you? Will you be with me always?*

Another drink.

Oblivion evaded him.

"I miss her," he confessed softly. "I didn't even… We didn't—" A sharp noise in his throat cut off his words, forcing him to swallow several times, the stars clouding above him. He dropped the bottle, not caring if it shattered. "I don't want to feel anymore, Tristan." The admission scorched his insides, fracturing his heart into a million pieces. He felt weak, broken, irrevocably damaged. Dampness touched his cheeks, tears falling of their own accord. He couldn't stop them even if he tried.

"I'm sorry," Tristan whispered. "I should have been there. I should have… I would have…" He bit out a curse that led to a string of Irish Issac didn't understand, but he conveyed the agony with his tone. "I never wanted this for you, Issac. Not like this."

"You hated her," Issac accused, the words coming from a vulnerable place inside that desired retribution. "This was exactly what you wanted—our end. Well, guess what? Jonathan accomplished the feat for you." The words tasted bitter, angry. He knew Tristan wasn't to blame, but he provided an easy target for Issac's anger. "You *wanted* this."

"Fuck, Issac. I may not have liked your relationship with the lass, but I didn't hate her." He ran a hand over his face. "I never wanted this. *Never.*"

Issac shook his head, unable to respond, the emotion thick in his throat.

Tristan sighed. "Have I been an arse? Yes. I wanted to protect my best lad from eventual heartache, from—"

"This," Issac finished for him.

They fell into companionable silence again, the wind rustling the nearby bushes. Centuries of friendship thrived between them, shrouded in understanding. Tristan's guilt over constantly taunting Astasiya was palpable, his deep regret over how it all ended equally tangible.

"I'll do whatever you need me to do, Issac. Just name it." The vow in his words was underlined in submission and remorse. "If I could bring her back, I would."

"She's dead," Issac whispered. "She's gone, Tristan."

"I know."

"She's never coming back."

"I know."

"I don't…" Issac swallowed. "I don't know what to do."

Tristan snorted. "You kill the son of a bitch who did this to her. That's what you do." A violent image plundered Issac's thoughts, courtesy of his best friend.

Jonathan strapped to a chair.

Screaming.

Blood.

Fire.

Archaic forms of torture appeared.

More blood.

A mere corpse coming back to life, only to have every heinous act repeated.

"You're quite imaginative," Issac said, his voice rough.

"That's just the beginning. By the time we're done with him, he'll be a shell of a man. A fucking ghost." His bright green-hazel eyes shone in the moonlight, pure malice dripping from his features. "He'll pay for what he's done."

"Yes," Issac agreed, sitting up slowly to mimic Tristan's position. "Do you suppose he's hiding behind his Sentinels?"

His progeny smirked. "Only one way to find out."

"What are you proposing?"

"A distraction." Evil intent graced his features. "Luc found two Sentinels who arrived late to the massacre. He kept them alive for questioning. I'm not convinced they've given up all the details yet. Maybe some sensory deprivation will help loosen their tongues."

Issac had been so wrapped up in funeral preparations that he hadn't visited the prisoners of war yet. He'd barely even thought about them. "I doubt they know much."

"Still, a fun distraction nonetheless." His shoulders rose and fell in an elegant shrug. "Why not give it a go, yeah? Perhaps it'll provide a new way to numb your feelings?" He nudged the empty bottles to punctuate his point.

Aya wouldn't like this, his conscience warned.

Aya isn't here, a darker part of him growled in response.

Issac glanced at her grave for the millionth time, taking in the headstone and the fresh dirt. He placed his palm above her, closing his eyes.

They took you from me.

Retribution is required.

You understand, right?

His heart panged in response to the silence. Fuck, he missed her voice. Her smile. Her touch. "You left me too soon," he whispered. "You promised me… *Always.*"

But those bastards intruded on the vow and took her away.

They killed her.

And now that the funeral was done, Issac could focus on the future. On his revenge. Starting with the two Sentinels Lucian had kept alive.

"I'll visit you, Aya," he vowed softly.

He opened his eyes to find Tristan standing several yards away, having given him a moment alone.

This was their final goodbye.

Issac's acceptance of her fate.

She's never coming back.

But we will meet again.

"I love you, Astasiya. Always." He stood, gathering the bottles. Tristan met him several steps away, his suit in far better shape than Issac's. "Find Jacque. I want to go to Hydria."

A twinkle of approval glistened in Tristan's gaze. "Of course, Sire."

~*~

Why is it so dark in here?
Because my eyes are closed.
Stas blinked.
No. That's not it.
What happened?
Why do I feel so weak?
She curled her fingers, numb from the cold.
What is that smell? Earthy. Her nose twitched. *Dirt. The hell?*

"Hel...?" Fuck, her throat resembled sandpaper. Dry. Unused. Everything felt raw. Her muscles were stiff. Her limbs unmoving. Her lungs hardly worked, each breath tasting of soil.

Her eyes burned as she tried to clear the lump from her throat, her body a foreign vessel. Almost like that time she woke up after Lizzie—

Stas's eyes widened as an onslaught of memories assaulted her.

The wedding.

The reception.

The Sentinels attacking the beach.

Fire burning in her veins.

Issac's agony.

Mom.

She'd found her in the afterlife, or in a dream. A nightmare. Her mother rambled on and on, talking about drowning, Osiris, Sethios, and then disappeared, only to reappear again with the same words. And always an apology.

We failed you.

But she never explained what she meant. Each time she started, she vanished. And when she returned, the gibberish restarted. Repetitive agony.

Hell.

Except, this was new—Stas waking up in a dark room.

She spread her fingers across the cushion beneath her, which ended only a few inches to either side. Where she hit a wall.

Uh.

Tingling erupted down her limbs, her toes wiggling.

Ever so slowly, sensation overwhelmed her, causing her stomach to churn. It felt as if she hadn't eaten in days. Her tongue, thick in her mouth, made swallowing impossible. Not to mention the rocks taking up residence in her throat.

What is happening to me?

She still couldn't see, despite her open eyes. Her heart beat loudly in her ears, the only sound in her strange space.

After several minutes, or maybe hours, her arms flexed, her wrists able to move to test the walls on either side of her.

Solid.

Weird.

She slowly—so, so slowly—trailed her fingers upward to find a similar wall above her face.

Her brow furrowed. *Am I in a box?*

How bizarre. Why would she...

"Oh," she choked out. "Oh no."

Ground.

Cushion.

Box.

Darkness.

Her heart stopped.

Her breath stilled in her throat.

No.

No.

No.

This cannot be happening.

She pressed against the wall, the surface above her face. It didn't budge.

No!

They wouldn't, couldn't… *Oh God.*

She started to squirm, panic overriding her stiff muscles. But she couldn't move. The box held her tight. The ground above her immovable.

A broken scream scratched her throat, hysteria strangling the sound.

"Issac!" His name hurt, her vocal cords belittling his name to a hoarse whisper. "Issac!" she tried again.

Oh, fuck.

They buried me alive.

They fucking buried me alive.

But I'm not dead!

Balthazar!

Anyone!

Help!

She yelled with everything she had, but the note left her on a breath. Tears streamed down her cheeks, her nails embedding in the material surrounding her.

I have to get out of here.

I can't…

This can't be happening.

"Issac!"

* * *

Oh God, not again.

Pitch-black.

Hell.

Stas's lungs burned, her mouth parted on a soundless scream. Because a voice required air, and this box… this box contained none. She'd used it all up days, months, years ago. Fuck, she had no idea how long she'd been trapped in this loop.

Darkness.

Suffocation.

A few minutes in the white space, sometimes accompanied by her mother.

Repeat.

Help me! she screamed the words in her mind, hoping someone, anyone, would hear them. *Issac...*

He gave her this necklace, saying to use it when she needed help. She turned it on at some point, right? But it didn't work. Or maybe she did it wrong.

Her fingers clasped around it yet again, finding it in the right position.

Please... Please come for me.

It hurt.

No air.

Yet her lungs kept trying to breathe.

And then bliss. These few moments of death, or wherever her soul went, were becoming her favorite.

"Astasiya," her mother murmured, agony in her voice. "I'm so sorry, sweetheart. I'm so sorry we failed you."

This again.

"I still don't know what you mean, Mom."

"I know, I know. We should have explained, should have made sure you knew... Oh, time is running out again. Love is worth the sacrifice. Your father and I, we'll never regret our decision, no matter what happens. I love you, little angel. Love..." She flickered and disappeared again, leaving Stas with no additional answers. Every speech was the same, all about sacrifice.

A tear tracked down Stas's cheek, followed by an agonized moan as she was sucked back into her own personal hell.

The darkness. Again.

Issac, she cried. *Anyone. Please.*

But there was no oxygen. Only pain.

Only... death.

* * *

STAS started counting.

Each visit to hell lasted just over three minutes, give or

175

take. The first ninety seconds provided her with the most mobility. After that point, her limbs began to fail and all she could do was wait for death.

Fifty.

Fifty-one.

She scratched at the surface above her face, her nails splintering and shooting pain up her arm. But she worked through it, knowing her time was limited.

Sixty-two.

Fuck, it hurt.

But no one was coming for her. She had to save herself. And this was the only way—to dig out of her prison.

What happens when the dirt enters the coffin? she wondered, not for the first time.

I start digging.

Or that was the plan, anyway.

What choice did she have? Sit here and wait? Die over and over again? No.

Seventy-eight.

Her muscles were already tiring, sweat stinging her eyes.

So dark.

So cold.

Yet her lungs burned, begging for oxygen that didn't exist in this small space. It felt as if she were collapsing into herself, her body spasming with a need that couldn't be met.

Eighty-three.

No, ninety-three.

Wait…

Her thoughts spiraled, her arms and legs convulsing. And still she tried to breathe, to pull in the air she so desperately craved.

Issac, her heart whispered. *Oh, Issac.*

Why had he left her here?

Why didn't the tracker work?

Why can't you hear me?

Please, Issac, her soul begged. *Please find me.*

But a logical part of her knew it was futile. He buried her

because he thought she was dead.
No one is coming for me.
I have to get out of here.
During her next round, she'd keep digging.
It's my only hope.

Chapter Twenty-One

"I miss dreaming. An odd admission, to be sure, but a fact. Aidan believes it's tied to my ability to control vision. I'm not sure I agree. It's almost as if there's nothing more to hope for in this world. A shame considering I'll live forever. Perhaps immortality is not as exciting as I once thought."

—Issac Wakefield
Vita mutatur, non tollitur

Everything burned.

It kept happening. Pitch-black, no oxygen, just a vacuum of insanity pulling him to consciousness only to drown him again.

Three minutes of agony.

Ninety seconds of opportunity.

Fuck, it hurt.

So much.

His nails bled as he fought at the confines holding him beneath the surface.

His arms shook.

His chest ached.

Suffocation drove his mouth to beg for air. An impossibility. A lethal fate.

Everything tingled, withered, died.

Only to come face-to-face with a pair of pleading green eyes, begging him to help in the midnight hour, to save her...

Issac woke on a gasp, his palm over his wildly beating heart. Fuck, that felt real. *Too* real.

Another bloody nightmare. He couldn't remember the last time he dreamed before this week, but every night since the funeral, he dreamt of Astasiya. Always the same—her begging him for help.

Guilt. He didn't save her, something he would forever live to regret. And it seemed his subconscious was nowhere near ready to grant him peace. Not surprising. He buried Astasiya only four days ago.

Her screams ricocheted through his thoughts, sending him to his feet. There would be no more resting tonight.

Balthazar knocked on the door. "Wakefield, Luc and Alik are in the living room watching some American football, if you want to join."

Apparently, Issac wasn't the only one having trouble sleeping. A glance at the clock showed it was just after three in the morning.

As sleep was no longer an option, he might as well distract himself.

"I'll be there in a moment," he replied, dragging his fingers through his hair.

"I'll make you some coffee," Balthazar offered, clearly aware of the nightmare that had awoken Issac.

"Cheers," he replied.

Astasiya's presence surrounded him as he moved around the guest suite of Balthazar's home. Her scent lingered on the pillows, her clothes in the drawers, even her toothbrush remained in the bath.

Tristan had tried to convince him to stay with them on the other side of the island, but Issac refused. He needed the reminder of Astasiya's life to stay grounded, to focus on the task at hand. It comforted him to keep her presence close. He could almost pretend she was still here.

Not the healthiest course, to be sure.

Pulling on a pair of jeans and a T-shirt, he met the others in the living area, not caring at all that he resembled an invalid. He hadn't shaved in a week. But why bother? All that mattered was killing Jonathan. The bastard wouldn't care if Issac used a razor or not.

"Wakefield." Lucian nodded from the recliner, a beer in his hand.

"Lucian," Issac replied, leaning against the wall rather than sitting. "Anything on Jonathan's whereabouts yet?" Mateo had spent the better part of the last four days trying to locate the son of a bitch, but to no avail.

The Hydraian King shook his head. "Nope. He's a ghost."

"We'll find him." Balthazar held out a mug of freshly brewed coffee. "Black. No cream or sugar."

"Thank you," Issac murmured, blowing across the steaming liquid.

"I still vote we just kill everyone at the CRF," Alik said, his focus on his phone, not the television. "It's the only place he could be hiding."

"Too many innocents," Lucian replied. "And it would be just like Jonathan to not be in the one place we expect him."

True. If Issac had learned anything about the bastard over the years, it was his penchant for doing what was least expected.

Like killing Eli.

And sending an army to attack a wedding party.

"The best plans take time," Lucian continued. "We will destroy him, Alik."

Issac agreed. As much as he longed to expedite the process, he understood the value in strategy. It was what Aidan would have recommended. And the best way to honor his Sire's memory was to listen to reason.

We need to lure him out of the city, Aidan would say. *To avoid conflict with the Conclave.*

Lucian had, of course, already suggested it, in addition to several ideas on how to coax Jonathan out of hiding. Most of the suggestions included Thomas. Jonathan's ego wouldn't be able to handle a missed opportunity to fuck with his son, something they all agreed upon.

Issac sipped his coffee. For all his faults, Balthazar certainly stocked his kitchen well. This aromatic blend tasted divine. Or perhaps it was the early hour improving the quality.

"Divine," Balthazar murmured, his dimples flashing. "Speaking of, I'll make pancakes."

Lucian snorted. "Inferior breakfast food."

"If you two start bickering, I'm out," Alik said, standing. "You all might not—"

A hum of energy caused the hairs along Issac's arms to dance.

What is that?

Lucian stood, Alik moving to his side protectively, gazes dancing about the room.

Everyone felt it, but the source remained unknown.

Had Jonathan sent another troop to—

Stark materialized in the center of the room, flanked by Ezekiel and a female with striking features.

Issac set his mug down as Alik withdrew a blade.

Ezekiel gave the latter a pleading look. "We're not here to cause issues."

"Yeah, I believe that," Alik drawled. "How about you, B?"

"Can't read 'em." Balthazar frowned at the trio. "I can't even sense them."

"But you heard us announce our arrival," Ezekiel said. "Something Stark and Leela didn't need to do."

The renowned assassin was notoriously cocky, yet always strategic. If he wanted to kill someone in the room, he wouldn't announce his presence first.

Balthazar and Lucian must have come to the same conclusions because they relaxed, but Alik remained alert.

Jayson and Jacque appeared, both holding weapons aimed at the ground, their gazes on the trio.

"Speak quickly," Issac suggested. "We're all a little on edge after last week." And there were no doubt several Guardians on their way. Alik being a telepath made him a great broadcaster for alerts, which Jayson had clearly received, hence his presence in the room with Jacque.

"We need—"

"Where is she?" Stark demanded, cutting off Ezekiel.

The assassin sighed. "Excuse his bedside manners. Despite my decades of work, he's still learning."

"Where is she?" Stark repeated, his focus on Issac and no one else.

He arched a brow. "Who?"

"Stas." The name from his mouth had Issac's fists clenching at his sides.

"I'm only going to say this once, Agent Stark. Fuck. Off."

Ezekiel rubbed his hand over his face. "See, this is why I suggested talking to them six months ago."

"Man has a point," the female replied, her voice as sultry as her appearance.

Balthazar cocked his head to the side, his brow furrowing. "Have we met?"

"I don't have time for this." Stark took a step forward, encroaching on Issac's space. "Where did you bury her?"

Issac's eyebrows hit his hairline. "Why the fuck would I tell you that?" And how did he know about Astasiya's death?

None of the Sentinels were alive enough to report back to Jonathan regarding casualties, and Issac sure as shit didn't inform him.

"Because she's giving me a goddamn headache. I already have one woman screaming in my head all the time. Now I have two. The first, I can't fix yet. The second one is on you."

"Yeah, I owe you fuck all."

Ezekiel chuckled. "I wouldn't be so sure about that."

"Where is Stas?" Stark repeated, his eerie green eyes flickering with inhuman power.

This man worked for Jonathan. Issac would sooner kill him than give him information about Astasiya. So he merely stared at him in response.

The female shook her head and laid a hand on Stark's shoulder. "Just tell him, Gabe."

Gabe?

Issac shared a look with Lucian.

As in, Gabriel?

He glanced at Balthazar as well, but the mind reader's focus was on the woman, his eyes narrowed with incredulity. Because of the name she used?

"I don't owe him or anyone an explanation," Stark growled, showing an uncharacteristic display of emotion. "Except for maybe Stas."

Stark is Gabe…

"Maybe?" Ezekiel repeated with a snort. "Try *definitely*. And a few apologies as well, I believe."

Thomas entered the house, a gun in one hand, with Amelia directly behind him. Her gaze went to Gabriel. "What are you doing here?" she asked.

"I'm trying to find out where your brother buried Stas," he replied, glancing at her. "But he's being stubborn."

"What do you plan to do with the information?" Lucian asked.

"Dig up her grave and set her free. Otherwise, she'll just continue to cry in my head." Gabriel pinned Issac with a look. "Considering you're nearly bonded to her, I'm surprised you can't sense her."

His brow furrowed. "What?"

"He doesn't understand bonds," Ezekiel replied shortly. "As I've mentioned several times over, they're all ignorant when it comes to Seraphim. If you would just take five minutes to explain, perhaps they would be more willing to assist."

"Stas is a Seraphim." Lucian again. "And you're suggesting she's alive."

"I don't deal in suggestions, only facts," Stark clarified. "Now, where is she?"

Issac's heart skipped a beat.

This had to be a trick.

Some cruel game created by Jonathan.

But how does he know about Aya? The same way he knew about the wedding?

"Can't you feel her?" Gabriel pressed, his voice dropping. "She's suffocating over and over because you buried her alive. Every three minutes, she dies. And comes back. She's trying to dig her way out."

A vision hit Issac square in the chest, knocking the breath from his lungs.

Astasiya's eyes begging him to save her.

The inability to breathe.

Counting the seconds…

"How do you know all this?" Issac asked, his throat rough with emotion. "How do you even know we buried her?"

"Because she's my sister," he replied.

Silence fell over the room as everyone froze.

Issac forgot how to blink.

Astasiya has a brother?

"You're Gabriel," Lucian marveled, standing.

"I am," he replied without looking away from Issac. "And I need you to take me to my sister. Now."

"She's alive, Issac," Ezekiel added quietly. "I vow it."

A promise from an assassin. Issac would be insane to believe it.

But Gabriel's description of the nightmares, he could hardly ignore.

"Incendiary bullets can't kill a Seraphim. They just knock you out for a few days while the blood regenerates." The female beside Stark glanced at Balthazar while she spoke, then dropped her gaze. "It hurts, a lot, but we recover."

"I swear we've met," Balthazar said, his attention solely on the blonde woman. "What was your name, again?"

"Leela," Gabriel answered for her. "We're wasting time. Every moment we stand here debating the veracity of my claims is another moment of agony for Stas. What she's shown you in visions and dreams is nothing compared to the experience of suffocating endlessly. She's in hell, Issac. Help me help her."

This is a game of some sort.

What if it's not?

Fuck, what if he really had buried Astasiya alive?

There was no option here. Yes, it could all be a clever ruse by Jonathan to capture Issac. But he didn't care. *If Astasiya's alive...* "Wakefield Estate, just outside of Chester," he whispered. "In the family cemetery."

Gabriel held out his hand. "Let's go."

Issac accepted the gesture on instinct alone, all rational thought fleeing on a hope he shouldn't dare tolerate.

But she might be alive.

His Aya.

Tristan opened the door just as everything around Issac spun, the world slipping into reddish hues. Soft fluttering filled his ears, just the barest hint of rustling. Or "misting," as Astasiya once called it. Similar to Jacque's teleportation, but without the tunnel atmosphere. This felt lighter, like flying, and held a softer touch.

Gabriel Stark really is a Seraphim.

Cool grass touched Issac's feet. Familiar. *Home.*

"Where?" Stark asked, releasing Issac's hand.

He couldn't reply, his vocal cords too strangled to form sound.

No one had jumped him when they arrived.

Only his estate.

Hope blossomed into devastation as reality crushed his soul.

I buried her alive.

And she'd tried to reach out to him, somehow, but he'd ignored her.

"Oh, Aya…," he whispered, his feet already moving, carrying him down the path as he sprinted toward the cemetery.

Jacque appeared with Lucian and Balthazar in front of the tombstones, then vanished.

Leela and Ezekiel were there, too.

Tristan.

Amelia.

Thomas.

Issac ignored them all, his gaze searching for a shovel. Anything. *Something* to dig her up.

Someone gave him one.

Several others began to dig.

Time moved too slowly.

His heart beat in his ears.

Aya.

They needed to move faster. Oh God, she was under so much earth. Suffocating. Dying over and over again because he buried her. What the fuck had he been thinking?

She was dead.

But she's not!

He should have known. Some part of him should have *known.*

I failed her.

The three words reverberated in his skull, solidifying in his heart, his palms clammy against the handle. She'd never forgive him for this. She *shouldn't* forgive him for this.

I buried the love of my life.

Alive.

She was never really dead.

But how could he have known?

It didn't matter. His soul knew. Some part of him, the part that allowed him to dream, *knew.* And he ignored the instincts. He ignored *her.*

His shovel hit her casket, the seconds stretching on like hours. He couldn't get to her fast enough, to save her…

The lid creaked as he yanked it open, the evidence of her escape attempt embedded in the wood. A nightmarish image of blood and nails that he would never forget, forever ingrained in his heart.

"Aya." It came out as a choked sound, barely audible above the pounding in his ears.

Her lifeless eyes stared up at him, displaying abject horror. Dead. But clearly not the way he'd buried her.

And then they blinked.

Her lips parting on a painful gasp that drove the dagger through his chest.

I did this to her.

Tears trickled down her face, her breathing coming fast as if addicted to the sensation. And then her lips parted on a scream so anguished it splintered him to his very soul.

Gabriel appeared beside him, his hand reaching for Astasiya.

And then they were gone.

No sound.

No sensation.

Just… gone.

CHAPTER TWENTY-TWO

"Aidan claims the world will always provide new opportunities and knowledge, despite our continued existence. Even the smallest details count in our quest for information, he says. I wonder if that will always be the case or if one day we will reach our maximum allowance for intelligence. That will be a sad day indeed."

—*Issac Wakefield*
Vita mutatur, non tollitur

Oh God, air.

Stas gulped in copious amounts, her chest expanding and deflating rapidly. She couldn't think or consider anything beyond the sensation, or the sounds leaving her mouth.

Her world shifted.

She didn't care.

Cool scents of the ocean swam over her.

She ignored them.

All that mattered was the oxygen flowing between her parted lips, down her throat, into her lungs. Beautiful, addictive, necessary. Her hands fisted at her sides, her limbs quaking, her body shivering from the onslaught.

I'm alive.

I think.

It doesn't matter because I can finally fucking breathe.

A conversation flowed nearby, two recognizable tones from a dream. And a third she never thought to hear again.

Don't think. Just breathe.

Yes.

Air.

The delicious, necessary essence of life.

Her eyes closed as searing light met her irises. Too bright. Too much. It knocked her off-kilter, crashed her into a wave of reality she didn't understand.

"…memories, Vera."

"You realize it's not that easy, right?"

"It's necessary. She needs to remember me."

Someone snorted. A woman? "Erase her mind, Vera. But only certain parts. Oh, now I need you to undo everything you've ever done. It's all just magic, right?"

"Are you done mocking me?"

"Never." A warm palm landed on Stas's forehead, causing her to jump, but bands of steel held her in place.

What's happening?

"You owe me, Gabe."

"I know."

"Good."

Stas tried to open her eyes, but the blinding lights made it impossible, her eyes too accustomed to the dark to see. And then she fell headfirst into an alternate dimension. A previous life. A memory.

"I want to see," Astasiya said, pouting.

"One day, my love," her momma replied.

"In about twenty years," a deep voice added. *It belonged to the angel she couldn't see because he was misting.*

"You're mean," Astasiya muttered. *"Hiding all the time."* She folded her arms and harrumphed in dismay.

"Sethios's influence is uncanny." The angel appeared before her, his wings invisible. 'Cause she shouldn't see them yet. Daddy said she had to grow into her own feathers first.

"How long before I see them?" she asked, looking at her daddy, who sat beside her, smiling.

"So eager to grow up," he murmured, touching a finger to her nose. *"And as your brother said, twenty years, give or take. You're only five."*

She pinched her lips to the side. *"Brother?"*

"Your angel friend," he replied, gesturing upward with his eyes. *"That's your brother."*

"Brother?" she whispered, her eyebrows lifting as she followed his gaze. *"But he's not very nice to me."*

Her daddy chuckled. *"That's because he's a Seraphim, little angel. He's afraid of emotion."*

The angel snorted. *"I fear nothing."*

"See, even now, he pretends to be big and scary," Daddy murmured. *"But he's full of fluff."*

"Fluff?" she asked, her eyes widening.

"Fluff," Daddy repeated with a decisive nod.

"Fluff," she said. *"Angel fluff."* Oh, she liked that! Her lips curled as she looked at her angel friend. *"Angel fluffy friend."*

"I prefer 'Gabriel,'" he replied.

She shook her head. *"Nope. Fluffy friend."* Because "brother" was too weird. This guy wasn't nice enough to be her brother. *"Be nicer, and maybe I'll call you 'brother.'"*

His lips twitched. *"You can't choose your siblings. That's not how it works."*

"I can too!" she argued. *"You're not my brother. Not yet. Not until you're nicer."*

He crouched down before her, his forearms on his knees. "I'm your brother no matter what you say, little angel. Deal with it."

"I will not."

He made a choked sound and shook his head. "Definitely Sethios's influence."

"Did you just laugh?" her daddy asked, sounding shocked.

"No," fluffy friend replied. "I do not laugh."

"You definitely just laughed. You almost smiled, too." Daddy looked to Momma. "Back me up here."

"It's okay to admit you love her, Gabriel," she said softly. "It's not a weakness."

"Love implies emotion, of which I do not feel." Fluffy friend stood. "I just came by to let you know nothing has changed. Skye's latest prophecy suggests we're on the appropriate track. If you need me, you know where to find me."

He vanished.

Astasiya pinched her lips. "Definitely not my brother. Not a nice man."

Stas blinked out of the memory, her palm over her heart, her back against a wall. Everything around her was too bright, too warm, too foreign.

Salt hung on the breeze, clouding her nostrils, confusing her thoughts.

Where am I?

She stumbled sideways, coming up against another wall.

"Stas," a familiar voice said.

His voice.

Stark.

No, Gabriel.

The red feather.

Her eyes flew open again, the glass windows before her showcasing a beach that led to miles of water. High ceilings hung overhead. A fan. Skylights. An oversized couch with a table in the center of the room.

What the fuck?

She gasped in another breath, her chest aching for a myriad of reasons.

"Here's a glass of water," someone murmured.

The approaching man was not one she ever expected to see again. His face swam beneath a wave of tears, the brown hues a sharp contrast to the white tones surrounding them.

"Owen?" she whispered, the wall at her back warm against her clammy skin.

Then the lights registered. Her new surroundings.

Oh, fuck.

I died.

Well and truly died.

Because her old friend was murdered months ago. Tragically. Burned alive and decapitated. But he stood before her now, looking refreshed and new in a pair of jeans and a flowery button-down.

Island attire.

She nearly snorted. Owen Angelton did not dress in *island attire.* The man adored his finer suits, designer jeans, tailored shirts. Not flowers and baggy pants.

So maybe she was in hell.

That would make more sense considering her lineage, right? Except, she never did anything to warrant her stay here.

"Stas," Stark said again, this time with more force, his arms folded. "Do you know who I am?"

She stared at him. Of course she knew him. "Stark."

"That's a nickname crafted by Ezekiel. What's my real name?"

Gabriel.

Wasn't that the name of the mysterious benefactor who funded Owen's bar?

But Stark worked for the CRF. Yet, he was her brother?

"I don't understand," she admitted, her words hurting her throat. Too much screaming. Shouldn't she feel less pain in the afterlife?

"Drink," Owen encouraged, handing her the glass. Well, it looked like water.

Isn't there some sort of rule about drinking in Heaven? Something about ambrosia? Stories about people giving in to temptation and dying?

She shook her head, ignoring all the gibberish in her thoughts. What did it matter? She'd already experienced hell in that coffin.

Issac's face graced her thoughts, his anguished expression as he stared down at her from above. Had he exhumed her?

Wait…

Something nagged at her, something important.

She sipped the water while she considered it, chasing the memory. It eluded her, hiding in the recesses of her mind, refusing her access.

"Who am I?" Stark repeated, drawing her attention back to him. Unlike Owen, he sported black pants and a tailored shirt. *That* was Owen's preferred attire. Why had they swapped places?

"Am I in hell?" she wondered out loud, curious as to whether either of them could tell her.

Owen chuckled. "Depends on your definition, Sassy." The old nickname warmed her heart. She hadn't heard it in far too long.

"Not helping," Stark muttered.

Owen arched an ebony brow. "What? I've been trapped here waiting for this moment for how long now? Can't call anyone. Can't visit. Everyone thinks I'm dead. Yeah, I'd say it's a lot like hell."

Stark actually appeared uncomfortable, dragging his fingers through his short blond hair and palming the back of his neck. "It was the only way."

"Yeah, yeah." Owen shoved his hands into his pockets and refocused on Stas. "You know, I expected some sort of reaction, Sassy. Either a hug or a slap across the face. Maybe even a punch. Not this boring shit. What the fuck has Wakefield done to you in my absence? You used to be so much feistier."

She finished her water and set it on the glass shelf beside

her. This entire house, condo, whatever, was decked out in elegant furnishings. And appeared to be surrounded by the beach. Even the air here tasted expensive.

"Seriously, where am I?"

"My home," Stark replied. "My real one."

"Somewhere in the South Pacific," Owen added. "Don't ask me where because it doesn't exist on a map. Seraphim are fun like that."

This time Stark snorted. "*Fun* is not a descriptor I would use."

"You're right. *Dull as fuck* is more accurate."

"That doesn't even make sense."

"Because you're too literal to work in metaphors, baby."

"Also doesn't make sense," Stark muttered. "And you wonder why I hardly visit."

Owen scoffed at that. "You visit plenty, trust me."

"You're derailing—"

"Gabriel!" The feminine voice came from elsewhere in the house. Loud. Demanding. Angry. "Where are you?" A gorgeous blonde woman stepped into the room, her hair flowing to her lower back.

Stas's lips parted. *I've seen her.* The Seraphim at the reception on the beach, shrouded in purple feathers. "You saved Balthazar."

A pair of light eyes blinked at her. "What? Oh, yes. I did. We'll discuss it properly after I finish admonishing your brother." She narrowed her gaze at Stark. "Right now, Gabriel."

"Dude, she full-named you," Owen said, tsking. "I wouldn't ignore her."

Stark glanced at him. "Thank you for the helpful advice, jackass."

Owen grinned. "There you go, Starky boy. About time you showed some frustration."

"Giving you a long-overdue nickname is not a sign of emotion," Stark replied. "And, Leela, I'm busy."

"Doing what? Bickering with Owen in front of a clearly

bewildered Stas?" Leela folded her arms. "This all could have been avoided had you stayed at the estate rather than taken flight without a word. Issac is beside himself thinking she hates him, and—"

"Issac?" Stas interjected, her heart giving a pang. "What did you say about Issac?"

Leela sighed. "He thinks you hate him because he buried you alive. Or maybe he hates himself. Regardless, it could all—"

"He buried me alive?" Stas repeated, the words striking home. Memories assaulted her, hours upon hours, days upon days, of not being able to breathe. The necklace not working. Her nails breaking as she tried desperately to free herself. "He buried me alive."

His distraught expression flashed behind her eyes again. A brief glimpse of pain in the moonlight above her grave. As she came back to life to finally find air.

And I screamed.

She glanced around again, her heart beating faster in her chest.

The conversation she barely overheard, something about her memories.

Stark being Gabriel—her brother.

This Seraphim, Leela, saving Balthazar.

Owen… "You're alive?" she whispered, meeting his chocolate gaze. "You've been here the whole time?"

"There she is," he murmured, a hint of sadness in his voice. "I'm sorry, Sassy. When you invited me to the graduation dinner, I couldn't say no. Stark did the only thing he could. He faked my death to satisfy Jonathan, then hid me here. Taking me to Hydria would have raised too many questions, and you weren't ready yet."

"You're *alive?*" she said again, her voice coming out on a squeak. A flurry of sensation overcame her, hot, cold, her hands fisting at her sides, her heart beating a mile a minute in her chest.

Owen isn't dead.

She spent all those months trying to figure out what happened to him, blaming herself for his murder, *mourning* him.

"I *grieved* you," she breathed, her throat thick with too many statements that all required a voice at once. She choked on them, her limbs shaking from the onslaught. So much to say. So many accusations. Hurt words. All coated in unmistakable happiness. *He's not dead.*

"Just as Lizzie grieved Tom," Owen replied. "Yes, I know."

Her lips parted. This was what Lizzie went through when she thought Tom was dead. Except that was probably worse because of the romantic feelings. No wonder she was so furious. Betrayal hummed at the surface of Stas's thoughts, her heart cracking and mending repeatedly.

Owen lied to me.

He's alive.

He tricked me.

But he's here and he's okay.

Her friend—former friend?—smiled sadly. "I've missed you, Sassy. More than you'll ever know."

"I thought you were dead," she spit out. "I thought the CRF killed you because of me!" Okay, so fury was winning.

His brow furrowed. "Why the fuck would you think that?"

"Because of the CRF files. They said you needed to be removed because of your ties to me, something about getting too close to the asset." She couldn't remember the exact wording. It'd been months since Mateo hacked into the CRF database. But one thing was certain. "You were marked for execution because of our friendship. So yeah, I blamed myself." And fuck, he was never even dead.

She took a step, then moved backward again, uncertain of where to even go. But she needed a minute. Something. To cool off. To not punch her formerly dead friend in the fucking face.

"And you," she growled, turning on Stark. "You're my

fucking brother? Don't you think you could have mentioned that at, I don't know, some point during the last two decades of my life?" Oh, but no. He had her memories erased. Memories that were now intact, including the day he asked an angel—Vera—to wipe her mind clean. Then left her on the Davenports' doorstep.

The laugh that escaped her throat sounded broken to her ears. Wrong. As if she'd forgotten to breathe. Which, hell, maybe she had. She'd been locked in a goddamn coffin for fuck knew how long.

By her boyfriend.

Who thought she was dead because she'd been shot several times by Sentinels.

"Why am I not dead?" she demanded, recalling the bullets that pierced her skin, licking a fiery path through her insides. "Why aren't *you* dead?" she asked Leela. "I saw you. They shot you at least half a dozen times."

"Seraphim can't die." Her voice was soft, her expression even softer. "Our lives reside in our souls. These bodies are just vessels, skin we take on in the corporeal form. But obviously our bodies can die, as you've noticed, and the harsher the death, the longer it takes to regenerate."

"A beheading can take up to a month to recover from, depending on age," Stark added. "Just as an example."

"Blood regeneration takes a few days." Leela shrugged. "Suffocation is, well, shorter."

"No shit," Stas deadpanned. "How long was I underground?"

"A few days," Stark replied, a hint of shame crossing his features. "I didn't know he buried you until a few hours ago. You telegraphed to me in a dream."

"I *what?*"

"It's part of the familial bond. You can convey messages while in certain states."

"Or all the time when blood-bonded." Leela gave Stark a look. "Which they're not, by the way, because he thinks he can't bite her."

"A topic for another day."

"See, now, that's where you're wrong. I came back here to tell you that Ezekiel is currently explaining everything to the Elders."

"Fuck." Stark ran his fingers through his hair again and blew out a breath. "I knew he would break."

"They're his friends, Gabe. And they deserve to know the truth." Her attention shifted to Stas. "Everyone does."

"The truth about what?" Stas asked. "What more is there to know?" Except, as she considered everything from the last few minutes, she realized she still knew nothing.

Seraphim can't die.

And I didn't die.

Did that mean…? "I'm a Seraphim." She blinked. This was all too much. None of it made any sense. Gabriel being her brother, Owen standing before her, Stas coming back to life over and over again.

Because I couldn't die.

She swallowed, the world dancing around her to a beat her mind refused to comprehend.

"I need Issac," she breathed. "I need… I need him."

Her knees wobbled, the wall at her back shaking. This reality she'd stumbled into made no sense. It had to be a dimension of hell. An alternate universe. *Something.* This couldn't be her life.

"Where's Issac?" she whispered, darkness creeping in around her. "I… I need…" Her legs gave out beneath her, strong arms catching her as she fell, a litany of curse words following. But the touch felt wrong. Foreign. Not the one she craved.

Where am I?

What am I doing here?

Who am I?

Her mind shut down.

Darkness ensued.

Sending her back to the hell she'd just escaped from. Except this time, her mom wasn't there waiting for her. Just a vat of nothingness. An empty hole created for Stas. Where she curled into the fetal position and cried.

Chapter Twenty-Three

Issac

"Living forever showcases everything in a new light. It's the shadows—the memories of those passed—that I feel the most. Most other things are trivial, disappearing in a blink of time, never to be thought of again."

—*Issac Wakefield*
Vita mutatur, non tollitur

"Say that again," Jayson demanded.

Ezekiel sighed, his jean-clad legs sprawled on the recliner chair, his trademark leather jacket unzipped at the top. The picture of ease despite the horde of angry immortals surrounding him. "This is going to be a very long day if you make me repeat everything, Jay."

"Then fucking explain it better," Alik suggested, his shoulder propped up against the wall as he twirled a blade between his fingers.

All the Elders, Thomas, and Issac's progeny had returned to Balthazar's house to settle in the suddenly too-small living area with Ezekiel. Issac stood in the corner, silent. Astasiya's scream played over and over in his head, making it impossible for him to focus.

She's alive.

Those two words warmed his heart while his mind berated him for his actions. Had she been awake while he lay across her grave, talking to her? Surely he would have heard her.

God, to suffocate over and over... Astasiya must hate him.

"Anything?" he asked, his question for Mateo beside him.

His progeny shook his head. "It's still spinning."

Upon returning, Issac demanded Mateo check the GPS in her necklace. She'd activated it *four days ago,* according to his records, but he'd turned off the tracker and alarm mechanisms after her funeral because there hadn't been a point to monitor her location.

Astasiya reached out for help.

And Issac had ignored her.

Another reason for her to hate him.

"What do you mean, Owen's not dead?" The hint of fury in Lucian's voice reverberated through the room. "And he was working for you and Stark by doing what, exactly?"

"Seriously, more repetition?" Ezekiel countered, shaking his head. "He was helping us guard Stas, hence the reason he befriended her at Columbia. And yes, he's very much alive."

The words rolled through Issac's thoughts, an image of the day he met Astasiya flashing behind his eyes.

A charred body on a chair.

Decapitated.

Unrecognizable.

Very, very dead.

But Issac had noted that day how the misshapen head no longer resembled the immortal he once knew. He assumed it was a result of the significant torture. Yet hearing Ezekiel's words brought up an entirely new possibility.

Gabriel staged the scene of grotesque remains that made it impossible to identify Owen.

Was he the one who texted Astasiya that morning? To enable her to find the body? The study date was prearranged, but the message was sent after the proposed time of death.

Or had it all been a setup?

No. That couldn't be it. Gabriel had no way of knowing Lucian would send Issac to investigate the crime site.

But someone had texted Astasiya—

"I don't believe you." Jayson folded his arms, his legs braced for a fight. "Just recently you expressed sorrow over his loss, saying he served a greater purpose or some shit, and that you missed him. Now you're saying he's alive?"

"Note that I never said he was dead, just that I felt sorrow over what happened to him." Ezekiel raked his fingers through his long hair, blowing out a breath. "Look, after Jonathan gave Stark the directive to kill Owen, he had no choice but to stage the young immortal's murder. Because, as I keep saying, Stark never truly worked for Jonathan. He's always worked for himself, primarily to keep his sister safe."

"Is that why he sent her the message from Owen's phone?" Issac asked, interrupting the conversation. "To ensure she showed up that morning? Was he planning to meet her at the apartment?"

Ezekiel smiled. "See, Wakefield is thinking outside the box. Well done."

"He wasn't there that morning." Only the two Conclave lapdogs were in the apartment. And then Astasiya.

"That you saw," Ezekiel corrected. "Stas ran into you first. He decided not to intervene."

"A risk," Issac pointed out. The Blood Laws required Ichorians to kill fledglings on sight, and Astasiya's immunity to his gift certainly classified her as distinctly other that day. Fortunately, Issac didn't much care for the archaic edicts ruling his kind.

"Yes, it was a situation we monitored carefully, I assure you."

Issac didn't like the sound of that. Gabriel being a Seraphim meant he could mist about without noise or an alert to his presence. How much had he witnessed? What private moments had he spoiled?

"Let's say I believe all this for a moment," Jayson said, his tone indicating incredulity. "If he didn't assassinate Owen, then who did he kill?"

"It was a body from the morgue." Ezekiel waved it off with his hand, suggesting the detail was unimportant. "Stark takes issues with harming innocents."

Thomas snorted. "You clearly don't know him as well as I do."

"On the contrary, young Fitzgerald, I know him far better than you do." Ezekiel cocked his head to the side. "Who do you think backed up your idea to take Amelia off-site last summer? Why do you think he did that?" He glanced at Jayson. "And do you honestly think he couldn't see you in the kitchen at Red's during that dinner? The one where he purposely left you the vial of her serum on the counter?" He tsked. "Really, while he's an ass for not bringing you all in the loop sooner, he's been helping you in every way he can." His attention shifted back to Issac. "And you have no idea what he's gone through to protect Astasiya. What we've all gone through."

"Because you've kept us in the dark," Jayson growled. "All of this could have been avoided had you stopped playing games and just been straightforward from the beginning."

"The prophecy dictated otherwise," a female voice chimed in just as Leela appeared in the center of the room. No misting energy preceded her arrival this time. She was just suddenly there. A Seraphim. In Hydria. Again.

"What prophecy?" Lucian asked, not missing a beat.

"You've not gotten to that part yet?" she asked in lyrical tones, the question clearly for Ezekiel.

"No." He actually sounded frustrated. A feat for the assassin, to be sure. "They keep making me repeat everything."

"What prophecy?" This time the query came from Balthazar, who had stood as soon as Leela arrived. He'd remained otherwise silent until now. Interesting that she provoked him to speak.

"*An unknown power is surfacing. She will possess the strength and will to destroy us all unless certain measures are put in place to curb her inclinations.*" Ezekiel shrugged as if the words meant nothing. "For those wondering, Stas is the unknown power, and the measures mentioned are the primary reason for keeping you all in the dark, as Jayson says."

"Astasiya required as human of an upbringing as we could give her, and she had to make her own choices." Leela's light gaze found Issac, her expression pained. "Unfortunately, it's worked too well, as we can't calm her down. I've been sent here by Gabe to fetch you."

"Hold on," Lucian cut in. "This prophecy—where is it from? And what does it mean?"

Ezekiel smiled. "That requires story time."

"Which you're welcome to begin after I'm gone." The Seraphim refocused on Issac. "We need your help. *She* needs your help." Leela held out a hand. "Please."

Tristan stepped between them before Issac could reply. "You'll take us both."

Leela's resulting laugh lacked humor. "You don't frighten me, young immortal. Nor do you know a damn thing about what I can do. And while I admire your loyalty, I will not bow to you or anyone else. I'm here to take Issac to Astasiya, something I imagine he wants as well." She looked over Tristan's shoulder to arch a blonde brow at Issac.

It wasn't even a question.

If Astasiya needed him, he would go to her.

Fuck logic. Fuck strategy. Fuck details.

"Take me to her," he said, not caring at all about the consequences.

"Issac, we need more information first." Caution underlined Lucian's tone. "We don't even know where she's taking you."

It didn't matter. "I'm going," Issac replied.

"Think about what you're doing, what you're risking." Tristan turned. "It might be a trap, Sire. Just because Stas is alive doesn't mean Jonathan isn't using her for something nefarious. Stark is his number one Sentinel, his right-hand man."

"Who has defied him at every turn," Ezekiel added. "Stark only took the job with the CRF to learn more about Jonathan's ties to Osiris and to keep an eye on the experiments."

"Without proof, those are just words," Tristan argued, his expression imploring. "Wait until we have more information, Issac. Who knows where she's taking you, Sire." He gestured to Mateo. "He can't even track Stas."

After everything they'd learned, everything they'd seen, no. Issac shook his head. "It's not a trap." Aidan had suspected Astasiya's lineage, just as Issac wondered at her birthright. Her blood tasted unlike anything he'd ever experienced, not to mention the lasting properties of keeping him satisfied. And she lived through something that would have killed all other immortals in his existence.

She's a Seraphim.

And she needs me.

"Take me to her," he said again, ignoring everyone else and focusing on Leela.

"Don't worry, young immortal." She patted Tristan on

the shoulder, causing his progeny to flinch. "I'll bring your Sire back in one piece. Or maybe Astasiya will."

She disappeared before Tristan could react.

Issac's lips parted in confusion, only to feel that odd sensation of flying again, just as he had on his way to Wakefield Estate.

Electricity hummed over his skin.

An oceanic scent grew stronger, surrounding him, infiltrating his lungs.

Heat encased him from the lowering sun, his sense of time and space completely thrown off, as if he'd been whirled to the other side of the world. And maybe he had. Day was breaking in Hydria. Here, night peeked at him over the horizon.

Sand hit his bare feet—he'd never bothered with shoes—and a beach house appeared before him. Quaint, equipped with a wraparound porch, palm trees, and a wide-open door with Owen standing on the threshold.

Definitely not a trap.

Leela led the way, her light hair flowing down her back in a cap of curls.

"If Gabriel is her brother, are you her sister?" he wondered aloud, noting that all three of them were blondes with light eyes.

She choked on a laugh. "No. Definitely not related to Gabe in any way, shape, or form. I'm from the fertility line. He's of the warrior line."

Right. That makes a whole world of sense.

"Wakefield," Owen greeted warily.

"You and I will be having a serious talk later," Issac replied. One that may or may not involve introducing his fist to Owen's face. "Where's Aya?"

"In the guest room." Gabriel appeared, expressionless. "She won't stop crying."

"I imagine she's rather overwhelmed." He couldn't help the sarcasm. The last week had been utter hell. He hadn't slept. His heart had been broken into a million pieces, most of which refused to mend without his other half. And he'd buried the love of his life alive. By accident. "Where is the guest room?"

Gabriel turned without a word, stalking through a living room shrouded in glass and skylights. The male clearly enjoyed his beach view.

The wide hallway beyond it boasted more windows, as well as sliding doors to the outside. A kitchen with stainless steel appliances appeared to the left, opening to a dining area with another exit to the outside.

This house was bigger than Issac realized.

Gabriel led him up the stairs, the dim sky filtering in through the glass overhead, casting shadows across the wood banister and furnishings.

Another corridor, this one lit from above, lined with doors. Gabriel stopped at the second one on his right but didn't open it.

"She's in here," he said quietly.

"Is there anything else pertinent that I should know before I talk to her?" Issac asked, his hand on the knob.

Gabriel sighed, the first signs of emotion creeping into his features. "She's not a Hydraian."

"I've gathered that. She's a Seraphim, like Elizabeth." Aidan implied the possibility of it during their discussions. Clearly, Astasiya had been genetically altered. By Sethios, perhaps?

"No, not like Elizabeth at all." Gabriel leaned against the wall, his arms folded again. "Caro, our mother, is a Seraphim. And Sethios is the son of a Seraphim, making him genetically compatible. From what I can tell, Astasiya is essentially a pureblood. Her wings should bloom any day now."

Issac's heart skipped several beats. "Sethios is the son of a Seraphim?" *And Astasiya is considered a pureblood? By birth? Not because of a lab?* Of all the scenarios Aidan and Issac had discussed, *that* was not one of them.

Just when he thought nothing else could shock him,

Gabriel said, "Osiris is the Seraphim of Resurrection."

The world stopped.

Time came to a halt.

Oxygen disappeared.

The Seraphim of Resurrection.

"His bloodline is why Ichorians and Hydraians exist." Gabriel's words were a murmur of sound obliterating Issac's senses. "That's why he can compel your kind. Astasiya, too. Because she's a direct descendant of the family hierarchy. The power is in her soul. She, too, could create immortal minions, if she desired it. But she's also partly descended from a line of healers and guardian messenger angels. Her combination of genetics is, to say the least, powerful. Without proper ties to humanity, she posed a great risk to mortal kind. Hence—"

"The reason the Davenports raised her," Issac finished for him on a breath.

"Yes. Sethios and Caro knew their fates from the beginning. They sacrificed everything to ensure Astasiya became the woman they knew she could be, and she's finally ready." Gabriel studied him for a long moment. "She could see my feather, right? With the gift I left?"

Issac nodded mutely, his mind too busy trying to process everything Gabriel had told him. Ezekiel, too.

"That's the final phase, her being able to view the ethereal realm." Gabriel pushed off the wall, starting down the hall. "Her blood isn't toxic, by the way. But I wouldn't bite her again, not until you both understand the bond."

"Bond?" Issac repeated, dismayed by the information.

Her blood isn't toxic. Because she's a Seraphim, not a Hydraian.

Astasiya was never unattainable.

And this bastard knew that the entire time.

Gabriel glanced over his shoulder at the top of the staircase. "Blood bond—a promise of eternity. The bond. You initiated it when you bit her. It's why she could reach you in your dreams. You're her chosen mate."

CHAPTER TWENTY-FOUR

Stas

"Aidan believes Seraphim are somehow linked to our existence, that perhaps they were the original immortals, who have since died off from old age. I'm unconvinced on both accounts. Knowing what I do now about Ichorian and Hydraian influence on the history of civilization, I wonder if Seraphim are a myth contrived by ancient beings. Similar to how Lucian and Balthazar influenced Greek and Roman mythology."

—Issac Wakefield
Vita mutatur, non tollitur

The barrel of the gun glinted in the daylight.

An eerie acceptance settled over her. She did this for love. For the future. But oh, it burned, the fire spreading through her veins. It sent her to her knees on an agonized scream. This wasn't part of the plan. She met her attacker's gaze, confusion radiating through her limbs. But a sadistic mask clouded his features.

"Incendiary bullets," Ezekiel explained casually. "Jonathan's researchers developed them for the Sentinels at the CRF. I don't think the science is quite right, though, because it's not meant to be obvious. And, well, this is pretty damn obvious."

Movement in the field grabbed her focus, a young angel with long blonde curls floating in the wind. Her little face morphed into one of shock and concern, her feet carrying her forward.

Is that me? *Stas wondered.* Why am I dreaming of myself like this?

Shock rippled through the bond, Sethios the source, followed by agony as he compelled his daughter to run. To hide.

The little angel's expression fell, torment twisting her features. But she obeyed because she had no choice. Her father's will commanded her to do as he urged, the last vestiges of energy channeled into the sole focus of protecting his little girl.

The image faded into a pair of exquisite light blue eyes, pleading.

And lips so similar to her own.

"Find him, Astasiya," the voice mouthed without sound. "Find your father. Save us all."

Stas gasped, sitting straight up in the small bed, her heart pounding a mile a minute. Her clammy palms stuck to the sheets around her, the shirt and pants she wore foreign against her damp skin. The female, whose name Stas couldn't remember—the one who saved Balthazar—had given her the clothes after a shower.

A shower in which Stas had spent the majority of the time sobbing on the ground.

Where am I now?

Another dimension of hell?

A hint of sandalwood teased her senses, lulling her into a false sense of comfort. The familiarity of it hurt her heart, stirring an ache deep inside—her soul craving her other half.

"Issac," she breathed, her eyelids falling closed on a sigh. Oh, she missed him. It felt as if they'd been apart for—

"I'm here," he replied, his voice low.

Her eyes flew open, her neck twisting toward the sound of his voice.

"You were sleeping and I didn't want to disturb you," he added softly.

The moon illuminated most of the room through the oversized windows, but not the shadows in the corner near the door. Issac leaned against the wall, his face hidden beneath a cloud of darkness. But she knew it was him. She recognized his long, lean form.

"You're here," she whispered, the words catching in her throat. Because him being here meant she was still dreaming. Which explained the weird surroundings. Her shifting of a memory that didn't belong to her to a world she didn't recognize.

A sob escaped her as she fell into the haven of pillows behind her and curled into a ball.

She hated this. Didn't understand it. Was lost to the overwhelming nature of life.

"Why?" she asked, begging the fates to explain this to her. "Why are you doing this to me?"

"Aya." Issac's arms wrapped around her, causing her to cry harder. To have him so near but to know none of it was real made this so much worse.

"I miss you," she admitted through her tears. "I miss you so much."

"Who, darling?" he asked. "Who do you miss?"

"You," she managed on a choked cry, her shoulders trembling violently. It hurt so fucking much. She needed him, which was why she'd conjured him into this dream. "But you're not real. It's all a cruel dream."

All of this. Being shot. Seeing her mom. The endless suffocating. Finally being saved. Being told she was a Seraphim. Dreaming about her parents from a body that didn't belong to her. Then this bizarre room.

"Aya," Issac said, pushing her to her back, his palm cupping her face. "This isn't a dream, love. I'm here. You're alive."

She shook her head. "I'm in hell." And she didn't know why or what she'd done to end up here.

"You're in Gabriel Stark's home." His thumb smeared the tears across her cheek, his breath warm and minty against her face. "This is real, love. I'm here."

His words only made her cry harder. This was some brutal joke created by her subconscious to fuck with her. Maybe she'd gone insane underground. "I couldn't breathe," she said, her throat aching from the memory. "But I prefer that over this… this… *pain*." She clutched her chest, her stomach cramping. "I miss you too much. And it *hurts*." Just admitting it out loud sent another stab through her heart, fracturing what was left of her soul.

Such a wicked, diabolical dream.

"Kill me again," she begged. "Put me back. *Please*. Don't make me wake up without you again."

Issac choked on a sound that severed her in half, his head falling to her neck. "Fuck, Aya." He shook against her, his fingers sliding into her hair and gripping her harshly, holding her to him. "I thought you were dead. I thought…" His voice broke, his body shuddering against hers. His tears soaked into her skin, rivaling the dampness beneath her eyes.

How could it feel so real and be all in her mind?

She cried out his name, her insides fracturing into a million pieces.

And he held her without fail, his agony etched into his shoulders, sending tremors down his spine, endless apologies falling from his lips.

I didn't know.

I shouldn't have buried you.

Fuck, I'm so damn sorry.

I'm so fucking sorry.

You were dead, Aya. I…

I can't believe I…

Will you ever forgive me?

The statements all blended together with time, the stars painting the sky above them. So many windows.

This place was unlike any she'd ever visited, making it impossible to conceptualize. Why would she choose this for her dream setting?

I wouldn't.

But clearly, she had.

Everything blurred, her vision sliding into shades of blue. Dark. Deep. Cold.

A mouth yawning on a scream.

Chains clasping her tightly beneath the surface.

So cold.

Alone.

Frightened.

Dying again.

"Sethios…" *A haunting voice hissing in her ears.* "Find Sethios… It's time."

Goose bumps prickled Stas's skin, skating a chill down her spine as the room resurfaced around her. Issac stared down at her, concern etched into his striking features, his eyelashes damp with tears.

Wow, even while crying, the man resembled a god. Maybe even more so.

No, not a god.

An angel.

She traced his perfect lips with her nail, adoring his soft skin. "You're the most beautiful man I've ever seen," she marveled. "The only one I've ever loved. I'll always love you, even in death. You know that, right?" She lifted to brush her mouth against his.

Divine perfection.

My angel.

She wrapped her arms around his neck to pull him to her, needing more. If her mind wanted to dream, then she'd make it a good one. It would hurt more later, but he tasted too good for her to resist.

He let her lead, his tongue gentle against hers, and not at

all what she craved.

How many days, weeks, or months had it been since he properly took her? All that dancing around fate, worrying that her blood would kill him, concern for their future standing in the way. And now that she had him on a playing field where they could do anything, be anyone, he kissed her softly? Tenderly? No.

She growled against his mouth. "Kiss me, Issac."

"I am," he whispered, his lips melting into hers.

"Harder," she demanded. "Kiss me like it's the last time you'll ever see me." This was their goodbye, the moment she would choose to remember. Always. "Please, Issac. Kiss—"

His mouth possessed hers on a growl that seared her insides.

Hot.

Dominant.

Issac.

His palm wrapped around her throat, holding her in place as he took her to heaven with his tongue. Dear God, she missed this. No restraint. No concerns. No ticking time bomb in the back of her mind.

Just pure, blissful passion. A mating of mouths so fierce it halted time and erased all the space between them. Her haven, her love, her *mate*.

She threaded her fingers through his hair, holding on for dear life as he devoured her. It was more extraordinary than any kiss in her memory, taking her to a new place of being, introducing her to sensations that shouldn't exist. Like they were flying, soaring through the clouds, their bodies as one. If only they could be in a place she adored, one where they could create a lasting memory for her to cherish for eternity.

Montana appeared in her mind, the cabin Issac had gifted her.

Yes.

She wanted to go there. To be with Issac in a place she considered home. *Their* home. A peaceful solitude surrounded by trees and snow and water. She could almost smell the fresh pine, the hint of wilderness teasing her nostrils.

Issac's grip tightened, his mouth demanding she focus and reciprocate. And oh, how she did, her tongue gliding against his in the expert dance he preferred. No holding back. Not now. No, she gave him everything and he returned it in kind, his touch a brand against her very soul. She belonged to him, and him to her, and there would never be another between them.

"Fuck, you're gorgeous." A hint of awe graced his tone, his palms sliding over her shoulders and upward, over a foreign part of her that tingled every fiber of her being. So, so good, whatever he was doing. She never wanted it to end.

Stas almost laughed, her heart beating with happiness because of *him*. This man, this alluring, beautiful man, completed her. *He's mine.* Fate couldn't take that away from her. Even if she suffocated a thousand more times, the price was worth it. For she would remember this feeling always, this sensation of being full of light. Carefree. Loved.

"They're so soft," he marveled, his lips stroking hers. "So fucking soft, Aya."

"What's soft?" she asked, smiling.

His sapphire irises flared with wonder as he met her curious gaze, his lips curling into one of his trademark smiles. It stole her breath, leaving her immobile beneath him, captivated by his handsome features. Almost as if she were seeing him again for the first time, recalling every magnificent feature.

"Your wings, Aya." His touch sent tingles down her spine again, his gaze lifting to his hand over her shoulder. "They're stunning."

"My…" She trailed off, her focus following his to the pale pink feathers splayed out across the bed.

Their bed.

In Montana.

Her eyes rounded.

"How did we…?"

He chuckled, his fingers combing through the plumes attached to her body. "You misted us, I think." His brow furrowed. "And somehow I can see you." His lips grazed her jaw, his nose going to her throat. "I don't even want to consider what it means. You're alive. You're here. That's all I care about."

Stas swallowed. "I don't… Am I…? Is this…?" She couldn't form a proper thought, the words all jumbled together in her mouth. Too much to say. Too many questions.

"You're a Seraphim," he murmured against her throat. "Gabriel said as much, but this certainly proves it." He kissed her collarbone, the column of her neck, back to her lips. "It physically hurts how breathtaking you are, Aya. And I love you, too. Always." His thumb traced her mouth, his gaze following. "There's so much I didn't say, so much we didn't do, before…" Tears shimmered in his eyes once again. "I thought you were gone forever."

She studied him, the scruff lining his jaw, the shaggy quality of his hair, the hollows of his cheeks. Still beautiful, undeniably so, but also… unkempt. And so very unlike her Issac. Even his outfit of a shirt and jeans didn't match the man she knew.

I would never imagine him like this—crying and disheveled.

She'd never picture herself with pink feathers, either. Lizzie, yes. Stas, no.

Issac's lips, warm and familiar, touched hers. Reverence and pain mingled in his kiss, a myriad of emotions traversing between their mouths.

This is real.

That was the only explanation. Because a dream just didn't fit.

"You're here," she whispered.

He nodded slowly, his thigh sliding between her legs, his hands running over her wings, her arms, as if memorizing her. "And so are you, my Aya. You're alive." His mouth covered hers before she could reply, his tongue dipping inside to claim her all over again.

She moaned, her heart thundering in her chest.

I'm alive.

Because I'm a Seraphim.

And Issac can see me because he's here.

She grasped his shoulders and wrapped one leg around his hips, her other leg trapped beneath him. But it didn't matter. Because he was really, physically, on top of her. And it felt amazingly right.

"I don't want to think about this anymore," she admitted. "I just want to be with you."

"Then be with me," he replied against her mouth. "Let me worship you the way I've craved for months. With my body, my mouth, my tongue." He punctuated the request with a deep kiss that took her breath away. "I've missed you, too, love. So fucking much. I need you. I need to know you're here. I need to *feel* you."

"Yes," she hissed, arching into him. "Everything. I'm yours."

"No, Aya." He nipped her lower lip, his royal blue irises radiating sincerity. "I'm *yours.*"

CHAPTER TWENTY-FIVE

"Imbibing blood is less difficult than I anticipated. It helps that women are otherwise distracted during the throes of passion. Each one possesses a different flavor, intriguing my Ichorian senses. I wonder if one day I'll taste everything this world has to offer, or if I'll continue to be amazed."

—Issac Wakefield
Vita mutatur, non tollitur

Astasiya's wings were the most marvelous sight of Issac's existence. He couldn't stop touching them, his fingers gliding over the silky texture, completely awed by her absolute beauty.

Her nails bit into the back of his neck as she pulled him

in for another kiss. He was helpless to stop her, his need far too great for him to consider any alternative.

Fuck, he'd missed this. The ability to take her the way he desired, to slide his tongue into her mouth without worrying about the repercussions. Mmm, she tasted so good, like his favorite dream only sweeter and more alluring. He deepened the embrace, taking charge on instinct alone.

Her throaty purr of approval went straight to his groin, his body on fire for her. He undulated his hips into hers to provoke the sound from her once more and smiled when she added his name to the mix.

"More." She sank her teeth into his lower lip, her reprimand clear.

"Persuade me," he dared, returning her bite with one of his own. "Tell me what to do to you, Aya." He wanted to feel her power, to luxuriate in the reality that they could do whatever they desired without consequence. Because her blood wasn't toxic to him.

According to Gabriel.

It might be a lie.

So what if it is? Issac didn't know if he cared anymore. Astasiya being alive was all that mattered. Her touch. Her gorgeous wings. Her blossoming smile.

"Undress me," she said, a hint of persuasion laced between her words, compelling his hands to move.

He allowed the command to drive his movements but worked them to his advantage and removed her clothes the way he desired—by gripping her shirt between his hands and ripping the fabric open.

Astasiya's nostrils flared, her legs clenching around his thighs. Arousal deepened her irises to a dark green shade, her eyelashes lowering as she gazed up at him expectantly. Mmm, she approved. As did he.

"More?" he asked, his palms already sliding to her hips as he shifted to the side.

She smiled and the sight nearly stopped his heart. So angelic, yet devilish. An intoxicating combination that left him aching to speed this seduction along. "Yes."

Ripping her pants wasn't an option, so he slowly drew them down her long legs, admiring her creamy skin as he went. God, he'd missed her. Not just for sex and intimacy, but everything about her. The teasing curl to her lips, the hungry gleam in her eyes, the way her muscles tensed as he ran his fingers up her thighs, and her adorable penchant for lace.

Her mind.

Her knack for words.

Her natural gifts.

And now these resplendent wings. Jesus Christ, how did he find someone so exquisite? So *perfect?*

He kneeled over her, kissing her soundly while toying with the lace decorating her hips. The elastic snapped with ease, earning him a hiss from Astasiya in the process—a hiss that lengthened as he slowly slid the fabric out from between her thighs.

"Feeling needy, darling?" he teased.

"I'm about two seconds away from demanding you fuck me."

He tsked. "That would spoil the experience, Aya." His hands skimmed her sides, her demand to undress her completely still very much in play. "I haven't had you the way I want in far too long. We're doing this right, love. And you're going to adore every fucking minute of it."

Her lacy blue bra contrasted beautifully with her pale skin. He bent to nibble the clasp between her breasts and unsnapped it with his teeth, eliciting a groan of appreciation from her throat.

Issac slid backward to admire her, to cherish the moment, to memorize every inch of her just because he could.

He thought her dead for seven horribly long days.

And now she lay before him very much alive. With soft pink feathers framing her nude form and a halo of golden hair falling around her shoulders.

"I've always thought angels were beautiful," he admitted. "But you take the expectation to an entirely new level of existence, Aya. You're bewitching, love. Perfection. Utterly alluring and so very much mine."

He took her nipple into his mouth, her reply coming out in an unintelligible sound underlined in pleasure.

The urge to bite her overcame him, his incisors aching with yearning.

What if—

No.

He cut off the line of thought and let instinct drive him, his mouth skating across her flesh, savoring, loving, enjoying. His tongue trailed downward, seeking her warmth, needing to remember her intimate taste. They hadn't done this in what felt like forever, the risk too great. But now, *now*, he could do whatever the fuck he wanted.

And he did.

He parted her legs, settling between her thighs, and licked her deep.

"Fuck," she groaned, her hips bucking upward to meet him. "Jesus, Issac. Can you...? Is this...? Oh God..."

She writhed beneath his mouth, her wet heat ambrosia on his tongue. He'd come so close to never experiencing this again, to never feeling her tense around him, to never hearing those delicious moans from her lips.

Never again would he take this for granted. He would cherish her always, lavish her in love and adoration every second of the day, and adore her with his mouth whenever she allowed. Such as now. He memorized her slick flesh, remembering all her favorite moves, and humming against her clit just to watch her squirm.

His Astasiya, his Seraphim, his mate.

He would forever belong to her.

Gabriel warned him against the bond, saying something about eternity. But Issac didn't care. This woman owned him heart and soul, just as he claimed her in return.

Her nails dug into his scalp, her thighs quivering on

either side of him. Passion thick in the air, her lips parting on a sigh of exquisite agony, waiting for him to say the words.

He smiled against her sensitive center, nipping her lightly and chuckling as she growled in response. "*Issac.*"

Part of him longed to prolong her torment, but he couldn't. He needed to see her shatter almost as much as she desired to fall apart. "Come for me, Aya. Scream my name."

Electricity sizzled between them, her wings rustling beneath her. She released him to fist the sheets, her back bowing off the bed as the most magnificent sound left her lips.

His name.

An echo throughout the room, the whole damn house, and permanently branding his heart. Gabriel was wrong. The bond between them already existed. Issac could feel the pull, the connection unfurling inside, the need to finalize the vows with a bite. He'd been avoiding it for months, this deep-seated urge to claim, but he no longer desired to ignore it. Instead, he wanted to embrace it.

Astasiya slowly returned to him, her gaze heavy-lidded as he crawled over her.

"More," she whispered.

"Yes," he agreed, dipping down to kiss her.

She tugged at his shirt, pulling it up and over his head. His lips returned to hers, his tongue still laden in her pleasure. He traced her mouth before slipping inside and kissing her deeply.

"Jeans. Off." She uttered the words between nips and licks, her demand sizzling down his spine. While he favored control, he adored this side of her—her ability to compel.

"You remove them," he countered, grabbing her hand and placing her fingers against the top of his pants. "Now." It fulfilled her compulsion while fueling his need for dominance.

Astasiya held his gaze and flicked open the button, then

dragged the zipper down, all the while saying nothing and everything with her eyes. Heat. Adoration. Respect. Desire.

He balanced on his palms on either side of her head—careful of her wings—and grinned. "All the way, my lady." He meant it to tease, but the flare in her pupils suggested she enjoyed it.

"As you wish, Your Grace."

He'd told her never to call him that.

Given the way his balls tightened with the formality—specifically, the sultry manner in which she'd said the title—he'd have to rethink his request.

Astasiya tugged the fabric lower as he lifted his hips, and used her heels to rid him of the jeans completely, leaving him naked above her.

"No boxers?" she asked, arching a brow.

"Are you complaining?"

"You always wear boxers," she said, gripping his cock. "But no, I'm not complaining."

"I've had an off week." Understatement of the millennium. He caught her wrist, stilling her movements as she began to stroke him. "I need to be inside you, Astasiya." And if she kept doing that, he'd not make it to that point.

She squeezed him and let go, her other hand wrapping around his neck and tugging him down for another mind-numbing kiss. He settled between her thighs, his elbows on either side of her head as he devoured her with his mouth.

Issac would never tire of this woman. Her flavor. Her essence. Her very being. With each swipe of her tongue, he hardened against her even more, his body tingling with the need to claim her.

He slid inside her in a single thrust, her body immediately accommodating his as if they'd never been apart. This was where he belonged, his soul forever connected with hers.

She raked her nails down his back, her lower body pressing into his, seeking deeper friction and urging him to move. He couldn't refuse her anything, especially not this.

"My Aya," he breathed, his body mating with hers in a rhythm they both adored.

"I love you." The heartfelt words were music to his ears, causing him to smile against her lips. They'd not vocally expressed their love much, if at all, during their time together. Mostly because it wasn't needed. They both knew how the other felt without the endearments. But now he wanted to say it on repeat, cherish each syllable with his last breath, and never stop telling her and showing her how much he adored her.

"I love you, too," he whispered, slowing his speed and savoring the moment. "I was lost without you." He shuddered with the admission, his limbs tensing.

Her alluring green eyes took on a haunted gleam. "It hurt, Issac. It hurt so much." She grimaced, her nails digging into his shoulders.

He lifted her off the bed, shifting their positions so they both sat up with her long legs wrapped around his waist, his cock still deep inside her. She held his gaze, her arms encircling his neck. "I'm sorry." He cupped her face, his thumb tracing her jaw. "I... I thought you were dead, Aya."

"I know."

"I wouldn't have..." He swallowed roughly, his forehead pressing to hers. "I should have known. Somehow, maybe I did, because I felt your presence. But I thought it was just my grief holding on to a lost hope."

Astasiya's lips feathered over his, lingering for a long moment, her breath warm against his mouth. "You had no way of knowing, Issac. I don't blame you." Another kiss. "You're here now. I'm here. That's what matters."

"I'm not sure I'll ever forgive myself," he confessed. "I—"

Her tongue silenced him. A deep, soulful, heated claim that sent a shock down his spine. She didn't relent, her mouth demanding against his, as if she needed him to ground her in the present, not the past, to solidify their mating rather than delay it. And he couldn't refuse her. He wanted her just as fiercely.

She *died.*

He buried her.

Said goodbye to her.

Planned to avenge her.

And now she sat astride him, her hips moving with his own, her lips whispering promises of forever against his mouth.

She's here.

She's alive.

She's mine.

He bit her lip, staking his claim, and shuddered as the sweetest essence slid over his tongue.

Astasiya.

Her blood.

He swallowed her gasp and sucked more into his mouth, missing this, missing *her.* She tried to push him away, but he didn't—*couldn't*—release her. His grasp on her hip turned to cement, his other palm gripping the back of her neck. He took another pull, groaning at the taste before pressing his lips to her cheek, then to her ear.

"I've missed this so fucking much, Aya. You. This. Us." He thrust upward, eliciting a moan from her throat. "No restraints. No rules. No requirements. I'm yours, love. Not just for now, but for always. If you'll have me."

She arched into him, her wings flaring around them. "You just drank my blood." A hint of awe filled her voice. "And you're still here."

He lifted from her neck with a grin. "Yes, I am."

"How? Isn't my blood...?" She trailed off, a hint of confusion stirring with the heat in her gaze. Apparently, Gabriel hadn't explained this to her, only to Issac.

"You're not a Hydraian, but a Seraphim." He stroked the underside of her wing, near her hip, for emphasis. "Your blood isn't toxic." Something Gabriel had mentioned and Issac had now proven. A risk, perhaps, but it was the only way to know for certain. And Issac trusted Astasiya never to hurt him.

She shivered, her pupils dilating. "Bite me again." Persuasion caressed the words, enticing the predator within him.

"Mmm, a command." He returned his mouth to her throat, teasing her pulse with his tongue. "I approve, love." His incisors pierced her skin, a growl lodging in his throat at the possessive need to reclaim his female—to mark her for everyone to see.

Too long.

Fuck.

More.

Her slick walls spasmed around his cock, her head falling back on a moan that went straight to his balls. Everything intensified—the heat, their pace, the urgency. His stomach clenched, her intoxicating blood flowing freely, satisfying an ache deep inside that he hadn't realized remained unfed. Not his Ichorian senses, but a new one. A cavern of desire and love and purpose. This woman was his other half, his reason for existing, the love of his existence.

Eternity would never be long enough.

He held her close, his mouth and body worshipping hers as his name fell from her lips on a benediction that went straight to his heart.

Her fingers wove through his hair, her eyes glazed as he pulled back to kiss her. It grew into a war of tongues, blood, and ardor between them. Each touch, each thrust, each lick and nip, all intertwined to carry them into a future of *always*.

"Never stop," Astasiya whispered, her wings folded around them, cocooning them in a halo of pale feathers. "I never want to stop."

Issac grinned against her mouth. "Then we won't."

"I need..." Her lips trailed across his jaw, her tongue laving the column of his throat. "I want..." Her teeth grazed his skin, stirring a shiver from his soul.

Fate whispered foreign intentions into his ear, his heart skipping a beat. They weren't so much words as they were instincts, a knowledge founded on a plane of existence he didn't comprehend. But the pull took them under, Astasiya's incisors puncturing his skin, his blood flowing into her moaning mouth.

It burned in the most delicious way, catapulting him over the edge into oblivion.

"Aya," he groaned, pleasure quaking throughout him, his orgasm stealing the breath from his lungs. His hand fell between them, needing her to join him, but she was already there, her body shaking on top of his, her feathers rustling across the sheets.

His breath caught at the beauty of the moment.

The shimmering colors, blinking in and out, her long waves of blonde hair cascading across her shoulders. And the sense of rightness overwhelming them both.

"Issac," she breathed, arching backward, her lips a delicate red.

He ran his palm down her breastbone to her hip, holding her against him as her wings shuddered at her back and disappeared. Her green eyes met his, drowsy and sated and bewitching. She smiled and kissed him, their blood mingling between their mouths, solidifying some kind of pledge.

No. A *bond.*

An everlasting connection binding their souls for the rest of time.

"I can hear you," she marveled, her palm against his cheek. "Your thoughts. You're *in* me."

He nibbled her lower lip, smiling. "Mmm." He could get used to this, had craved it since meeting her. But now that he was inside her, he realized how much it didn't matter. Issac didn't require access to Astasiya's thoughts to know how she felt. It was written in the way her body accepted his, the way she looked at him, the way she touched him.

Love.

So much love.

Kissing her again, soundly, he opened his mind to hers, his heart, his very being, and allowed her to feel all his emotions, everything he kept harbored away, including the pain of last week and his joy at finding her again, and his regret for not saving her sooner.

She responded with a wave of acceptance and forgiveness, her fierce love mending all the pieces of his broken soul and soothing the aches of his heart.

This relationship, their *bond,* surpassed all logic and pretenses, reaching an area of the universe no one had ever touched.

The future wasn't just theirs to experience, but theirs to create.

So much power, emotion, *life,* rippled between them, their connection not of this world. It blew Issac's mind, leaving him shivering beneath her. But his Aya, she took it in stride, pushing him onto his back and placing her palm over his chest as she straddled him.

Her winsome smile melted him inside, her eyes holding a devious gaze that belied her angelic nature. "We're fucking again," she said, already moving.

He chuckled and rolled her beneath him. "No, Aya. We're making love again. All night." Because now that he could see inside her? He would never be able to stop touching her, desiring her, adoring her.

Mine.

Mine, she agreed, joy radiating in the thought. *Take me, Issac.*

To the stars, Aya.

Chapter Twenty-Six

"Death's fragrance does not appeal to me, but I'm learning there are those of my kind who crave it. I understand why fear lurks in the dark, why there are those who never trust. Because I've witnessed such intense brutality this evening, yet I didn't attempt to dispel it. Instead, I remained outwardly calm while screaming on the inside. I suddenly fear for my humanity and what millennia will do to my mind. For it has clearly rendered Osiris mad."

—Issac Wakefield
Vita mutatur, non tollitur

"My wings are pink." Stas pinched her lips to the side, recalling the way her feathers felt against her back. They'd disappeared during sex, but the memory was vivid in her mind. Specifically, the color.

She shook her head, irritated.

Well, at least Lizzie will love them.

"*Lizzie.*" Her heart gave a pang. "Does she know I'm alive? Is the baby okay? Is *she* okay?"

"She's all right, love. Jayson has taken excellent care of her," Issac murmured, glancing sideways at her from the pillow. "She was distraught, but I'll be honest, I didn't really pay much attention. Not with…" He trailed off, swallowing. "I couldn't much focus at all."

Pain trickled through their connection, a pain that rivaled her experience in that coffin, one that threatened to crush her heart and destroy her very soul.

She shivered beneath the onslaught of his torment, the thought of her death fresh in his mind.

Cold.

Lonely.

Broken.

Guilt prickled her insides. "I'm always acting before I think," she whispered, recalling the events that led to her demise. Her running across the beach to Lizzie's side, being distracted by that Seraphim in front of Balthazar, and then using the last of her energy to take all the Sentinels down.

I didn't think.

I acted.

And I hurt everyone in the process.

"You also saved several lives," Issac murmured. "The Sentinels wore runes on their fatigues that repelled our gifts. You were the only one who broke through."

She shook her head. "But I caused so much pain… I hurt you, Issac. Just like in Bora Bora with Lizzie. I keep making all the wrong choices."

"Who's to say what's right or wrong, love? Blaming yourself for this is the same as me blaming myself for burying you alive. How were we to know? How could we have anticipated the results of that day?" Issac sighed. "We could dance in circles of *what-ifs*, but all it will do is damage our history. We need to think about the future and how to better react, how to use our experiences as strengths."

Her heart warmed at his words. "You sound like Aidan." *Who also died,* she remembered, the warmth inside her turning to ice in an instant. "Oh, Issac…"

"Shh." He silenced her with a kiss, his lips soft against hers. "Aidan lived for thousands of years. To say he enjoyed a full existence would be an understatement. While I mourn his loss, I also celebrate his life." He smiled. "It's as he would want it. He saved the next generation—Elizabeth and Jayson, and their unborn child. He would be proud of that."

Stas moved to her back, her palms digging into her eyes. "Fuck, I missed so much." How many others died? How many lives did that bastard take from them? She nearly growled. "Tell me John is still alive…"

Issac made a noise of pure disgust. "He is. The bloody coward is hiding, but I'm going to find him. We all are. And he will pay for what he's done."

Good. "It needs to be painful."

"It will be."

"And bloody," she added, picturing her former mentor's head on a stake. Stas didn't typically lean toward emotions of hatred, but for John? Oh, she loathed him entirely.

"Absolutely," Issac agreed, falling silent beside her.

She removed her hands to gaze up at the high ceilings, the events of the last however many days or weeks rolling through her mind. Such as her becoming a Seraphim.

A Seraphim with wings.

How do I make them appear again?

Frowning, she searched for a muscle or a physical trigger but found none. And her feathers—her *pink* feathers—remained hidden.

"Ugh," she groaned. Maybe her inability to make the wings appear again was a good thing. "My feathers are fucking *pink.*"

Amusement shone in Issac's gaze. "That's your primary

concern at present?"

"What? They're *pink*, Issac."

His responding chuckle blossomed into a laugh that shook the bed beneath them, causing her to glower at him.

"It's not funny."

"You're right," he said between laughs. "It's hilarious."

She sat up and smacked his arm. "You're not the one with rosy plumes coming out of your back." Although, they appeared to be gone now. She didn't really understand how it worked. "Do you think they change colors?"

He continued laughing, his handsome face too alluring for her to smother with the pillow. It was a crime to be that beautiful. Truly.

"I'm serious," she said. "Do you think they're always going to be pink?"

Tears glistened in his eyes, his long fingers flicking them away from the corners. "You find out you're a Seraphim and your biggest concern is the color? Not how you misted to Montana? Or how the feathers grew? Just the color."

"They're pink," she growled. "It's like Valentine's Day threw a party on my back."

His laugh erupted again, followed by more tears that left her sighing beside him.

"Well, you're helpful." She tried to slide off the bed, but he caught her by the waist and yanked her underneath him, his thigh sliding between hers as he went to his elbows on either side of her head. All while chuckling.

"We're in the middle of chaos, love, and you're focused on a color. It's amusing. But you're right. I should be taking this more seriously. Pink is certainly..." He trailed off on a chuckle, then bit his lip to keep from laughing more. She could feel his amusement through the bond, the hilarity of the moment. And the stress residing just beneath the surface that required his humorous outburst.

She palmed his cheek. "I think we both need to eat something." They'd been in bed for... hours... days? Who the hell knew? And they hadn't contacted anyone.

"Yes, reality," he murmured, trailing his nose across her cheek. "Although, I feel well satiated at the moment."

She smiled. "After all that biting, I imagine you would be."

His eyebrows danced as he hummed, "Mmm." He nipped her earlobe. "How do you feel about breakfast, darling?"

"It's a meal I enjoy," she replied, glancing at the dark windows. "Even at, uh, midnight?"

"No idea what time it is," he admitted, sliding backward onto his heels. Naked. Glorious. The body of a god, both outside and inside the bedroom. His lips curled. "Oh, I do enjoy that look on you. But I thought you desired a break?"

"I'm not sore, if that's what you're implying." If anything, she felt rejuvenated.

"No, the beauty of immortality is our ability to heal." He winked and slid off the bed. "Let's eat something, perhaps off of one another, in the kitchen." He held out a hand. "Assuming there's still food to prepare."

Hmm, yes. They'd left the house a few days… uh, or weeks, ago, maybe? She frowned. "What day is it?"

"Honestly? I haven't the slightest clue at the moment." He caught her ankle and tugged her across the sheets. "Let's have a wander and find out, yes?"

She giggled as he lifted her off the bed, setting her on her feet before him. He dipped his head to brush his mouth over hers, then led her to the closet. Her eyebrows lifted. "Where did all these clothes come from?" It was empty when they visited, and she'd left with her full suitcase.

"I may have called in a few favors to have the house stocked for future use."

"And you ordered me all dresses?" she asked, incredulous. Her entire side of the closet looked like something Lizzie would prefer to wear, not Stas.

Issac smirked. "I like your legs."

"And I like jeans."

"Top drawer, love." He gestured with his chin toward

the second dresser at the back of the bedroom-sized closet.

Sure enough, several pairs of jeans sat on top. As well as some yoga pants. She opted for those instead and paired it with a tank top and sweater she found in another one of the drawers. Issac pulled on jeans and a T-shirt, his hair artfully messy—from her fingers running through it—and his scruff thickening around the edges of his jaw.

"I kind of like this version of you," she decided. "You're… relaxed."

He snorted. "I'm an unkempt mess, but thank you for accepting it." He gazed down at her, his palm against her lower back, holding her close. "After we eat, I need a proper shower and a shave. *Mountain man* is not my preferred appearance."

"It's cute, though." She was partly teasing, partly telling the truth. Issac could pull off almost any look he attempted, including this one.

"It's disturbing," he countered, tapping her on the nose. "And my jaw is itching like crazy."

"Did you want to shower first, then?" she suggested as he walked her backward out of the closet. "Trim up the man scruff?"

His lips curled. "Darling, if I give in to that idea, we'll never eat. I'll just fuck you in the shower all day instead."

"I'm not sure I'd object to that." Her shoulder brushed the bedroom wall as she headed toward the shower, not the stairs.

Issac spun her so she faced the right direction and slapped his palm across her ass. "Food first."

"I thought you were 'well satiated'?" she teased, using his words from earlier.

He yanked her back against him, his palm demanding against her lower belly, his lips at her ear. "You were the one who suggested food. Now I have to feed you. It's in the rules, love."

"Rules?" she repeated.

"Ask Balthazar." He nudged her toward the stairs.

She glanced at him from the top step. "Balthazar, huh? You're friends now?"

"We've always been friends."

She snorted and started downward. "Yeah, I believe—" She froze as the living room below came into view. Specifically, as the oversized couch and recliner chairs appeared. One of the end table lights was on, showcasing a lounging Stark, who held a book in his lap, his long legs crossed at the ankles.

He glanced upward from his lazy position, one of his arms tucked behind his head, propping him up against the pillows near the end of the couch. "There's coffee in the kitchen" was his greeting. He went back to his book, completely unconcerned.

"*You.*" She stomped down the stairs, ready to kill him. He knew about her Seraphim status from the beginning and never told her. He *saved* her all those years ago, had someone alter her memories to hide it all, and allowed her to think her parents were *dead.*

Oh, but she remembered everything now.

Every fucking detail.

How he found her in that field, took her away, and promised to come back to her. Promised to help her find her mother. Then stole her memories without her permission, claiming it was to *protect* her. Then this asshole had the audacity to become her trainer at the CRF? And still didn't tell her the truth? No.

"This is *your* fault," she snapped. "You… You kept me in the dark. You didn't tell me shit. Issac buried me alive because you never told any of us the truth!" She lunged at him, but the bastard went angelic and misted behind her, his arms crossed, those red wings splayed behind him.

"Stop being a brat."

"A *brat?*" Oh, now she understood the color of his feathers. This man wanted to bleed. Well, she'd paint him crimson.

Her fist connected with his jaw before he could phase

again, and he stumbled backward with a shocked expression.

Issac whistled behind her. "Took the action right out of my hands, love. Hit him again, yeah?"

"Happily." Except the bastard disappeared again, this time landing with a finality on the wood platform at the bottom of the stairs.

His hands were on his hips. "First of all, nice hit. Second of all, could one of you please use the phone on the coffee table to phone Jacque? He's teleported in three times now to check in and only left me alone because I promised one of you would call him when you finished"—he waved upward—"upstairs."

Stas's cheeks warmed. "You've been here the entire time?"

He snorted. "No. I've left on over a dozen occasions. No one wants to hear those noises from his little sister."

Oh my God. She nearly fainted into Issac's waiting arms. He didn't seem to share her embarrassment, his chest solid against her back as he held her against him.

"What the fuck do you want, Gabriel?" he demanded, his voice low and simmering with rage.

Stark didn't appear fazed in the slightest, his expression as stoic as ever. "To discuss our future. We have several tasks to handle."

"We?" Issac repeated, and she could tell from his tone he'd arched a disbelieving brow. "What makes you think we're interested?"

"Because it involves rescuing Sethios and Caro—Astasiya's parents. It involves destroying Osiris. And I also know how you can take down Jonathan." He tilted his head to the side. "Do I have your attention yet? Or should I also point out that I'm the only one who can help Astasiya learn how to control her new abilities?"

Stas swallowed, only the beginning of his statement sticking in her thoughts. "My parents...?"

"Are both alive and in a great deal of pain," he finished

for her. "They sacrificed themselves to protect your legacy. The prophecy never gave the rising power a name and Osiris assumed it was our mother, but it's always been about you."

"What prophecy?" she asked, her throat dry.

Stark ran his fingers through his light hair and sighed. "I need to start from the beginning. Do you want to do that over coffee? Or shall we remain standing?"

Issac's grip loosened. "Astasiya requires coffee."

Normally, she'd argue against someone making a decision for her, but Issac was right in this case. She did need coffee. "Black with—"

"Brown sugar," he said, releasing her with a wink. "I know, love."

Of course he did. He was in her head, her heart, her very essence. He knew everything.

Issac winked at her again as he passed Stark, clearly having heard her thoughts.

"If I sit down, are you going to attack me again?" Stark asked, his voice void of emotion.

"Are you going to call me a brat again?"

"Are you going to act like one?" he countered.

She narrowed her gaze. "You kept me in the dark my entire life, stole my memories, faked my friend's death and kept it from me, and you failed to mention that you're my *brother* for the last several however many fucking months of our acquaintance. Oh, *and*, I was buried alive because you didn't tell anyone I was a Seraphim. So yeah, I'm entitled to act however I fucking please, thank you."

His lips fucking twitched.

Twitched!

"This is not funny."

"No, it's not, but you remind me so much of Mom right now." He made a strangled noise, the sound foreign to her ears.

"Are you...? Is that your laugh?"

It grew louder, his shoulders beginning to shake.

"Oh my God, you're actually laughing." The man didn't even crack a smile in the months she'd known him, and now he laughed? "Who the hell are you?" she asked, not recognizing this version at all. It was meant to be rhetorical, but naturally, the tone went over his head.

"Gabriel Stark, Seraphim of the warrior and messenger lines." He misted to the couch again, kicking up his legs and relaxing. "You're a Seraphim of the resurrection and messenger lines."

"I don't know what that means," she admitted.

"I know." He picked up the phone from the coffee table and began typing while speaking. "Our mother is a messenger, meaning she delivers edicts on behalf of the council. She also possesses a dormant healing gene, one I inherited that you might as well. Most didn't see her as very powerful, but having spent the better part of two decades around humans, I think our kind has belittled her skill set because of the guardian qualities."

Stas finally sat in one of the chairs, her gaze narrowing. "You're going to need to start from the beginning, Stark. What's an edict? Who is the council? And what guardian qualities?"

"Coffee first," Issac said, sauntering up behind her with a steaming mug of heaven. He handed it to her. "Someone stocked the fridge. Should I make something? Breakfast, perhaps?"

A glance out the windows lining the living area displayed a moon hanging high over the lake. Definitely the middle of the night. Not that it mattered. "Breakfast sounds—"

"All right," a deep voice interrupted. "I have my phone, Red. Just hold on." Jayson and Jacque stood in the dining area. Well, just Jayson because Jacque had already disappeared.

"I want to see her, Jay," a female voice said over speakerphone. "I *need* to see her."

"I know, sweetheart. Just give me a second." Dark brown eyes gazed imploringly around the living area, landing on Stas. "You. Phone. Now."

Nice to see you, too, she thought. But the desperation in his features had her setting her coffee down, standing, and moving toward the phone. Lizzie's face peeked up at her from the screen.

"Stas?" she breathed, her brown eyes wide. "Are you okay?"

"Hey, Liz." She took the device from Jayson's hand and smiled. "I'm here. Alive. Are you and the baby—"

A haunting screech came over the phone as Lizzie burst into tears.

"Fuck," Jayson muttered. "I thought this would help, not make it worse." He looked to the heavens as if to beg for assistance while Stas watched her best friend fall apart on the phone.

"Lizzie, I'm okay," she assured her. "I mean, I have pink wings, which, well, you'll love. But I'm all right, I swear."

More sobbing, followed by unintelligible words involving some convoluted mix of Stas's name with Issac's, something about Stark.

"I can't—"

"Ah, hell. He gave in, didn't he?" The female voice came from the background. "Come on, darling, you need to breathe. In and out, that's it. Shh…"

The phone image blurred, followed by Lizzie crying out, "Stas!"

"I'm still here," she replied, her brow furrowing at the shifting colors on the screen. "Lizzie?"

A blonde woman with striking features appeared—the Seraphim who saved Balthazar. *Leela*, her memory supplied.

"Lizzie needs to calm down or there will be complications," she advised in soft tones. "Her pregnancy is abnormal enough without all the stress, something I just told Jayson five minutes ago."

He sighed, visibly agitated. "She needed proof that Stas was alive."

Leela's lips twitched. "And you caved."

"Technically, you told me not to teleport her. You said nothing about coming here myself and showing her Stas is alive."

"No, I told you not to stress her out more," Leela corrected, sounding nothing like Stark, who always spoke in stoic tones, and every bit like an irritated female. *Odd.*

"Look, she was already a mess over Stas. And then she grew demanding, leaving me—"

"*Demanding?*" Lizzie repeated, her voice strained.

"Yes, Red. You were shouting at me to find Stas." He spoke the words in the most timid tone Stas had ever heard from him. "I did what you asked, okay, sweetheart?"

"No, I wasn't." She sniffled. "I mean, I didn't mean to. I just… I just… I missed Stas. And all this is s-so confusing." Another sniffle followed her words.

"Mood swings," Jayson mouthed, shaking his head.

"I heard that," Lizzie snapped, the tears gone in an instant. "You try carrying this… this…. *angel baby* inside you!"

Leela smiled, the expression indulgent. "I'll handle it from here. Visit your friend soon, Stas. She needs to see you." The screen went dark, the Seraphim having hung up on her.

"Why is that woman with Lizzie?" Stas asked, confused as hell.

"She's a Seraphim of the fertility line," Stark replied from the couch. "She helped our mother give birth to you, and she's volunteered to assist Lizzie now. I gave her all the records from the CRF as well. Including the ones Mateo couldn't hack."

Stas's lips parted as Jayson's gaze narrowed. "Still doesn't make me trust you, asshole."

"That implies I care about what you think, which I do not," Stark replied, his focus on his phone. "Go back to your wife, Elder. She needs you."

"I could hear her screaming from my house," a deep male voice said from the kitchen. Balthazar stepped into the dining room, a stack of pizza boxes in his hands. "Jacque helped me procure these."

"Yup. Save some for me. Gotta grab Luc and Alik, and take Jay back to Lizzie first." The teleporter stood beside Jayson already, his floppy hair mussed from the wind of zipping back and forth. "Good, Jay?"

"No," he muttered. "Lizzie didn't seem satisfied at all."

"Pregnancy does that to a woman," Balthazar murmured, a devious twinkle in his eyes. "I can't wait until little LJ is born."

Jayson glowered at the mind reader. "We are *not* calling her that."

"Perhaps you're not, but I am."

"No, you're—" Jayson's retort disappeared on the wind as Jacque teleported them both out of the dining area, leaving Balthazar chuckling in their wake.

"So, who's hungry?" he asked, the picture of innocence as he set the boxes down on the oversized dining room table.

"I am," Issac said, his lips curled into a boyish grin. "And I smell pepperoni."

Since when do you get excited over pizza? Stas wondered.

After the marathon of sex upstairs? I'm excited to eat anything.

I thought you were well fed? she teased.

He smirked over his shoulder. *I was, and now I'm starving. I suspect this is going to be a very long day, Aya.*

"Well, that's new," Balthazar mused, his gaze swinging back and forth between them. "And what's fascinating is, while I know you're speaking, I can't *hear* it."

Issac's eyebrows lifted. "You mean I finally have a way to keep you out of my head? Brilliant."

"They've bonded," Stark said from the couch. "Despite my warning to the contrary, I might add."

"Because your cautions impact so many of my decisions," Issac deadpanned.

"Bonded?" Balthazar repeated, stepping closer.

"Seraphim blood bond." Stark stood, his expression

blank. "Issac just joined the Seraphim of Resurrection's bloodline, via Astasiya. Congratulations. I'm sure Osiris will be thrilled."

PART THREE

Seraphim Bonds

"A new Seraphim has risen from the ashes of despair.
He will bring with him a Wrath unlike anything this
Earth has ever seen, and She will reign even in death.
Kingdoms will fall. New powers will emerge. The
endgame begins now."

–Prophetess Skye

CHAPTER TWENTY-SEVEN

Stas

"ISSAC IS TURNING INTO A SERAPHIM," Luc repeated, his tone incredulous. He'd arrived with Jacque at the tail end of Stark's explanation—an explanation no one in the room understood.

"Sweet." Alik collapsed into the recliner chair, kicking it back. "Hope it gives him some additional powers. Oh, and since no one else has said it, glad you're alive, Stas."

"Yes, I'm thankful you're still with us," Luc said, his gaze still on Stark. "So you're saying by completing this blood bond between them, it's initiated some sort of transition process?"

Stas wasn't offended by his immediate return to the topic at hand because she wanted an answer, too. They could all celebrate her life *after* they learned more about Stark's cryptic statements.

"The process started the first time Issac bit Stas. It's why he didn't need to feed. Her blood cured his inherent curse, allowing him to survive without the essence of a mortal. And now that they've completed the bond, his soul has joined with hers. He's no longer an Ichorian; he's transitioning into the ethereal realm."

"I don't feel any different from before." Issac stood in the living area, his elbow resting on the mantel above the fireplace. The pizza remained untouched in the dining room, everyone having lost their appetites—Stas, too. "I can still see everyone's visions, apart from yours and Astasiya's, and I certainly haven't grown any feathers."

Stark snorted. "The process takes decades, not hours. Why do you think it took Stas twenty-five years to reach maturity? And she was born a Seraphim. You were not. It will take two decades for you to fully phase into your ethereal state, likely longer."

"Stas was born a Seraphim?" Luc repeated, frowning. "Ezekiel mentioned Osiris is a Seraphim, but Sethios's mother was mortal. Doesn't that make him a half-breed? Genetically speaking, I mean."

Stark shook his head. "You're working in terms of mortal expectancies. Seraphim may resemble humans in our corporeal state, but there's nothing human about our genetics. The blood contains our elemental properties, which override mortality in every way. Sethios was predominantly Seraphim because of his father's genetic influence, not a half-breed. As such, Stas was born pure because Caro's bloodline overruled what little mortality Sethios carried in his system."

"How is one predominantly Seraphim and not completely Seraphim?" Luc asked.

"By mating a Seraphim *to* a mortal," Gabriel replied. "Sethios maintained just enough mortality to straddle the boundaries between the human realm and ethereal realm.

Meaning he could see Seraphim but could not fully phase. Although, I suspect he's completely transitioned now as a result of the bond."

"And the process takes several decades?" Issac prompted.

"Yes, it's a gradual evolution, but you'll eventually become a purebred Seraphim—meaning your human DNA will dissolve as the superior essence takes hold. New powers will manifest over time. You could develop skills that rival Stas's bloodline, or perhaps your visionary abilities will morph into something spectacular. We have no way of knowing for sure."

"Fascinating," Luc marveled.

While Stas agreed, she had a more pressing query. "Can you go back to the part about Osiris being a Seraphim?" Because that was news to her. Everyone had speculated at Sethios's origin, but no one had guessed Osiris to be anything other than an Ichorian.

"Yes, he's the Seraphim of Resurrection." Stark lifted his ankle to his opposite knee and relaxed against the couch, his arms sprawled to either side as he sat like a king. "There are hundreds of Seraphim bloodlines, all defined by their abilities or supernatural talents. Each offspring falls into one of the familial lines based on their superior gift, just as each bloodline has a figurehead who is considered the most powerful being of that group. In your case, Osiris is the oldest and most influential Seraphim of the resurrection family. As he's only procreated once—meaning Sethios—it stands to reason that Osiris is the strongest being."

"And his blood is what has created Hydraians and Ichorians," Luc added, shocking Stas even more.

"*What?*" She needed to sit down. First, the news on Issac. Now, whatever the fuck this was. Yeah. Okay. She collapsed into the love seat that was catty-corner to the couch Stark lounged upon. Issac joined her, his arm encircling her shoulders and pulling her close, sensing her need for comfort.

Luc took the opportunity to sit as well, but not in the only open chair. He sat on the brick fireplace stoop, directly across from Stark, his gaze intense. "Ezekiel said Osiris created a handful of the first Ichorians—himself and Aidan included—and the curse, as he called it, spread from there."

"Yes. My kind refers to it as a curse because your kind should not exist. You're all abominations of the human race, brought back to life through the magic of resurrection. It's why Osiris can persuade you all. Stas can, too, because she's a descendant of the same line."

He made it sound like she could only compel Ichorians and Hydraians because they were resurrected. "But I also compelled Osiris and humans, and they're not resurrected," she said as Balthazar rejoined them. He handed Stas a fresh cup of coffee—her old one was still on the end table—and also gave one to Issac before joining Luc at the fireplace.

Stark scratched his jaw, his brow furrowing in thought. "There are varying degrees of persuasion. Osiris's control over the beings he's created is vast, meaning his compulsion holds regardless of time and space until he actively releases the command."

"Okay." She swallowed some of her coffee, needing the warmth.

Talking about Osiris's power had her stomach in knots. The immortal redefined the meaning of *cruel*. And the reminder of her relation to him unsettled her insides. She did not want to be compared to him in any way. Alas, they shared a similar power.

"So." She paused, clearing her throat. "Why can I compel him if he's not my creation?"

"Osiris's bloodline isn't just about resurrection, but also about creation," he clarified. "You control life and existence, Stas. Those of your bloodline can persuade anyone and everyone. It's one of the most powerful gifts, which is why Sethios and Caro felt strongly about grounding you in humanity. You need to appreciate life to respect it. Otherwise..." He spread his hands as if to say, *You know the rest.*

"You become Osiris," Issac translated, taking a sip of his drink.

"Exactly. He was sentenced to ten millennia on Earth after using his gift of persuasion on others to complete nefarious acts. I wasn't alive then and therefore didn't witness his atrocities, but everything I've observed over the last fifty-five years suggests his exile was warranted."

"You're only five decades old?" Luc asked, his brow lifting.

"Nearly six, actually." He shrugged. "I'm young but well trained. I've already risen in the ranks of my paternal line, surpassing several who are millennia older, because my father, Adriel, is the Seraphim of War. While I maintain abilities from Caro's messenger bloodline, my true strengths are in combat."

"I can see that," Stas muttered, recalling all the grueling hours of having her ass handed to her on a mat. "No wonder you're such a hard-ass."

His lips twitched. "No, you're just untrained, little sister. But you're improving every day."

The endearment sent a jolt through her bloodstream. *Little sister.*

Gabriel Stark is my older brother.

What the actual fuck is happening in this world?

She considered him the enemy for so long—Jonathan's pet Sentinel—but now she didn't know what to think. He'd kept everything from her, led her to believe her parents were killed, but the logical part of her understood his actions. The manufactured history in her mind about the death of her parents forced Stas to hide her abilities out of fear of repercussions. And living with the Davenports had taught her to value human life, had essentially given her a conscience that Osiris clearly lacked.

"But what about my father?" she wondered out loud. "Is Sethios like Osiris?"

"Yes," Luc and Alik answered simultaneously.

"No," Stark countered. "Sethios sacrificed everything to protect you, Stas. Osiris would never make such a choice for anyone except himself."

Stas recalled the memory—the real one—in her mind, seeing her father's eyes as he mentally compelled her to run. He'd been in such pain…

Green irises, radiating hurt and fear, focused on Astasiya. Persuasion shook her being, forcing her legs to move, to run—

"I can see him," Issac marveled, pulling her from the thought. "I can see Sethios."

She blinked up at him. "The memory?"

He nodded. "Every detail."

"Yes, you're bonded," Stark interrupted. "For eternity."

Issac merely smiled. "You say that as if it's a bad thing, mate." He shifted his focus, his arm around her shoulders tightening. "Are you concerned about my intentions for your sister?"

Stas busied herself with the caffeinated beverage in her hands, needing the liquid energy to fortify herself for this conversation.

Stark snorted. "You should be more concerned about Sethios's reaction."

"I'm not afraid of Sethios." The certainty in Issac's voice matched his resolve inside.

"Regardless, there are a few things you need to understand about the bond. First, it attaches your soul to hers, which is why you'll eventually evolve into a Seraphim. Right now, you can see into our plane of existence—"

"I could see Aya before we completed our bond," he interjected.

"Yes, because it was already initiated. But you couldn't see me. Now you can."

Issac's chin dipped. "All right."

"And you'll eventually be able to go ethereal as well, but not until the transition is complete, which we already discussed."

"Indeed. But I'm still not seeing your concerns,

Gabriel," Issac said, taking a final sip from his mug and setting it aside. "Everything you've listed thus far is a perk."

"Fair enough." Stark shifted his attention. "Stas, do you dream of being underwater? Drowning? Screaming for help with no one to hear you?"

His words sent a shiver down her spine, vivid images flashing behind her eyes of their own accord. The cup in her hand suddenly felt cold. Bitter. She placed it on the table and wrapped her arms around her middle.

"Yes," she admitted, haunted by the visions flooding her mind. The nightmares were almost as bad as being buried alive, almost as real.

"That's Mom telegraphing through the bond," Stark said flatly. "I see them, too, but only when I sleep. Sethios, however, feels her agony every single second of every single day. Through the bond. And what's worse? He has no idea why."

"He doesn't know he's bonded?" Luc asked, his brow furrowing. "How is that possible?"

"Osiris compelled him to forget everyone and everything, right in front of Caro. Wiped her from his mind completely. Then threw her to the bottom of the ocean."

"Where?" Stas demanded, her hands in fists. "And why haven't you helped her?"

"You don't think I would if I could?" His tone finally held a note of emotion—incredulity—and it matched his features. "I have no idea where Osiris left her, and this planet is mostly water. Ezekiel doesn't know, either. Which is why we need Sethios. He's the only one who can find her."

"Because of their bond," Issac said softly.

"Yes." Stark held his gaze. "Now you understand the complication. If something ever happens to Astasiya, you will live in agony until the problem is resolved."

"I would be miserable regardless of the bond." Issac tilted his head to the side. "Something I believe this last week has shown everyone." His palm slid up and down her arm, as if reminding himself she still sat beside him.

Stas leaned into his side, laying her head on his shoulder and nuzzling his throat. *I'm here.*

I know.

I love you.

His lips curled. *I love you, too, Aya.*

"Seriously bizarre," Balthazar said, his chocolate gaze swirling with admiration. "I know you're speaking to each other, but it's muffled."

"You have no idea how much that thrills me," Issac replied. "I've finally found a way to tune you out."

"So I need to bond with a Seraphim to kick him out of my head." Alik spoke the words as if he were plotting his future. "Added benefits are intense immortality—since, apparently, Wakefield can't die now—and I might sprout wings." He nodded. "Sold."

Stark didn't appear amused at all. "It's not just a bond; it's an eternal mating. Sacred and rare and requires intense commitment. Issac will never be able to romantically react to another being. His soul belongs to Stas and vice versa."

A hint of satisfaction slithered through the bond, Issac pleased at the idea that Stas could never look elsewhere. She sent a blast right back at him.

You're the playboy billionaire, remember?

He snorted. *That's a long-dead image I have no intention of ever resurrecting.*

Good. Because I'll kill anyone who touches you. She had no idea where the possessive instinct came from, but no way was she quelling it. Issac was hers. She would not be sharing him. Ever.

He arched a brow. *I might actually enjoy that, Aya.*

Don't tempt me, or I'll return the favor and flirt with Balthazar.

His gaze narrowed. *Touché, love.*

"All right, you mentioned freeing Sethios as a next step. What about Jonathan? You worked with him the longest. Where's he hiding?" Luc had somewhat relaxed, his back up against the brick lining the fireplace, his long legs stretched out before him.

"Better question—why didn't you warn us about the attack?" Alik asked, a blade playing between his fingers. "If you were on our side, you would have said something."

Stark didn't flinch despite the clear threat lurking in Alik's gaze. "John assigned a different Sentinel to lead the mission. I didn't even know about it until it was too late."

"But Leela was there," Stas said, frowning. "I saw her."

"Yes." Stark's jaw clenched. "We rotated watching over you, and that was Leela's week. She's the reason I found out about the attack. She misted to my house right before dying from the bullet wounds. Owen took care of her and called me. I went to John to find out what the fuck happened, then requested a two-week vacation to clear my head."

"And he didn't question that?" Luc asked.

"I want to know how Leela was shot," Balthazar cut in. "Can Seraphim take bullets in an ethereal state?"

He doesn't know? She blinked. *Of course he doesn't. He couldn't see her.*

See who, darling? Issac asked, hearing her thoughts.

Leela. She protected Balthazar. That's why I was so distracted— I saw her wings. Then I heard you calling my name, and... She swallowed. *You know the rest.*

Stark shifted, uncrossing his legs and leaning forward to brace his elbows on his knees. "Yes, Seraphim can sustain damage in an ethereal state. And no, John didn't question it because I told him there wasn't much for me to do at the moment so I wanted a break. Since I've never taken vacation days, he gave them to me. But he expects me back soon."

"Which presents us with an opportunity," Luc murmured. "Interesting. Ezekiel tells me you can alter the wards at the CRF headquarters?"

"Yes. Osiris created them. I know how to update them and have done so on numerous occasions."

"So Jonathan knows you're a Seraphim?" Luc asked.

"No. He has no idea. Osiris is unaware as well. I updated

the runes without their knowledge and have kept my identity a secret for the better part of a decade. John thinks his genetic modifications worked on me." Stark gazed at Luc. "Did Ezekiel share all the research files? To give you insight into the Sentinel updates? John's been very busy at the CRF using Osiris's money and Seraphim resources to create more abominations, some incredibly lethal."

"That's something I don't understand. Why has Osiris entrusted Jonathan with all these projects? What's his goal? He's advocated for conflict between Hydraians and Ichorians for nearly two millennia, has even led a war on one side and killed hundreds of his creations. What is he trying to accomplish?"

"That should be obvious." Stark cocked his head to the side. "You're all foot soldiers crafted for his own personal use. He's sharpened his tools through thousands of years of bloodshed, killing off the weak and keeping the strong, and he keeps you all on edge so you continue to train. He's amassing an army, Lucian. And the projects John has worked on are just another line of defense—humans with Seraphim genetics."

"Like Lizzie," Stas breathed.

"Yes," Stark confirmed. "But she was created for a different purpose."

"To breed," she muttered, recalling everything Lizzie had told her.

"Specifically, to breed Osiris's progeny. He views her current pregnancy as a test of survival. He also assumes any child she bears will be of use to him later. However, in a future state, his goal is to replace Sethios—whom he sees as a broken lieutenant after his dalliances with Caro. That's why Lizzie was genetically modified to conceive."

"But why?" Stas pressed. "I mean, he created my father with a mortal, right?"

"Procreation amongst Seraphim is very rare. I suspect he's attempted to produce another progeny using similar methods and failed. Hence, he assigned John the task of manufacturing a female with enough Seraphim genetics to carry his child."

"Is Lizzie similar to my father? Or is she transitioning into a Seraphim?"

"Leela would be better tasked to answer that. The way Elizabeth was created defies the supernatural order. She's a mixture of bloodlines, both Seraphim and mortal alike. I don't know that she has a definition."

Stas shivered. "Does that mean her future is unknown?"

"In essence, yes. She's one of a kind. The CRF Sentinels used for experimentation were only given small amounts of Seraphim alterations to strengthen their mortality. Elizabeth was effectively manufactured in a lab."

That sounds ominous, she thought, another shiver traversing her spine.

But not hopeless, Issac murmured reassuringly. *Elizabeth is resilient. We'll figure this out.*

"You mentioned procreation is rare," Luc said. "Is there a specific reason why?"

"There are a multitude of reasons. First, Seraphim rarely fornicate because my kind doesn't see a point. Second—"

"Whoa, hold on. You don't see a point?" Balthazar's eyebrows were in his hairline. "As in... Yeah, no, I can't even finish that because it's unreasonable. How is there no point to sex?"

"It's a predominantly human act done for selfish reasons that bear no practical recourse aside from producing an heir, which I was about to say is uncommon because it requires timing and an appropriate blood match."

Balthazar blinked at him. "Pleasure is *selfish?*"

"It's impractical."

"No wonder you Seraphim are so damn stoic. Clearly, you don't know how to live. Direct me to your leaders, as I'll be happy to provide a few tutorials. Pleasure can most certainly be a gift when applying the correct methods." Balthazar glanced at Luc. "Can you believe this? It's like an entire realm of untried opportunities—the mother of all challenges."

Alik snorted. "Not everyone lives and breathes sex, B."

Balthazar waved at Stark. "Clearly."

"Again, it's impractical. Seraphim only fornicate when the Fates have predicted an ideal coupling. Such as when Caro and Adriel were prophesized to create me."

"Are you a virgin?" Balthazar asked, incredulous.

"That bears no consequence on this conversation."

"I beg to differ," the mind reader pressed. "Your virginity would explain your narrow-minded view, something I'll happily fix for you. Just say the word."

"No."

A flat response.

No elaboration.

Just an emphatic denial of the suggestion, or perhaps a response to the virginity question. Not that Stas wanted to know. At this point, she just wanted a break. Or some alcohol. Or maybe a really long nap.

"You mentioned the Fates?" Luc prompted. "What are they?"

Stark cleared his throat. "The Fates are our oracles. They dictate the future, but there are some who believe they might be corrupt." His gaze flickered to Stas. "They tricked our mother into delivering an edict to Osiris, knowing Sethios would intervene. That's how you were conceived."

"That might be too much information," Stas muttered.

"But it's important because the Fates wanted Caro to become pregnant and failed to warn her of that intention. Instead they set her up on a false errand. Then the Fates— and the council—wanted you raised among Seraphim, but our mother refused. It would have required terminating Sethios in some fashion. However, Skye prophesized the need to keep him in your life, to teach you the importance of humanity, to ground you to the earth."

"And Skye is the prophetess in Osiris's custody," Luc added, scratching his jaw. "How do you know which seer speaks the truth?"

"I don't," Stark admitted. "Caro and Sethios chose their path, and from what I've seen thus far, it appears to be the right one."

Chapter Twenty-Eight

Stas

I'M GETTING DIZZY, Stas admitted. *This is… a lot. I just wanted to have a snack and go back upstairs.*

Issac chuckled in her mind, pulling her close and kissing the top of her head. *Do you think I'll have pink feathers, too?* he mused, effectively distracting her.

She scowled at him. *I don't want to think about* that, *either.*

You don't think I could pull off rosy plumes? His use of her earlier description was not lost on her. *Maybe mine will be fuchsia.*

I really hope they are. Then you'll regret ever suggesting it and maybe understand my sorrow.

Another chuckle. *Poor darling. Maybe you're right. Maybe they'll change colors.*

I'll pay you back for taunting—

Feathers appeared in her peripheral vision, sending her scurrying to the side of the couch, eyes wide. "Oh my God…" Issac had wings. *Pink* wings. Neon in shade and gaudy and, holy crap, his were worse than hers.

And very fake, he whispered across her thoughts.

They disappeared as Issac rolled to his side on a boisterous laugh.

She pressed her palm to her beating heart. "That… What? How?"

He wiped tears from his eyes as he met her gaze, his smile radiant. "Vision" was all he managed to get out before collapsing in laughter again.

She glowered at him. "You manipulated my sight?"

Issac's responding chuckles were not words of apology. Nor was the amused gleam in his gaze. "Your face…"

"How does my face look now?" she countered, picturing a stake driving through his heart.

He responded by adding wings again and fanning them out around them. She wasn't sure what pissed her off more—the color or the fact that he still looked good despite the fuchsia plumes sticking out around him.

She tackled him against the couch, only to end up in his arms, pinned to a cushion beneath her. "Gabriel, I'm most disappointed in Astasiya's sparring skills. I don't think you were hard enough on her."

Stas arched a brow. "Yeah? How about—"

His lips covered hers before she could unleash a demand.

I can still think one at you, she pointed out.

His tongue slid into her mouth, slowly and purposely. *Mmm, not if I distract you, love.*

Warmth slithered through her veins. *You don't play fair.*

Never with you.

Luc cleared his throat. "Right, so you're saying Osiris is creating an army to fight the Seraphim."

"Specifically, the High Council of Seraph," Stark replied.

"They are the ones who exiled him and continue to issue edicts in regard to taming his behavior. He has no interest in complying and every desire to destroy them. His ultimate goal is to take power over Seraphim kind and humankind alike."

"He's been playing the long game," Luc murmured.

A very long game, indeed, Issac thought, his lips still covering hers. *Shall we rejoin the conversation or continue ignoring them?*

I could mist us upstairs. Maybe.

His smile warmed her mind. *Mmm, I like that idea.*

She almost giggled as he continued kissing her. It made her feel young, alive, *new.* She hadn't acted like this in, well, ever—just letting go, in front of an audience… one that included her brother.

Okay, maybe not.

"Stas…" The familiar male voice sent a jolt down her spine.

You do realize this is the second time in our relationship that Thomas has interrupted my kissing you, yes? Issac released her with a smirk, shifting on the couch and helping her up into a seated position beside him.

An image of the restaurant lobby where she shared her first kiss with Issac flashed behind her eyes in reference to his words. *That hardly counted.*

His eyebrows lifted. *Excuse me?*

The limo was better.

His lips curled. *I did enjoy that dress.*

I know. She finally refocused on Tom, who stood dumbfounded at the edge of the room with a beaming Amelia at his side.

"Hi," Stas greeted lamely. What was one supposed to say after rising from the afterlife? Good to be back? "I'm alive." Was she supposed to stand and hug Tom now? Amelia, too?

Issac's arm fell around her shoulders, making her decision for her. He obviously wasn't ready to stop touching her. She understood because she felt the same way, which she showed by placing her palm on his thigh and relaxing into his side.

"You're alive and a Seraphim," Tom said, awe in his voice. "I'm… It's so good to see you again."

"We're all thrilled you're back with us," Amelia added, tears in her eyes. Stas suspected the emotion was related to her brother in some way.

She's relieved for me, Issac whispered. *I think I worried her.*

It's the mountain-man look, Stas teased. *Scares people.*

He pinched her side. *Careful, Aya.*

Or what?

Or I'll find a clever way to punish you with the scruff. Perhaps between your legs? All that sensitive skin? Could be fun…

Her cheeks heated. *You wouldn't.*

Oh, Aya. You know I would.

"Right. So Stas bonded with Wakefield, which not only grants him full immunity from death but has also reverted him to a horny-teenager phase of being." Alik shrugged. "That's the summary of what you've missed. Oh, and Osiris seems to think we're going to play the roles of good little soldiers in his war against the Seraphim. Which, spoiler alert, will not be happening. Ever."

Tom gaped at the Elder. "I think that's the most you've said to me since you warned me not to hurt Amelia."

Alik glanced at him. "I've not required many additional statements since my first worked so splendidly. Keep up the good work, baby immortal, yeah?" He stood. "Right. Are we going to do anything proactive this evening or just continue talking while Stas and Issac make out? Because the way I see it, Starky Boy here knows how to alter runes. I say he pops on over to the CRF headquarters, does some rearranging of the wards to allow our gifts to work, and then we storm the place and bring Jonathan to justice. Good?"

"Do we even know if he's there?" Tom asked. "And you trust Stark not to double-cross us?" He snorted. "Because I sure as shit don't."

"Better question." Stark relaxed into the couch, the

picture of ease. "What makes you think I would ever desire to help in this scenario?"

"Because you will," Stas replied, not missing a beat. "You'll do it for me."

His brows rose. "I will?"

"You will." She held his light green gaze. "You altered my memory without my permission. You lied to me—repeatedly. And you fucked with my life in countless ways. Because, at this point, I assume my roommate assignment freshman year was a result of your tampering, just like my friendship with Owen was always planned, not fate." She paused to wait for him to deny any of it.

He didn't.

"Okay, so while I can believe you did all of this to enhance my humanity and fulfill some sort of prophecy—that I still do not fully comprehend the goal of, by the way. But anyway, as I was saying, while I can understand your motives, you still betrayed me at every turn. Issac buried me alive because none of us knew my true nature, something you could have told me last year without any impact on who I am today. So don't give me the bullshit that you waited until the right time. The right time was when I joined the CRF. The right time was after I spent an evening at the Conclave. The right time was before I fucking died and was buried alive."

He stared at her. "Would you like an apology?"

"No, Stark. I want you to help us get the bastard who tried to *kill* me. Who killed our friends. Who murdered Issac's Sire—Luc and Amelia's *father*. To take vengeance on the asshole who subjected my best friend through countless years of God knows what kind of torment. Who faked Amelia's death and tortured her for years. I want *you* to help us destroy him and everything he stands for. And you will, if you ever want me to even consider forgiving you for the last two decades of my life." Her hands were fisted in her lap by the time she finished, her breathing harsh with exertion.

And her wings were flickering in her peripheral vision.

Because she'd apparently gone ethereal.

Again.

My wings are still pink.

They're beautiful, love, Issac whispered through her mind. *You're gorgeous.*

Everyone else in the room was blinking in confusion except for Stark, who appeared bored. "We're going to need to work on your emotional ties to the ethereal realm, sister."

She narrowed her gaze. "We're going to need to work on a hell of a lot more than that, *brother.*" She spit the word out like a curse, but he didn't react. No, he remained as unfeeling as ever. Stoic. A man behind a mask of nothing. Stas couldn't even tell if her rant seconds ago had registered.

"All right." Two words. Toneless.

"All right?" she repeated.

"I'll help." He shrugged. "If that's what you want, consider it done."

Stas blinked, surprised he agreed.

And her wings disappeared in a flash.

His lips twitched, causing her breath to catch. An actual facial movement to express amusement? Holy crap.

"It's like walking. You'll get used to it."

"Walking," she repeated slowly, her brain still focused on his display of unexpected emotion. "Uh-huh. Right."

The flicker of a smile disappeared as he addressed Luc. "Apparently, I will be assisting you in this plight. For Stas."

"Liar," Amelia accused, stepping away from Tom. "You may have them all fooled, Gabriel, but I know you care. We have history, you and I."

He glanced at her. "I was only doing my job."

She smiled, moving closer. "As a Sentinel? Or as a guardian angel?"

His lips flattened. Another display of emotion. "You've been talking to Leela."

She sat beside him, still grinning. "I have, and she explained how the messenger line inspired myths of guardian angels. You were mine at the CRF."

He said nothing.

"Is that true?" Tom pressed. "I know you helped heal Amelia. She said you gave her drugs. What else did you orchestrate?"

Stark ignored them both in favor of Alik. "When do we leave?"

"Now?" Alik suggested.

Balthazar chuckled, shaking his head. "Try telling him that out loud."

"He won't listen," Luc muttered in reply. "How many millennia have I attempted to teach him the importance of strategy?"

"About three too many." Alik continued twirling the blade between his fingers, his stance ready near the foot of the stairs. "Come on, *King*. Let's do this. I'm ready to kick some Sentinel ass."

"I see that. And what if Osiris finds out?" he argued. "I'll tell you what will happen—the treaty will be forfeit and we'll go to war. Again. People will die. *Our* people. All because we didn't think this through."

Alik snorted. "According to Starky Boy, Osiris wants us alive to fight the Seraphim. He won't care if we take out Jonathan and his minions."

"Stop calling me Starky Boy."

"Nah, I think I like it."

"Me, too," Tom agreed, waggling his brows. "Starky Boy."

"All right, Fitzy," Stark returned.

Tom stopped smiling. "Fuck that."

"Nah, I think I like it," Stark deadpanned.

Did he just make a joke? she asked Issac.

I believe he did, yes. His astonishment trickled through the bond, rivaling her own. *It seems there's a lot more to your brother than meets the eye.*

No shit.

Alik rubbed his hands together. "All right, what are we

doing? Because if we're not going tonight, then I'm out."

"We're not going tonight," Luc stated flatly.

"Fine. Jacque?" Alik called.

The teleporter appeared in a blink. "'Sup?"

"Let's go." Alik held out his hand. "Call me when you're ready to blow some shit up."

The duo vanished, leaving Luc to sigh in their wake. "One day he'll understand strategy."

"Doubtful," Balthazar replied, patting his friend on the back. "But we can discuss strategy all night. We'll figure this out together."

A long moment passed before Luc nodded. "Yeah." Stas caught a note of sadness in his gaze—there and gone in a flash.

Aidan, she realized, her heart giving a pang. That was who he would usually converse with regarding plans and ideas. But he couldn't. Because his father was dead.

Luc's features hardened as he stood, clearly pushing away the emotions. "You're coming with us, Stark. I need to know as much about these runes as possible. I also want a detailed layout and suggestions for entry."

Stark shifted forward, his elbows on his knees again as he studied Stas. "Think about where you want to go and the ethereal plane will appear to guide you. Similarly, think about being corporeal and you'll become physical again." He stood. "I'll meet you all in Hydria after I check in with Owen." A cloud of red feathers whirled around him as he dissolved into thin air.

"Thanks for the lesson," Stas muttered after him.

Issac brushed his lips against her temple. "Don't worry, darling. We'll figure it out."

"Glad you're confident," she grumbled. Because she certainly wasn't. It seemed her wings only appeared in moments of high emotion. But when she wanted to go ethereal, she didn't.

Luc smiled at her. "It really is good to have you back, Stas."

"Yeah, we missed you," Balthazar added, his expression holding a secret she immediately understood.

You were there for him just as I asked, she thought at him, her mind instinctively opening to his ability.

It was strange. Before, Balthazar had unfettered access to her musings. Now, she had to actively allow him entry, almost as if she'd opened a door and invited him inside. It wasn't tied to her Seraphim genetics but to the bond between her and Issac. As if they'd formed their own cloud of being that no one else could access unless granted entry.

But it worked, as the subtle nod from the mind reader confirmed that he'd heard her.

Thank you, she whispered to him, her heart in her throat. *Thank you for being there for him.*

Another nod, this one accompanied with a small smile.

I can still hear you, Issac murmured, his lips at her temple. *But Balthazar told me your dying wish was for him to be there for me.*

It was. I asked him to say goodbye when I couldn't.

His mouth lingered against her skin, his body shuddering beside her. *Don't ever leave me again, Aya.*

Never, she vowed. *We're in this for always.*

Always, he repeated softly. *For eternity.*

She smiled. *Yes. And apparently, Stark thinks you'll live to regret it.*

Issac snorted. *Never going to happen, love.*

I know. And she did. Because this relationship—this bond—between them ran far deeper than anyone could ever fathom. It shattered all expectations, surpassed any perceived rule, and cemented them together in a connection not of this world.

"So does anyone want any cold pizza?" Balthazar asked. "I have a few boxes."

"We'll pick up a few new boxes on our way to Hydria," Luc said. "We have a lot of planning to do in a short amount of time. I want to use the Stark connection to lure Jonathan out of hiding, preferably sooner rather than later."

"It's a smart play," Issac agreed. "He still assumes

Gabriel is his right-hand man."

"Exactly. Let's use it to our advantage." Satisfaction lit Luc's gaze, his lips curling. "Jonathan's days are numbered."

A round of agreement sounded through the room.

Approval radiated from Luc's expression. "Let's get the bastard."

Chapter Twenty-Nine

Issac

THREE TEAMS.

A-Team—led by Alik.

G-Team—led by Gabriel.

T-Team—led by Thomas.

Each with a different purpose and entry point. Issac and Astasiya were on Gabriel's team with Tristan. Their primary objective was to capture Jonathan alive.

"I've arranged a meeting with him in thirty minutes," Gabriel confirmed, his shoulder braced against the wall of Balthazar's living area. The same wall led into the dining area and open kitchen, providing an oversized room for everyone to fit into. "The wards have also been altered to allow your gifts to function."

"On it." Jacque disappeared in a flash, taking Ash with him. She'd been assigned to Alik's team due to her penchant for playing with fire.

"And you're sure Osiris won't notice?" Lucian asked from his position at the dining room table. He and Balthazar were reviewing the layout—*again*—searching for any last-minute strategic alternatives or potential threats.

"He didn't notice when I changed it after first starting at the CRF. Nor did he notice when I made updates last summer to allow Stas's gifts to flourish underground." He shrugged. "There's no reason for him to check considering he assumes I'm just a human with genetic modifications."

"Wait, you updated the wards so I could compel?" she asked, frowning. "But Issac and I tested the wards before I met with John in June. Before I became a Sentinel."

Issac recalled the afternoon vividly. That was the day he found out about Amelia's captivity, via the camera Mateo had attached to Astasiya's blouse. It was also the day he realized how much he trusted Astasiya.

"Was that test performed above ground?" Gabriel asked.

"In the parking area, yeah."

"Had you tried it in the basement, you wouldn't have been able to persuade. That's a Seraphim's only weakness. We can't access the ethereal realm, the source of our gifts, while underground. Not without proper runes, anyway. Which is why the wards are there to begin with—Osiris needed them to be able to mist in and out of headquarters. I just altered them slightly to grant me the same access, and you."

Her eyes widened. "That's why Mom's trapped."

"Correct. You can't create a ward in water. And she can't mist because she's trapped underwater, way below sea level."

Issac wrapped his arm around Astasiya as she shivered. They both stood next to Gabriel in the living room because the majority of the seating was already taken. Most of those involved in the pending action had gathered in Balthazar's house for the final review of the plan. Alik's team would stir up hell and distract the Sentinels. Thomas's team would handle freeing any hostages or test subjects. Gabriel's team would capture Jonathan.

No deviations.

No arguments.

No offhanded missions.

All strategically planned and driven by Lucian, who expected everyone to return alive. And they would. With Jonathan in tow.

Jacque reappeared near the front door with Ash beside him, his smile radiant. "Checked it out. We're good to roll, people."

A flame flickered in Ash's hand. "This baby worked just as expected."

"Brilliant," Lucian murmured, still reviewing the schematics. "And all the players are where Stark and Tom predicted?"

"Yep," Jacque replied, his lips popping at the end. "Most of the Sentinels are near the armory, guarding the basement entry point. I didn't see Jonathan, but I also wasn't looking for him."

Gabriel shrugged. "He's probably in his office."

"Didn't go near there," Jacque confirmed. "But everything else is ready."

"Good enough for me," Alik said, jumping off the kitchen counter overlooking the dining area. "I'm ready to kick some Sentinel ass."

"Don't kill them all," Lucian reminded him.

Alik cocked his head to the side. "Sorry, what was that? Did anyone else hear bullshit flying about?"

"I certainly did." Tristan sat in the recliner chair, mischief in his gaze. "Sounded something like 'Don't kill the enemy despite everything they've done to deserve it.' Clearly, a misguided edict."

"The goal is to extract Jonathan without raising alarm," Lucian said, sounding exhausted. "Chaos equates to future war. I would like to avoid said war."

"According to Starky Boy, war is inevitable. Why not kick it off early?" Alik tugged on the lapels of his leather jacket. "I'm ready to burn some shit up."

Lucian sighed. "Try to remember that not all of the Sentinels are guilty."

"He's right," Thomas agreed, his arm around Amelia on the couch. "A lot of them have been essentially brainwashed by my father. They don't realize they're being led by an asshole of epic proportions."

Gabriel pushed off the wall, his hands falling to his sides. "Not sure I agree with that assessment, Fitzy."

Thomas narrowed his gaze. "Fuck off, *Starky*."

"Clarify that, Gabriel," Issac said, genuinely curious. "You don't think there are innocent Sentinels?"

"I can name the ones I believe *might* be good men on one hand. The others enjoy killing and haven't bothered to seek the facts. They've just followed the commands because they enjoy them." Gabriel focused on Thomas. "Tell me I'm wrong."

The former Sentinel clenched his jaw. "Some of them are good men."

"How am I supposed to tell the difference?" Alik interjected. "I'm a telepath, not a mind reader."

"That's why I'm on your team," Balthazar said. "I'll let you know if any of them are innocent."

Lucian glanced at him. "I still don't like you going. Doesn't feel right."

Balthazar clapped him on the shoulder. "You're just upset that you have to stay here with Mateo. I've got this."

"He'll be fine," a feminine voice added as purple feathers erupted in the center of the room. Bright, fluttering, gorgeous. But nowhere near as alluring as Astasiya's.

Liar, she breathed into his mind. *Leela's feathers are exquisite. Mine are pink.*

He chuckled, amused that after three days, that was still at the forefront of her thoughts. *Try misting again, darling.*

Maybe they've changed.

If I knew how to mist, I would. But unlike what Stark says, it is not as easy as walking.

Do you remember your first steps? Because perhaps it's similar to that experience, he suggested warmly, brushing his lips against her temple. *Give it time, Aya. You'll figure it out.*

"I'm joining the A-Team," Leela announced as she took on a corporeal form.

Balthazar's eyebrows rose. "Why?"

"My reasons are my own." She cocked a brow at Gabriel as if expecting him to object.

The Seraphim merely shrugged. "If you want to play, then play."

"We could use another being capable of teleportation," Lucian murmured. "Yes, this balances the plan nicely." He started humming as he shifted a series of papers around on the table, his lips curling in triumph. "This increases our odds of success. Thank you, Leela."

"Sure." She touched the hilt of a sword strapped to her hip. "Can we leave soon?"

I think I'm going to like her, Aya mused softly.

Me, too. The Seraphim wasn't stoic like her counterpart. She seemed to have a personality and fire beneath her wings. Were there more like her? Or did her ties to fertility somehow influence her emotions?

"Sweetheart, we can do just about anything you like," Balthazar murmured, his appreciative gaze running over Leela.

Her lips twitched. "You can't even begin to handle me, love. Don't even try."

"According to Stark, your kind requires more handling. Something about pleasure being a selfish need?" He cocked his head to the side. "Where do you fall on the spectrum of experience? Being the fertility goddess and all?"

She sauntered toward him, her blonde hair swaying as she walked, her curves attracting most of the male eyes in the room. One hand went to Balthazar's hip, while the other pressed into his chest to push him up against the wall.

"My experience has over a millennium on yours, Balthazar," she purred. "Trust me, lover. If anyone is going to handle anyone, it will be me handling you." She trailed her nails down his sternum to his abdomen and lower, stopping at his belt. "But not today."

She pushed away, but Balthazar caught her around the waist, yanking her back to him. "We've met before," he said, his gaze searching hers. "Tell me when."

Some of her bravado seemed to fade, her shoulders tightening. *Do you think he recognizes her from the beach?* Issac wondered.

Maybe. But I don't remember her taking corporeal form. Astasiya sounded just as intrigued.

"Your conversation is going to need to wait," Mateo said, entering the room with one of his tablets. "Jonathan's credentials were logged about twenty minutes ago at CRF's headquarters, confirming he's there. There are no cameras for me to grab a visual, so this is the best I can do."

"We have the verbal confirmation that he'll meet Stark as well," Lucian murmured. "It's our best opportunity. Let's take it."

Issac nodded. "I'm ready."

"Me, too," several others said in unison.

"Fucking finally." Alik shook out his arms and rolled his neck. "Ash, Warrior Angel Chick, Balthazar—you're with me. Comms on." He clicked the button inside his ear, initiating the technology Mateo had created specifically for this mission. The earpieces and respective mics would allow them all to communicate in the underground and report back to Lucian and Mateo on Hydria.

"We're not done with this conversation," Balthazar murmured, his palm against Leela's back as he nudged her toward Alik.

She wrapped her palm around the back of his neck and pulled him down into a kiss that silenced the room.

Holy crap, Aya marveled. *She's like…*

A female version of Balthazar, Issac finished for her, equally amazed.

"Consider that the end of the discussion," Leela replied, her teeth snagging on his lower lip. "You're not ready for me yet."

He threaded his fingers through her hair as she tried to step away, his mouth coming down on hers in a practiced move even Issac found impressive.

"I need two new volunteers for my team," Alik announced, glancing around the room. "Anyone?" All the others were already assigned, making no one actually available to join.

"I'm ready, sweetheart," Balthazar said. "And I've definitely kissed you before."

Leela visibly shivered. "Only in your dreams."

"Mmm, no. I remember your mouth—vividly—but can't place the memory. You will tell me. Eventually." He released her with a smile. "Until then, I'll enjoy our flirtatious foreplay."

"Oh, are you two done?" Alik asked, feigning disbelief. "Because I thought we could kill at least another five minutes by fucking about in your living room."

Balthazar gave the slightly shorter male an admonishing look. "I would require more than five minutes to provide a proper demonstration. You know that, Alik."

He snorted. "Can we go now?"

"I've been ready. We're just waiting on you to say the word." Balthazar embodied the picture of innocence, causing Alik to roll his eyes.

"Jacque. I really need to kill something now." He extended his arm, palm up.

"Do not—" Lucian stopped on a growl as Alik disappeared from view, Jacque having already teleported him and Ash from the room. "He's going to kill them all, isn't he?"

"I'll rein him in," Balthazar vowed, holding out his hand for Leela. "Shall we?"

She slid her fingers over his. "Hold on, lover. We're about to go for a ride."

His lips curled. "Oh, I do like you."

"I know," she replied, her violet feathers flickering around them, casting color across the room.

Unreal, Issac thought. In regard to both the feathers and the intense dynamic between Leela and Balthazar.

"We better go before they burn down the CRF," Thomas said, standing with Amelia at his side. "Assuming Jacque is coming back for us?"

"Yep," the teleporter replied, his dark hair windswept and curlier than usual. "Alik's team is already in position. You're up."

"Be careful," Issac murmured, his words for Amelia. She'd been adamant on going, wanting to help free any of Jonathan's test subjects who may have suffered her fate. Issac understood her need for closure, and he trusted the team to aid and protect her as needed.

She smiled. "Tom won't let anyone touch me."

"Damn right," Thomas agreed, his hand holding hers. "Let's go."

"I need to find Nadia," Jacque muttered, glancing around. "Hold on. I think she's with Clara." He disappeared.

"We can't wait on them." Gabriel glanced at his watch. "I'm always early and John knows it."

Issac nodded. "Right, take us to the rally point." The plan was for them to await Gabriel there as he entered the headquarters through normal means.

"Alik's team is in place," Lucian murmured. "Turn on your comms, Wakefield."

Right. Issac touched his ear, initiating the communication device. Astasiya repeated the action, as did Gabriel.

"We're on our way," Issac announced.

"Hurry up" was Alik's terse reply. "I'm already bored."

Gabriel's crimson feathers fanned out around them. He

grabbed a silent Tristan first, then Astasiya and Issac, whirling them all through space and time to the CRF headquarters.

"Ladies and gentlemen, it's time to play," Issac said as they arrived in the hallway.

Chapter Thirty

FLYING WITH STARK FELT WEIRD. Wrong. Like Stas should be able to do it on her own but required training wheels to move. And she severely disliked the sensation. It left her hairs standing on end, even after he disappeared to enter the CRF through normal means. Or maybe it was the basement of the CRF giving her the creeps.

Tristan stood across the corridor, hands tucked into his black trousers, his shoulder braced against the wall. He hadn't looked at or acknowledged Stas since she came back. It was as if he hated her even more, something Issac had also noted. Not out loud, but in his mind.

When they finished this mission, she planned to ask the Ichorian what the hell his problem was with her. She'd done nothing to deserve his treatment, and she no longer posed a threat to his best friend. He had no reason to be such a reclusive jackass.

It's like he's sulking, she muttered, more to herself than to Issac.

Don't worry about him, love. He'll come through when we need him. Trust me.

Trust was the only reason she hadn't requested Tristan be moved to another team. Issac's faith in his progeny was heartfelt and true, and she couldn't help but believe in the man as well. Even if he was acting like an ass.

"Stark just passed through security downstairs," Leela murmured through the comms. Someone had obviously given her a communication set. Likely Balthazar.

Such a strange dynamic between them, one Stas intended to investigate more later. Specifically, she wanted to know why Leela had saved him on the beach that day. And more importantly, why she'd not mentioned it to anyone.

Issac tilted his head to the side and smiled. *Ready, darling?*

You know I am, she replied, returning his grin. They stood in the hallway adjacent to John's office. Tristan masked any sounds associated with their presence, while Issac hid them from view. Not that anyone had ventured this way since their arrival.

Do you sense John?

Issac considered, his lips twisting. *I'm not sure. It's hard to identify everyone in my mind, and there are too many in an office setting right now for me to distinguish his sight from the others.* He provided her with a glimpse into his power, all the "monitors," as he called them, showcasing different scenes, none of them identifiable except those he was attuned to most—like Tristan. As Issac rarely played in Jonathan's mind, he didn't appear to have his frequency identified.

She nodded. *Hopefully, one of them is John.*

"T-Team is on site," Tom said through the comms.

"About fucking time you joined the party," Alik replied.

"I thought we might have to start the show without you."

"Jacque had trouble locating Nadia." From Tom's tone, he was not pleased by the delay. It seemed odd considering everyone else had reported on time.

"Clara was having a breakdown," Nadia muttered, her voice far away and indicating she'd not been given a comm.

Issac grimaced beside Stas. *She's not taken Aidan's passing very well.*

I thought she wasn't really part of their, uh, arrangement? Issac once told her that while Clara lived with Aidan and his harem, she wasn't really a participant in the sexual side of things.

I think she cared for him in a familial sense, like a father.

Yeah, that's not creepy at all, she thought, shivering.

They were hardly intimate, darling. He cupped her face. *It's not a dynamic we will ever choose.*

She leaned into his touch. *Good.*

The heat from Tristan's gaze practically scalded Stas's skin, causing her to glance sideways at the well-dressed Ichorian. Both he and Issac sported dark dress pants and button-down shirts. Very unlike everyone else, who had chosen jeans and casual shirts—like her.

She arched a brow at him, daring him to say something.

He lowered his eyes in response.

Seriously, what is his problem?

I'll talk to him when we return, Issac murmured in her thoughts. *Let's focus on Jonathan for now.*

As if hearing those words, Stark appeared at the end of the hallway. He didn't pause as he passed them, just tilted his head in a way to indicate they should follow.

Stas swallowed. This was it. The moment they'd been waiting for—vengeance. She waited for a lightness to fall over her, some hint of excitement, even a skipping of her heartbeat.

Nothing.

Only a clammy sensation against her palms.

And a twist in her abdomen.

Something… isn't right. She couldn't explain what or how or where the sensation was coming from. It seemed to start in her chest, spreading outward to her limbs, cramping her legs as they walked. *I don't feel a hundred percent.*

Issac slid his hand to her lower back, offering her support. *Talk to me, love.*

It's… I… She couldn't find the words. *Nerves, maybe?* No. That wasn't it. Bile lined the back of her throat, her brow furrowing. *Issac—*

Stark knocked on the door.

Stas grabbed her stomach.

"Come in, Sentinel," Jonathan called, but he sounded eerily far away.

Issac's arm slid around Stas as she swayed, her vision blinking in and out. *I don't like this,* she whispered.

I don't, either, he admitted. *Because I don't sense anyone in that office. Especially not Jonathan.*

She gaped at him. *What?*

I thought I did, but it's not—

Stark pushed open the door.

Beyond it sat an oversized desk with a computer monitor.

And no Doctor Fitzgerald.

No, that wasn't right. Doctor Fitzgerald was there, but not in the way they wanted him.

He grinned up at them from the screen. "Ah, so it's true," he murmured, his lips twitching. "You know, when my source told me you were actually a Seraphim and aiding the Hydraians, I thought it had to be a lie. But seeing Issac and Stas behind you now…" He waved a hand as if to say, *Well, there it is, then.*

The camera on the monitor flashed a little green light their way. And Issac couldn't manipulate a captured image via technology. So yeah, game over. Jonathan could definitely see them.

Stark leaned against the threshold, his posture saying, *I don't give a fuck.*

"Oh, please, all of you, come inside. Sit down. Let's have a chat." Jonathan flashed one of those charismatic grins, one she used to adore and respect and now loathed.

"It's a trap," Stas said. "All of this was a setup."

"What?" Tom asked through the mic. "Wh…" *Crackle.* "…me…?"

Stas glanced at Issac. *Something's interfering with the comms.* And she still felt off, almost weak.

My gift is still functioning. He pressed against her back, nudging her forward. *Let's play along for now.*

"Jonathan," Issac greeted, guiding Stas into the office and to a nearby chair. Stark remained by the door. As did a stone-faced Tristan. "Good to see your face."

"Likewise, Issac." He smiled. "I'm impressed. I honestly didn't suspect you knew the truth all these years. How did you manage to withhold your rage?"

"It's simple," Issac replied, his lips curling. "I imagine the way you will eventually die—by my hand—and it brightens my mood considerably."

"So confident."

"Indeed," Issac agreed. "So, is there a purpose to this diversion? Or should we continue waiting?"

John chuckled. "I've always enjoyed you, Issac. You almost know how to play this game as well as I do. Alas…" He shrugged. "I do hope you had an escape route in mind. The elevators should be closing right about—"

Boom!

The explosion rattled the underground, shaking the equipment on the desk and flickering the lights above. Jonathan's face dissolved into static, the room around them quivering from the aftershocks.

"Shit." Issac was on his feet, and Stark and Tristan were already out the door.

But Stas couldn't stand. Her legs resembled rubber, refusing to work. And fuck, her head *hurt.*

I really don't feel well, she whispered to Issac.

He grabbed her hand, but she hardly felt it. "Aya? Oh,

shit." His touch moved to her forehead, then to her neck. "Gabriel!"

"Some… ong…" The words tasted funny. No, they *sounded* funny. Tasted? Maybe. Hmm.

She glanced around. Everything had gone dark.

Oh, she didn't like this.

The last time she experienced a lack of light, she'd suffocated.

Over and over and over again.

No, thank you.

A tremble rocked through her, followed by a harsh shake that had her eyes flying open to see a pair of sapphire orbs. *So pretty.* She reached out to touch them, but no, they were too far away. Oh, but he had a nice mouth. Saying her name, she thought.

What is wrong with me?

Such a weird dream.

No, reality.

Wait… *Where am I?*

A foreign room surrounded her. Dirt-laden walls, resembling an archaic dungeon apart from the beautiful sky above her. Chains clamped around her wrists. Her legs were encased in cement. And oh, it burned! Yet she kept pouring the scalding liquid into her confined space because it's what *he* told her to do.

She frowned. *Why would I do such a thing? How did I get here?*

Astasiya! The blast ruptured her vision, cascading her into a room encased in windows. The ceiling. The walls. So open. So beautiful. And the scent of the ocean, ah, she loved that.

Stark's house, she recognized. Or the place she'd seen shortly after being pulled out of the ground. Wait… Was this some sort of time loop? Had she just woken up again? *Am I in a nightmare?*

"Here," a familiar voice said. *Owen.*

"Cheers," Issac replied. The scent of coffee drew her attention to the mug in his hand. He held it toward her.

"Drink, Aya."

"Why?" She coughed, the sound coming out hoarse and painful. Fuck, her throat hurt. *How?* She took the cup, sipping the warmth into her mouth and swallowing. *Heaven.* What the fuck had happened? *Where's Jonathan? The CRF?*

"Everyone's fine," Issac assured her. "The mission wasn't a complete wash. But Jonathan destroyed his own building."

Her eyes widened. "What?" Her voice came out slightly more normal.

"He detonated the lobby, causing the building to collapse. It's honestly a miracle we all escaped alive. But you were knocked out." He touched her temple. "One of the ceiling panels fell on your head."

She blinked, not remembering anything other than the explosion and everything going dark.

And the really weird nightmare about cement.

Stas shivered. "And everyone…?"

"They're all fine. Amelia and Thomas were in the process of freeing some former Sentinel from a cage when the building collapsed. Jacque teleported the T-Team back to Hydria. Gabriel took us here. And Leela—"

"Decided to give us a vacation," Alik finished for him. "A-Team is on the beach. Well, except Balthazar. He's with Luc." He shrugged. "I opted to stay here. Gives me the opportunity to kick Owen's ass a few times before Luc grants him immunity."

"*If* he grants me immunity," Owen muttered. "He might not."

"He shouldn't," Ash said from the doorway. "You broke the vow."

Stas glanced between them, her head still pounding. "What vow?"

"Unspoken agreement to honor the Elders and your fellow Hydraians. Always." Owen had the grace to look sheepish. "When I agreed to help Ezekiel and Gabriel, I went behind Luc's back. It's seen as a betrayal, even if I did it for the right reasons."

Ash snorted and walked through the open glass doors.

"Yeah, everyone hates me," Owen mumbled. "Honestly, I'm not all that eager to go back right now."

"They'll come around," Alik replied. "After you let us kick your ass a few times." He clapped the guy on the shoulder and sauntered off to the kitchen, where Tristan stood nursing a beer.

"Where's Stark?" Stas asked, completely at a loss for her surroundings. She was lying down. On a couch. Using Issac's thigh as a pillow. If she kept losing time and space like this, she might just lose her mind.

"He's sulking upstairs." Owen collapsed on the chair beside her. "Stark isn't one for visitors, and his property is overrun with guests right now."

"We won't be here for long," Issac murmured, brushing Stas's hair away from her face. "Once Astasiya is feeling better, we'll return to—"

Alik swore.

Issac tensed.

And Ezekiel appeared in the center of the room, panting. "Stark!" he shouted, his eyes wild. "Stark!"

"I'm here." Stark's red feathers flickered in the incoming light. "What is it?"

"It's Sethios," Ezekiel breathed. "Osiris... *Fuck*. Osiris is... he's... he's killing Sethios."

Chapter Thirty-One

"JONATHAN HAS AN INFORMANT WORKING on the inside." Luc sat at the head of the table, his hands clasped over the CRF's worthless schematics. The entire fucking building had collapsed. All those people—dead.

A terrorist attack, according to the media.

Tom shuddered. His father was an evil son of a bitch—a selfish bastard who cared nothing about innocent lives. Tom's jaw threatened to break from him clenching it so hard. *When I get my hands on him…*

"We knew this after the wedding but thought it might be a lower-ranking Hydraian," Luc continued. "We now know that isn't the case. Only a handful of people knew about our operation at the CRF today—something we kept secret on purpose. And Jonathan still knew. It's the only explanation for the trap, as well as his knowledge of Stark being a Seraphim."

Tom agreed, frustrated that their plan went up in flames. At least he and Amelia were able to save one of the research subjects. All the others were undoubtedly destroyed by the collapsing building.

His hands tensed on the table, furious at his father's actions and even angrier at whoever had betrayed them. Too many lives lost. Friends, and employees Tom had likely met or smiled at in passing, were all *dead.*

Alik reported that only a handful of Sentinels were left to guard the entry. Which meant those bastards knew what John intended to do and left all those people to die. That, or he'd given them all an assignment out of office. But Tom very much suspected the former. Those men didn't have souls.

And they're supposed to be humanitarian aid soldiers.

"Who do you suspect?" Jay prompted, his dark eyes holding a hint of exhaustion. Lizzie's pregnancy was escalating quickly, leaving the Elder concerned for her health. Many of them shared his worry, but if anyone would survive it, it would be Lizzie Watkins. That woman was resilient to her core.

Balthazar shook his head. "Both seem unlikely." He'd clearly overheard the names from Luc's thoughts. It was only the four of them in the dining area of B's house. Everyone else had been excused, except for Amelia, but she had chosen to check on Lizzie instead of staying for the meeting.

"Who?" Jay demanded.

Luc leaned forward. "Nadia and Tristan."

Balthazar shook his head. "I just don't see it, Luc."

"Think about it, B. They were both in Athens during the attack—"

"As was Alik," he interjected.

"Yes, because they asked him to go out with them. And

we know it wasn't him."

"I know, but I'm saying, I don't think it's Nadia. Or Tristan, either. It doesn't feel right."

"Then explain Tristan's behavior of late. And Nadia—what the fuck was that earlier?" Luc asked, his tone lacking his usual patience. "She didn't show up at the required time. She half-assed her participation, according to Tom's report, and she's been incredibly distracted. She also used to be friends with Jonathan."

All true and fair points. But Tom somewhat agreed with Balthazar that it didn't feel right. Tristan was too obvious a choice. He might be an ass, but he clearly cared about Wakefield. All his actions, even the darker ones, served a purpose of supporting his Sire. What motive did he have to aid John? Other than maybe his jealousy over Wakefield's relationship with Stas, but that couldn't be morphed into a need for revenge. At least, not on a logical level.

And Nadia, well, her emotions seemed to be fucking with her ability to focus. Tom didn't know the woman well, but he gathered from her less-than-stellar performance that she had a lot on her mind. Maybe she'd known about the impending attack and worried for her life, but he didn't get that read from her. She just seemed sad.

"By that account, we're all suspects, Luc," Balthazar pointed out. "Because we also used to be friends with Jonathan."

"But she was closer to him. Tristan, too."

"And Clara," Balthazar added. "If you're going to accuse Nadia, then you have to accuse Clara as well."

Luc sighed. "That woman is broken over my father's death. You said it yourself."

"Yes, as is Nadia, whom I also mentioned in that conversation."

"Fine." Luc ran his fingers through his hair. "Then who do you think is responsible? Because someone—someone close to us, to our movements—is feeding information to Jonathan. Only a handful of people knew about today's mission, and Clara wasn't one of them."

"Unless Nadia told her," Tom murmured. "That's where Jacque found her."

Luc heaved another deep breath. "I've narrowed it down to who it's not—the four of us, Alik, Amelia, Stas, and Wakefield are definitely not involved."

"Leaving Stark, Ezekiel, Leela, Mateo, Jacque, and Ash as possible suspects as well," Balthazar surmised. "That's everyone who definitely knew about our plans today. Plus, Tristan and Nadia."

"It's not Jacque or Ash," Luc said, confident. "Ezekiel?"

Tom sat up straighter, his shoulders tensing. "Yeah, where was he when the building exploded? He knew about the plans but didn't volunteer to help."

"He had to report back to Osiris," Luc said.

"Which is rather convenient." Tom scratched his jaw, considering everything he knew about the notorious assassin. "He's proven to be working against Osiris, yet he always crawls back to the bastard like a loyal lapdog. Do we know why?"

"When I asked him, he claimed Osiris has his heart." Balthazar folded his arms, his biceps bulging beneath his T-shirt. "I'm not sure what that means, but I suspect he's referring to Skye."

"The prophetess?" Tom asked, recalling the name. He'd only heard it a few times in passing, always in regard to Stas's future. "Is she, like, a seer?"

"I believe she's an Ichorian with the ability to see future outcomes," Luc replied. "Stark mentioned she's a descendant of the Fates. Apparently, all our abilities—both Ichorian and Hydraian alike—can be linked to one of the Seraphim bloodlines. There are hundreds of them."

"And where are they?" Tom prompted. "We've only met two, three if you include Stas."

"They have an entire society in the South Pacific that is hidden from view by wards." Intrigue deepened Luc's voice. "It's fascinating."

"And completely off topic," Jay grumbled, running a hand over his tired face. "Look, as much as I would love to learn more about the Seraphim, now isn't the time. As far as Ezekiel is concerned, everything that man does in some way benefits himself, and I really don't see how tattling to Jonathan benefits him in the slightest. Also, let's not forget that whoever the culprit is informed Jonathan that Stark's a Seraphim, something Jonathan clearly did not know until this week. Why would Ezekiel expose Stark now after keeping his confidence for over twenty-five years?"

The man had a point. "He could be playing the long game," Tom said. "But I agree; it doesn't seem to benefit him."

"Unless Osiris is compelling the truth from him," Luc suggested. "However, in terms of betrayal, neither Ezekiel nor Stark makes much sense. And by association, I'd rule out Leela as well."

"It's not Leela," Balthazar said, certain. "I'd bet my life on that."

"You're slightly clouded considering your obvious interest in the female, but I'm inclined to agree here," Luc murmured. "Which brings us back to Mateo, Nadia, and Tristan. As Mateo was literally with me the entire time, I don't see it being him."

"Unless he sent an electronic communication that we couldn't hear or see." Technology allowed for all manner of innovation, something Tom knew well from his time at the CRF. "The comms did go bad as well," he added.

Luc shook his head. "He explained all that to me. It had something to do with the detonation interfering with radio signals. I really don't think he's working with Jonathan."

"He's never done anything suspicious, has always helped Wakefield and us when we asked, and is also too young to have any positive ties to Jonathan." Balthazar relaxed in his chair. "Not him."

"Agree," Jayson said. "Leaving Nadia and Tristan, as Luc said. And maybe Clara."

Silence fell over the table, all of them contemplating how to proceed. Alik had purposely stayed with his team at Stark's place so he could keep an eye on Tristan, aware that Luc questioned the man's loyalties. Nadia was with Clara again.

"Someone needs to keep an eye on Nadia," Tom said.

Nods around the table.

"I can do it," Balthazar murmured. "The girls trust me. I can also monitor their emotions and thoughts, listen for anything out of the norm."

Luc inclined his head in agreement. "Meanwhile, we need to narrow down Jonathan's potential locations."

"Uh." Mateo cleared his throat from the living area, having apparently entered while they were all deep in discussion. "Yeah, about that, I have his location."

All four of them turned toward the voice, shock rolling over all of them except Balthazar. The latter nodded at Mateo, clearly having heard his thoughts upon approach.

A little heads-up next time, yeah? Tom thought at him.

Balthazar merely shrugged, unapologetic.

"I know you said not to disturb you, and, yeah, I get why now, but… I, uh, thought you'd want to know that I found him." Mateo swallowed. "So, should I show you, or am I still on the potential mole list?"

Luc sighed. "We know you're not the mole, Mateo."

"Good. Right. Of course." Another clearing of the throat. "'Cause I could show you proof that I'm not, if you needed me to. And I've never much liked Jonathan. So if you need some evidence to the contrary or anything, just—"

"Mateo, we know you're not the mole," Luc repeated, authority ringing in his voice. "Now tell us what you've found."

"Cool. Yeah." He stepped timidly into the room and set his laptop on the table. "He's in Upstate New York, in a place—"

Tom cursed, immediately recognizing the location on

the screen. "Of course. I should have known. That fucker." He shoved away from the table and began pacing, his hands in his hair. "I'm going to throttle him. That's Rosalie's house."

"Rosalie?" Balthazar repeated. "Like your former aunt?"

"One and the same." His father had used her to lure him out of hiding once, only to reveal that Rosalie had worked with him the entire time. The poor woman had believed his father's lies and had paid the ultimate price—with her life. And now it seemed the asshole was using her house as a safe haven. "You're positive he's there? That it's not another trap?" Because it almost seemed too obvious.

"I tracked the communication from his office to this address. He routed through several locations first, enough to mask his whereabouts from most sufficient hackers. But I'm good." Mateo smiled. "Actually, I'm the best."

"What were some of the other locations?" Luc asked slowly. "Can you list them?"

"Uh, yeah, of course. But he's not there."

"I understand that, but I might have an idea."

"Okay." Mateo scrolled through his computer and listed over a dozen physical sites the message pinged before finally connecting at the CRF headquarters.

"Do you recognize any of those places, Tom?" Luc asked.

Tom nodded. "Several. The one in the Caribbean is a property he owns. I'm pretty sure the same goes for that address in Arizona, too. Also, the Calgary location, as well as the Munich condo, are known CRF safe houses."

"Which one would you find more plausible for him to be at? Hypothetically, I mean."

"Any of them," Tom replied. "Although, the CRF safe houses would be more likely because his estates are too easily found. And he'd have access to weapons and potential personnel at those locations." Assuming he hadn't killed everyone involved with the CRF.

Amelia and Tom had only been able to help one person

escape alive—Blake. Luc assigned the unconscious male to the same cell Tom had occupied only a few months ago after helping Amelia reunite with her family.

They had no way of knowing what kind of mental condition Blake was in yet. However, John Fitzgerald's penchant for psychological torture made it safe to assume the former Sentinel was not in great shape.

"I like that," Balthazar murmured, responding to something in Luc's thoughts. "It's a good test of faith."

Luc scratched his jaw. "We tell Tristan we're heading to Calgary to catch Jonathan. Then we give Nadia the Arizona address, but switch it up to Munich last-minute."

"While allowing her enough time to notify Jonathan," Balthazar added.

"Exactly," Luc agreed. "Assuming he's set traps like he did at headquarters, we can base the findings on whichever one implodes."

"And if he didn't arrange anything?" Mateo asked, causing Tom to shake his head.

"Not my father's style. He loves a good game of cat and mouse. I can guarantee he's set traps at all those locations, but he'll only be monitoring one—the one he suspects is about to go up in flames. Because he'll want to admire his handiwork."

Luc grinned. "Meanwhile, we'll sneak up on the cat while he's on the prowl." He rubbed his hands together. "All right, Alik will lead the team with Tristan because he's probably the only one who can subdue him if he's our culprit. Jay and B, I want you to team up with Ash to manage Nadia. Then Fitzgerald, Wakefield, and I will get Jonathan."

"Amelia, too," Tom said, adamant. "She's earned her spot on this team, and I go nowhere without her." If anyone had earned the right to exact vengeance, it was Amelia. No way would Tom ever take that opportunity away from her. "She's coming. And I imagine Stas will want in as well."

"All right," Luc replied. "But I'm counting on you to keep my sister safe."

"She doesn't need me to do that," he replied, smiling. "The woman is a natural sharpshooter." His heart warmed at the thought. His little asset had blossomed into quite the warrior—a total turn-on in the bedroom, too.

Balthazar cleared his throat. "Going to cut you off right there, Fitzgerald. Got it. She can handle herself. Done. Moving on."

Tom smirked. "I never thought you would be such a prude, B."

"Do you want Luc to punch you, Tom?" he countered. "Because he will. A single mention of what you want to do to his little sister and—"

"Understood," Tom interjected. "Weren't we discussing a tactical plan?"

Balthazar grinned, his gaze saying, *That's what I thought.*

"I was about to suggest we call Wakefield," Luc said, completely unfazed by the conversation.

"Tristan will overhear the discussion," Mateo warned.

"Yes, I already have a way around that," Luc said, playing with his phone. "All right. Tom, go find Amelia and inform her of the plans. Jayson, go love on your wife for a bit. She needs it. Balthazar will brief Ash. And, Mateo, we need separate communication devices and frequencies for each group. Oh, and keep an eye on Jonathan. If that bastard moves, I want to know immediately. Meanwhile, I'll handle Wakefield."

"Good luck," Balthazar said softly. "He's not going to take your accusation lightly."

Luc gave him a grim expression. "I know, but right now, Tristan's actions prove him to be the guiltiest suspect."

"For what it's worth, I don't think it's him," Mateo said quietly. "But I'll look into all their phone records to see if I can find anything telling."

"Good." Luc glanced around, his expression stern. "This goes without saying, but Jonathan's location stays between us."

Everyone at the table voiced their agreement.

Luc stood. "All right. The bastard played us once. Now it's our turn. And I refuse to lose twice."

The energy in the room darkened, all the Elders craving John's blood. He'd hurt too many people, including loved ones of those in the room. Tom's father deserved this fate.

He's a monster.

A terrorist.

A cruel manipulator.

But he's also my father.

Tom glanced out the window, his fingers curling into fists in his lap. He hated John Fitzgerald for all that he'd done. But a small, minute voice kept reminding Tom that he wouldn't be here today had John not created him.

He sent me to military school.

He constantly tested my abilities by almost having me killed.

He crafted me into the perfect weapon—for his own personal use.

He hurt Amelia. Tortured her for years. Mercilessly.

The list was endless, each point digging a deeper grave for the man who fathered Tom. There were no redeeming qualities, no reason for John to be kept alive.

But would kidnapping and torturing the monster make any of them feel better? It wouldn't change history. Sure, an outlet for everyone's rage might help temporarily.

Alas, wouldn't tormenting someone change a person on a psychological level? Was that how John started down this path? And if Tom participated in his father's persecution, would it drive him down the same path? Clearly, the malevolent genes lurked within him somewhere. What if these actions brought that side of him to the forefront?

Tom shivered. *I don't want to become my father.*

A hand landed on his shoulder, Balthazar's intense gaze yanking him from his thoughts. "You won't."

Tom blinked. The others had already left for their tasks, leaving the two of them alone in the dining area. "Oh, sorry. I sort of—"

"Do you remember the first time you took a life?" Balthazar interjected, his hand keeping Tom seated even as he tried to stand.

A memory from Tom's childhood sent a chill down his spine. "Yes." He recalled the incident vividly, the way his father taunted him into pulling the trigger, the churning in Tom's gut after the body fell lifeless to the floor. "I didn't even know the man's name. Or why."

"But you mourned the life you took afterward, right?"

"I always do," Tom replied, his throat constricting around each word.

He always tried to avoid death when he could, just incapacitating the individual for long enough to escape. But on occasion, there was no other alternative. And even when those beings deserved their fates, Tom still grieved their passing.

"It's what keeps me human," he added, recalling a similar conversation he had with Amelia after she killed Doctor Patel a few months ago. *It's when you start enjoying the kill that you have something to be concerned about,* "he'd told her.

"And that's where you and Jonathan are different," Balthazar said quietly. "He enjoys hurting others. You do not."

"But I'm his son. What if that part of him is in me somewhere?"

"I've overheard enough of your memories to know what your father did to you as a child. And yet, you survived all that with your heart intact. You know what that tells me, Tom?"

He swallowed, shaking his head slowly. Thinking about his history churned his stomach, especially the upbringing Balthazar referenced. Tom preferred to avoid the topic, only mentioning it when the experience was relevant. Or when Amelia asked him something specific.

"It tells me that your mom is just as much a part of you as Jonathan is. It tells me that you're a good person, Tom." He squeezed Tom's shoulder and released him. "Unlike your father, you value love and family. Use that to empower you. I know you've been raised your entire life feeling like you didn't belong anywhere, but you do belong here. You're one of us. Allow our knowledge and guidance to sharpen your future, not your relation to a soon-to-be dead man."

Tom sat, stunned. He hadn't realized how much he needed to hear that until Balthazar said it.

I belong here.

His father constantly taunted him that he would never be accepted anywhere, not by the Hydraians and definitely not by the Ichorians. However, not only had the Elders proven his dad wrong but they'd also allowed Tom into the/their inner circle. They trusted him. This meeting today proved that—they'd included *him* because they valued his opinion and experience. And sure, it was mainly because he knew the most about John, but they also listened to him. They treated him as an equal, not an informant or a weapon, but an actual being of importance.

"Thank you," Tom said, some of the tension leaving his limbs.

Balthazar nodded. "Anytime." He started to leave, then paused on the threshold of the living area, turning back to meet his gaze. "And if you don't want him to be tortured, Tom, then kill him. The others will get over it. Because if anyone has earned the right to deliver Jonathan's judgment, it's you."

Chapter Thirty-Two

EZEKIEL PACED, knives twirling dangerously in his hands. "Skye had a prophecy," he explained. "She predicted Sethios's death by Osiris's hand."

"That's impossible," Gabriel replied calmly. "Seraphim don't die, and Sethios has to be fully transitioned by now."

"Well, her prediction says otherwise," Ezekiel replied, wild energy pouring off him in waves. "And I can't find him anywhere on the property."

"It has to be a misunderstanding." Gabriel studied him. "What exactly did Skye say?"

"'One power falls as another rises' was her exact phrase. Then she blinked and told me Osiris was going to kill

Sethios. I tried to find him to warn him, but he's nowhere to be found. And the only way he could have left is if Osiris compelled him to."

Astasiya stiffened beside Issac, an image of a gravesite flashing through her thoughts. *What is that?* he asked, studying the vision.

The nightmare I just had while knocked out, she breathed into his mind. *You don't think it's my dad, do you? Like how my mom has projected to me from under the water?*

Show me again.

More detail came through this time, the dirt siding and a pale blue sky. Some of Astasiya's emotions trickled through with it as well, including a deep-seated need to pour cement over her limbs. He flinched at the sensation, causing her to pull back.

Was that part of your dream? he wondered. *That compulsion?*

She nodded, shivering. *It felt… real.*

He opened his mouth to comment, but a buzzing in his pocket caught him off guard. "It's Lucian," he said. "I need to take this."

Tristan perked up from the kitchen, his ability to control sound allowing him to hear the call. Issac nodded his approval, knowing his best friend would want to be apprised of the Jonathan situation as well.

"Tell him I'm bored and in need of something to destroy," Alik requested from the dining area.

Ignoring him, Issac answered the call. "Lucian. Ezekiel just arrived with news of another prophecy. It appears Sethios's life is in jeopardy."

"Seraphim can't die," he replied, echoing Gabriel's sentiments.

"It seems Osiris may have found a way around it," Issac said, eyeing the pacing assassin. Those knives in Ezekiel's hands were a little too close to Astasiya for Issac's comfort.

"Unlikely," Gabriel said, shaking his head. "It doesn't make sense. You can dismantle a Seraphim and put him underground to cut off his access to the ethereal realm, but he'll never die. The soul always finds a way back to the host."

Astasiya grabbed Issac's knee, squeezing. "I think that's what Osiris has done," she breathed, her nightmare replaying again.

Ezekiel stopped moving. "What do you mean?"

"I... I had a nightmare, or a vision, while unconscious about a grave and pouring cement into it because... because someone told me to." She shuddered. "It... it felt like when Mom talks to me." The words came out on a whisper, her focus on Gabriel. "But I think, maybe... maybe it was my dad?" *Do you think that's why I felt so off at the CRF headquarters, Issac? Is that where the dread came from?*

You've never experienced that with your mom, have you?

She shook her head. *No. But maybe he—*

"Where were you in the dream?" Ezekiel demanded, cutting her off. "Describe it to me."

"I-I don't know. I was already in the grave, with only the sky above me."

"Daylight? Night?" Ezekiel pressed, his panic tangible.

Issac located the assassin's mind and took control of his visual receptors to display the image Astasiya had shared. The man stumbled as a result, catching the back of a chair to stabilize himself near one of the open windows. He shook his head as if to clear it.

"What the fuck is that? What just happened?"

"You're seeing the location from Astasiya's nightmare," Issac replied, showing every detail he recalled from her vision—the dirt, the sky, the sun. Even the cement pooling in the ground below.

"How is that possible?" he asked, his breathing hitching. "I've seen enough. Turn it off."

"Of course." Issac released Ezekiel's vision, allowing him to see in the present again.

"It's the bond," Gabriel said. "The rune Osiris gifted you only protects you from his creations, of which Issac no longer qualifies. He's of the Seraphim realm now."

"Fascinating," Lucian said into his ear. "Your power is already growing."

"Indeed," Issac murmured, switching the phone between his hands so he could wrap his arm around Astasiya. She trembled against him, her father's name repeating in her mind with a series of questions and scenarios. "Can you provide me with a quick update on Jonathan?" Issac asked, needing to return his focus to the woman at his side.

"Fuck Jonathan," Ezekiel interjected before Lucian could reply. "We have to find Sethios. Right now."

Gabriel shook his head. "We need Stas and she isn't ready. She can't even mist yet."

"Then fucking teach her," Ezekiel snapped, his calm veneer disappearing into a heated wave of scalding emotion. "I've watched my best friend suffer for almost two decades, and I vowed that I would protect him. Now Skye has prophesized that he's going to die. I can't just sit back and wait. I'm done working at your pace, Gabriel. I've done everything you've asked, and I'm calling in all my favors today. Sethios needs us. He needs us *now*."

"He's right," Leela added, appearing in the doorway. "We've all done this your way, and while I agree that Stas has been raised adequately as a result, it's time to rescue Sethios."

"It sounds like there's a lot going on over there," Lucian said quietly.

Issac eyed the assassin glowering at a still-stoic Gabriel. "Understatement."

"Then I'll be quick. Mateo just sent you a message that might be of use. Do me a favor and read it." The casual way Lucian spoke had Issac's curiosity piquing. The Hydraian King didn't throw words around lightly. He always possessed a motive or a strategy of some kind.

"One moment," Issac replied, eyeing the screen. The messages weren't from Mateo but from Lucian.

Don't outwardly react, the first one read.

We discussed the mole situation and have narrowed it down to two culprits, potentially three. And you're not going to like our findings.

Issac typed back, *Tell me.*

Based on timing and knowledge, Tristan is our primary suspect. Nadia and Clara are also potentials.

Issac read the message four times before the words resonated. They were accusing most of the Ichorians currently residing in Hydria. Ichorians who had been friends and allies for decades, if not centuries.

And Tristan?

No bloody way.

Issac knew his progeny better than anyone else. The man was his best friend. He glanced at him now, a note of concern touching his features. He'd obviously caught the request and wondered at the notes on the screen. Tristan was an ass, but not daft. He had to know Lucian meant to convey a message that he couldn't overhear. And the hint of sadness creeping into his expression confirmed it.

They all knew there was an informant among them. Tristan had been playing this game with Issac for a long time; he, out of anyone, would know what a secret message meant—a removal from the inner circle. It implied a lack of trust, something his progeny had done nothing to earn. Apart from being a bit rude lately.

It's not Tristan, Issac replied, refocusing on his phone. *He's loyal to a fault.*

"I'll be outside," his progeny informed him flatly, his shoulders stiff as he walked out the door. Alik followed him without a word, but Issac knew it wasn't to talk to him. No. Lucian had assigned the Elder to watch the suspect, something Tristan would discern immediately.

Fuck. Because Issac needed another problem to deal with at the moment.

His phone buzzed with the response.

We have an idea to test loyalties. Alik's already been briefed. He and Tristan are headed to Calgary. Nadia is being told another address but will be taken to a third. And we have Jonathan's actual location, which is the real reason I called.

Issac's heart skipped a beat. "You're certain?" he asked out loud, the phone already at his ear again.

"Positive," Lucian replied. "We leave in thirty minutes."

Astasiya's nails dug into his thigh, grabbing his attention. *They found Jonathan*, he told her.

I've been following along, she whispered back to him. *And I don't know if you heard, but Stark just agreed to help Ezekiel find my father. They want to leave. Now.*

Issac lifted his gaze, realizing he'd tuned out the entire conversation around him.

"…estate?" Gabriel asked, the initial part of the question lost to the harsh cadence beating in Issac's ears. They had another opportunity to grab Jonathan, to finally make that bastard pay. He needed to leave now if he wanted to join them, to finally see his revenge come to fruition.

"That's where he was last," Ezekiel replied.

"Then that's where we'll start." Gabriel focused on Astasiya. "You're not ready to face Osiris, but we can't do this without you. You're the only one with the power to break Sethios's compulsion."

Her lips parted, shock trickling through their connection. "B-but I don't even know how to mist or even how to properly persuade. The last time I faced Osiris, we only won because he walked away."

Which now made a hell of a lot of sense knowing that Osiris wanted the Hydraians and Ichorians to fight on his side of a war against the Seraphim. Destroying the Elders would have removed some of the most powerful pawns from the board. Osiris needed them alive. Astasiya, too.

"The power is in there; you just have to let it out," Leela said softly.

"And you expect me to do that by going up against Osiris?" she squeaked, her body tense beneath Issac's arm. *Have they lost their minds? I can't do this, Issac. I… I want to, but this is insane.*

If anyone can do it, love, it's you, he assured her, meaning it.

You were born for this, Aya. You're the most powerful being I've ever met.

Aside from Osiris, she corrected. *Or has everyone in this house forgotten him?*

Not all strength is measured in supernatural ability. You have love, darling. Osiris only has ego. He brushed her racing pulse with his thumb. *You can do this, love. I know you can.*

She shook beside him, doubt and incredulity clouding her aura.

"Issac?" Lucian's voice reminded him of the phone in his opposite hand. He'd completely forgotten the task at hand when Astasiya reached for him, her need trumping everything and everyone else without cause.

"My apologies," Issac said, resituating the device against his ear. "The conversation here distracted me. Your information is intriguing, though I question the accuracy." Meaning the bit about whom they suspected.

He trusted Tristan implicitly.

Also, Nadia and Clara were family. Issac could not see either of them turning on Aidan. Of course, he didn't know them as well anymore, having spent the better part of the last decade building his presence in New York City. A presence that had all but halted over the last month. Fortunately, he had a protocol in place for prolonged absences that kept his company in working order.

"We'll know more about the accuracy of our information soon," he replied. "That said, we need to move on the information. Are you in or are you out?"

Issac glanced at Gabriel and Leela before looking to Astasiya. Even terrified, he knew what decision she would make. Sethios was her father. Her loyalty would never allow her to let him down, even if she felt unprepared. The only reason she hesitated now was because her previous decisions on similar situations had ended badly. He could hear the concern in her thoughts—if she acted impulsively again, it might evolve into another horrendous outcome, and she refused to lose or hurt *him*.

He sighed.

She wasn't the only one left without a choice, because he could never allow Aya to enter a dangerous situation without him by her side.

"I'm needed here, Lucian," Issac said quietly, his decision already made. When it came to supporting Astasiya or fulfilling his need for vengeance, he would always select the former. They were a team. Always. And for eternity. "I'm sorry."

"Given the circumstances, I understand and admire your resolve. But, Issac?"

"Yes?"

"Try not to get yourself killed. We need you alive."

Issac grinned. "Didn't you hear, Lucian? I'm invincible now."

He snorted. "Don't let that bullshit go to your head." A pause. "Seriously, be safe. I need you, brother."

"Likewise, Lucian. Good luck."

"Not needed. You know I don't lose without purpose." Lucian hung up, sending through a message right after that read, *I'll send you the outcome as soon as I know.*

It's not Tristan, Issac returned, certain.

I hope you're right.

Issac didn't need hope. He knew without a doubt that Tristan would never betray him.

"They've found Jonathan," Issac said, pocketing his phone. "Alik and Tristan are needed in Hydria."

"I can take them," Leela replied. "I need to pick up something anyway." She looked meaningfully at Gabriel.

He nodded. "Yes. It's time."

"Good." She glanced at Ezekiel. "You go back to the estate, see what you can find. Try to talk to Skye again, if you can. I'll meet you on the perimeter in sixty minutes."

"You want me to go sit on my thumbs," he translated.

"We can't mist in until the wards are altered." Gabriel glanced at Leela. "I'll take Stas with me so she can at least see how it's done, then we'll wait for you before we enter."

"You'll be taking me as well," Issac informed him. "I go wherever Astasiya goes."

Astasiya shivered. "Yeah, but I don't even recall agreeing."

"You're the only one who can break Osiris's compulsion over Sethios because of your familial bond to him, Stas," Gabriel explained. "Without you, we have no guarantee that Sethios will even be able to leave with us."

Owen walked in holding what appeared to be a scotch and sat in the recliner closest to Astasiya. "Do you remember that professor from our junior year who started class the first day without a syllabus and just expected us all to know what the fuck was going on?"

Astasiya stared at him. "What?"

"I'll meet you at the perimeter near the tree line, Gabe," Leela said quietly, disappearing.

And there goes Tristan. Issac sighed. He'd follow up with his progeny after the others dealt with the Jonathan situation. Because he would be proven innocent. Issac was certain of it.

Ezekiel nodded at Gabriel and vanished without a word, the plan already defined between them.

If Owen noticed everyone departing, he didn't show it. "That jackass who asked you about the reading that we didn't even know we were assigned, then proceeded to call you lazy for not being prepared?"

Astasiya frowned. "Of course, I remember that. I wanted to punch him."

Owen nodded. "So that jackass is like Stark here. He doesn't have time for a proper introduction or a course guide, mostly because he dillydallied in getting you the course notes, right? But he needs you to take an exam today. And your entire grade will be affected by the results."

"That's not helping me feel better."

"Then I'll put it another way." He set down his untouched drink. "If there's one thing I've learned, it's that Skye's prophecies usually come to fruition. So if you don't get over this lack of confidence—and soon—then your father is going to die. Either you help him or you don't. You dictate his fate."

She glowered at him. "Really not helping."

"Just sayin' it like I see it, Sassy." He relaxed, resting one ankle over his opposite knee.

"You're making me want to punch you now," she retorted. "Which you more than deserve for faking your own fucking death."

He shrugged. "Honestly? I'm not worried. I mean, given this pathetic mood you seem to have fallen into, I doubt it'll hurt much."

She gasped. "Excuse me?"

Issac tightened his grip, more to give his hands something to do than to hold Astasiya back. She wasn't the only one suddenly fancying a bit of violence. *Pathetic mood?* That was a bit harsh and unnecessary.

"What? You're over there moping instead of being proactive. What happened to the sassy woman I knew a year ago? The one who compelled that jackass professor to trip over his feet three times during our first lecture?"

Okay, now that made Issac's lips twitch. Astasiya recalling the memory didn't help since it played vividly through his mind.

"I did not!" she exclaimed, but her thoughts proved that to be a lie. It seemed she'd chalked it up to coincidence but was now realizing the truth.

Naughty student, Issac teased.

Ughhhhhh was her reply.

He snorted. "Yes, you did. I heard you muttering under your breath."

A rose colored her cheeks. "He tripped of his own accord."

"Bullshit. *You* did that. You're a hell of a lot more powerful than you realize. Which, I mean, clearly, since you're too afraid to help your father."

Ah, so that was the point of Owen derailing the

conversation. He was trying to motivate Astasiya. Issac relaxed, approving.

"I don't see you volunteering to come with us," she muttered.

"If I thought I could be of any use, I would. And I don't even like Sethios. Yet, I would go because he's your father. I would do it for *you*." He cocked his head to the side. "The question is, can you put aside the nerves and do what feels right? Because the Stas I know would never hesitate to help those who needed her. You risked your life by befriending Wakefield, and yes, you did it to learn more about your powers, but I know you also did it to find out what really happened to me. Find that woman, and bring her out to play. Her father needs her."

Astasiya went eerily still beside Issac, her shoulders stiff, her mouth flattened into a line. "I'm not that girl anymore, Owen. I've died—*twice*. Both times from making an impulsive decision to help others. Forgive me for needing a few minutes before I jump at the opportunity to die again."

"Well, if that's your mentality, then I can see why you don't want to go. You've already failed."

"I'm trying to be smart."

"No, you're being a coward," Owen countered. "I get that this is all overwhelming, that you haven't fully grown into your wings yet, but your father needs you. Why else would he project to you?"

She swallowed, her guilt slithering through their bond. Issac rubbed her arm, offering what little comfort he could. Because while Owen wasn't being the gentlest communicator, his tactic seemed to be working. Astasiya needed the boost in courage, a reminder of her strength.

It's not an impulsive decision, love, he whispered to her mind.

I want to help him, Issac, she admitted. *But I'm terrified of failing.* The bit that bothered her the most—he could see it in her mind—was that she never doubted herself. Yet, she lacked confidence now. Primarily because of the last few weeks, everything she'd endured, and she couldn't stand the thought that she might not be able to help him. And then she berated herself for thinking that way, claiming it was a weakness in her thoughts.

To acknowledge all potential outcomes is intelligent. It doesn't make you weak, he told her. *But you need to remember your power. You stood up to Osiris once. You can do it again. Remember, you have love on your side. That's one of the most powerful motivators of all.*

She swallowed, nodding. "All right," she said softly. "All right." She looked at Owen. "I still want to punch you."

He chuckled. "Good. You can punch me when you get back."

"Repeatedly," she added.

"Fine. Just not in the face." He winked. "It's my best feature and all that."

"It won't be when I'm done with it," she said.

He grabbed his chest as if she'd wounded him. "That's just mean, Sassy. You love my face. Don't threaten me like that."

"If you're done, we need to go," Gabriel interjected. "Dismantling wards takes time, and we've already wasted ten minutes."

"And why do we have to dismantle them?" she asked warily.

"I'll explain once we get there." He held out a hand. "Come on. Both of you."

Issac glanced at Astasiya. "I go wherever you go," he told her. "If this is your choice, then let's kick some ass."

Thank you, she breathed, the words wrapping around his heart and warming him from the inside.

Never thank me for doing what's right, love. It's you and me. Always.

Always, she agreed, her lips curling softly.

"Well?" Gabriel prompted, completely unaware of their private moment. Or perhaps not caring. "It's now been eleven minutes."

Astasiya took a deep breath and stood. "Right. Okay. Anything I need to know?" she asked, her gaze on Gabriel.

"Of course. I'll brief you on-site." He grabbed her hand and Issac's wrist. "See you soon, Angelton."

"I'll be here doing noth—" His response was cut off by the wind whipping around them.

Issac closed his eyes, steadying his breath, waiting for the ground to appear beneath his feet. It did within seconds, blowing his mind with time and space. It was as if the Seraphim could just imagine a place and make it appear.

I hope you figure out how to do that soon, Aya, he admitted. *We could have some fun.*

She didn't reply, a note of shock traversing through the bond. He opened his eyes, locating her beside him.

Aya?

She felt cold, their bond brittle between them. And her eyes were on the man standing three feet before them.

No, not a man.

A Seraphim with giant black wings etched in fire.

Osiris.

"Welcome, Stas," he greeted. "Allow me to provide you with the grand tour."

Aya's scream echoed inside Issac's head as darkness fell around them.

Oh, fu—

CHAPTER THIRTY-THREE

Tom

TOM HANDED AMELIA A GUN. "This one doesn't have a safety."

"Rule number one: know how to use a weapon before you handle it," she parroted back at him.

He chuckled. "You're such a good little student."

She snorted. "You mean hot. I'm a hot student."

An image of her in a schoolgirl uniform formed behind his eyes. A welcome reprieve from the murderous scenes playing through his mind. "Are we role-playing?" he asked, arching a brow. "Because I might enjoy that. 'Professor Tom' has a nice ring to it."

"So does 'Dead Tom,'" Luc replied, entering the room.

"Which is what you're going to be if I ever find you enacting that scene with my little sister."

Tom sighed. *Fucking spoilsport.*

Amelia rolled her eyes as she secured her gun—just like he'd taught her. "It's like they all want me to be a right prude," she muttered.

"A nun, actually." Luc selected a firearm and loaded it with bullets. "Tom briefed you on the plan? Or was he too busy writing his future obituary?"

Tom snorted, saying nothing. This was between Amelia and her dick of an older brother.

"You're worse than Issac," she accused. "And yes, he provided me with the schematics of Rosalie's home and our entry points."

"Good." Luc attached the weapon to his belt and selected a wicked knife to twirl between his fingers. All the Elders seemed to possess a penchant for blades.

Tom preferred bullets.

"All right, then we're ready to roll. Let's go," Luc said. Tension lined his wide shoulders as he exited the armory, his long legs moving quickly.

Amelia pinched her lips to the side. "I'm worried about him," she admitted softly. "He's not usually this abrupt."

Really? Because in all the time Tom had known him, he'd always been short and to the point. Then again, Luc didn't seem all that pleased by Tom fucking his baby sister. And, of course, there was the addition of him replacing the man's best friend—Eli.

"I don't think he's really mourned," Amelia added. "He's just kept it all inside. That's not healthy."

"Everyone handles grief differently," Tom replied, pressing his palm to her lower back to guide her from the room. "All we can do is be there for him when he's ready." *If* that time ever came. Something told Tom that when Luc fell apart, it would be in private and away from everyone else on the island.

Amelia paused just outside the door, her blue eyes

glowing as she tipped her head back to gaze up at him. "Luc won't grieve until after we've found Jonathan."

"Then we better find him." He traced his thumb up her spine to the back of her neck. Wrapping his palm around her nape, he tugged her into a kiss. "Are you sure you want to do this, sweetheart? To face John on his own turf?" They'd discussed it at length already, but he had to be certain this was what she wanted. Or maybe he was the one who required reassuring.

"Are you?" she countered, her eyebrow arched knowingly. She was the only one in his life who could read him so easily.

He sighed, dropping his forehead to hers. "He's hurt a lot of people, Amelia. If we don't stop him, he'll hurt a lot more." Words he'd said before, words he believed, and yet, the ache inside him remained.

"That doesn't tell me if you're ready to face him," she murmured, cupping his cheek.

"I don't know that I'll ever be ready," he admitted softly. A dark part of him desired to inflict pain on the man who tormented him for most of his life. The other part just wanted to be done, to no longer have to worry about what terrible torture his father would dispense next. But one thing Tom knew for certain. "We need to finish this. And the endgame begins now."

She agreed. "It's the final play."

"It is." He brushed his lips against hers, seeking her warmth and comfort. "And it's a play we're going to win."

Luc appeared at the end of the hallway, an expectant look on his face. "Coming?"

Right. The Hydraian King was clearly eager to get moving. And as the other teams had left twenty minutes ago, Tom understood why.

"Yep." He stepped away from Amelia and tugged on the lapels of his leather jacket. His weapons were holstered beneath, as always. And he had a knife in his left boot, tucked under his jeans. He reached for her hand, squeezing it once before threading their fingers together.

"Good," Luc said, leading the way.

They wandered down the stone corridor and up the stairs to meet Mateo and Jacque outside. Luc locked the iron door behind them and pocketed the key. Apparently, there were only three in existence. Jay and Alik managed the other two because apparently, Balthazar didn't want one. If anyone needed access to the weapons, they had to go through the Elders.

"Everyone is in their respective locations," Mateo said as he handed Tom and Amelia their earpieces. Amelia assembled hers first, testing the microphone once and nodding when the frequency appeared correct. Tom followed suit, giving a thumbs-up after testing his own. Jacque and Luc were already prepared to go.

"Tell them to hold," Luc advised.

Mateo keyed something into his tablet. "Already done."

"Brilliant." Luc glanced at each of them, clearly cataloging every detail—Amelia's gun, Tom's loose jacket, and the metal hilt sticking up over Jacque's shoulder from the sword strapped to his back. "All right. Set us about a block away."

"Scoped and ready." The teleporter held out his arm. "Latch on and don't let go."

Tom kept one hand in Amelia's and used his free palm to grip Jacque's wrist. Amelia grasped his forearm. And Luc took the man's shoulder.

The world whipped around them—literally—as Jacque teleported them to Upstate New York, to a street Tom hadn't seen in years. But one he knew well.

Stars twinkled overhead, the dimly lit neighborhood silent for the night.

No cars.

No witnesses.

And about a foot of snow.

Great.

Tom nodded his head to the left, indicating that he was

taking the lead. While the team technically belonged to Luc, the turf belonged to Tom. He knew this neighborhood like the back of his hand, already aware of all the places he would hide a Sentinel if he were in John's shoes.

The four of them ducked behind a house with oversized hedges, where Tom hunkered down. "Amelia's with me. Jacque, you and Luc need to come around from the back, just like we discussed."

Both men nodded.

"See you in the middle," Tom said, smiling.

This was his playground. The game he'd been created to play. And now it was time for the protégé to become the master.

Adrenaline pumped through his veins as he crept silently through the backyards with Amelia right behind him. They were definitely creating a trail—courtesy of the fucking snow—but the Sentinels shouldn't be lurking back here. The team would be closer to Rosalie's home, and hopefully lazing about because no one suspected this attack.

He continued along, the house at the end being his first target. It provided the perfect vantage point for a sniper rifle with unfettered access to the entire street, including Rosalie's driveway.

He paused at the trees hedging the back of the property, his gaze on the roof. *There you are,* he thought with a smile. With a signal, he told Amelia to stay in place and remain vigilant. She nodded, remaining by the outskirts of the yard while he crept forward to handle the Sentinel on top of the house.

Being silent was key, both to not alert his target or the people inside.

Fortunately, they had a two-tiered deck.

He carefully hopped up onto the snow-covered railing of the first level and gripped the icy platform above him. Good thing he enjoyed pull-ups, because this one was a bit tricky. He hoisted himself up just enough to view his surroundings—a closed balcony door and more snow.

Awesome. He gripped a slick post to guide himself the rest of the way up and stood on yet another snowy railing to grab the aluminum gutter lining the roof.

I do not miss snow, he decided as he quietly maneuvered his way upward to the frozen metal shingles. Thankfully, the roof wasn't too badly slanted, or he'd be on his ass in the grass right now.

He squatted low, eyeing the Sentinel perched on the edge—facing the wrong direction.

Justin.

Seriously? *That* was who his father assigned to sniper duty? *For fuck's sake, old man, Justin's barely out of training school.*

With a silent sigh, he edged his way toward the poor kid. Killing him wasn't an option. Maybe he knew the truth about the CRF bombing. Maybe he didn't. His father had probably claimed it was a terrorist attack or blamed the immortals. Or perhaps he'd given them the truth. Regardless, Tom was not here to play judge, jury, and executioner with his former teammates today.

He crept up behind the unsuspecting male—who was still facing the wrong fucking way and not being at all careful of his surroundings. Tom shook his head, withholding a tsk. He needed this to be mostly silent.

Which was totally ruined when Justin finally glanced over his shoulder.

The young man's eyes widened. "Sh—"

Tom jumped on him, his pistol already in his right hand, and clocked the asshole over the head. He fell limp to the roof below him.

Tom pulled the earpiece from Justin's ear, listening intently for any chatter.

Nothing.

Checking his jacket, Tom found his microphone. *Off.*

Thank fuck.

"Jacque, I have a pickup on three," he said softly, noting the number they assigned this location on the map.

The teleporter appeared at his side, grabbed the

unconscious Sentinel, and disappeared without a word. They'd agreed that any men captured alive would be deposited in the cells in Hydria. Apparently, there were several.

"A teleport down would have been great, by the way," he muttered as he started the silent trek off the house.

Amelia's lips were squeezed tight with laughter by the time he returned to her, his curses having been clearly heard through the communication link.

He glowered at her, which only made her smile bigger.

"One and four are clear." Luc's voice was soft but clear over the comms. "And the street appears to be empty as well."

"What about two?" Tom asked.

"Closer to you," Luc replied.

"Checking it out now," Tom murmured, indicating with his head for Amelia to follow him. He'd punish her later for laughing at him.

The snow stuck to his jeans, making him thankful he'd chosen boots. Amelia had chosen similar footwear, as well as a sweater that hugged her curves and neck, keeping her warm. He approved, and not just because she looked sexy as fuck in her outfit. Although, that was an added benefit.

She arched a brow at his blatant appraisal, causing him to grin and continue moving over the wintry ground. Almost to the road. The next location was—

Crack!

Tom staggered, pain shooting up his side.

"Fuck," he muttered, his knees giving out beneath him. Icy pavement bit into the side of his face as he fell, his heart hammering in his ribs. "Ow."

Amelia's shout was lost to the thundering in his head, his eyes misting from the collision. Shit, he couldn't breathe. His lungs burned, his mouth open on a silent groan.

He lifted his hand, touching his side, finding the source of the pain. Right through his motherfucking jacket. And he liked that coat, too.

Another shot rang out, this one too close. And loud. It rang through his ears, clearing his mind.

Gotta move, he told himself, trying to sit up.

A string of curses hit him next as Amelia fell beside him, her hands roaming over his body. She inspected his arms, his neck, his chest, moving downward to his abs and up under the black sweater he wore beneath his jacket.

"Lower," he encouraged with a cough. Argh, that hurt. No more moving. Not yet.

"Christ." Her forehead fell to his. "You scared the shit out of me, you arse!"

He tried to laugh but couldn't, his side aching from the bullet hitting the thin vest Mateo had created for everyone. "Armor works," he managed to say, his voice higher than usual.

"Good. While I appreciate you testing it for me, try not to get shot again, yeah?" Mateo asked.

"Sure," Tom replied. "On the list." He tried to sit up, but the world spun around him. Amelia caught him around the shoulders, lending him her strength. She had a wild gleam to her eyes that made him want to kiss her.

"I shot him," she whispered. "I… I just reacted."

And there went the inappropriate urge. He followed her gaze to the body lying facedown a few yards away. The stocky build and dark hair suggested it was Greg. That damn Sentinel was always jumping the gun and trying to play hero. It seemed he'd finally paid the price for his brash actions.

Tom forced himself to move, his body complaining even while healing. The vest Mateo manufactured blocked all bullets—including the incendiary one Greg had fired at him. Good thing, or Tom would be dead right now.

Amelia stood with him, her hands clasped in front of her, lips twisted.

"You did the right thing, sweetheart," he assured her as he slowly made his way toward the body.

Definitely Greg.

And he was still breathing.

"He's not dead." Tom knelt beside the unconscious Sentinel. He'd fallen in front of a house toward the end of the block, suggesting he'd been patrolling the sidewalk when Tom and Amelia had waltzed into sight.

Tom shook his head. *Rookie mistake.* He should have checked his surroundings before emerging from between the houses.

"He's alive?" Amelia asked, sounding surprised.

"Yeah, just knocked out from the impact against his vest." Which probably should have happened to Tom as well, but he'd focus on that detail later. "Jacque, cleanup about thirty meters southeast of two."

"On it." The teleporter appeared with a nod of acknowledgment before disappearing with Greg's body.

Amelia stood with her arms wrapped around herself, shaking. Tom pulled her into a quick hug, pressing his lips to her cheek. "We need to—"

"Dude. Turn on your fucking radio," a deep voice said from behind them. "John said to keep the mics off unless something came up. Not the whole fucking set."

Charlie.

Tom pointed to the closest porch, telling Amelia to hide while he ducked behind a nearby bush. The Sentinel appeared within seconds, his gaze sweeping the front yard. He'd clearly followed Greg's footprints, which meant his eyes went straight to the spot his friend fell. Pretty obvious what happened considering the male-shaped imprint in the snow.

Charlie whipped out his pistol, carrying it low with both hands, his training and form on point. He tracked the patterns along the ground while Tom quietly maneuvered to the side, away from the bushes and into the shadow of the awning overhead.

Come a little closer, he urged, wishing he had the power to compel like Stas. Alas, all he had were his thoughts. *Just a few more steps, Charlie. You can do it.*

The Sentinel continued along the path, aiming his gun at

the bushes Tom had just occupied. But he didn't fire. No. Charlie was smarter than that. He crept forward, vigilant, and used the barrel of his gun to part the branches and peek into the empty space behind them.

Tom used the brief distraction to his advantage, pouncing on the Sentinel and hitting the gun out of Charlie's hands. It went sideways, disappearing into the white earth, as the two engaged in a brawl of arms and legs.

"Fitzgerald," Charlie growled as he tried to win the upper hand.

"Miss me?" Tom asked, his fist connecting with the Sentinel's square jaw. Charlie responded with an upward knee jab that almost hit the family jewels, and a clever ankle hook that sent Tom to his back. "Shit, you've learned to fight."

"I always knew how to fight, asshole." Charlie slammed his elbow into Tom's chest, knocking the wind from his lungs. That, coupled with his still-aching side, made him begin to reconsider his plan of the hand-to-hand combat.

A flash above them had Tom's gaze narrowing just as something crashed into Charlie's head. Twice.

Is that a bat?

Amelia swung it a third time, sufficiently knocking out the Sentinel. He landed with a thud beside Tom, sending red splatters across the snow.

"Shit," Tom breathed, gazing upward at his avenging female. "Nice form, asset."

"Found it on the porch." Her chest rose and fell in quick succession, the metal bat falling from her hands. "I still bloody hate baseball. But I'll concede that it provides useful weapons."

He laughed, amused as hell despite the pain ricocheting through his being. "I told you she didn't need me," he said through the microphone. "She's saved my ass twice now."

Luc snorted. "You don't deserve her."

"You're not wrong," Tom replied as he pushed himself up off the ground. "Final pickup, Jacque."

"Wait," Amelia said when the teleporter appeared.

He arched a bushy black brow. "Yeah?"

"I have an idea." She pulled off her sweater, revealing the vest she wore beneath—with nothing else. And began unfastening her pants.

Tom stepped in front of her, blocking the teleporter's view. "What are you doing?"

"Changing," she replied. "I need Charlie's clothes."

He frowned. "Why?"

She met his gaze. "Because I'm going to shift into his skin and then enter Rosalie's house."

Chapter Thirty-Four

Amelia

"HOW DO I LOOK?" Amelia asked, her voice deep and masculine, exactly like the Sentinel that Jacque had just teleported away.

"Horrible," Tom replied emphatically. "You resemble Charlie, which is not attractive."

Her lips twitched. "You mean you don't want to kiss me right now?"

He stared at her. "I love you, but no. This is not a memory I want to keep."

"Then we'll make it a quick one," she suggested, leaning in to kiss him on the cheek. He grimaced in reply, causing her to giggle. "I'm ready, Luc."

"You are to go in, determine if there are other Sentinels

in the house, and then leave," he replied through the comms. "Do you understand?"

Seriously? "I can take care of myself, Lucian." As she'd just proven by aiding Tom. Sure, she was still learning, but she had one hell of an instructor—one she'd just assisted *twice.*

"Do you understand?" her brother repeated. "I went through the experience of losing you once. I will not live through that again." While he uttered the admission in a stern voice, she heard the hint of emotion on that final word.

She sighed, understanding. This wasn't about his lack of trust in her abilities but about his fear of losing her. He hadn't even begun to mourn Aidan. She couldn't add to that misery, refused to give him another reason to close himself off from everyone.

"All right, Luc," she murmured. "I won't do anything rash."

"Good. I'll meet you around back, Tom."

"Roger that," Tom replied, grabbing Amelia's hand and giving it a squeeze. "If you suspect for one second that he's caught on to who you are, shoot him."

She nodded. "Shoot to kill, not to wound." That was part of an early lesson between them—never try to incapacitate an attacker; that only works in the movies.

"Such a good student." He winked. "Try to make it quick. This face really isn't doing it for me."

She stuck out her tongue, making him laugh.

"I take it back. *That* is amusing."

Amelia snorted. "Go meet my brother, arse."

"As you wish, asset." He took a step away, then turned to grab her around the waist, yanking her up against his hard body, his lips at her ear. "Be safe."

Ah, she couldn't handle him being worried about her, too. She needed his confidence, his strength, his reassurance that everything would be fine. She swallowed, searching for a way to lighten the tone. If she allowed nerves to overtake her now, she'd never be able to do this. "Try not to get shot again," she suggested.

He snorted and slapped her on the ass. "You'll just save me."

Yes, much better. "Damn right I will."

He grinned and pulled away. "Next time I see you, I hope it's your real face."

"I'm going to stay like this for a day just for fun." Complete and utter bollocks, of course. She much preferred her own skin.

He scoffed at that. "I give it an hour." He waggled his brows. "We both know you can't resist my lips on you, sweetheart." He blew her a kiss and wandered off, leaving her sighing in his wake. Because he was right.

Arse.

She wiped her clammy palms against her jeans and took a deep breath to calm her insides. *You can do this,* she told herself. It was a solid plan—walk into Rosalie's home, search for additional Sentinels, and leave to report back to Tom and Luc.

Amelia could do this.

Easy.

She swallowed and began her trek through the thick snow. Fortunately, the road was paved. Same with some of the sidewalks and the driveway leading up to Rosalie's home.

Jonathan may not even be here, she reminded herself. *Mateo could be wrong.*

But she suspected he wasn't. Especially as they found several Sentinels lurking about already. Why would they be here without Jonathan?

Okay, so he's here, she thought. *That's fine. I can handle him.*

Perspiration dotted her brow as she approached the porch, nearly a decade of memories flooding her in an instant.

All those attempts to harvest her gift of being able to shift her appearance.

The lab tests.

Jonathan's endless torture.

She shivered, her stomach revolting.

"You can do this, sweetheart," Tom murmured in her ear. "I'm right here."

How did he know?

She shook her head, her lips threatening to curl. The man always knew. He was her heart, her better half, the one who brought her back from the darkness every time.

"Take a deep breath," he continued softly. "And walk up those stairs as if you're me. Put some swagger into it."

She almost laughed. He and Luc had obviously repositioned themselves to watch the house from the front. The temptation to glance over her shoulder hit her hard, but she forced herself upward instead.

I survived hell, she thought as she approached the door. *Now it's time to seek vengeance against the devil. Against Jonathan.*

"Don't knock. Just walk inside," Tom told her. "You're supposed to be there. Own it."

She nodded, agreeing.

The knob shifted beneath her oversized hand, the door opening without hesitation. Beyond it was a foyer with a dull rug, a small wall table, and a staircase off to one side. A living area opened to the other, the quilts and tapestries giving the room a homey feel. This was the sort of home that should hold the aroma of apple pies or freshly baked cookies, not cigar smoke and aftershave. But that was all she scented as she slipped inside.

Dust had gathered on the photos decorating the corridor. Amelia spotted one of a young Tom. He wasn't smiling the way a boy of that age should. No, he stared at the camera like an emotionless soldier, his military school uniform adding to the overall vibe.

Amelia's heart panged uncomfortably in her chest at the reminder of his not-so-warm childhood. She at least had a mother and a father who adored her. While she missed Aidan, she cherished their memories together—all fond, loving, and nurturing. If she had to choose fates, she would pick hers every day of the week.

She continued deeper into the home, reaching a room with an oversized couch that opened into a small breakfast nook and kitchen. Sliding doors behind the dining table opened to the backyard. And to her left was another set of stairs that led downward.

Not a Sentinel in sight.

And the house was silent, too.

Where's J—

"What are you doing?" a deep voice demanded from behind her.

Think of the devil and he shall appear.

"Repeat after me," Tom said into her ear. "Just looking around."

She cleared her throat and faced the familiar devil behind her. "Just looking around," she parroted, her deep baritone sounding wrong to her ears.

"I needed some water," Tom added.

She repeated the phrase.

Jonathan gave her a bored look. "Then go grab a water." He gestured to the kitchen. "Did you find Justin?"

"Yes," she replied, turning stiffly toward the kitchen. Placing her back to Jonathan felt wrong—dangerous. She swallowed twice, maneuvering into the room and opening the fridge to search for a bottle. Thankfully, one sat on the top shelf. She popped the tab and took two swigs. "I'll just be outside."

Jonathan frowned. "Why?"

"Tell him you want some fresh air," Tom replied, his voice warm and comforting in her ear.

She answered as he directed, causing Jonathan to shrug. "All right. But I need you… Hold on." He slid his hand into the pocket of his black dress pants and pulled out a phone. After reading the information on the display, he answered, "Yes?" He held up a finger, telling Amelia to wait while he listened to what sounded like female chatter over the line.

It would be so easy to unholster the gun on her belt and shoot him. He stood close, only about five feet away, his hip casually leaning against the counter beside the stove.

One shot.

Between the eyes.

And he'd be dead.

Her fingers itched to react, to put this man in his grave, to pay him back for everything he'd done to her. But she couldn't do that to Tom. To Luc. To Issac. Everyone had a right for revenge. Taking it from them would be selfish.

"That's interesting," Jonathan murmured. "Thank you for informing me. Yes, my dear, I'll see you soon." He pocketed the phone with a smile. "Sorry about that. What were we discussing?"

"I was about to go outside," she replied, taking a step in that direction.

"Right. You know, it's funny; I was just reminded of that time in Bulgaria. Crazy déjà vu. Do you remember that mission? The one with Alan?"

"*Fuck.*" Tom's curse jolted down her spine. "He knows. Get out. Get out now!"

Amelia swallowed. "I, uh, I don't," she replied, answering honestly as she took another step toward the exit. "Remind me of what happened?"

Jonathan chuckled. "You know, I'll show you instead." He lunged for her, grabbing her by the shoulders and shoving her back against the wall. The bottle slipped from her hand as she tried to go for her gun, but he got there first, pulling the pistol from her hip and placing the end of the barrel against her head.

"Shift back, Amelia." A lethal command punctuated by the metal digging into her skin. "I've always adored your pretty face. Show it to me."

She couldn't move, her heart hammering against her ribs, her arms loose at her sides. One twitch and he'd send an incendiary bullet into her brain.

"Now, Amelia," he snapped.

Her limbs trembled as she resumed her natural form, shrinking by several inches in the too-big clothes. The gun followed, Jonathan's lips curling into a triumphant grin.

"Is that my son whispering in your ear?" he asked, eyeing the small device tucked just inside her ear canal. "Do send him my regards."

No response from Tom.

Or Luc.

"I hear all my Sentinels have been transferred to Hydria. That's disappointing." Jonathan trailed a finger up her sternum, his other hand as stable as ever with the gun against her skull.

When he reached her throat, he circled it with his palm, giving it a squeeze. She trembled in response, his touch cascading a myriad of memories over her, all laced with pain.

Knowledge, some part of her whispered. *Use that knowledge.*

But she stood frozen, her heart in her throat, unable to move or speak.

Jonathan had captured her again. He had her pinned to the wall, his palm encircling her throat, a device meant to kill her in the opposite hand.

He's going to kill me.

"You've caused so many problems for me, darling Amelia. You seduced Tom, converted him into this weakling, and convinced him to turn his back on a bright future. Not to mention all the issues between myself and Issac now, and I suppose Lucian and Aidan. Well, the latter is dead and no longer a concern. Such a shame, as I hadn't meant for him to be a target." He shrugged. "But it's hard to control angry men, Amelia. I believe we've had this discussion before, yes?"

Countless times, she thought. The last of which had been after something Issac had done that pissed Jonathan off. He'd shattered her ankle and punched her repeatedly, yet he never broke the skin. His punishments were always internal. Always agonizing. Her blood too toxic to him to spill.

Until Stark healed her.

But he wasn't here now.

There would be no remedy tonight.

Only death.

"You're thinking about it." He cocked his head to the side. "All the times I mastered you."

Hatred boiled inside her. Blind rage. But her throat remained closed, his grip constricting to just the right point where she could barely breathe. He wanted to prolong the torment, to draw out her suffering.

That's our advantage, she realized. *His arrogance.*

He wouldn't shoot her until the perfect moment, until he destroyed her resolve. Anything else would leave him unsatisfied. If she fought back, he'd be forced to work harder to put her in her place.

She actually smiled. Probably a result of the delusions, the years of torment, the finality of the moment, but her lips fucking curled. And his lifting eyebrows displayed his surprise.

"Fuck. You." She spit the words into his face, not caring at all how they rasped against her windpipe. As long as she possessed her spirit, he lost. That was what she'd forgotten when he caught her, the situation momentarily rendering her stupefied. But now she remembered his greatest weakness—he hated to lose.

No matter what he did to her, she'd never break.

That was why he kept her alive for all those years. The experimentation was all a guise. He had everything he needed, apart from her soul. And the monster in him wasn't satisfied without it.

She started to laugh, the sound coming out as a croak, then disappearing altogether as he tightened his hold, stealing her breath.

"You court death, do you?" he taunted. "I'll grant it. And when you wake up, I'll grant it again."

Her chest continued to vibrate with silent laughter, even as her airways begged her to inhale. It only seemed to infuriate him more. So much so that he didn't notice the man creeping up behind him.

Tom grabbed the gun beside her head, yanking it upward and to the side before Jonathan could react. She gasped as Jonathan released her, her legs unsteady.

Curses and crashes occurred as Tom wrestled his father to the ground, landing a punch against the other man's jaw that sent blood spraying across the room. "You fucking bastard!" Tom snarled, his expression crazed. Another punch, this one Jonathan blocked as he sent his fist upward. But it didn't faze Tom, rage pouring off him as he clamped his fingers around the other man's throat. "I'm going to fucking kill you!"

Jonathan sputtered, his eyes rounding as he gripped Tom's forearms.

Amelia sucked in a breath, her lungs aching. She couldn't speak, her throat still healing from the damage Jonathan had inflicted.

But Tom wasn't letting up, his chest heaving from the exertion, his muscles bulging with the effort as if he were trying to rip Jonathan's head from his body.

"You killed Mom. You killed Rosalie. You killed all those innocent people. You're a monster. You deserve this. You can't... you can't *remain*. Everything you've done, everything you continue to do." Tears poured from Tom's eyes, a violent tremor ricocheting down his arms. "Fuck, I have to. You'll just hurt more people, do more horrible things. To Lizzie. To Stas. To Amelia." He shook. "Fuck!" His grip loosened, his head falling. "Why couldn't you be normal and care? Be a real dad? All I ever wanted was your approval. But you never fucking gave it."

Tom released him, his shoulders shaking, more tears falling as Jonathan gasped. He remained trapped beneath Tom's stronger form, pinned to the ground. "Son," he breathed, his voice in tatters, reminding Amelia of her own.

"You deserve to die," Tom continued in a whisper, ignoring that single word. "But I can't be like you. I refuse that fate. I will never be you." He slammed his fist into

Jonathan's face, knocking the man out. "I can't kill him." He looked at Amelia. "I... I can't."

She knelt beside him, her hands on his cheeks, pulling him into a hug as Luc walked into the kitchen. He took one look at Jonathan and nodded. "The house is clear." Quiet words. "We need to secure him." He knelt to fish the phone from his pocket. "And I need to get this to Mateo. Whoever called him is our mole."

Jacque appeared, his expression grim. "To the cell?" he asked.

Luc nodded while Amelia said, "No."

Both men looked at her. "What?" Luc arched a brow. "What do you mean?"

"No," she repeated, her hand locating the gun on Tom's waist. Her mind was made up. If he couldn't even kill his own father, how would he withstand the torture? He'd feel guilty. He'd worry about turning into the monster who created him. And that part of him, the history, would forever be there to haunt him.

But if Jonathan died, that history went with him.

"No," she said again, her voice raspy but clear. "That's not who we are, Luc. It's not who Aidan would want us to be. We have to move on from this, to move forward. Not live in the past. Not torture a man to make us feel better. We'll never get past this if we keep him around. The worst punishment we can give Jonathan is to forget him."

She removed the weapon from Tom's belt.

"Amelia," Luc cautioned.

"No, Luc." She glanced up at him, tears in her eyes. "I love you, big brother. I do. But this is the right way. He needs to die. He needs to be forgotten. He needs to burn in the sins of the past. By himself. Don't you understand? Don't you get it? As long as he's here, he'll haunt us. Torturing him will do nothing but bring more sorrow. This is the right path."

And the longer they debated it, the more satisfaction it would give Jonathan. He didn't have to be awake to broadcast that achievement. He would just know, for as long as his soul remained, he had a hook in them all. It gave him an importance, one she refused to allow him to keep.

She wanted her life back.

He'd held it captive for long enough.

Amelia didn't wait.

She lifted the gun.

And pulled the trigger.

Tom jumped beside her. Luc cursed. And Jacque… just smiled.

It was done.

"He's dead," she whispered, marveling at the charred blood pooling between his closed eyes. The incendiary bullet had worked instantly, rendering his insides to ash.

Jonathan Fitzgerald would never breathe another word again.

Never hurt anyone else.

Never be the source of another nightmare.

Amelia was free. They all were. "He's dead," she repeated, handing the gun back to Tom. He gazed at her with adoration and respect and sadness.

"He's gone," he said, as if he needed to say it as well. "He's finally gone."

She cupped his cheek. "It needed to be done."

"I know." He leaned into her. "But I couldn't do it."

"That's what makes you so strong," she whispered. "Even after everything he's done, you still care. That's called love, Tom. Never lose sight of that. It's what makes you who you are." She pulled him into a hug, her arms wrapping around his muscular shoulders, holding him tight while he silently grieved.

Luc and Jacque left them to their peace, to allow them their moment of shared understanding. And Amelia loved them both for it.

Jonathan may have been a monster, but he created Tom.

All sons and daughters deserved their right to mourn. Something Luc knew, even if he hadn't taken his moment yet.

"I hated him," Tom whispered. "God, I hated him so much."

What was left unsaid were the words, *But I also loved him.*

Amelia parted her lips on a reply as Mateo's voice came over the comms. "Uh, guys? I just received a call from Owen. He hasn't heard from Stark in over two hours. And Stas just activated her tracker, but the location's unknown. Something's wrong."

Chapter Thirty-Five

Stas

AYA.

God, it was cold. And wet. And that smell, like rust mating with sulfur. Ugh. Stas was not a fan at all. Her nose crinkled, her muscles cramping as she tried to roll to her side.

Aya.

Slick stone abraded her skin through her thin shirt and jeans, sending a shiver down her spine. Her stomach heaved, jolting her across the hard floor. *This sucks.*

Aya.

The male voice sounded impatient. She couldn't find the source, her surroundings too dark. And so damn frigid. *Where am I?*

In Osiris's dungeon. I need you to focus.

She blinked. *What?* Who was talking to her and how? *Wait…* Another slow blink, a yellowish tint forming. Something splashed between her eyes. More of that stench infiltrated her lungs. *Oh, yuck.*

This place reeked. And, God, what was she lying in? Some sort of icy liquid that seeped right through her clothes.

Stas shifted to her back, trying to sit up, but her head pounded. What the hell had knocked her out? A wrecking ball? Fuck. She swallowed, her throat dry. She needed water. No, she needed to determine what the hell happened.

With as much energy as she could muster, she levered herself up off the ground and forced her eyes open. A set of metal bars filled her vision. Beyond it lay an archaic room littered with stone walls and haphazard lighting.

What had the voice called it? A dungeon? Yep. That was exactly what this was. An old one with rusty metal, stagnant water, and… blood stains.

She scrambled backward, away from the remains to her left, the back of her hand at her mouth. *Oh God.* That was the smell—rotting flesh. *Fuck. Fuck. Fuck.* Her stomach churned, her mind whirring. *Where the—*

Aya, a voice snapped. Male. Familiar. Stern. *Breathe and focus on me. I'm one cell over.*

She glanced left at the gray wall. *Issac?*

Other side, love.

The same view overwhelmed her vision as she shifted her head in the opposite direction. *How do you know?*

Based on your vantage point of the chamber outside the cells, he replied. *Do you still have your necklace?*

Her brow furrowed. *Necklace?* She touched the heart pendant hanging from her throat. *I've never taken it off.*

Good. Can you activate the tracker?

She shook her head. *It doesn't work. I tried that when, uh, you know.*

It works, he replied, sounding sad. *But Mateo had turned off the monitoring after… the reception.*

Oh. Right. She pressed her thumb to the metal rung at the base and shifted it to the side. *It's on.*

When Osiris returns, be sure to deactivate it just in case he scans you. Although, I suspect he already did.

She shivered at the thought of that man touching her. *What happened?* The last thing she remembered was misting onto the property and coming face-to-face with Osiris. *He ambushed us.*

Indeed. Issac fell quiet for a long moment. *Someone set us up. Only a handful of people knew where we were heading.*

You're worried Tristan betrayed us.

More silence, then a soft and hesitant *Yes.*

Where's Stark? she wondered. *And Ezekiel?*

Gabriel is in the cell on the other side of you. He keeps showing me images of potential escape plans.

She frowned. *Why doesn't he just mist us out?*

We're underground. But he's working on a rune. Except, well, he's having to use his own blood to draw it.

Her mouth fell open. *What?*

There's nothing else to write with, Aya.

She glanced around. *What about water? Or…* Her gaze fell to the rotting body in the corner. It wasn't exactly a skeleton, more of a zombie-like form.

That's what happens when an Ichorian is left to starve for a very long time, Issac murmured.

Are you telling me that thing might be… alive?

Possibly. I'd stay away from it.

Yeah, that was advice she didn't require. Stas slid backward until she hit the wall beside Stark. *We can't just sit here,* she said. *There has to be something we can do, something we can use.*

She grabbed one of the edgier stones jutting out above her and used it to pull herself up. Standing made no difference in her ten-by-ten-foot cell. Nor did it reveal anything additional beyond the bars. But sitting on her ass seemed pointless.

Stas reached for her power, searching deep inside, and

came up against a wall of nothingness. *Wait. How are you using your visual gift?* she wondered.

Great question, he replied. *I don't actually know but, I suspect it has to do with not being fully transitioned yet. My powers have always worked underground.*

A tremor rocked her to her core. *Does that mean you're not entirely immortal?*

Possibly. He didn't sound concerned. *You know, I just realized why Osiris built the Conclave beneath the Arcadia—to prevent Seraphim from entering. He chose a powerful safe haven for his creations. Fancy that?*

If you're asking me to admire the monster, it's not going to happen. She trailed her fingers over the bars of her cell, searching for a weak link.

It just further proves what Gabriel said about Osiris amassing an army. He's been preparing for several thousands of years. And no one had a clue. The admiration in his tone reminded her a bit of Aidan. He, too, would have found the reveal fascinating.

The clank of metal had Stas freezing in place, her gaze searching for the source. *Did you hear that?*

Yes.

Another creak sounded.

Then footsteps.

Loud.

Heavy.

Authoritative.

She pressed her thumb to the tracker, deactivating it just as Osiris sauntered into the room.

"Oh, good, you're all awake," he said by way of greeting. The elegant cut of his suit acted as a façade for the evil lurking beneath. He almost appeared approachable and friendly, even with the ghastly halo reflecting around his bald head. "I trust you all slept well?"

No one replied.

He chuckled. "Well, I have to say, I'm actually impressed. Especially with you." He focused on the cell to her left. "I honestly never suspected you of being a

Seraphim, Gabriel. I just assumed the genetics we implanted took. How did you fool the researchers? I know they drew blood samples, but everything came back mortal."

"They were easy enough to swap with a local hospital." Stark sounded as bored as ever. "Nothing to be too excited about."

"You're right," Osiris agreed. "I'm just thrilled you managed to hide your identity for so long. It proves you might be useful to me. But your misting about with Ezekiel, well, that's a shame. I honestly thought him to be tamed long ago. Alas, here we are. Poor Skye. She'll bear the brunt of his transgressions, learn to hate him more. Such as my compelling her to give that fabricated prophecy about Sethios to Ezekiel. I mean, I can't kill him. Trust me, I've tried."

The way he said it, as if he expected them to pity him, had Stas biting her tongue to keep from saying something sarcastic back to him. Now was not the time to taunt the monster.

"Fortunately, it worked, didn't it? You're all here now, just as I planned. Well, and as she predicted. Such a useful little prophetess. And it served as a fun punishment for Sethios as well. Win-win all around, yes?"

He paused on a smile, allowing his admission to settle over his audience.

The prophecy was a lie.

A way to force them all to react, to fall right into Osiris's waiting hands.

The bastard had played them all brilliantly, and his cocksure expression said he knew it, too.

"Ah, well, one day Ezekiel will truly heel. I just have to finish breaking him first."

"And my father?" Stas asked, folding her arms. "Is that what you're doing with him?"

His green eyes flickered beneath the lights, his lips flattening. "Sethios is a lost cause. You, however, I have hope for. And knowing you bonded to Issac has provided me with the most delicious training module."

How does he know about our blood bond? she wondered, shocked. *Is it something Seraphim can sense?*

That, or someone told him, Issac thought back at her, his tone underlined in fury. *My suspicion is it's the latter.*

Which means he might not know for sure…

"I'm not sure how much use I'll be to you," she said, an idea forming as she uttered each word. "I can't even figure out how to mist."

He gave her an indulgent smile. "You're still young. A baby, really. I'll teach you what you need to know." He shifted his focus to the cell beside her. "The offer stands for you as well. I've always been impressed by you and your practical stance on life. There's a future here, if you desire it."

"Assuming I can earn that future," Issac added, his tone calm. "Betrayal is hard to overcome."

"It is, yes," Osiris agreed. "That you even acknowledge that fact proves my point. You're valuable." He glanced around, his lips curling into one of his charming grins that made her queasy inside. "You all are, actually. We'll come to an understanding over the next few centuries. I'm certain of it."

Ice trickled through her veins, her heart threatening to stop in her chest. *Centuries?* Stas glanced at the ghastly remains beside her. Was that her fate? Would she wither and decompose here? Become a husk with a soul floating about without a host?

She shivered, the image desolate, numbing.

I'll become my mother.

A vision of the ocean floor appeared around her, the seaweed climbing up her limbs, holding her beneath the surface. Trapped for eternity. Dying over and over again. A fate worse than death.

Just like the coffin.

Suffocating.

Except Stas could breathe here.

How long before her body began to shut down? Her mind?

No.

That is not *my fate.* She didn't accept it. Refused to even acknowledge it.

Life flickered within her.

Creation.

Power.

I will not die here.

Energy swirled within her soul, spilling into her veins and flooding her limbs. Her fingers twitched.

Osiris said something, but she couldn't hear him over the roar in her head—a lioness begging to be let free.

And she opened the door.

Literally and figuratively, her mind was no longer hers to control. It belonged to the powerful being inside her.

The iron snapped under *her* will, sending Osiris backward a few steps. His eyebrows rose, not in fear but in awe. She pushed him back with a mental shove, sending him toward the stairs.

"*Walk,*" the Seraphim inside her commanded. This went deeper than persuasion—a control unlike anything she'd ever felt—and Osiris succumbed to her power with a smile.

"Beautiful," he said, his feet taking him backward. "Absolutely stunning."

He wouldn't be saying that when she overtook him, when she *destroyed* him. They moved upstairs, Stark and Issac behind her. She barely felt them, couldn't hear them, her entire focus on the monster before her.

"More," he encouraged as they stepped outside.

Night had fallen.

The stars a reassuring glisten above her.

"Show me your wings," Osiris demanded. His power washed over her, causing the feathers to burst from her back, her soul retreating into the ethereal realm. She nearly stumbled, her heart in her throat. But the impressed note in his expression had her steeling herself, her spine straightening.

"I am not yours to command," she told him, another wave of authority washing over her. "You will not own me." Her wings beat at her back, sending a gust of wind toward him, the move instinctive and powerful.

But he responded in kind, his ebony feathers blossoming around him as he sent another burst back at her, forcing her a step backward.

Keep him busy, Issac said. *Don't let him see.*

She didn't know what he meant, too focused on the task of battling Osiris. His ancient spirit pushed against hers, some bizarre force trying to belittle the light inside her. It hurt, sending spasms down her spine as her soul fought for purpose.

This went beyond psychic energy. He was attacking her in the ethereal realm. And she didn't know how to fight him. She barely knew how to fan out her wings, how to fly, how to *mist.*

And she sensed that he was going easy on her.

He saw this as a test.

A lesson.

Osiris wanted to explore her skill set, to determine how best to sharpen it for his own personal use.

No! She would not allow it. *I am not yours!* She sent another blast of air that he countered with a flick of his wing, his expression pure joy.

"You will make a fine lieutenant indeed," he murmured. "Again."

She growled, searching inside for more, something to shock him, to put him on his ass. But he met her compulsion with commands of his own, counteracting her every step of the way, leaving her dumbfounded and exhausted.

Her back ached, her wings strained from whirling on the grass and dancing with the stars. He took her to planes she didn't understand, her soul leaving her body and returning in waves, the confusion of *what* he was doing baffling her senses.

And all the while, he encouraged her to push harder, to show him everything she could do, forcing her to continue this lethal game she hardly understood.

She fell to her knees in the grass, her breathing harsh to her own ears, her wings broken around her. Osiris stood before her, triumphant, his inky feathers encircling them both as he gazed down at her.

"Ah, you impress me, Stas. Breaking your fight will be my biggest achievement." He petted her hair, cooing her name. "You'll be my most impressive—" He jolted backward, his focus shifting to the side. "*Vera,*" he growled.

"Hello, darling." A Seraphim with navy wings appeared, her smile radiant. "You really should pick on an angel your own age." She tsked. "Poor form."

He collapsed, a sound of pure rage ripping from his throat. "I'll—" The words died as he rolled to his back, his wings disappearing and his eyes falling closed.

"Well, that was easier than I expected," Vera said. "You exhausted him for me, Stas. Well done."

Stas couldn't reply, her own fatigue taking over. She had no concept of time or space or even what had just happened.

"He buried him two miles that way," Vera said, pointing through the trees. "Look for the fresh grave at the base of the mountain. Beneath the dirt is a cement tomb. But hurry, Gabriel. I can't hold Osiris for long." Her head fell back on a shudder, power rippling through the air around her. "And Skye..." She rolled her neck, her voice hollowing. "The lake, near the docks. There's not enough time—"

"Go," Stark said, his voice oddly close but far away.

"But Sethios—" That sounded like Ezekiel.

"Issac and I will handle it," Stark interjected. "Save Skye."

Ezekiel's reply was lost on the wind roaring in Stas's head. She felt shattered. Alone. Confused as hell.

"Skye will be the one he torments because she's not

expendable." *Is that Leela speaking?* "Save her. We'll deal with the compulsion later. It's her only hope."

Another harsh gust, something fighting for access. To take control. To command. *Osiris*, she realized. "He's…"

"Get her out of here," someone snapped.

The world shifted, Stas's surroundings melting into the night and reappearing in a blink.

"Here!" The masculine voice warmed her heart. *My Issac.*

"I need some space to break through the concrete," Stark said, sounding distant and cold.

"You can do that?"

"I'm a warrior Seraphim. Now hold Stas."

Another whirlwind.

The stars swimming overhead.

Warm arms circling her. Protecting her. She snuggled into the familiarity, luxuriating in the sandalwood that infiltrated her senses. *Love.*

I'm here.

I know, she whispered back to him. *I feel you.*

Gabriel is using his wings to shatter the concrete holding your father. A shock wave followed his words, causing her to flinch. *I was wrong before. I should fear your brother.*

She wanted to laugh, but that required energy she didn't have.

And then they were moving again. Fuck, she was dizzy.

"How long will this last?" Issac asked.

"It depends on how much Osiris damaged her soul." Exhaustion lurked in Stark's voice. From demolishing the concreate, maybe?

"You said a Seraphim can't die."

"That doesn't mean a soul can't be attacked," Stark replied. "Come on, Sethios. Wake up."

Issac sighed. "Shouldn't we move—"

The arms around her tightened, yanking her backward as a wave of power stole her breath.

Energy.

Strength.

A lethal purpose.

Her eyes flew open, her heart beating a mile a minute. She *recognized* that essence, had dreamt of it a thousand times.

Green irises identical to her own narrowed in her direction. "Who the fuck are you?" he demanded, his voice rough with disuse.

She swallowed.

Daddy, the little girl inside her whispered, *knowing* him. Even with the unkempt tangles of dark hair, scruffy beard, thin build, and dead expression, she *knew* him. "Dad," she breathed, her heart in her throat.

He flinched. "Excuse me?"

"Osiris compelled him to forget," Stark reminded him. "Make him remember."

Her heart pounded. "How do I do that?" She could hardly hold herself up, could hardly focus on the present, and Stark wanted her to overpower Osiris's command? "I… I don't…" She swallowed again, her chest aching.

He doesn't know me.

But I know him.

I remember everything.

She thought of the times he called her his *little angel.* All the times he held her, told her stories about her mother's wings, how beautiful they looked when they fluttered. She pictured him chastising her for using compulsion inappropriately, sharing ice cream cones in secret, and playing hide-and-seek outside. He taught her so much in such a short period, had embedded a sense of purpose into her that she hadn't understood until recently.

He was her savior.

Her father.

The one who sacrificed everything for her.

And now he didn't remember her.

Didn't remember her mother.

Couldn't recall anything he stood for.

A shell of a man beneath Osiris's influence.

She hated that, hated everything that evil being had taken from her, from *them*. He was a monster. He destroyed. He hurt.

Because of him, she didn't have a childhood. He stole years of her parents' lives, had forced her to grow up without her father.

I'm your little angel, she wanted to tell him now. *It's me, Astasiya.* But she didn't know how to voice the realizations, not with him looking at her as if she were nothing.

He doesn't know me.

Her heart threatened to break.

God, he has no idea who I am. A tear trickled down her cheek, hopelessness brewing inside her. *How do I make him see?*

More memories flooded in, her mind fracturing beneath the assault. The last time she saw him, he commanded her to run, to leave him to his fate. "I didn't understand," she whispered, breaking. "I didn't know why you made me run. But I felt your pain. Oh, God, I *felt* it." And she could sense it now, shattering inside her, torturing her soul. "I still feel it."

Her knees gave out beneath her, Issac's arms catching her as she fell.

She couldn't do this.

Didn't know how to undo it.

All she felt was immense torment. A broken piece of her being, forever unhinged. She pictured her mother, begging beneath the waves, allowing it to fuel her agony. The suffering, the sorrow, the grief spilled through, ripping a cry from her throat. *It hurts,* she moaned. *Oh God… it hurts!*

"Caro?" her father breathed, falling to his knees before her, his hands on her face, forcing her attention upward. He blinked in surprise, rearing back. His pupils widened, his lips parting. "*Astasiya?*"

The earth rumbled beneath them, a quake that knocked everyone off balance.

"Osiris is awaking," Stark said. "We need to go."

Her father gaped up at him. "Gabriel?"

A brief smile flitted over his features. "Good to have you back, Sethios." He grabbed her father's shoulder. "Hang on."

Stark's opposite hand came down on her shoulder, Issac's arms tight around her waist as time and space moved again.

But it was too much.

She couldn't keep her eyes open, couldn't focus.

Sand touched her senses.

Followed by a soothing cloud of masculine energy.

Sleep, Issac whispered. *I'll be here when you wake.*

Chapter Thirty-Six

Issac

ASTASIYA WAS ICE COLD, her mind vacant.

Issac laid her on the couch in Gabriel's living area, kneeling at her side. "What's happening? Why can't I hear her?"

"She's healing." Gabriel collapsed in the chair beside them, his expression ragged. "Fighting Osiris took a lot out of her. As did shattering his hold over Sethios."

"What year is it?" Sethios demanded, his hands in his overgrown hair. "What the fuck? Why the hell are you touching my daughter like that?"

"They're bonded," Gabriel replied, his eyes closed. "And she's twenty-five. Do the math. I need a nap."

Sethios started pacing, his energy surprisingly strong for

someone who had just been encased in cement. Issac had no idea how that man had healed so quickly. It had to be related to his Seraphim genetics and ancient bloodline.

And Astasiya.

Holy. Fuck.

She'd glowed like a goddess on that field tonight, her wings flaring with a power unlike anything Issac had ever witnessed. And she was wrong—her feathers weren't pink, but opal. They sparkled in the moonlight, cascading an array of colors across the sky as she battled with Osiris on a plane of existence that baffled his mind.

Osiris had all but forgotten everyone else the moment Astasiya's power took over, his sights on his granddaughter alone. Issac understood. Astasiya had captivated him with her beauty, her strength, her very existence. So when Gabriel tasked him with remaining by her side, to keep her grounded and lend her his strength, Issac hadn't argued. It was the only option—to support her and observe in complete and utter awe.

"How did she do that?" Issac marveled, recalling the way her skin had glowed in the dungeon. Even her hair had lit up, turning a white-blonde that flowed around her like a silken cape.

Gabriel squinted at him. "You'll need to be more specific."

"Astasiya, underground. How did she free us?"

"Why were you able to manipulate vision?" he countered. "Runes, Wakefield. Osiris leaves them everywhere. She tapped into that extension as a member of his bloodline, and it granted her power. Just as you did."

"But she couldn't at first." He'd heard her try and fail through the bond. "Why was I able to access it before her?"

"Because she didn't believe in herself. Osiris pushed her over the edge." He shut his eyes again. "As to why you didn't suffer the same confidence issue, it's because you're used to tapping into his runes."

Sethios snorted. "The Conclave. I have not missed that

circus per—"

A shriek outside cut him off, Gabriel immediately on his feet. Sethios followed him outside as Owen came running down from upstairs. "I told Mateo you're all okay, but he's trying to call you," he informed him on his way out the door.

Issac frowned, pulling out his phone.

Seventeen missed calls.

Over a dozen text messages.

Mateo's name flashed on the screen. Issac pressed the button to answer the call, placing his progeny on speakerphone. "Is everyone all right?" he asked, concerned. Either everyone had worried about him—and rightly so— or something had happened. "Did you get Jonathan?"

"Your sister killed him," Mateo replied. "Shot him between the eyes with an incendiary bullet."

Issac's eyebrows lifted. "Did she?" He nearly smiled. "Well, I can hardly fault her for that." Even if it did remove all elements of revenge. Far too easy a death for such a psychopath, but Issac felt oddly at peace with that. Perhaps because he was too exhausted to feel much else at the moment. With everything else occurring around him, it was almost a relief to have one less item to worry about.

The screams outside grew, causing Issac's brow to furrow. "I may need to call you back, Mateo."

"Hold on," his progeny said. "You need to know that we've identified the mole."

"Who?" he demanded.

"Clara."

He blinked. "Are you certain?"

"Yes. She called Jonathan during the attack to inform him that his Sentinels were in Hydria. She had sensed their auras when Jacque dropped them off, and apparently recognized one of them. Her actions nearly cost Amelia her life."

Issac's hand tightened around the phone. "And she was the source of the other links?"

"Affirmative. I'll send you the detailed report, but in

summary, I was able to link the data from Jonathan's phone and computer back to her. She gave him everything, and it would seem he provided the notes to Osiris."

"Which explains how he learned about Ezekiel's activities with Gabriel," Issac replied, his jaw clenching. "Did she play into Lucian's plans at all? Alerting Jonathan of one of the other sites?"

"Yes, but he didn't act on the information. Tom believes it's a result of being short on Sentinels after the explosion at headquarters and the wedding reception massacre. Jonathan was watching his properties remotely, and I suspect a few of them were wired to explode, but the teams never entered to find out."

"Right." Issac palmed the back of his neck, grimacing at the memories of that night. "So everyone's all right?"

"No casualties," Mateo reported. "All the Sentinels are alive and locked away. The only one who died was Jonathan."

"Good." Maybe they should add Clara to the casualty list. How could she do this to Aidan? To her friends? Her family? To Issac? What the ever-loving fuck was the woman thinking? "Do we know why Clara did it?" The words came out harsh between his teeth, his need to throttle the woman something fierce.

Mateo blew out a long breath. "From what Balthazar has gathered from her mind, she's been working with Jonathan for months. They're both outsiders, with him not being Aidan's real progeny, and Clara not being a member of the harem. Because, you know, she was made for you."

"Are you fucking serious?" Issac cut in, livid. "She didn't even want me!"

"Perhaps not, but she never felt like she belonged, and it seems Jonathan played on that. While Aidan may have adopted him, he didn't *make* him. Apparently, they bonded over it. A lot."

"Why the fuck wouldn't she say anything?" he demanded. "How did no one know?" Not even Issac had suspected Clara as being capable of such treachery. She always seemed so… *happy*. "We're certain?" he asked again, needing him to say it.

"Yeah, there's sufficient proof and messages. I even found a note about your bond to Stas, which, apparently, she overheard Tristan talking about to Nadia. It's bad, man. She gave Jonathan everything."

Issac resisted the urge to punch something. He focused on Astasiya. Her beautiful, complacent features. Her perfect lips. Her soft, blonde hair.

After several breaths, he felt the anger dimming inside. "I never would have suspected her of this," he admitted. "Fuck, Mateo. How could she do this?"

"Nadia is astounded and pissed," he replied. "Tristan, too. Fuck, everyone is, Sire. They're calling for blood."

"Rightly so." Issac didn't condone killing, but if Clara had been betraying them for this long? "She deserves it."

"Yes," Mateo said softly. "Lucian and the others are still debating her fate. As with all the Sentinels in custody. This is going to take days, maybe weeks, to sort."

Issac rubbed the back of his neck. "Yes. It will."

Leela appeared in the doorway, her blonde hair in tangles around her head. "I need you right now."

"Is there anything else?" he asked.

"Nah. We're knee-deep in pissed-off Sentinels at the moment, and Clara's been apprehended. Honestly, the rest can wait. But I wanted you to know that it wasn't Tristan."

"I never thought it was," he replied, standing. "Thank you, Mateo."

"Sire." He ended the call.

Issac slid the phone back into his pocket. "What do you need, Leela?"

"For you to put Skye out of her misery." She waved him forward. "Stas is fine. Skye is not."

He assumed that was who was screaming outside. As he stepped through the threshold, his suspicions were confirmed. A woman with black hair stood bellowing on the beach, both of her wrists shackled by Ezekiel's hands as she tried to drag him into the water.

Issac tapped into her vision, curious as to what she was thinking, and stopped breathing.

Chaos whirled through her mind.

Images of suicide.

Begging on her knees.

Weeping.

Drowning herself in the ocean.

Osiris shackling her to the bottom of a lake. Ezekiel saving her. A vision of a blonde goddess whirling in the clouds. Lightning.

Back to the desire to slit her wrists.

A gun—Ezekiel's—firing into her brain.

Issac couldn't tell what was real versus what was desire. And the blonde goddess was dancing again, power thriving around her, opal wings flashing.

Aya.

Blood.

Aya's head rolling across the ground, her eyes dead.

Issac stumbled backward, yanking himself from the woman's mind, his heart racing. "What the fuck?" He grasped his chest. "*What the fuck?*"

"Make her sleep," Leela said. "She's going to drive herself insane."

"She is insane!" He pressed himself against the side of the house, then peered through the windows to reassure himself that Aya still slept soundly. Her mind was quiet— too quiet. "Jesus." He never wanted to see that vision again.

"Osiris compelled her to kill herself if anyone ever took her from his custody. Her mind is the result of that compulsion. Make her sleep until we can figure out how to override his power."

"But he's not here." Shouldn't that lessen the effect? "Gabriel said Osiris can't reach us here." They were technically within the Seraphim realm, of which Osiris was banned. The others had all been granted access through wards or runes or whatever magic Gabriel had performed. Issac was too damn exhausted to analyze it all now. They were safe. That was all he cared about.

"It doesn't matter. She's an Ichorian. He created her and therefore his coercion remains." Leela grabbed his shoulder. "Get yourself together and put that woman to sleep. Right now."

God, she made it sound so easy. "She just envisioned Astasiya's severed head rolling across the ground. Give me a bloody minute."

Leela gasped. "What?"

"Yeah."

"Here?"

He swallowed. "No. It wasn't in the sand." He ran a hand down his face. "Was it a prophecy?" he asked softly, hoping like hell he'd misunderstood the outcome.

Leela shook her head. "No, prophecies are spoken aloud. She's done nothing other than scream in agony. The Fates work in odds. They *see* everything, all potential outcomes. Only those spoken aloud are the destinies they believe will come to fruition."

"And she's never prophesized Astasiya's death?"

"Not that I'm aware of, no."

Well, that made him feel somewhat better. He shook off the residual shock and glanced inside again. His Aya remained unmoving, her face soft with sleep.

"All right," he murmured. "I'll try to help her sleep." But it wasn't going to be easy.

He carefully accessed her vision again, flinching at the gory image flickering in her thoughts. "She's envisioning a blade piercing her own heart," he muttered.

"One of the many ways she's died," a new voice informed him. Female. Vera. Her navy wings fluttered at her back as she appeared beside them, her gaze tired. "I can see the day Osiris unleashed this command, but I can't rewrite it. He's stronger than me."

"Can Sethios override it somehow?" Leela asked.

Vera shook her head. "He's not strong enough in his current state. His release from Osiris's control is too recent."

"Stas?" Leela suggested. "Once she wakes, I mean."

"She certainly has the power, after what I just witnessed, but I doubt she'll know how to accomplish it. Perhaps the two of them together?" She sighed. "I'll contact some of our allies, see if anyone has any suggestions. For now, I agree with putting her to rest." Her silver eyes lifted to him. "Show me your usefulness, youngling."

"Youngling?" he repeated.

"You're only a few centuries old, right? A baby in my time. But show me what you can do. Make me understand why one as powerful as Stas has chosen you as her mate." She nodded to Skye. "Help her."

"Sure. Then you can explain what you did to Osiris." Whatever she'd done had sent the ancient being to his knees and knocked him out. Issac wanted to know how so it could be done again. But he focused on the task first, locking on Skye's visual receptors and easing her into unconsciousness.

Her screams quieted, her lashes fluttering closed as Ezekiel caught her in his waiting arms. "What the hell just happened?" he demanded, his gaze feral as he searched the beach.

Comprehension settled into Issac's mind, the puzzle pieces all coming together.

Skye was the reason Ezekiel had chosen to remain with Osiris.

The assassin loved her.

And Osiris had used that to his advantage, just as he had planned to use Issac against Stas—to train a new pet.

"Ezekiel," Vera called. "Issac has calmed Skye's mind to grant her a temporary reprieve. Tell him what you want her to dream about."

The assassin's ebony gaze flashed to Issac. "What is she dreaming about now?"

"Nothing," Issac replied.

"Good." He lifted Skye into his arms. "Please keep it that way for as long as you can." He carried her toward the house and paused on the threshold, glancing back at Issac. "Thank you."

He gave the man a nod. "It's the least I can do." And he meant it. After everything all these people had done for Astasiya, the trials and torment they'd survived, helping a prophetess sleep seemed trivial in comparison.

"To answer your questions about Osiris, I dismantled his mind by rewriting his history," Vera explained. "The trauma is what knocked him out. That, coupled with what Astasiya had done to him prior to my involvement."

"She manipulates memories," Leela translated. "And she's very good at it."

"So you warped his past?" Issac asked, his brow furrowing.

"Yes, but only temporarily. He's too strong for it to be permanent. Astasiya is the same way. She'd unraveled several of my distortions over the years, to the point that giving her back her memories the other day was actually quite easy."

"Someone bring me up to speed," Sethios said, approaching from the beach, his expression sheltered. "My recollection of the last few decades is… fucked up."

"I'll bring you up to speed once you take a shower, shave off that hideous beard, and cut your damn hair," Vera replied. "You look terrible."

"Gee, thanks for the concern, Vera. Now tell me, where the fuck is Caro?"

Leela and Vera visibly flinched.

Gabriel folded his arms. "At the bottom of the ocean somewhere."

"*What?*" Sethios blinked, his gaze taking on a faraway gleam. His lips flattened. "I can't feel her." His eyes flickered around, his palm grabbing his chest. "Why can't I feel her? God, why didn't I notice?" He grabbed his hair, pulling on the filthy strands. "What the fuck has happened these last…?" He trailed off, his focus shifting to inside the house.

Sethios started moving, prompting Issac to follow, as the seemingly deranged male was headed straight for Astasiya.

But he stopped abruptly, causing Issac to nearly face-plant into the man's back.

"Astasiya," he breathed, falling to his knees beside the couch. "Dear God, she looks like Caro." He lifted his hand as if to touch her but stopped himself partway. "Twenty-five?" he asked.

"Yes," Gabriel confirmed from the doorway.

"How is she? Did everything go according to plan?" he asked. "Is she fully transitioned? Does she have wings? Are they blue like her mother's?" He had tears in his eyes as he looked at Gabriel. "Does she even know about me? About Caro?"

"She knows who you are and aided us in helping you escape," he replied, sitting in the chair closest to the couch. "She's still learning about what she is, how to compel, everything. We managed to keep her out of the supernatural world until last summer when she met Wakefield."

Sethios stiffened, his attention shifting. A pair of green eyes—so similar to Aya's glorious green—locked on Issac. "And you're now *bonded* to my daughter?"

"I am," he replied, unfazed by the brutality lurking beneath the notorious male's skin. Sethios was renowned for his cruelty, being Osiris's right-hand man, and having the ability to influence. Most were terrified of the man.

As it was, Issac couldn't give two fucks about the man's powers.

"Astasiya is beautiful and loyal—sometimes to a fault. She cares about others more than herself, and she's one of the strongest women I've ever met. She faced Osiris to free you, channeled the heartache of losing you and Caro to shatter the remains of your father's compulsion, and reached out to me for comfort in her final seconds before shutting down. I promised her I would be here when she wakes, and I will not be breaking that promise." He arched a brow to enhance his statement, ensuring Sethios read between the lines.

You will not come between me and my Aya.

"Remind you of anyone?" Vera asked, hiding a smile behind her hand.

"Yep." Leela smirked. "Those two are going to get on famously, I think."

"Or kill each other," Vera murmured. "Shall we take bets?"

"You two haven't changed in the slightest," Sethios remarked, his gaze still on Issac. "And we'll see if he proves himself worthy."

"He already has," a groggy voice replied from the couch, Astasiya's tired eyes on her father.

Issac knelt beside her, his palm going to her cheek. "Are you all right, love?" He still couldn't hear her, which concerned him.

"I'm just tired," she murmured, leaning into his touch. "And all of you keep talking."

He smiled. "Sorry, darling. Would you like me to take you upstairs?"

"Mmm." Her eyes fell closed, her fingers reaching for him. "Please."

Gathering her into his arms, he stood and met Sethios's gaze. "We'll continue the discussion after Astasiya has rested."

Approval gleamed in the other man's eyes as he nodded, but he didn't move out of their way. Instead he lifted his hand to trace her jaw. "I'm proud of you, little angel," he whispered. "Thank you for saving me."

Her lashes lifted. "Little angel," she repeated, a smile teasing her mouth. "I've missed that name. And you. And Mom."

"I've missed you, too," he replied, tears in his eyes. "Now rest. We'll catch up after you've slept. And then we'll talk about your mother."

"Ocean," she mumbled, shivering. "So cold. And alone. But she told me to find you. And I did." She yawned, her eyes barely open, her body limp in Issac's arms. "I found you."

"You did," he agreed. "And together, we'll find your mom."

She nodded, snuggling into Issac's shoulder. "Yes. Sleep. Mmm. You smell good."

Issac chuckled and nuzzled her cheek. "We'll go have a nap, darling."

"'Kay," she murmured, her eyes closing.

Sethios moved out of their way this time, his expression soft as he studied his daughter. But as Issac started down the hallway, he overheard the man saying, "Tell me they can't procreate."

"Is that a command or a question?" Leela asked, humor in her voice.

"Whatever will get you to answer," he growled. "Astasiya is too young to be pregnant. She's barely an adult. And fuck, she's *mated?* You all were supposed to protect her!"

Laughter met his outburst. "What do you think that man has been doing?" Vera asked, humor in her voice. "He's been guarding her since the day he met her. And as to the procreation bit, ask the fertility queen."

Leela snorted. "Fertility queen? Really? I'm still mad at you for what you did to Balthazar. He fucking remembers me, Vera."

"You told me to rearrange his memories and I did. That doesn't mean I removed every single detail."

Well, *that* was interesting.

"Can we focus on the procreating part?" Sethios cut in. "I need to know that my daughter isn't going to make me a grandfather in the middle of this chaos."

"Relax, Sethios. The fertility cycle for Seraphim revolves around centuries, not days or months. Well, unless Jonathan alters your genetics, apparently."

"What?"

"Long story involving Stas's best friend," Leela murmured. "Anyway, as far as your daughter goes, she won't be fertile until she's at least five hundred or so. But if you really want to have the 'birds and the bees' talk with her, I can give you some pointers."

"Jesus Christ," he muttered, sounding even more upset. "She was *seven* yesterday. To think about having the sex talk…"

"Worried Issac is doing to your little girl what you enjoy doing to Caro?" Vera taunted. "Don't worry. I've not seen any knife-play in her memories."

Oh my God, I do not need to hear about my father playing with my mother! Astasiya shouted into his head, causing him to nearly drop her.

Well, at least the connection wasn't broken.

Sorry, love, he replied, shaking his head to clear the buzzing she'd left behind. *Heading upstairs now.*

Do we know who the mole is? she asked sleepily as he laid her down on the guest bed—the same one he'd found her in what felt like a century ago.

Clara. The name came out on a mental growl. *I don't know why yet, but rest assured, the Hydraians are handling it.*

Will they kill her?

I don't know, he admitted. *It depends on her motive and if she regrets it.*

He pulled off his soiled dress shirt and pants, then repeated the action with her jeans and shirt. Her eyes opened, a smile playing in their depths. *Are you trying to seduce me? Because I don't think I'm up for a performance right now.*

"You need sleep first," he murmured. "I'm just making sure we're properly prepared for when you wake up."

"So you *are* seducing me." Mirth sparkled in her green depths.

"It's a preemptive seduction." He tucked her into the blankets and slid in beside her. "Hmm, and I can influence your dreams now, too. That may make this even more interesting."

She shivered, her pupils dilating. *Is it considered an abuse of power to infiltrate a woman's mind while she sleeps?*

Only if she's unwilling. He raised a brow. *Are you?*

She snuggled into him, her face going to his neck, her lips gently brushing his pulse. *Consider me always willing.*

Likewise. He pulled her close. *You were absolutely radiant today, love. But I have to tell you something. It's rather important.*

She tensed. *What?*

Well, it's about your wings, he hedged, fighting a smile.

What about them?

He sighed. *They do change color.*

She gasped inside his mind. *They do?*

Yes. They're opal, not pink.

Opal? she repeated.

He kissed her temple. *Yes. Opal.*

I like that more than pink.

His lips twitched. *I thought you might.*

She fell silent, her mind quieting again. He realized now it was a result of exhaustion, of her soul requiring rest. But their connection thrived, her heart beating in time with his. She even breathed at the same pace.

They were forever linked.

Eternally bonded.

And nothing would ever come between them. Not even Osiris.

You're my always, Aya, he whispered, hugging her to him. *Whatever you need, I'm here. Wherever you go, I'll go. We're a team, you and I. No matter the obstacle, no matter the trial, I will never leave your side. That's my vow to you, always and forever. Across the universe and beyond, I will love you.*

She remained quiet for so long that he thought perhaps she'd fallen asleep. But then she asked, *Why does that feel like a proposal?*

He smiled. *It's not.*

Oh. She almost sounded disappointed.

It's my wedding vow, he whispered. *During Elizabeth and*

Jayson's ceremony, I couldn't stop thinking about what I would say to you, how I would convey my feelings. And the words just came to me, the certainty in them completing me in a way that just felt right. I'd intended to say them to you that night. I didn't get a chance, so I'm saying them now.

She rolled in his arms, her tired gaze finding his as she cupped his cheek.

"You're my always, Issac," she said, her voice soft yet clear. "I promise to honor you, to cherish you, to be honest with you, and to respect you. To work with you, not against you. To forever remain by your side, regardless of the trial or task. And to trust you, always and forever. Across the universe and beyond, I will love you."

Emotion burned in his eyes, his throat thickening as he whispered, "Always."

"Always," she replied. *You may now kiss the bride,* she added in his mind, causing him to grin.

The perfect wedding, he whispered to her.

To the perfect man, she agreed. *My always.*

My always, he repeated, his lips claiming hers. *I love you, Aya.*

I love you, too.

Epilogue

Sethios

ASTASIYA STOOD OUTSIDE, her face tilted back to enjoy the sun blazing overhead. She kept flickering in and out of her ethereal state, her gorgeous wings flaring around her and disappearing and flaring again. Her childlike smile said it was on purpose.

"She's finally figured out how to mist," Issac murmured, joining him at the sliding glass door. "She wants to visit Elizabeth first."

"Her friend, right?" Sethios asked, recalling the name from Leela's rundown about Astasiya's current life. "She's pregnant?"

Issac nodded. "Yes. I don't think she's due for another month, but it's all very strange. Leela seems to have it handled."

"She would. She helped Caro birth Astasiya as well." He studied his daughter's excited expression. "I need to find Caro."

"And you want Astasiya's help," the intuitive male beside him surmised, his intelligence somewhat respectable.

"Yes."

"Then tell her," he replied, making it sound like the simplest task in the world.

"How?"

It felt weird asking another man how to talk to his own daughter, but these weren't normal circumstances. And after everything Sethios had endured, he wasn't quite sure how to talk to anyone, let alone his own flesh and blood.

"By being honest and forthright." He faced him. "She's still a bit miffed over being left in the dark all these years. The truth will go a long way."

Sethios nodded. "That I can do. I—" The appearance of two males on the beach cut off his words, his hackles rising at Astasiya's resulting frown. She took a step back as the taller one approached her. "Who is that?"

"My progeny," Issac murmured, his gaze narrowing. "Tristan."

An Ichorian. Sethios didn't recognize him. "What can he do?"

"Control sound," Issac replied, satisfaction radiating from his expression.

"Can you hear him now?"

"Not directly. But Astasiya is complacent, which tells me everything I need to know." He gestured with his head. "Let's join them."

"'Sup," a floppy-haired male said as he passed them, his gray eyes looking Sethios over with interest. "Papa Stas. Cool." He waltzed into the house without a backward glance.

Sethios frowned. "Who the fuck is that?"

"Jacque. Hydraian. Teleporter. Lucian's primary

Guardian." Issac glanced at him. "You'll be seeing him a lot."

"Right." He dragged his fingers through his hair—which was shorter now, thanks to Vera's intervention with a pair of scissors. Apparently, she felt cleaning him up was more important than finding Caro. The only reason he'd agreed was because his angel hadn't contacted him yet.

Where are you, darling? he thought at her for the thousandth time.

Nothing.

She'd clearly severed the link, but he didn't know how. Gabriel suspected it to be related to trauma and her wanting to protect Sethios.

Eighteen years.

A blink for someone his age, yet it resembled an eternity in his heart.

I miss you, angel.

"…make him happy. Thank you." The male's Irish lilt sounded old and tampered with age, perhaps an influence of living stateside for a while.

"That might be the nicest thing you've ever said to me, Tristan," Astasiya replied, smiling. "Careful, or I'll consider it a request for friendship."

He snorted. "I wouldn't go that far, pet."

"Yeah, that's what I thought." Astasiya shook her head. "Your best friend is still an ass, but a tolerable one."

Issac chuckled. "Noted." He glanced at Sethios and then back to the one called Tristan. "Fancy a walk, mate? I believe we have a few details to discuss."

A somber note overcame the male's features as he nodded. "Of course, Sire."

The formal address seemed to tighten Issac's shoulders. "Make that several details." He leaned in to kiss Astasiya's cheek. "I'm going to be a while."

She nodded. "I figured."

Issac glanced at Sethios. "Sethios."

"Issac," he returned.

Astasiya watched the two men walk away, her heart in her eyes.

Sethios refrained from commenting on his opinion and instead decided to open with a query. "Gabriel tells me you were raised in Havre."

She smiled. "Yes. With the Davenports." Her brows rose. "Oh, I should call them. They're probably worried sick about me."

His brow furrowed. "Why?"

"Because I haven't spoken to them since the holidays. That was…" She frowned. "God, I don't even know what day it is, or month for that matter."

"No, I meant why would they be worried? I thought they knew everything." That was what Gabriel had implied, anyway.

"What? No. They know nothing about this world." She started to laugh, but the sound slowly died. "Wait, why did you think they knew?"

"Your brother told me about them last night while bringing me up to speed on things. He mentioned them knowing about your ability to compel, so I just assumed that meant they were aware of, well, everything."

"*What?*"

Gabriel chose that moment to mist in, his red feathers glistening in the sun. He frowned at the expression on Astasiya's face. "What's happened?"

"The Davenports know I'm a Seraphim?" she asked, her voice shrill.

"Oh. That." Gabriel's wings disappeared as he took on a corporeal state. "Uh, no, not exactly. It's complicated."

"Uncomplicate it," she demanded, reminding Sethios of Caro. He nearly smiled at the familiar fury radiating in her gaze but managed to cover it with his hand.

Gabriel sighed. "Think about it, Stas. They couldn't possibly have raised you without a little knowledge. So I gave them everything they needed to know. Such as your ability to compel. And I may have told them you were a descendant of angels who would always be watching over you."

Her jaw was on the floor by the time he finished.

Except he wasn't done.

"Vera helped keep it in check over the years, altering their memories as needed. As an example, when you left for college, she erased all the details about your ability to compel. And when you started working for the CRF, she removed their memories of me. Which, in theory, means they know nothing now."

She gaped at him. "You've been fucking with my parents' heads for *years*?"

"Technically, Vera did that," Gabriel pointed out.

Sethios crossed his arms, amused.

"Vera," she repeated. "You're going to blame Vera?" She charged at him, causing Gabriel to disappear and reappear on the other side of her.

"Violence"—he misted again to avoid her punch—"is not"—another mist—"the ans—argh!"

Astasiya had anticipated his next movement and nailed him in the face with an impressive punch while in an ethereal state. Gabriel landed on his ass with an *Oomph*.

"Nice form, little angel," Sethios praised.

She stood over Gabriel, her hands on her hips. "Is there anything else you haven't told me yet, jackass?"

"Why do I get blamed for everything?" Gabriel asked, his hand rubbing his jaw. "Ezekiel, Sethios, Leela, Vera, even *Mom*, were all part of this."

"But we left you in charge," Sethios pointed out.

The male grumbled something as he pushed himself up off the beach. "I can't even retreat to my own fucking house because it's overrun with guests. Seriously, what did I do to deserve this fate?" He stalked off toward the back door while Astasiya glared at his back.

"I think I hate him."

"That's too bad, little angel," Sethios replied, tilting his head to the side.

"And why's that?"

"Because we're going to be spending a lot of time with him in the future weeks, possibly months." He touched her on her nose, the way he used to do when she was a child. Typically, after misbehaving. "We need him to help us find your mom."

A memory flickered in her gaze, her features softening. "He promised me once that we would search for her together."

"He didn't lie." Sethios tucked his hands into the pockets of his jeans and glanced up at the sky, his thoughts on the woman he adored, the angel of his dreams.

Where are you, love? Why have you blocked me from your mind?

When she didn't answer—again—he met the gaze of their daughter. "That's actually what I wanted to talk to you about."

"Mom?"

He nodded. "And looking for her." His chest ached, guilt settling in the pit of his stomach. Had his angel severed the link because he'd failed her? Because she'd felt the torment Osiris had inflicted upon him? Because she'd lost faith?

Sethios swallowed. He could spend days debating the cause. But none of them would bring his angel back.

"I need your help in finding her," he admitted softly. "Please." He didn't use that word often, but it felt appropriate now. "I know I'm practically a stranger to you, that trusting me won't be easy, and clearly, Gabriel has done a shit job of earning your trust as well."

Yeah, he wasn't explaining this right. Or even really asking in a comprehensible manner.

He ran his fingers through his hair, expelling a long breath.

Time to try again.

"What I mean to say is, working together—as a team— is the only way we'll locate your mother. Because I know, without a doubt, that my father has hidden her somewhere difficult and impossible to find. But I've left your mother to suffer for—"

"Dad," she interjected, the single word a caress against his frozen heart. "You don't need to explain. I want to find her, too."

Oh. Right. "Have I mentioned how much you remind me of your mother?"

"A few times." She smiled, her expression even more reminiscent of Caro. "When do we leave?"

He studied her. "As soon as possible."

"Good." She took a step back. "Then I better perfect the art of misting." Her wings appeared. "I'll be right back." She vanished, causing him to shake his head.

You'd be so proud of her, Caro, he thought, smiling. *She's just as brave and as fearless as you.*

Nothing.

His shoulders fell, his eyes falling closed. *Come back to me, darling. I miss you.*

He took a step, his soul weeping inside, when a distant whisper prickled the back of his thoughts.

The words were faint, as if carried on a breeze.

Free me, Sethios…

Free.

Me.

SETHIOS AND CARO WILL RETURN IN BLOOD SEEKER...

An unexpected connection led to a forbidden affair that ended in blood. Now Sethios will stop at nothing to find his mate, even if it means risking his life and love in the process.

Caro's mind is fractured, her body destroyed, her heart broken. She thought he would come for her, save her, free her from this nightmare. But her hope flees with every wave, her soul teetering on the brink of madness.

Will Sethios arrive in time? Or will other powers intervene?

A new prophecy is rising... One that will threaten to destroy them all.

IMMORTAL CURSE SERIES
WHAT'S NEXT

Dear Reader,

Thank you so much for reading *Angel Bonds*. I consider this book the end of a major story arc, one I lovingly call the "Jonathan Is An Arse Era." And now he's dead.

This was the most emotional story I've ever written, and I'm fairly certain my husband thinks I'm nuts for all the hours I spent crying in front of my computer. But it was worth all the tears to finally give Stas and Issac the beginning of their happily-ever-after.

Did you catch that? My little hint that they're not done yet?

Waggles eyebrows

I have so much more to explore in this world, from relationships to Seraphim bloodlines to Osiris… It's going to be a whirlwind, and I can't wait.

If you have any theories about future plotlines or relationships, be sure to join my reader group and/or the Immortal Curse discussion group on Facebook. You'll find me hanging out there often :)

So, up next is *Blood Seeker*, which follows Sethios as he searches desperately for Caro. You'll hear from Stas, Issac, Stark, and others along the way, too.

Oh, and the Elders might become uncles soon… Can you imagine them with a little version of Lizzie and Jayson running around? Ah, I'm in love with the idea already!

Until next time, feel free to join my <u>newsletter</u> for sneak peeks, early chapter reveals, and special excerpts. I may have some deleted scenes coming your way soon, too.

Thank you again for reading!

Cheers,

Lexi C. Foss

ACKNOWLEDGMENTS

This book nearly killed me. Without the people mentioned below, I don't think I would have survived. A lot of people don't realize how much emotion goes into writing. It takes months to craft the right words, and an army to perfect it.

My husband is the person I always thank first. He's the one who puts up with my crazy deadlines and insane sleeping habits and reminds me to eat often. He also plies me with caffeine, which alone is a great reason to list him first. But in seriousness, I could not pursue my dreams without him, and I'm very thankful for his support and love.

And then there's Bethany. My editor. The Obi-Wan of Punctuation. Without her, no one would be able to read this book. It'd just be a bunch of nonsense scribbled on paper. Ask her. She'll tell you. So thank you, Bethany, for perfecting my art and allowing me to run rampant with deadlines. One of these days, you will receive a manuscript on time. No, it'll be early. Just don't die of shock, okay? I need you!

Right up there with Bethany is Allison, my alpha reader, who drops everything to help me when I'm running late on a deadline. (Does anyone else sense a theme here?) She's the one who keeps me honest, finds my double words, and makes me explain things that I don't want to explain. Like, seriously, who cares if Balthazar somehow has three hands? I'm sure he uses them wisely.

Tracey: Thank you for reading *Angel Bonds* in pieces and providing feedback. I really hope you're wrong about the voodoo dolls…

Casey: Thank you for allowing me to kidnap you for hours on end and plot. We should probably go on a drive soon… I have more ideas to discuss. I'm looking forward to the series bible!

Louise and Melissa: I love you both to the moon and back. Thank you for keeping my social media alive when I need to disappear. I appreciate you both more than you'll ever know.

Barb, Joy, Katie, and Laura: Thank you for proofreading! I don't know how y'all do it, but I love you for it.

Julie: Gah, this cover. I love it! Thank you, Goddess of Cover Art. I appreciate all your designs, especially for this series.

Thom: Thank you for "playing" Issac for me. He approves of the covers so far in my head, so I think we'll release another one soon. ;)

Dan: Thank you for being my "weapons expert" on the fly. Tom approves.

Famous Owls: Y'all keep me alive. Thank you for your support, social media tags, shares, comments, love, and friendship.

And to the readers: Thank you for trusting me with Stas and Issac's story. Hopefully, you didn't hate me too much…

Thank you all! <3

ABOUT THE AUTHOR

USA Today Bestselling Author Lexi C. Foss is a writer lost in the IT world. She lives in Atlanta, Georgia, with her husband and their furry children. When not writing, she's busy crossing items off her travel bucket list. Many of the places she's visited can be seen in her writing, including the mythical world of Hydria, which is based on Hydra in the Greek islands. She's quirky, consumes way too much coffee, and loves to swim.

www.LexiCFoss.com
https://www.facebook.com/LexiCFoss
https://www.twitter.com/LexiCFoss

ALSO BY LEXI C. FOSS

Immortal Curse Series
Blood Laws
Forbidden Bonds
Blood Heart
Elder Bonds
Blood Bonds
Angel Bonds

Blood Alliance Series
Chastely Bitten
Royally Bitten

Dark Provenance Series
Daughter of Death
Son of Chaos

Mershano Empire Series
The Prince's Game
The Charmer's Gambit